THE SECOND CORTEZ

CHADWICK WALL

ENCHANTED INDIE PRESS

THE SECOND CORTEZ

a novel by

CHADWICK WALL

ENCHANTED INDIE PRESS

Austin

PUBLISHER'S NOTE

Copyright © 2018 Chadwick Wall
Interior formatting for print and digital editions:
Tosh McIntosh
Cover design by: Rafido

Printed and Published in the United States of America
by
ENCHANTED INDIE PRESS

Digital Edition (v1.6)
ISBN-13: 978-1-938749-45-2
ISBN-10: 1-938749-45-6

Paperback Edition (v1.6)
ISBN-13: 978-1-938749-44-5
ISBN-10: 1-938749-44-8

for my friend Ernesto Mendoza

"What I fear most is power with impunity. I fear abuse of power, and the power to abuse."

—Isabel Allende, writer and activist

1

The trio of men entered the café laughing. Boys they were, really, between the ages of eighteen and twenty-one. Two had Kalashnikovs slung over their shoulders.

Nicolás Nolano sat at the bar, the remnants of his dinner before him as he finished his wine.

"Well, *Profesor*," the bartender said under his breath as he leaned toward Nicolás. "Now cartel soldiers have officially been in my café."

Another boy of no more than nineteen walked past the trio. Slight of build, and with long bangs dangling below the bridge of his nose, he wore pants and a University of Veracruz T-shirt. The cartel boy without a Kalashnikov shoved him from behind, hurling a volley of profanities.

Nicolás recognized the boy in the college T-shirt. Enrique Ponte, from his British and American literature class last spring.

"My work always follows me," Nicolás said. "I can never escape it. That boy they've got—he was my student last year."

Nicolás lurched to his feet and approached them. Time seemed to slow. A touch of anxiety heated up within him, but he smothered it by quickening his steps.

All three boys were taunting Enrique, leaning forward into his face.

"Prissy boy," one snarled. "One day you'll be working for us anyway."

One cartel boy, then the second, and then the third registered Nicolás's approach. Their chins perked up, their eyes flashing with menace.

"Enrique, are you bothering them?" Nicolás uttered the words as soon as he could invent them. As the faces of the cartel boys turned to each other and lengthened with shock, Nicolás placed his arm around Enrique's shoulder and whisked him forward.

A hand pushed the back of Nicolás' head, sending his long, combed-back bangs into his eyes. He ignored it, instead ushering Enrique around the bar and into the next dining room. When the kitchen's swinging doors came into view, he pushed the boy through them and hurried with him past the chef's line, topped with food-laden plates.

"Faster, faster, damn it!" Nicolás said, as he jerked the knob of the outside door and pushed Enrique into the cool night air. The unlit parking lot was almost full of cars, but no one was in sight. Nicolás pointed at his car, parked meters away. "The Alfa Romeo, get in. Hurry."

Enrique hesitated, and then Nicolás pointed again at the car.

"Now you're going to get us killed, man," Nicolás said. "Move!"

Enrique sprinted to the car, and Nicolás pursued him, while clicking the keychain controls. Enrique yanked the passenger door open and collapsed into the seat, while Nicolás swung around to the driver's side and followed suit.

Nicolás stabbed the key into the ignition. The engine hesitated, turning over once, and then twice.

Oh God no. Not now.

He shot a glance at Enrique. Despite the dim light, Nicolás could see his face had turned a sickly pale.

At last the engine growled to life. Nicolás cursed, then jolted the car backward out of its spot and steered it through the parking lot onto the road.

Nicolás slowed. A vintage *segunda clase* bus, surely filled with any combination of chickens, pigs, and passengers.

"Is anyone following?" Nicolás shouted. "Enrique?"

"No, *Señor*. No one."

"Still, I've got to pass him," Nicolás said, checking to ensure the opposing lane was empty.

Nicolás slammed the accelerator hard and they surged around the bus, shot down the avenue, down a side street, then down another avenue.

Enrique clapped three times and let out a celebratory whoop.

"Sorry I was rude," Nicolás said. "Close one, back there. So where do you live? I'm taking you home."

"I live with my parents," Enrique said. "I'll show you the way. Keep on this road for a few minutes. Anyway, I'm impressed with how you pulled that off. So glad my girlfriend wasn't there to see them messing with me."

"Well, look," Nicolás said, recalling his own embarrassment that he had fled the three Segundo Cortez boys, despite their rifles. "We all suffer humiliation from time to time. And defeat."

There was a pause. The hum of the engine remained the only sound in their ears, beyond Nicolás being halfway out of breath.

"Damn, I need to start exercising," Nicolás said.

Enrique cleared his throat, leaned toward him, and stared. He seemed more mystified than curious.

"*Profesor* Nolano, was all that because you remembered me? That literature class?"

"It was the decent thing to do. And I remember you, too, Enrique Ponte," Nicolás said as he lowered the window a bit. He fished a cigarette out of his sport coat's inside pocket, put it between his lips and lit it.

"You were a good student. Always with fresh insights. You have an original mind."

"How have you been?" Enrique said. "Everyone knows about your brother, Esteban. And your mother. That they're activists against Segundo Cortez. I guess we're lucky those guys didn't recognize you."

"My goal's been to keep out of all of that business," Nicolás said, shaking his head. "And out of the public eye. Just to concentrate on my profession."

"Sir, I hear your brother filed a lawsuit two days ago against the head of Segundo Cortez."

"He sure did," Nicolás said, releasing a sigh.

"And your mother sir, she's a *curandera*, right? Doña Lucinda? Giving talks against Segundo Cortez? I saw her speak on television."

Nicolás paused. Was this kid the Grand Inquisitor?

"Well," Nicolás said. "I tried to stop her."

"Hey, *Profesor*, can I please have a cigarette?"

"Not a chance. It's a vice you don't want."

"What do you smoke?"

"Lambert and Butler," Nicolás said.

"British cigarettes? Well, you are an English professor."

"Have you declared a major?"

"Accounting. I'm in my second year."

"Good for you, Enrique. Keep at it."

Yes, maybe the boy would graduate and move away, and set up his practice in safer city. God willing.

"Now, *Señor*, if you could turn right at that next stoplight up there. Then take your second left, at the red brick house."

When Nicolás pulled up to the curb, Enrique extended his hand and Nicolás shook it.

"All right, Enrique. Stay out of that place back there. I will, too. I've never known it to be a cartel spot. Wouldn't surprise me if they're being racketeered."

"My knapsack is still there. My father will want to go back and get it. Tomorrow sometime."

"Your father, not you," Nicolás said. "You know that family that was kidnapped last week? They're still missing. The parents and the boy. No doubt it was the cartel. Anyway, get some sleep. See you on campus sometime."

"Thank you, *Profesor*," Enrique said, and then paused. "*Señor?*"

"Yes?"

"Is it true that you attended the *colegio* with Ivan Méndez?"

The name pierced the moment like a spear. To this boy, what was the answer worth?

"That is true," Nicolás said. "Unfortunately."

"What was that like?" Enrique said, watching him intently with wide eyes.

"Enrique," Nicolás said, feeling a flash of irritation spread over him. "Please."

"I'm sorry, *Profesor*."

Nicolás paused. In his mind he saw the fresh-faced boy of the mid-nineties, an unmistakable innocence beaming outward from the eyes. To think that—as the years wore on— such a nearly untainted soul could grow so monstrous.

"At first, Ivan was a good child. Then he changed. It was not pleasant. He became the class bully. And I could tell he would get much worse. Now we have what he is today."

"May God help us," Enrique said, opening the door and stepping outside. "Thanks again, *Profesor*."

Enrique shut the door. He headed up the walkway to the house, and Nicolás watched until he was safely inside.

As he drove through the night, Nicolás kept finding himself shaking his head. The student was so full of questions, but his curiosity about Ivan and the cartel was justified. Veracruz suffered more and more as Segundo Cortez spread, dumping bodies all over town in the wee hours. Disgusting. Infuriating. His brother Esteban, his adopted mother Lucinda, and the priest who watched over them always, Padre Manolo—perhaps they were wise, after all, to rebel. To ratchet up their open activism.

Segundo Cortez. The Second Cortez. The second invasion by Cortez. He had to give Arturo Méndez that—he had coined the most original name of a cartel ever. Brilliant yet perverse. Hernán Cortez, the Spaniard who appeared one day in Veracruz like a magical knight and, within months, had slaughtered, infected with disease, or subjugated the entire culture around him.

Nicolás mashed out the cigarette into the console ashtray.

Damn, I need to quit these things. I just don't know how.

Though it was Saturday night, Nicolás knew he should be back at his apartment. He still lagged a day or two behind grading papers, and the upcoming events of the Easter Week Festival would consume more of his time. Almost everyone in the city turned out for the festival, and though it was not Nicolás's favorite, it would be hard to escape. And he did have Sunday brunch the next day with his mother...at their usual place. Still, the night was calling him. With all its pleasures, to relieve his loneliness. He could not resist its draw. Just not the same place; he must seek out a different venue. No more running into Segundo Cortez.

Nicolás had always been so lucky, to the point that it surprised him. That run-in back there ...maybe it was a fluke.

When Nicolás pulled into the parking lot, he saw that the nightclub was packed. A line snaked out of the door. He just hoped there was no trace of Segundo Cortez around. Or of its chief's son. After all, he knew Ivan was another addict of nightlife, and of the life of pleasure.

Yes, Ivan Méndez. To think they had once been friends, those many years ago.

2

An entire week had passed in Veracruz without one body being dumped. And the Easter Week Festival arrived. Nicolás sat at the small table in the bright seaside café, finishing a cigarette. He stroked his stubbled jaw, looking out through his sunglasses at the plaza crowded with families. The day was splendid throughout: sunlight flooding the stone floor of the plaza despite its canopy of palms, the cerulean sky devoid of clouds, freighters and sailboats moving across the ocean in the distance. Frequent laughter erupted from the throngs outside. Often he would savor such a spring day in his hometown. It might even match his vision of paradise. Yet the sunlight flowing through the open sliding door of the café seemed to enflame his already sharp hangover. The shouts, laughter, and chattering made his temples throb more. He knew it would worsen when his mother grilled him as she did here—at every Sunday brunch —about his lifestyle, his habits, and his avoidance of any civic activism against Segundo Cortez.

"You need to take it easy, son," Doña Lucinda said. "You know you even do this sometimes on weekdays."

"I know, I know. Don't tell me."

"And you're drinking this minute. And smoking."

"This drink's a necessary remedy, Mother. For the head. Why aren't you enjoying one, like most of the people here?"

"You know the reason." Her strong voice belied her petite frame. "Only on special occasions. Alcohol effects the energy and spirit all throughout your body. It dulls them both."

He smiled inside, noting her straight posture in her floral bohemian dress. He caught her strong scent of sage. He remembered the incense she burned for her healing rituals, this extraordinary *curandera* he loved who once adopted him and his brother from the orphanage.

The waiter appeared, setting down their food before them. Nicolás admired the colorful plates and presentations, and stamped out his cigarette in the ashtray.

"Are you at least feeling better?" she said. Her love really was unrelenting.

"By the minute."

A cumbia band struck up into sound across the plaza.

"*Viva!*" she exclaimed, raising her hands from the table. She gave him a broad smile. He loved how she would often call out her favorite word.

A hand fell on his shoulder.

He flinched, remembering the cartel goons from the evening before. Turning, he saw his younger brother looking down at him, the end of his mouth turned upward in a tight-lipped smile.

"Snuck up on you, Pato," Esteban said.

Damn the mockery in that word. The nickname Esteban coined—Duck. Such an uninspiring, gentle bird.

Esteban kissed the top of Doña Lucinda's head and took a seat just across from Nicolás. Still in his courtroom clothes, minus the suit coat.

"You look drained. Wait," Esteban said. "Are you hungover again?"

"I was," Nicolás said. His stomach clenched as it often did the last several times he and Esteban talked.

"Out late again."

"It was my day off."

"So what was her name, Pato?" Esteban said, shaking his head, a trace of a frown playing about his mouth.

"That's irrelevant, I will submit to the court," Nicolás said, running his hands back through his longish hair. His face began to heat up from more than the sun. Hours earlier he stirred awake to see a nude woman beside him and realized he couldn't recall her name. The first time that had happened he'd blamed it on his hangover. But this third or fourth time—he knew a pattern had formed.

And the irony. He pursued these women out of lust and loneliness. But his loneliest moments were when he waked next to these strangers...

"You can't pull that saintly act on me," Nicolás said, smiling and shaking a finger at him. "I know you and that hot journalist have been rolled up into a sweaty ball at least every other night for a while now. Carla. Carla de Echegaray."

"Me? With her?" Esteban touched his chest in mock surprise. "You have the wrong guy."

"A pair of lovers leading the rebellion," Nicolás said. "Hell, I think she's after the cartel as much as you."

"One matter we've discussed," Esteban said. "Segundo Cortez has been very silent all of a sudden."

"Maybe there's some...internal strife," Nicolás said.

Esteban rolled his eyes at his brother and said, "It will start up again soon. They're just lying low since I filed the suit against Arturo Méndez on Thursday."

"You know how much I've been worried about you, Esteban? And after those Segundo Cortez men beat you senseless in December? And after all those times lately you've been trailed by police cars? I love you both. *Mamá*, he won't hear a word about it. And neither will you. You speaking to groups in your house about Segundo Cortez. And Padre Manolo doing the same. Over and over, to his entire congregation. Padre fanned your flames. He knew he was inciting you two. He knew you were already the most outspoken activists in the whole damned city."

"You should get involved, too," his mother said. "You used to be more engaged in things. Until Segundo Cortez came around. Now take your stand, at last."

Nicolás slapped his hands down on his thighs with a grunt. Their overtures would never end. He admitted it to himself: he strived to ignore Segundo Cortez. Most of its atrocities seemed to meld into one grotesque act, a crime too horrific to contemplate. And he just knew that if he resisted the cartel out in the open, he, too, would end up as one of those atrocities. It was his only reason not to rebel, and it was more than enough.

"You know," Esteban said, the expression in his eyes going from proud to thoughtful as it often did, "that, for many years, I used to look up to you. And it can become that way again. Look, brother. You've been given so much. Me too. Now it's time to give back. I can construct solid arguments. And I can write op-eds, well, adequately. But not as well as you. You're the writer. Come on, man. I really could use your help."

"I fight the cartel in my own way. In private comments to my students."

"That's not enough. The irony of it, man. Me, the idealistic attorney. You, the cynical literature professor. Damn, just like when we were boys. You always off in your bedroom, in your own universe, your nose in a book, dreaming. While I was out living. Making dreams into reality."

Damn that pride in him.

"You're so high on yourself," Nicolás said with a scornful laugh. "Always have been."

Esteban's eyes erupted into rapid blinks. For a second, his nostrils flared as he began to stare. Then he closed his eyes. Exhaling, he placed his hands, fingers outstretched, onto the table.

"There's safety in numbers, brother. If enough of the people speak up and don't fold, that'll make the difference. Damned cartel can't get us all."

The crowds roared in the distance, a great din unlike anything Nicolás had heard that morning. It was no collective cry of exultation like before.

It was terror.

The muscles in his abdomen tightened. Barreling down the avenue between the sea and the plaza, as the crowds shrank back, was the caravan of four vehicles. Mercedes and Porsche SUVs, and one midnight-blue commercial van. Atop an SUV's antenna, that dreaded scarlet banner of the Segundo Cortez cartel flapped in the wind.

At the table, Nicolás stood, his mother and brother with him. He could feel it as his heart pounded faster—something was about to change. Time was slowing down. It was not a mere passing of a cartel caravan.

If only he had stayed home that morning. He could have been safe in bed, lost in oblivion.

A few shrill screams erupted—female voices.

"Wait here," Esteban said. As the crowd surged forward, he shot out into it.

"Esteban!" Nicolás yelled. "Stay back! Stay back till they leave!"

He had disappeared. Doña Lucinda bolted through the café's open sliding door into the edge of the crowd. Nicolás cursed, jerked his body away from the table and by instinct began to sprint toward her. He could see the last SUV pass—a Mercedes with its windows down. Inside, hockey-masked men held

Kalashnikovs upright in their laps. He drew alongside his mother and grabbed her around the shoulders.

"Wait! Wait a second, Mother!" She writhed in his arms with a surprising ferocity. He held her tight until the caravan had passed for several seconds. He let go. She worked her way through the crowds, and he followed just behind, mumbling profanities.

Nicolás could hear the onlookers. Some argued with great emotion, while some swore in disbelief and outrage. A few even wept.

He must reach his mother and Esteban, immediately. The thought presented itself: He could lose them both forever, right here and now.

"Lucinda! Esteban!" he screamed, as he elbowed his way through the crowd.

Seconds later the crowds were behind him, and Nicolás spotted his brother just meters away, staring at his feet, his hands on his hips. Esteban bit his lower lip as he shook his head.

Nicolás saw the bodies. There were four of them. Two men, their severed heads resting nearby on the asphalt. And just a step or two beyond them, from where he and the edge of the crowd watched and stood, there was something else.

Oh God no. It could not be.

A woman lay in her bra and panties, her throat slit, her body covered with bruises. And just beyond her, a boy, about twelve years in age.

No mercy could be found from Segundo Cortez. No quarter. And no honor.

So Segundo Cortez had moved on from leaving *encobijados*, or corpses wrapped in blankets and electrical tape. These were nearly nude bodies in plain view, amidst a festival. A woman and child? Segundo Cortez was becoming like other cartels, that just years ago had started to kill women. And he remembered, in the north, in Juarez or Tamaulipas, another cartel had turned a teenage birthday party into a massacre.

His heart pounded as he noticed the boy's head twitch. Doña Lucinda let out an agonizing cry and shot forward into the opening toward the boy. Nicolás shoved his way past an onlooker, sprinted toward the boy, and stopped just one meter shy of his small frame. He knelt.

The boy's eyes had been put out.

Nicolás's throat burned. He became aware of the smells invading his nostrils: sweat, human waste, and the metallic smell of blood. Rarely in a Segundo Cortez dumping had there been a female. And never before a child, or a live body. His stomach threatened to turn itself inside out.

Doña Lucinda burst out in loud wails, hugging the boy to her and sitting him up as she inspected him for further wounds. There were none. The crowd sighed as she held the boy's head to her breast. She whispered to him in that assuaging tone she used in her healings. A shadow spread across the boy. Nicolás looked upward.

Esteban stared down at the boy, then back at the dead woman, and then again at the boy. His mouth moved, but no sound emerged. Never had he seen Esteban so stunned. So helpless.

Doña Lucinda wedged her purse under the boy's head, atop the surely scalding asphalt. The crowd crept closer.

"Yes, they're watching right now," Esteban said with anger. "At least one of them. Or they're returning in the next few minutes. To do a drive-by or to watch our movements."

Nicolás knew how it was. No ambulance would come for thirty, forty-five minutes, even sixty minutes. In many parts of Mexico, even the paramedics feared the cartels returning, though children and their parents alike would stand and gawk.

"We need to get him to the hospital now, Esteban," Nicolás said, shooting to his feet. "I'm going for my car."

"His left side's bleeding," Doña Lucinda said. She tore a large hole in his T-shirt. "See? It's a puncture wound, a blade. Esteban, get down and apply some pressure to it."

Esteban knelt, found the wound, and slapped his palm onto it.

"Press hard," she said. "And yes, go for your car, Nicolás. Hurry."

Then she stood, screaming, *"Cobardes! Cobardes! Bárbaros!"* Her bloody fists were raised, with her throat choking as she turned in a circle, looking over the crowds as if searching for an unseen foe. For a moment, she faced Nicolás as she turned. It was almost as if she was screaming the words at him.

Shame crept over him. Perhaps he should have acted, or have spoken out, long ago.

Fear had fused his feet to the pavement. The uncensored photos in the news were nothing like seeing it in the flesh.

But he must save the boy.

He nodded at his brother's widening gaze and sprinted down the avenue toward the parking garage.

3

That evening, Nicolás steered his car uphill along the oyster-shell drive, through the steaming forest thick with palms. He parked before the church rectory, just beside Padre Manolo's Volvo; Padre and Esteban had returned long before them from the hospital.

As Nicolás and his mother stepped outside he tried to place it —that Volkswagen beside the Volvo. Why yes, of course. Esteban's new flame Carla would be joining their tradition, the Padre's Sunday-night dinner. Nicolás once loved the tradition, but as of late he had been tempted to abandon it due to his family's pushy overtures. And now he would have to sit with one of the top new photographers of the Veracruz *notas rojas*. Those papers with their gory photos—what disgusting excuses for news publications. Lower than yellow journalism.

He turned and glanced at his mother. Her head of gray-streaked black hair drooped from fatigue as they stood at the rectory door. It had been the longest day, for her and for them all. Nicolás was worried about her but knew that Padre's cooking would make it somewhat better.

He rang the doorbell. Approaching steps caught his ear, and

the door opened. Padre Manolo stood there, still dressed in his customary black short-sleeved shirt and white collar.

"There you are," Padre said, his face exuding a quiet peace that mirrored Lucinda's. Despite the man's harassing him to join his activism, Nicolás loved the Padre as he always had since boyhood.

Just inside the house, a remarkable aroma greeted Nicolás.

"Welcome," Padre said. His usual merry tone had flattened into solemnity. "Just in time. Take a seat."

Doña Lucinda and Padre sank into their chairs at the heads of the table. Each gazed at the other with a version of the same preoccupied expression. Nicolás sat between them, beside Juan, the print reporter Carla photographed for, with his large, morose eyes.

"Hello, Carla...Juan," Nicolás said. He raised his gaze across the table. Esteban and Carla, seated beside one other, each forced a smile.

"I suppose the boy was still sedated when you left," Esteban said with an air of gravitas.

"Yes he was, praise God," Doña Lucinda drew out her words, her speech more fatigued than it had been almost two hours before, at the hospital. "Poor child. He will be out until morning, the doctor told us. His aunt and uncle and cousins are still there, though, you saw them. I'm returning tomorrow morning to visit him. And I can help with his healing. The hospital will care for his body. I will take care of his spirit."

"Never have I seen anything so diabolical," the priest said. "Veracruz...the situation is changing."

Nicolás felt the guilt return. Should he join their cause at last? No, by no means. It would be insanity. His family was about to come at him hard. He would have to fight them.

"This is why we need my brother on our side," Esteban said. They've already started in. And this early in the dinner.

"You were great today, Nicolás, running for the car," Esteban said. "And rushing the boy to the hospital. But could anything more convince you of what we are up against?"

"I know this very well," Nicolás said. "That's exactly why you should all be laying low. Each time you condemn Segundo Cortez to a group, or file suit against it, you get more in its crosshairs."

"Laying low and biding your time is not how change is won in the world, I keep telling you," Padre Manolo said, running his finger along his priest's white collar.

Nicolás said, "You know they killed two students at the university. And they have moles everywhere. Look, resistance needs to survive to be powerful. You know you're all setting yourselves up for tragedy."

As the others stared at him, Carla leaned forward and cleared her throat. She was indeed captivating. Those flashing eyes seemed as if a roaring furnace lay somewhere just behind them. With high cheekbones, glowing skin, and an impish smile, Esteban's quip was right: She belonged not just behind the camera, but also in front of it.

"With all you could offer to Padre and your brother and your mother," she said, "you shouldn't stand on the sidelines. Your writing, your position at the university. And you would be even more impactful because people would know they were hearing from Esteban Nolano's brother."

Nicolás could feel the blood rising into his face.

"You don't deserve to say that. You spend your days and nights on call for the next cartel kill. Then you speed to the scene and photograph the victims up close. You did this to those two students. Do you have any shame? Would you want someone to do that to you? Your mother, your brother?"

"Nicolás!" Esteban shouted.

"The people have a right to know," Juan said, raising his eyebrows at Nicolás.

"No," Nicolás said. "That is not an actual right a person is born with. That violation of dignity. Today I bet you two got there right after I drove the boy out. How many up-close photos did you take of the other bodies for next morning's rag? You don't even see this practice in the American tabloids. Not even in the British ones."

"You don't need to insult them," Padre said.

"But you know I'm right," Nicolás said. "I don't need to defy Segundo Cortez behind the podium. I can keep doing it in private. And eventually one cartel will gain supremacy and absorb or eliminate the others. Then there will be only one true cartel in the nation. It won't be Segundo Cortez. And Mexico will coexist with one group as she has before. Things will be calmer."

Esteban shot to his feet. "Coward."

Nicolás felt his ears growing hot. He glanced at the young woman beside Esteban and saw her looking up at her lover with admiration. Absurd.

"Coward? Sit back down in your chair," Nicolás said, smirking up at his brother. To think that Esteban once respected, even admired him. This thought ate at his core. He was infuriated at Esteban, but even more, he felt disgust at his fling with a *notas rojas* photographer.

"Esteban, sit down now and stop that," Lucinda said.

Padre reached over and tugged Esteban's wrist. Esteban paused, and then sank back into his chair.

"Nicolás makes his own decisions," Padre said. "Do you hear me? We have asked him enough. Now, I made this dinner and want us to all enjoy it. Talk about other things while I bring it out. Understand?"

He shot a fiery glance, one by one, into the eyes of each guest.

"Yes, fine," Esteban said, shaking his head with a blink.

"I totally agree," Nicolás said.

Padre disappeared into the kitchen. He brought in the plates, two by two, and said, "*Huachinango a la Veracruzana.* With papaya salad and rice. Almost as good as Nicolás' cooking, I'd say."

He then moved around the table, pouring more Rioja Tempranillo. Nicolás felt his mood lift. The local dish was among his favorites: red snapper in a spicy red sauce with green olives and onions, capers, and garlic.

They ate in tense silence. Doña Lucinda returned his gaze with a gentle smile. Her eyes were soft, their irises jet-black, yet they were as piercing as any eyes of the lightest blue could be. He often got the sense they plumbed the farthest depths of his soul, that in the end he could hide nothing from her. She knew all of his faults well, but she loved him nevertheless. Perhaps she still loved the innocent boy he once was.

As Nicolás resumed eating, concentrating on savoring each mouthful, he could no longer contain what still burned in his heart.

"Esteban, you're my brother and I love you," Nicolás said. "Padre, you always have been like my father, and Lucinda like my mother. I'm worried about you three in a way someone only does if they truly love you. I don't sense it improving for you. Unless you reverse course, and stop resisting for a good while, I see it getting worse."

"It may have to get worse before it gets better," Padre said. "That's probably inevitable."

"I worry about that police car following you everywhere, Esteban," Nicolás said. "And one followed Lucinda the other day. Maybe trying to intimidate. Maybe something worse. You know they've infected the police."

"Stop worrying," Esteban said. "Start being brave."

Whenever Nicolás was starting to feel guilt, his brother always cut it short.

"You know, honestly, I'm disgusted by your arrogance, Esteban. Judging me with such harshness. Calling out my entire character for not joining your crusade—"

"Crusade?" Esteban said. "We're not on any crusade. We are reacting in the way a dignified, well-adjusted human being should. You're the one on the wrong path."

Nicolás sighed and shut his eyes. How humiliating. And in front of the journalists. He rose and tossed his napkin beside his plate. "Esteban, you often did think too poorly of others, too highly of yourself. And Padre, *Mamá*, you both enabled it."

"Fine, just go then," Esteban said with irritation. "I'll take Mother home."

Nicolás marched down the foyer and out the door. On the gravel drive, he paused. How rude to not say goodbye to Lucinda. And to Padre, who had even prepared the meal. He would just catch up with them tomorrow.

An ocean breeze threaded its fingers through the night as Nicolás drove toward his apartment. Where the shell drive adjoined the avenue, he stopped, and fished another cigarette from his sport coat breast pocket. As he lit it, his eyes focused on something about ten meters before him. His adrenaline surged. A police car had parked across the two lanes, its lights off.

He shook his head. It was just another sign he had been right to stay on the sidelines.

Nicolás turned left onto the avenue and accelerated. He counted to thirty, and when he saw the patrol car did not pursue him, he pulled his cell from inside his sport coat.

"Padre Manolo?" Nicolás said. "A little warning. I'll tell you what I just saw..."

4

Nicolás closed the hardback volume on his lectern and looked out at the young faces before him. How hopeful, innocent, and untried so many of them appeared.

"All right. There you have it," he said, smiling. "Remember, your essay on Robert Jordan and the last chapter of *For Whom The Bell Tolls* is due next Wednesday, after Easter. Don't forget to examine the significance of the bridge, and the symbolism of detonating that bridge."

His students paused, then trickled out of the class. Among them was Mar, slender yet curvy, with her finely chiseled face. She was so distinct: his quirkiest, most beautiful, and perhaps his brightest student. As she neared the door, he spotted her hemp sandals, multicolored yoga pants, navy-blue pea coat, and a red scarf encircling her neck.

"*Hasta luego, Profesor Nolano,*" Mar said, flashing her smile of white teeth.

"Take care, Mar. Good luck on the essay." She was a senior, and twenty-three, but—despite her flirtations and all of his desire for her—he still could not step across that line.

Ah, Fate. If only they had been undergrad students together.

After all the students departed, Nicolás swept his palms back across his hair, and then shut the door. As he organized his papers, his thoughts returned to last night's dinner. His guilt grew over leaving with no goodbye. And over that last statement to his brother before he had walked out. Then there was the worry—the police car waiting near the rectory—just the most recent of many such sightings. Something was building.

He needed to apologize—to Esteban and the Padre and Lucinda. It nagged at him all day.

He looked at his watch. Two-thirty. First, he would phone his mother, as that call was the easiest. But there was no answer. He replaced his phone in his pants' front pocket. He would see Lucinda anyway that afternoon.

In fact, he would leave early. His last class had ended, after all. He missed Lucinda—yesterday was the first time in a week he had seen her. He jammed his papers into his leather bag and locked the classroom.

Yes, he missed her all right, he thought, as he turned his key in the ignition and headed out of the faculty parking lot into the traffic. He even missed the odd and sometimes bizarre rituals he had witnessed since his childhood, employing anything from sprinkled rosemary and basil to burning sage and sandalwood incense, to used coffee grounds and rare Catholic saints' relics. Some of her rituals had proved curative, he had to admit. It was utterly inexplicable.

Half an hour later, he noticed the front door of her house was open, just a crack. She must be mopping again, and airing out the den. He would have to gently chide her for leaving the door not just unlocked, but ajar.

He pushed the door open, smiling. He would apologize, crack some jokes, and all would be fine again.

Yet something wasn't right.

Wait. Was it not a smell? What in creation was it? There it

was again in his nostrils—that strange unforgettable smell from the day before—of blood and human waste.

"*Hola, Mamá?*" he called, his voice wobbly in his ears.

In reply, there was only silence.

"*Mamá?*" he called again, his heart already racing. More silence.

He took brisk steps inside. The smell intensified, and as he crossed the dining room he found himself pinching his nose for a moment, by instinct.

In the living room, he spotted an odd shape on the hardwood floor, poking out from behind the coffee table.

Please God, just don't let it be that.

His heart felt squeezed, as if by some invisible hand. The shape on the floor was familiar to his eye, and his reason produced the dreaded explanation, but a voice within him denied it. He forced himself to approach, on tiptoe—he knew not why. Was it not his brother's black wingtip?

Nicolás focused his eyes on his own feet as he drew near. Then wincing, his shoulders raised high in a shrug, he turned his head slowly to the side and downward, squinting as if a wild dog could leap out at any moment.

His stomach tightened, then wrenched at the sight of the three bodies.

No, no, no...please *Mamá*, take me away from here.

The plea sounded within his mind, something from decades back in his childhood. But neither his mother nor Padre Manolo could take him or his brother away. All three lay below him, and no longer inhabited the world.

Forward onto his kneecaps he fell, then onto his forearms, his forehead touching the hardwood floor as he wept in a loud convulsion. Faint tremors commenced in his forearms and spread throughout all of his limbs and torso. With one hand, he gripped his stomach. He could not bear to lift his face from the floor.

His throat burned with sorrow and rage. There it was again in his nostrils—the smell was almost overpowering.

Nicolás pulled himself to his knees, then onto his feet, and forced himself to step over to the closest body. Collapsing again onto his knees, he felt Esteban's neck for a pulse that was not there. For the first time in his life, he cradled his brother's head like an infant's in one hand. The closed eyes and slightly opened mouth almost gave Nicolás the impression Esteban was sleeping. Forcing himself to draw in and release deep breaths through his mouth, he ran his eyes across the many crimson spots in his brother's gray pinstripe suit and white, starched office shirt.

Esteban was all he had ever had. They never knew their blood parents. Padre Manolo and Doña Lucinda raised them with such selflessness, and gifted them with a stellar education. Now they were all gone.

A memory from many years past surfaced in his mind: him as a boy of ten, waking as an eight-year-old Esteban stood beside him, begging him to share his bed. They had just seen a violent action film that night, and Esteban could not sleep. But he had ordered Esteban from his room in irritation. Yet another moment residing in the immutable past, a film he longed to rewind, then edit.

He remembered those last cruel words to his brother over dinner the night before. If only they had never escaped his mouth. Now there could be no retracting them, no apology.

Pivoting in his kneeling position, he placed a hand on Padre's shoulder, and then muttered a prayer as he felt for a pulse. Nothing. He could not help but notice the great wound in Padre's forehead, just above his open eyes, and groaned. The blood congealed into a common pool between the corpses. A fly buzzed overhead.

As he closed Padre's eyes with his fingers, something caught his peripheral vision. A cardboard sign, propped against the coffee table, bore an inscription in red permanent marker. It was a narco hit, after all. The *sicarios*, or hitmen, always left such *narcomantas*. The words sent his already pounding heart into a wild dash.

CIERREN LA BOCA, PINCHE IDIOTAS
LOS QUE PIENSAN QUE PUEDEN CHINGAR AL
SEGUNDO CORTEZ
NICOLAS, ERES EL PROXIMO

His teeth clenched at the message, threatening anyone who challenged Segundo Cortez to keep their mouths shut or face death. Warning Nicolás that he was next. Outrage rose within his throat like vomit until he swore aloud.

After mustering the will for a few moments, he turned toward the third body. He found himself weeping with even more passion.

He forced himself to do what was the most difficult: to step the few meters to his mother. She lay on her side, her back facing him, the crimson stain halfway between her shoulder blades. He could not bring himself to turn her over, or to cross over her body so he could face her. Instead he knelt and, holding his breath, reached around for her neck, to check her pulse. There was none. Like the others, her skin was lukewarm to the touch.

At least they had not disfigured or dismembered the bodies, as in many of their other hits. That would have crushed him; his heart would have stopped. Nicolás slammed the door behind him and bolted across the lawn toward his car.

That sign they left. Damn them to hell. And despite all his years of neutrality—they announced they were coming for him.

Tears continued to trail down his cheeks and drip from his jaw as he reached the driveway. Never again would he see his mother, brother and Padre alive. Saying goodbye, and asking forgiveness, was now beyond his power.

Get the hell away, Nicolás. Before Segundo Cortez returns for you. Before their puppet police detain you.

No. He must change. He had to.

Someone or some people would die for this act—Arturo Méndez, his son Ivan. And their enabler, Police Chief Hector Pantano. He could not, would not, let them win.

As he sped away, he clenched his hair in his fist. Surely he could only get one of them: Pantano or the cartel's own chief, Arturo Méndez. But he must choose, as once one fell, the other would come for him. There could only be one, and then he must flee.

No more tears came. Would Esteban have chosen the police chief? Méndez committed evil with impunity and made no pretense that he was good. But Pantano masqueraded as the city's heroic protector yet proved corrupt to the core. He'd obstructed Esteban for years in all of his attempts to prosecute Segundo Cortez and its protectors in law enforcement.

Nicolás recalled how Esteban received that late-night call a week before. Some mystery caller ordered him to cease all investigations into Segundo Cortez and the local and state police forces, threatening him with death. And of course, there was that police car trailing Esteban, from the courthouse to his law office to his house to many other destinations in Veracruz.

But Nicolás knew that he must choose Méndez. He was the source.

Yet this was all nonsense. He was powerless to take the life of either of these men. Had he forgotten he was merely a professor?

Then he hit upon it. He knew what he must do, as insignificant as it was. Pulling over, he exhaled a long breath into the stillness of his car. He checked his watch. Three-thirty. A few errands awaited. But one thing was certain: Going home was not an option. Neither was staying in Veracruz. In fact, he knew that, for now, he must leave the country. He could not hide in some far-off corner of Mexico. It had grown too compromised by the cartels. He just knew it. The longer he stayed, the sooner Segundo Cortez would find him. Whether in Baja California, Chihuahua, Tamaulipas—there could be no refuge within his homeland.

It must be America.

His mind shuddered at the thought, at the enormity of the move he was poised to make. One thing was sure. If he survived this next act, his life would prove unrecognizable in a matter of days.

Realizing his head was trembling, Nicolás slapped his palms onto his face.

Was his entire psyche on the verge of breaking?

5

Hours later, Nicolás eased his car forward to a mere crawl, its headlights extinguished despite the fading twilight. Beside the chain-link fence, he came to the point closest to the warehouse on the opposite side. He braked, then scanned his surroundings. Not a guard in sight.

All of the errands—to the bank to withdraw all of his cash and convert most to dollars, to the home improvement store, to the gas station to refuel, to another store for a knapsack, knife, water, cigarettes, and dried food—they had not expended an ounce of his energy. Every bit of adrenaline his body could produce—he felt it coursing through his veins in preparation for this moment. This last act before fleeing was the least he could do, for now. Even it proved only a gesture of retribution, and defiance.

He recalled his brother, his torso ripped with gunfire, his eyes closed, and mouth agape.

Arturo and Ivan were probably not nearby. But he knew from Esteban that this was one of their depots for their product. True revenge would come later, but they would feel this in the gut.

Wedged between his thighs were the three prepared Molotov cocktails. He could not miss. Each one must count.

He opened his door, wrapped his hands around the bottles and alighted from his car. Near the front bumper, he set the three bottles down onto the asphalt. He pulled the lighter from his back pocket.

He felt as if he was about to be sick. But he closed his eyes and drew in and released several breaths, hoping to calm his nerves and stomach. For a second he recalled the famous work by the street artist Banksy, with the protestor hurling the Molotov cocktail containing a flower. His own work he was about to create would not be so gentle in expression. He rolled a bottle in his palm until he found a good grip.

This one is for Lucinda.

He drew in a deep breath, lit the rag, and hurled the bottle over the fence at the roof of the warehouse. It came up short, breaking apart against the side of the warehouse, catching a small patch of it aflame.

He lit and hurled the second, sending it into an arc over the fence, shattering the large office window. Shouting reached his ears. His heart thundered faster as his stomach turned, threatening to go into full revolt. He recalled his feeling from earlier that day, in Lucinda's house: that all along he had been so powerless, so ineffectual. He knew he could alter that course forever. If only this one bottle would hit the mark.

Please God, send this one inside. This last one is for all three.

He threw the third. It rose, arced, and entered the cavity of the broken window. As black smoke billowed upward, the shouting intensified. He dove into the car and sped off.

Trickling sweat cooled his face, his arms, back, and chest. His whole world had morphed, seconds before, into something even more unrecognizable. Strange territory surrounded him, and he was its sole explorer. He was going it alone, companionless, with no ally.

Nicolás swung onto Calle de Almagro, gunned his car a few blocks, and then down a few side streets toward the truck stop. He jerked the wheel and shot across its parking lot.

At last a sense of victory welled up in his breast, since the Méndez clan would hear of this attack, loud and clear. And mere hours after their hit on their three activist gadflies.

His elation gave way to the fear from hours before. Was Segundo Cortez on the cusp of finding him? Nicolás imagined that caravan from the festival reappearing, speeding into the parking lot.

But nothing yet had diverted him from his plan. With keys left in the ignition and the engine still running, one of the many homeless who congregated here would take the wheel in no time.

He yanked his coat and backpack from the passenger's seat and pushed his newsboy cap low over his eyes. Once outside, the chirping of birds caught his ears. The sound of a tranquil joy, and perhaps, of promise. Would he really make it out alive?

Shutting the door and leaving it unlocked, he crossed the lot toward a trucker about to climb into his cab.

"*Señor?*" Nicolás called.

"*Sí?*" the trucker said, looking down at Nicolás with fierce eyes. He was a large man, tall for a Mexican, stocky, and broad across the shoulders. His head was a greasy dome devoid of even stubble.

"I lost my home this week," Nicolás said. "Please, help me. For the love of God. I need to get to America. I have family there."

It was not such an unbelievable lie. Yet the man hesitated.

"Where are you headed?" Nicolás said.

"I'm headed all the way to Tijuana."

"Here, how's fifty American dollars?" Nicolás handed a wad

of cash to the man, who seized it and shuffled it in his fingers without counting it.

Some engine roared in the distance. Had Segundo Cortez uncovered his location?

"Can you just stow me in the back?" Nicolás said in a stammer, feeling fresh sweat popping out on his brow.

"Deal. I'll get you there, *guey*," he said, leading Nicolás toward the back of the truck. He opened the bolt and motioned for Nicolás to climb inside. "I'll let you out at stops to hit the bathroom. Just don't piss in my truck."

"Never," Nicolás said as he climbed inside. Perhaps he would reach the border after all.

The massive metal door closed and Nicolás heard the bolt turn. Despite the coolness within the truck, his sweat returned. Now he had relinquished all control. Hope, and prayer—it was all that remained.

Surely it couldn't be this simple. Could he trust this stranger? Would the cartel or police intercept the truck and search it? Could the driver himself be a cartel trafficker? He had no other choice.

Never before had he felt so vulnerable. In Lucinda's house hours before, he had felt so powerless. But this new feeling was different. Never before was his life so at the mercy of another man, a man whose heart and character were unknown quantities.

Nicolás sat between what he could feel were two pallets of crates. He drew his knees against his chest and enclosed them in his arms. Allowing his eyes to shut, he drew in one long, profound breath. Then he released it into the darkness.

Lucinda, Esteban, Padre Manolo—they were forever lost. His soul throbbed with grief, and the loneliness of his new flight. The only thing that shoved the pain below, if only for now, was the dread of being caught, tortured, killed. As if in a nuclear reaction, these emotions coursed through him from various points, colliding in massive combustion.

He forced his mind to concentrate on the arson. Surely there was some triumph in that. Was there not?

He must believe, and keep believing. He must believe that his full escape—and later revenge—would occur. His northern passage to America, and through America, had begun.

6

Nicolás's eyelids jerked open as the wheels below him squeaked and ground to a halt. A moment later, he heard the great bolt move in its case. The door swung ajar.

Sunlight streamed into the cargo hold, forcing his eyes shut. His back ached, but he sat upright. His watch showed eight nineteen in the morning. At least he had found sleep for a few hours.

"I need some more money," the man said, standing just outside the truck bed. "Otherwise I must unload you here, in Monterrey."

Nicolás's stomach wrenched as he imagined himself deserted. "I see your game. I paid you well. You gave me your word you'd take me to Tijuana. Now you'd just ditch me here."

Once again those fierce eyes glared straight at him, the lips pursed.

"You must pay me a tip for the ride. Everyone does."

"But you're taking me to Tijuana," Nicolás said. "I already paid you."

"*No importa*. I deserve a bigger payment."

Nicolás paused. What could he do? He considered his predicament, and his goal. He imagined the cartel speeding toward him, newly tipped off by the shifty truck driver.

"How much are you asking for?" Nicolás said.

"You are using dollars," the man said. "So fifty American dollars."

"Thirty dollars. And first I need to hit the bathroom," Nicolás said. "You know how long I've been locked in there. You never stopped for me to relieve myself, you know. Then I'll pay you the cash."

"Fine, *guey*."

Nicolás let himself down onto the pavement, eyeing the driver. Then he walked across the grass to the truck stop, his pack strapped across his back. He lit a cigarette and puffed it as fast as he could—over fourteen hours had passed since his last.

As he departed the bathroom, he saw the driver entering from the other end.

Nicolás waited by the rear of the truck, smoking his cigarette, when the driver appeared, moments later.

"Open the door back up," Nicolás said. "And let me inside, and I'll pay you."

The driver's eyes narrowed with irritation. He unbolted and opened the door and Nicolás stepped up and scrambled inside. He pulled the wad of bills from his coat pocket and handed it to the trucker, who took and shuffled it in his hands.

"Good. This is fair. Now let's get back on the road," the man said.

Nicolás shook his head. Fair?

He took a couple of steps backward, turned, and walked farther inside the truck. Reaching the pallets, he turned toward the door.

The trucker squinted at him, a smile twitching at the edge of his mouth. He grasped the handle and swung the door shut, his gaze never leaving that of his passenger.

In the next several hours, the driver let him outside to urinate twice. They proved welcome breaks from his situation. Though the metal floor of the truck bed was cool under his back, it jerked and jolted at random. Only after many hours was he able to find sleep, this time a light, dreamless slumber.

Nicolás woke to the sound of the truck door opening. Past the pallets the man stood, staring at him in the darkness.

"Come out," the trucker said.

"What is it?" Nicolás asked, as he hopped onto the gravel. They were at a roadside, not at a truck stop. Through the dusk, past the driver's shoulder, Nicolás saw the glimmering lights of a town. Surely they were nowhere near Tijuana.

"Where are we?" Nicolás said.

"That is the town of Sonoyta. We're a few miles south of the border, south of Lukeville, Arizona," the driver said. "I need more money for the trip. Or you'll have to walk here. Trust me, Sonoyta's a town you don't want to enter. Even at one in the morning, like now."

"I can't believe this," Nicolás said. "Scoundrel. Thief!" He spit at the man's feet, as his eyes locked onto the driver's. In his coat pockets, his hand felt for his new hunting knife, in case the man rushed him. "I'd rather die than give you another peso, *pinche ladrón.*"

Nicolás was glad he was wearing his backpack and his coat, his cash sewn inside. He had been prepared for this treachery each time the truck stopped. He took brisk steps backwards and then turned and marched toward the lights, away from the swearing trucker and his eighteen-wheeler.

"I will warn you again," he heard the man call out. "You'd be wise to pay and come with me. You do not want to go anywhere near that town. You just don't understand."

"How could I ever trust your word?" Nicolás shouted back at him. "On anything?"

As he proceeded down the silent dusty road toward the lights, the semi's engine gunned up far behind him.

Esteban, Doña Lucinda, and Padre Manolo appeared in his mind, as if they dwelled there, in living form. An unexpected memory emerged: Padre bringing wrapped gifts that Christmas to the orphanage visiting room. His little brother squealing with delight and ripping off the wrapping paper. The memory had not faded into oblivion. He was five, and Esteban was three.

He thought of that last meal at the church rectory, and then tried his best to purge the memory from his mind, at least for the moment. But this conjured up the faces of the reporter and the photographer. How did Juan and Carla escape the narco hit? At the rectory, did he not hear them say they would join the meeting at Lucinda's house the following day? Despite their anti-cartel stance, were they spies?

He must go into hiding, then find some income and stability, somewhere far to the north. Then he must return to Veracruz—after he somehow acquired weapons and training—to strike at Segundo Cortez. And if he was even bolder, at Pantano. And if they were accomplices, he would find Juan and Carla.

As he cut through the streets, Nicolás came to a plaza. A group of men smoked and drank around an old Suburban's tailgate.

"Hey, you there!" a man shouted. "What in the hell are you looking for, *hombre?*"

Nicolás felt his heart accelerate. "I am looking to cross the border. Just have to figure out where to do it."

The group erupted into laughter. There was something about them—all muscles and gaudy jewelry—he had seen their type before in Veracruz, as Segundo Cortez caravans passed.

The man reached around toward his lower back and pulled

something from his belt. It was a semiautomatic pistol, and now the man trained it on him.

"Know who we are, *cabrón?* Get over here. Now."

Every cell of Nicolás had frozen in time. Save for his heart, which seemed on the verge of bursting. He had made it so very far north, to the border at last. He could not die now.

Surely these were cartel men. But they were not Segundo Cortez. The Méndez footprint did not stretch this far north. But did it matter much?

"Put your hands up, *pendejo!*" the man yelled. "Move."

Nicolás raised his hands in the air and stepped toward the cluster of men. As he approached, second by second, he felt the presence of evil nearing. It was unmistakable.

One of them opened the back door of the Suburban, just behind them. Nicolás was two meters away from the cluster when it unraveled. Half of the men swung behind him, pushing him into the open door.

"Get in," a voice said in a growl. "And keep your mouth shut."

As the Suburban jerked into motion, and sped down the road and then cut through the town's narrow streets, Nicolás did not raise his eyes from his lap. In his nostrils swirled four smells: old sweat, tequila, beer, and cigarette smoke.

"Now, listen to me," the voice said from the front seat. It was the voice from before.

"Look up, *guey.* See those two tents, those two camps ahead?"

Nicolás raised his head and looked though the windshield, aware that the first cartel soldier was staring at him from the front passenger's seat. Ahead stretched a wide parking lot, flanked on opposite sides by two massive tents. Under each were blurry forms of people, some seated and some pacing.

"Only we can get you to where you're going, *guey.* If you have enough money, get under that tent on the left. If you don't, you get under that tent on the right. Try to escape, and you'll regret it."

"You'll get this," a voice said from the driver's seat. Nicolás saw a hand leave the steering wheel for a moment, then reappear, holding aloft a massive knife, its sinister silhouette threatening him through the darkness.

7

"But what have you *found*?" Ivan Méndez said, staring straight at him.

Pantano eyed the Segundo Cortez bodyguards beside him, and then glanced back at Ivan. But the young man now gazed at his own reflection in the wall mirror. That old vanity Pantano recalled from decades before had never left Arturo's elder son, now thirty-two. No doubt it was a face that usually gave him pride. But now all about the eyes was darkness: the whites around the black corneas and pupils were bloodshot, and the lower lids crowned semicircles of dark gray. Between that warehouse arson and his father then suffering the massive heart attack, the man probably had not slept a wink all night.

"Tell me, Pantano," Ivan said, "so I can get back to the hospital."

"Well, we finally recovered the car," Pantano began. "Nicolás Nolano's Alfa Romeo. A thief had it. At first he wouldn't divulge where he got it, but after a bit of physical manipulation, we were able to get him to spill everything. Thief was a boy of seventeen, a pauper. Found the car running at a truck stop near Sor Juana Park. The keys were in it, and the engine was still running.

Almost like Nolano wanted someone to steal it as soon as possible."

"The car was stolen within minutes, seconds?"

Odd query. This young upstart was so naïve. Nothing like his father.

"Our city has more than a few desperate people, *Señor.*"

Pantano shot a look beside him at a bodyguard. In the man's blank stare, he detected shock.

"Pantano, you ingrate. I don't need your sarcasm," Ivan said. "That amusement—I can see it all in your eyes. You forget my father really lined your pockets. And until he recovers, guess who runs Segundo Cortez? You will have to reckon with me. You know, ironically, my father never would have founded and built this organization if your police department had just promoted him at least once. You know he was one of your best cops. And he was your good friend. Your best friend, even. You got promoted to lieutenant, and eventually he quits. And then soon after, you're the chief. And you didn't even try to bring him back into the force. You permitted his humiliation. You know it dishonored my family."

Silence ensued. Ivan was right. He couldn't rehire a former cop who had fallen into the drug game. But he also knew that as police chief he would never admit it. And the kid didn't deserve it. Thirty years younger than him and talking to him like chattel.

"So," Ivan said. "Any indication as to Nolano's whereabouts?"

Pantano hesitated, and then said, "We believe he hitched a ride on a semi." A tone of reluctance registered in his own ears.

Come on, Hector. Be firm.

"Ivan, we combed through every centimeter of that apartment. And the church rectory. And the house of the *curandera*. No laptop, no evidence. Nolano emptied his checking and savings accounts yesterday."

"How much?"

"Everything. Thousands. Late afternoon yesterday, he called the vice chancellor, asking for a leave of absence. Then he turned off his phone. Never turned it back on. We know he never returned to his apartment or his brother's house yesterday evening. Or the church rectory."

"And that's all we know?"

Pantano nodded ever so slightly, with a slow blink.

"My," Ivan said. "I now fully realize that I cannot depend on you."

"Ivan...*Señor* Méndez," Pantano said. "You need to respect us, and me, as well. We'll be in power as long as you."

Ivan closed his eyes and let his chin sink onto his chest. In a flash, his eyes burst open. He snatched the vase from the corner of his desk and hurled it at the door, shattering it into a momentary haze of a thousand grains and shards.

Good God, was a lunatic now at the helm of Segundo Cortez? Pantano knew it was a foolish move to come to their hacienda. His first invitation ever.

"Very well," Ivan said after a long pause, his hands on his hips. Then he looked at one of his bodyguards. "Chuy, escort the good chief out. Then leave me alone here. So I can think."

8

Nicolás sat under the massive tent, smoking a cigarette at last. He stared out through the dusk at the other camp, sitting and standing about a hundred meters away under its tent.

How much he had seen and learned in the last hour. How fortunate that he had money for the crossing. That other camp—it had to be hell.

Most of its inhabitants were young women. Next were middle-aged women and children, with a few men.

"It looks so different from our camp," Nicolás said.

"You know why, right?" Mateo said. By the look of his fresh face and acne, he could be no more than eighteen, but he seemed to know the crossing process quite well. And to be wiser than his years.

"Why?" Nicolás said.

"You know they've got no money to cross, so they'll have to be—"

"Indentured servants?"

"I don't know what that means. Slaves are what they'll be. The girls and young women, many will be forced into prostitution. Even some of the children. And the men will do labor. Roofing or construction, if they're lucky, but usually unskilled labor in the fields. Eventually they can earn their freedom. Some will die before that."

"Mother of God. How do you know these things?"

"This is my third crossing. My third attempt, right through here. I've been caught by *la migra* and deported twice in the last year. I know this world. And it's dark. So dark. And you know what?"

"What is it?" Nicolás said.

"The true slaves," Mateo said, "are the women and children pushed to sell their bodies."

Nicolás could not bring himself to answer. His throat burned with rage. After almost a minute, he said, "You say this is run by that cartel from Sinaloa?"

"Yes," Mateo said. "Gangs of coyotes used to dominate this whole border crossing business, the *coyotaje*. They still do, but more and more the cartels charge them fees to use their territory. A lot of the coyotes even work for the cartels, and use crossers as drug mules. And force people to sell their own bodies. They saw all the big money in it."

A wave of nausea hit him, and then subsided. He yearned for that moment when he had traveled northward enough to be free from the reach of any of these cartel or gangs. The mere thought of them—it was infuriating, maddening, annoying, terrifying all at once.

After a long pause, Mateo continued. "Consider yourself lucky. We are lucky. We have the money to cross. I had an uncle with enough money for my crossing. And you were lucky you brought enough. Otherwise you'd be under that tent over there. And you know if you tried to cross elsewhere or leave this place, they would execute you. I've seen it several times."

Nicolás made a puffing sound out of his nose. He stared across the pavement at the children and the young women, wishing he could do something, and the helplessness and vulnerability he felt inside the semi's cargo hold returned. He saw a man holding an assault rifle. If only he could wrest it from the man's grip and turn it on the guards, then somehow set the two camps free. If only he had power, something he had never prized, opting instead for knowledge, adventure, and pleasure. Soon in America he must attain power. With power of the right kind, with force, he could return and change what was before him, even just by a little.

Nicolás turned to his left. She still sat, gazing out at the opposite camp. Mateo had said she was from El Salvador. Or was it Guatemala, or Nicaragua? One of those humble nations to the south. Her face was youthful, with striking doe-like eyes, and would have been attractive except for the harelip.

At least she had paid her fee and would not endure what others might, across the way.

"Another thing," Mateo said. "Like the guard told us, all smoking stops in this tent. You can bring your cigarettes, but if you light one up while we cross, they see you as jeopardizing our position. You'll get stabbed, because a bullet is too loud. I've seen it happen. They don't want anyone to blow our cover."

A whistle pierced the night. A group of five men approached. Each was stout, athletic, and holding a rifle.

"It's our time," Mateo said with relief.

Nicolás felt his breath stop in his chest. This was it. So why was he so on edge? Fear of the unknown? Perhaps of being killed?

The men stopped just short of the tent's edge. One of the five coyotes, with a salt-and-pepper buzz cut and five-day beard, cleared his throat and made a shrill whistle with his mouth.

"*Escucha!*" the man said. "Everyone, look at me. You need to gather what you're bringing, and I hope it's light. If it seems too much, we will make you leave it behind. We're setting out to the wall in two minutes. Form four lines right here. If you lag behind, if you get us found out, I promise you will regret it. Do not be so foolish as to light a cigarette on this entire trip. Do everything I say, and you will arrive with me at your destination. Now follow me."

All those under the tent grabbed their packs and bags, and began to line up. After the coyotes counted them, they pushed forward en masse, in a steady march out into the night. Cartel men, rifles in hand, brought up the rear. Adrenalin surged within Nicolás. What would the border look like? He knew it varied in appearance depending on where one crossed. It might be a tall chain-link fence with razor wire, a four-meter-high metal wall, a simple linear marker on the ground, or something that resembled a sort of metal split-rail fence.

In minutes they were there. He was surprised at the wall outside Sonoyta. Before him stood what seemed at first to be a joke: a metal screen fence just over four meters in height. Someone had placed a ladder against the fence. And just beside this ladder's peak, he could see the top of another ladder, on the fence's opposite side.

One by one, the crossers began to climb one ladder, and descend the opposite one. When his turn came, Nicolás was surprised at how very easy it was. In less than one minute, he was part elated, part frightened as his sweating feet touched down in the dust on the opposite end of the wall. He paused for a moment, and then jogged north a few meters to join the mass of waiting crossers. When the last migrant emerged over the wall, joined by the last two coyotes, he recognized the coyote with the salt-and-pepper hair and beard.

"Listen up. Our other men are about to collect these ladders. As for us, we will move fast at first, and then we'll slow a bit as we leave the wall behind us. Now, follow me."

Their brisk walk commenced into the brush-spotted desert. His heart raced, despite the near silence and the dark that cloaked them. Border-patrol agents and park rangers could appear at any moment. The thought spurred his feet onward at a steady pace, and ensured they did not slow, or falter.

Yet a pang of guilt reverberated through his soul. He survived, while he drew farther and farther from the troubled land he loved still.

9

Just when Nicolás thought they would stop—as surely even his captors needed rest—the coyotes would push them farther into the desert, into the night. His legs cramped. His lower back ached. Never had he walked so far in his life. Never had he been forced to turn his back to a drawn rifle.

He could not pause. One of the coyotes had kicked a heavyset man who had fallen behind. Without turning to check, Nicolás knew three young coyotes brought up the rear, while two older ones marched ahead of the group. The crossers had learned to scan the ground hard with their eyes and meander around large stones, bushes, and cacti, but every hour or so one would miss and cry out or swear.

Yet he was grateful for the cool air of the desert night.

"I can only imagine," Nicolás mumbled to Mateo at his side, "how very high the temperature will soar, after daybreak."

"You couldn't imagine it in summer," Mateo whispered. "Good thing is…I hear that on the new route, the coyotes have this cave for us all to sleep in. Just before dawn."

An hour later, they reached the cave. After a coyote searched it with a flashlight for rattlesnakes, he emerged and ordered everyone inside.

When Nicolás found a flat spot far within, near the rear, he heard Mateo's voice, a step behind. "*Guey, escucha.* Wrap yourself completely in that blanket you have, and your coat."

"Rattlesnakes?" Nicolás whispered.

"And scorpions."

"*Mierda,*" Nicolás cursed. He put on the coat and then wrapped himself in his blanket, forming a pouch.

Sleep eluded him for one hour, two hours—he knew not how long. Thoughts of scorpions jamming their barbs into his skin tormented him, as did thoughts of his mother, brother, and Padre Manolo, their bodies by now encased in something far different than blankets and coats. Who had buried them, or who would? Was this what the grave was like—as damp as it was within his blanket from his own breath?

With all his might, he attempted to purge such thoughts from his mind, thoughts that further pushed out any chance of sleep. Yet somewhere in that waking nightmare, he lost his hold on consciousness.

Nicolás woke to someone making a hissing sound, over and over. Nicolás unwrapped the blanket from over his head and around his body. That crisp air again, cool on his cheeks and forehead.

"Time to get up," a coyote said. "We head out in ten minutes. If you have to piss or worse, you do it now. Try to escape and you'll end up dead."

His bladder was full, so he stepped around the stirring masses to the sunlight-filled mouth of the cave. His watch showed a few minutes past noon. They had been in the cave around six hours.

He walked for about ten seconds, then paused, ensured each crosser was behind him, and urinated into the dust. As he returned to the cave's opening, he spotted the boy staring into the horizon.

"Mateo?" Nicolás said. The boy pointed into the distance, his eyes flashing with a barely contained fury.

About thirty meters ahead, a lone figure approached in a sort of stumbling gait, its arms wrapped around its sides. Just behind it were two larger figures, their rifles leaning against their shoulders. As they neared they grew taller, like dark towers growing from the desert floor.

Their identities were now unmistakable. The silhouette holding itself—he recognized the Central American woman, her shoulders slumped like before, with weariness and defeat. No doubt those were two coyotes escorting her.

Something was not right. Alarm sparked and spread within him.

"What? What has happened? Mateo?" Nicolás said.

"It's what always happens with some women on the routes. Any one of them remotely desirable. The coyotes take her. I saw them come to get her. You were sleeping."

"Rape? Why did you not tell me?" Nicolás spat.

"What difference does it make?" Mateo said. "What would you do about it? These coyotes can do whatever the hell they want, *guey*."

"Damn it," Nicolás growled. "Damn them all to hell. And you're ruined. Cynical. Way before your time."

"Oh yeah?" Mateo said. "You tell me what you would do."

Nicolás wished he could somehow rebut the boy's words.

Yes, the crossers were powerless. As long as those five gun-toting parasites were anywhere nearby.

Nicolás said, "I cannot wait for the moment when I am away from the reach of the cartels and gangs, hell, even from any trace of my homeland."

"Now, that last part's going too far, *Señor*," Mateo said. "You know it."

A pang of shame shot through his core. He threw his pack hard onto to ground before him. It just made him all the more resolved for that day when he would exact vengeance on Segundo Cortez, and any such group he would encounter. The last day had bolstered his pledge to gain the expertise, and the means—the right weapon—to make it real. After all, America was the land of arms. It was a nation even forged by the gun. Somewhere ahead, he would make it all happen…

He heard a *ssst* sound behind him, and spun around.

"Now, everyone up!" said the graying coyote. "In ten minutes, you'll form lines again and get counted. Then we leave. We are halfway to the truck. Once we reach it, you can rest inside. When we park, you'll be in Phoenix. The trip you paid us for will be over. You'll be free to go."

They dashed to gather belongings, to relieve themselves, to again form four lines. Then they resumed their way—part march, part trudge, part stumble—through the desert.

And then just when he thought his legs would at last give way beneath him, the interstate emerged in the far distance. Vehicles coursed along its spine and vanished over a ridge, then appeared just beyond it. What seemed to be a gas station stood beside the roadway.

His heart lifted, and all around him, crossers sighed and released exclamations of joy. Their pace quickened, just a bit, until it was clear. Gas station indeed.

One of the coyotes, walking about twenty meters ahead, pulled his phone from his pocket. He spoke into it, for almost a minute.

"Look," Mateo whispered. "Guy's calling the truck. They'll be waiting."

Could it be? Deep inside, Nicolás offered up a silent prayer of gratitude.

Minutes later, when the crossers stepped from the scrub-dotted dust onto the asphalt of the rear parking lot, one of the coyotes pointed at a semi. Its rear door had been rolled up and a wide ramp connected it to the pavement.

"Every one of you, inside," he said. "Hurry!"

In two minutes all crossers were stowed inside. A coyote grabbed the rope attached to the door's handle, and down came the accordion-like metal until it was like before. He might as well have been in the cave once again.

The stench of sweaty bodies and the frequent sounds of coughing, sneezing, and snoring grew less irritating as Nicolás edged closer and closer toward sleep. Even the three men seated at the opposite side of the truck no longer bothered him with their chatter. Nicolás held his flashlight, listening to Mateo beside him expound on the jobs one could obtain in Phoenix, until his limbs and head grew too heavy to sit up. He turned off the flashlight, wedged his pack beneath his head and let go.

In his dream he was a boy again. He ran, giggling down the jungle trail that meandered around the great trees, chasing his little brother, who must have been no more than eight years old. Esteban tripped and fell. Nicolás heard a pause, then weeping, and he ran faster. Followed a bend around a massive tree, he saw Esteban as a man of thirty, lying dead once again in his pinstriped gray suit and tie. He collapsed onto his knees on the trail, dumbstruck and powerless as he panted out of breath. His eyes scanned the scarlet spots. And then he snapped awake.

A woman was screaming at the opposite end of the semi, where the three men were. He shot up into a sitting position.

"*Señor*, it's those crossers," he heard Mateo said with urgency, somewhere nearby. "They have Harelip now."

"No," Nicolás said as he thrust his hand into his pack, then bolted to his feet. "Not again."

He lurched toward the opposite end of the semi, gripping his flashlight in left hand, the other held close to his side. He stepped quickly over several crossers, who gasped when they saw what he clutched in his right hand. Someone screamed, and then another.

One of the men stood from the prostrate woman, her clothes halfway off, and spun around to face him.

In his mind he saw his mother's killer, standing over her body in her living room. Inside he felt something strain under great heat and tension, and then break.

The man swore when he saw the unsheathed hunting knife at his side. He had reached into his own pocket, when Nicolás shoved his blade deep into the man's abdomen.

The man released a muffled groan. Nicolás pulled the knife clear, then lunged at the man lying over the woman. As the man struggled to rise, Nicolás drove the blade downward into the man's back, sending a wild shriek across the cargo hold.

He pulled the knife free. The third man rolled away and then dashed into the nearest corner.

Nicolás dashed to the end of the cargo hold furthest from the door. Screams of horror and terror—and a few of pain—intensified around him.

And now I am inflicting bloodshed, and perhaps death. I must steel myself to it—you know it won't be your last time…

The truck slowed, then swung to the right. His legs came out from under him, and as he crashed onto the metal truck bed, he held the knife away from his body.

The truck surged forward, then swung leftward and ground to a halt. He pulled himself up into a crouching position, his knife held outward.

The rolling upward of the door met his ears. Daylight blinded them all. Nicolás struggled to keep his eyes open, vigilant.

"Stop! Stop!" Nicolás heard a man shout, just outside the truck. "You knifed two of our crossers, *pendejo*! Put down the knife!"

It was the graying coyote.

"No chance," Nicolás said, rising and trudging to the rear of the truck. After stuffing the flashlight inside, he hoisted the pack onto his back. He was ready to leave and did not care what awaited outside the semi.

"Ask these people," Nicolás said. "Those men there were trying to rape that woman. Wait, nothing you coyotes haven't done before, you—filth."

"Get out of the truck and leave, then, damn you," the man said, training his gun on him. "You already paid us."

With a deep breath, Nicolás gripped his pack tight and, knife held outward, he jumped down onto the asphalt and stepped sideways and then backward, away from the truck and the two more coyotes that had appeared. He looked back toward the rear of the semi. She stood inside, staring out at him with eyes watery with fear.

"Will you join me, *Señorita*?" Nicolás called out. "And Mateo? We can still get to Phoenix."

"You have quite a walk, *idiota*," the longhaired coyote said.

"*Señorita*, it will happen again. Unless you come with me," Nicolás said. She lowered her eyes to the ground with resignation, turned, and paused. Then she shuffled toward the back of the truck.

Was this real? She was willing to accept it, just to reach her destination?

"And you, Mateo?" Nicolás said.

The boy lowered his eyes toward his feet, and shook his head.

"How you like that, *pendejo*?" the graying coyote said, sneering at Nicolás. Climbing up into the opening, he then pulled the cord. As the door came down the two coyotes swung around toward the cab of the truck, the longhaired one turning back toward him.

"Have a pleasant walk. I'd steer clear of the highway. *Migra* or cops will get you, *cabrón.*"

The engine erupted into a growl, then a roar. The wheels jerked into motion as the semi rolled away.

It was apparent. Once again, Nicolás found himself all alone —in one very strange landscape.

10

Eleven a.m. arrived on his second day after leaving the smugglers' semi. Nicolás turned from what he assumed was a northward course and trekked what seemed to be due east—over a dry plain alongside a canyon. His mission to find some store or gas station selling water was driving him to the brink of madness. To a lesser extent, he longed for food, and perhaps some shelter, at least for a night. All the while, he knew full well that *la migra* might find him and toss him in jail, then deport him to Mexico.

He paused, laid his pack onto the sandy desert floor, and sat upon it. Raising the plastic jug to his cracked lips, he sipped the last of the water. It was like hot soup on his lips. Damn the heat —he might as well be sitting in flames. He longed for the cool of a cave. If only he could encounter a *tinaja*—a watering hole—here amid such desolation. At least for water to cool his skin. To think that he was walking on the seabed of what was the Permian Sea, 250 million years before.

He tossed the plastic jug into the dust. At least he had tried to save the girl. At least he had intervened. And he held fast to his values, in the face of death. How tragic that she was so desperate to make Phoenix with its jobs that she chose to confine herself to that hell of the semi, once again. Surely one or more of those men had assaulted her, moments after the doors had bolted shut. He could think no more of it.

High noon's fierce sun smothered the landscape with merciless heat. No water could be found in the arroyos. Nicolás saw tracers. Then the hallucinations became truly frightening. A giraffe chased a buffalo amidst the cacti of stout saguaros, the *chollas* with their lone barbs, the prickly pears, the slender ocotillos. Parrots crowned the thorny paloverdes and the black ironwood stumps.

Hours later, his thirst grew too strong to bear. He dashed down into a shadowy wash and ripped open a prickly pear with his fingernails and teeth, leaving its spines stuck into his chin and fingers. But there was no water within—it was more like slime. His bone-dry lips swelled, peeled and cracked. His eyelids stuck. Dizzy, he vomited three times, and fell several times more.

Nicolás sensed that the end was near, but he still could not accept it. He pushed himself a few paces farther, but his coordination began to disintegrate. Tripping, he sprawled onto the cracked hardpan, scraping it with his palms and chin. Seconds later, his eyes opened. A pack of demons ran across the horizon and disappeared. He was sick of the hallucinations. Closing his eyes, he prayed for a swift death.

Yet the image of the bodies in that living room, and the blinded boy, kept him conscious. He must continue. He must live for all of them. For vengeance. But there was far more—for aiding his city, for living a long and fruitful life. Even if it meant risking time in an American or Mexican jail. Perhaps he could make some sort of signal, and some good Samaritan would find him, take him to water, shelter.

It took him nearly an entire minute to reach down and withdraw the lighter from his pocket and to lean over, ready to ignite the large bush. He paused. This would change everything. It would alert any *migra* within several kilometers. He continued to contemplate his decision for one minute, then another minute.

The flapping of wings, a stirring of air somewhere around him sounded in his ears. A brownish bird with a whitish underbelly, not small and not very large, landed on its yellow feet in the sand a few meters away. An amber eye squinted at him, just behind the hooked grayish beak. It was no vulture, but a bird of prey. An eagle, a hawk. Those tail feathers jutting from behind it—they were reddish, like a dark orange, and white at the tips. Yes, as Mateo had described. A red-tailed hawk of the desert. It squinted its keen eyes further at him, turning its head to study him. Nicolás smiled, and felt his upper lip crack and smart. The bird erupted into the air, flapping its wings, pushing a hint of a breeze against his sunburned face. Then it climbed and soared away, northward it seemed, over a bluff.

Yes, his own passage must mimic this beautiful bird's, northward. But only after he got east enough to find the interstate once more. And water, food, and rest. Then a ride. In that order.

Nicolás inhaled a profound breath, and then crawled several meters. He drew himself up onto his feet, paused, and walked in a slow but steady gait toward what he assumed was the east. An hour, two hours, three hours passed. His legs gave way, and he crumpled to the dust.

How many more times would he fall before he could never rise again? He recalled how very far he had fled from Veracruz. At first he had thought himself fortunate to evade *la migra*. After all, he had made it so many kilometers into Arizona.

He knew he was disoriented. It had been hours since he'd completely lost his bearings. Now he would lose everything.

Nicolás could not raise his head from the searing ground. His breath came weaker, though strong enough to upset the dust, which rose into his face. Now he felt what Cervantes had described, how Don Quixote's brain baked in the sun to the point of madness. All about him sounded the music of his far-off Veracruz, *marimbas* and *danzón* with xylophones, tambourines, strumming guitars, and stomping feet in Zamora Park. The carnival crowds roared. The waves crashed onto the brownish-gold beaches with their thatch-roofed seafood shacks. As the *norte* gusts blew in from the gulf, the rich aromas of the boardwalk drifted about him: the scent of cigars, fish tacos, and fresh corn tortillas. He grew feebler as consciousness began to slip from him, minute by minute.

He heard his brother's voice. It was screaming down at him. What was Esteban saying?

Peering up into the fierce sunlight, he saw his brother, more hologram than actual matter, dressed sharply in a black suit and red tie. His face contorted into the most frantic expression of worry—and outrage—he had ever glimpsed. Esteban was like a boxing trainer, yelling down at the fallen fighter before him on the canvas.

"Get up, Nicolás! Get up, just one more time, for me! Then you'll make it, I promise you! Don't surrender here, damn it. Don't let them win! You haven't finished. You haven't completed it!"

Nicolás jerked himself to his knees as he felt his last adrenaline surge through his body.

Was this what a risen human looked like? Or had his brain in its delirium conjured up a ghost?

Again he looked up, then all around him. Esteban had vanished. He clenched his teeth and forced one foot in front of the other, until he had regained a sort of rhythm.

Minutes later, he gave into the temptation to rest, and fell to his knees. As he teetered there, at the point of falling forward, he spotted a small dark mass far off in the distance. It was some sort of edifice, squarish and low, with smaller, rectangular masses moving into and out of it. A gas station? Surely another hallucination.

11

Pantano pulled the police cruiser into the hospital parking spot, eyeing first his hulking nephew Gustavo beside him in the passenger seat, then the three police cruisers in his rearview mirror.

Shock still pervaded him. Arturo Méndez had summoned him, through his brat son, there to his own deathbed. A second heart attack in seventy-two hours. Surely this was the end. Did his old friend and enemy want to insult him? Forgive him? Divulge some unexpected news? Pantano was used to enjoying some measure of control, but this was utter chaos. It was maddening.

"Stay close, Gustavo," Pantano said. "I don't think they would try anything. But we never know, right?"

"Don't worry, *Tio*," Gustavo said with a slight smile, holding up his hand almost as if in a wave.

They emerged from the cruiser. The nine other officers, already parked, joined him and Gustavo beside their cruiser.

"Men, I don't need to tell you this," Pantano said, breaking the silence. "But be vigilant. Be ready for anything. You know that older son of Arturo's has a head as hot as lava. Gustavo and Grijalva, Briones and Escudero, you accompany me into the room. The rest of you stand guard in the lobby."

"We've got your back, *Jefe*," said the voice just behind him. Without having to turn, he knew it was Sergeant Grijalva, one of his best officers. Gustavo was the most dependable and physically powerful. But Grijalva was the best with pistols. Ten years with the Marines had not been the worst thing for him.

The trip up to the hospital and through the lobby seemed like forever. He wished he were back in bed, or even back at the station. Anywhere but in this place and time.

Amidst the elevator's silence, Pantano drew in a profound breath. He was wrong. Despite everything that had transpired over the last two decades, it would be no easy task to see Arturo breathe his last. His throat burned as memories flooded back of his time on the force. Their friendship had formed as partners assigned to the same detail. They were there for each other for years—he often forgot—through so many life-or-death situations. Even when they were reassigned separate beats, and were no longer partners, their friendship had deepened. How many evenings had they spent over beers, in cantinas and bars? Pantano was even present at the church christening for Ivan Méndez. To think of it: Arturo had even asked him to be the godfather to his firstborn child. Back when Ivan was a harmless infant, when there was no hint of the monster he would become. Ivan the Terrible, as so many in Veracruz had come to call him.

If only he could have seen the future, twenty years ago. To think his best friend would become his greatest rival and adversary, a man who hated him, and to a degree, a man he hated in turn. But underneath it all, he realized many times through the years, there still breathed an ember of brotherly love and affection.

Truly this was the strangest hour of his life. He prayed he would not become emotional in front of his men.

The elevator surged to a halt. The bell dinged and the doors rolled open on their tracks. The sight before him caused him to draw in, and hold, a quick breath.

12

Nicolás sat on the shady cool pavement, his back against the rear wall of the gas station. At first he had vomited, the water and the tacos proving too much at once. But bit by bit, he had ingested enough to bring him closer to normalcy—a bite of taco and a swig from the jug until they were all depleted.

He had escaped death and rejoined civilization. And he knew he would go on living. Moxie, grit and intuition had pulled him through. But now he must find transportation north to Phoenix. Then he could seek shelter, and work. He could regain his bearings.

Phoenix, he thought as he rested there. The mythological bird rising from a bed of ashes. Like he himself had done. Like that mysterious bird back there in the desert.

Yes, the red-tailed hawk. Nicolás realized his survival was no mere product of his bravery and determination. Something from above was watching him, steering him to this point, forcing him upward from surrender on the desert floor…

His eyelids grew heavy, signaling the need for one very long nap, despite the many hours of sleep he had enjoyed behind the gas station dumpster. Somehow, though, he could not rest until he was on the road. He rose to his feet, slinging his knapsack over his shoulder, and grabbed the aluminum taco wrappers in his hands. Good God, how could these people eat this? Plastic food, nothing like the tacos back in Veracruz. At first, the gas station tacos had tasted like heaven for all his hunger. Minutes later, he realized how unappetizing they truly were.

With his first step, Nicolás became aware again of the heaviness of his limbs—especially his legs—and grimaced at the burning in the soles of his feet and in his face. Surely he must be blistered to oblivion. As he rounded the corner, he encountered a trash can and tossed the wrappers and empty jugs inside.

Who could take him on the road north? He would start by hitchhiking, but he had to stow himself somewhere, hidden from the eyes of any police or *la migra*.

He took in the sights in the distance, past the gas pumps. In the crisp morning light undulated a great expanse of hills, carpeted with yellow flowers and punctuated with yuccas and tall, thick saguaro cacti. He had seen natural scenes of stunning beauty in Mexico, but this new vision held a special rank. No wonder the Americans had fought with such ferocity to make this land theirs, back when it was part of Mexico. This landscape seemed as beautiful as the desert days before had been unsightly.

An elderly white man in a button-down shirt was gassing up his truck at one of the pumps. Nicolás stepped toward him and gave a friendly wave and smile. His lips smarted.

He must summon his best English.

"Sir, could I trouble you for a ride? Are you are bound for Phoenix?"

The man glanced at him, and then looked far past him, as if into the horizon.

"Sir, please. I've lost everything. I only have my pack here, and a little water."

The man looked downward, his wrinkled hand still gripping the nozzle. He cleared his throat and shook his head.

How embarrassing. Nicolás nodded and walked on. The person at the next pump was a pale, middle-aged man in a western shirt and jeans, his dark hair streaked with gray, staring at him with light blue eyes.

"Sir, may I trouble you for a ride? I have lost everything. Everything except this pack and some water. I'm just hoping to get to Phoenix."

Just as the words left his mouth, he regretted them. He shouldn't have even approached the man. Something about him was not merely callous—in his expression was an air of hostility, of violence.

"You don't fool me, bud," the man said. "Even though you learned some really good English. I know a man who's illegal when I see one. Ain't about to help another one of you take another one of our jobs."

Nicolás felt it return—the fear from that first stowaway ride. Would this man alert the police?

"Sir, I am legal. I'm a citizen. My wallet was stolen in Tucson."

"Right," the man said with a smirk. Then his eyes narrowed in a cruel squinting stare. "Now step away, boy."

Nicolás stepped backward, then turned and walked away. Shame built within him. He would return to the rear of the building to rest. As he crossed the parking lot toward the side of the station, he noticed an old man gassing up his truck at another pump, his gray hair pulled back into a ponytail, his skin dark brown and crisscrossed by a network of deep wrinkles.

Nicolás smiled. The man's stare was formidable, yet the eyes were wise, kind, in shape like those he had seen for decades, yet different—not Mexican, more Asiatic. The face alone made him miss his hometown, filled with the descendants of the Olmecs and Toltecs.

This would be his last try for now. Then he would take a break and try later. If the gas station attendant didn't order him off the property first. Or call the police.

"Sir, please," Nicolás said. He could hear the desperation and defeat in his own voice. "I implore you—may I hitch a ride north? I have lost everything except my pack here. My wallet was stolen as well, in Tucson. I have no ID. So I cannot ride a bus."

He caught the scent of some familiar fragrance—an incense smell. Burning sage. He remembered his mother's rituals.

"Where you tryin' to get?" the old man said.

"I need to get to Phoenix," Nicolás said, sensing a ray of hope breaking through. He studied the man for a moment: the light blue jeans and western boots, the indigo blue shirt with the top two buttons undone. Then he saw it.

A necklace holding a single red feather, whitish at the tip.

"Sir, that feather," Nicolás said. "Is that from a red-tail hawk?"

"Sure is," the old man said. "It's a special bird in my tribe. The Tohono O'Odham tribe. We also were called the Papago."

"I saw one on my way here. Just as I was about to pass out, and give up. It landed just in front of me. As close to me as you are. It was just—staring at me. Then it flew away."

"Hmm," the old man said. The nozzle clicked and the old man pulled it from his truck and placed it back into its cradle. "You were given a good omen."

He then turned back to face Nicolás. "I am heading to Phoenix. But I'll tell you, young man. I don't pick up hitchhikers. One of my rules."

"Please sir," Nicolás said. "How then can I make it to Phoenix?"

The old man hesitated. Nicolás stared at the lone feather.

"I will give you some cash," Nicolás stammered and pulled off his backpack. He set it on the concrete and unzipped it feverishly, pulling his clothes from it. Under the knife he felt the bills, and pulled some from the stack and inspected them. Four twenties.

"Please," Nicolás said, holding out the cash.

The old man paused, then glanced and smiled at the bills. "My wife would skin me alive, if she knew."

He pulled the cash from Nicolás's fingers.

"Lay down in the truck bed, son. I'll get you to Phoenix. Just don't, you know, pee in my truck."

13

Every half hour or so, Nicolás would pull his newsboy cap off of his face and squint upward from the truck bed through the fierce sunlight. He had seen two overpasses, buzzards flying overhead, semis passing. Now he saw something new altogether: skyscrapers towering high above him in the sharp glory of their glistening glass and steel. He thought of Monterrey with its modern office buildings. Monterrey, a center of opportunity—one of the last of the great Mexican cities to be infiltrated by the rot of the cartels.

A siren erupted nearby. Was it not right behind the truck? It sounded like a police siren. Had he been spotted, as flat as he was laying in the truck bed? Sweat broke out all over him.

Good God. It was directly behind the truck. He put an index finger into each ear. All of this way for naught. Prison awaited, and an early death...he could feel it. The siren seemed to grow louder. Then it swung around the side of the truck and proceeded forward, its volume decreasing every few seconds. He withdrew his fingers from his ears. It had passed.

The pickup turned and slowed, passed over a bump, accelerated to a degree, then turned again and stopped. A palm tree loomed overhead. Nicolás sat upright and then got to his feet, pulling his pack around his shoulders. Slapping the hat atop his head, he swung himself over the side of the truck onto the pavement.

All around him stretched a parking lot, which abutted a small park. Bordering the park on all sides were tall office buildings. In the near distance, sitting and standing under a couple of the park's largest trees were groups of men and boys, and a few women, all Hispanic.

The truck door creaked open, and the old man emerged.

"Here you are," he said as he approached. "Downtown Phoenix. I know you said you lost everything. If you need work, this is one of the prime spots where contractors and business owners will scout for day laborers. Those men over there can tell you all about it."

A pang of grief shot through him. Would he ever teach again? Not just at a university, but in any capacity? Day labor—was that all he could do in America?

"Thank you, sir," Nicolás said as they shook hands at the side of the truck.

"William. Or call me by my native name, Kwewu."

"Call me Pato. Perhaps I'll see you again!" he said with a wave, and pulled a cigarette from a pocket in his backpack and lit it. Then he walked toward the figures under the limbs of the nearest large deciduous tree.

As he neared them, he saw that only women sat on the park bench. Around them sat and stood about fifteen men and boys. They observed him with various expressions: curiosity, mistrust, welcoming, and amusement. He became conscious that he was the fairest-skinned person in the vicinity.

"Good afternoon," Nicolás called out. "How are you all doing today?"

Chatter followed, then muffled laughter, a grunt or two. A large, older woman on the bench smiled.

"Well, how are you, sir?" she said. "Puebla, Veracruz?"

"Veracruz, yes," Nicolás said. "Good guess. I'm Pato."

Damn it—he had divulged his home city. And his nickname. He needed to settle on a pseudonym, and fast. Then again, only Esteban had called him Pato...

"I see you got a ride from one of the natives," said a stocky, middle-aged man in a straw hat.

"Yes," Nicolás said. "Don't know how I pulled that off. Maybe he felt sorry for me."

By now he was within a few meters of the group. "Anyone know where I can get some work around here?"

"We all worked today, got started very early," a boy said. "They already let us go."

Damn, I already missed it. I wonder how early they start...

"What kind of work could I find, maybe tomorrow morning?" Nicolás said.

"*Chico*, almost anything," said the man in the straw hat. "Roofing, cleanup for a construction crew. Janitorial work indoors, you name it."

Nicolás felt his spirit sink within him. Janitorial work?

"Anything a sane man wouldn't want to do," said a young man, tossing a soccer ball up into the air and catching it, once, then twice.

Several in the crowd laughed.

Nicolás said, "What do you think I could get paid for this work?"

"*Pues*, siding jobs aren't common but they pay the most," the man with the straw hat said. "Next is roofing. If you can learn it quickly, you can make one hundred dollars a day, cash. It's hell on the back, arms, joints though."

His spirit sank further.

Talk about a brave new world. I must be ready to adapt, even more than before.

A very short, swarthy man cleared his throat with irritation. "About seventy-five or eighty dollars a day if you were a Salvadoran. Or a Guatemalan like me."

Some in the crowd jeered at the man, and some grumbled.

"Why less?" Nicolás said, shaking his head.

"Because they know we are more desperate," said the Guatemalan. "I'm not a Mexican like you people."

"That's so unfair," Nicolás said. "What about the other jobs? Cleaning, carrying things, or whatever. How much could I expect to make?"

"Less than six dollars an hour, *Señor*," said a teenage boy with a haggard face, a lit cigarette dangling between his lips. "Maybe five."

"Oh God," Nicolás said.

A wave of laughter rose and rippled through the crowd.

"Especially this close to the border, *hombre*," another man said.

Indignation burned in his throat. He must swallow, force it back down, and ignore it. He could not keep losing what cash remained.

"What if," Nicolás said, "I want work tomorrow?"

"Show up here," said the woman on the bench who had greeted him. "At six tomorrow morning. Different businesses will come for us."

"Just watch for the police," the Guatemalan said. "You never know when they will single you out. New law here in this state. They can stop anyone on the street and demand their ID or papers. You're one breath away from deportation."

"Damn," Nicolás said. "And what if I want to go to New Mexico? Utah? Colorado?"

"You can't ride one of those buses if you don't have a good

fake ID," said the man in the straw hat. "But a crosser can pay one of the Mexican gangs to let him ride in one of their transport vehicles. To Albuquerque, wherever. They take ten, twenty at a time."

"Ah, no," Nicolás said. "No."

"Why?" said the man in the straw hat.

"I'll be damned if I'm going to pay one dollar to a gang."

"*Pues*, actually, *Señor*," the Guatemalan said. "The Mexican cartels run many of them now. Many of the gangs are their arms."

Several of the men laughed.

"Absolutely disgusting," Nicolás said. "They're like vampires that suck our blood."

"Let that stay here," said the Guatemalan. "Don't go saying that around town. One of them finds out, and you're done."

"I hear you," Nicolás said. "Thanks."

He turned and walked away, stunned. As he traversed the park toward the avenue, he could hear them chatter about him. Some resumed their laughter.

At the avenue, he stopped, watching the cars whiz by and people course up and down the sidewalks. His people were everywhere. In suits, bearing briefcases. One in medical scrubs, several in business casual. In Phoenix he knew there was opportunity, a place to recalibrate, to prepare to return to Veracruz to attack. And after that, Phoenix was a place of promise if he wanted to return.

Yet his intuition shouted that he must leave, and keep moving, far away from the stench of any cartel. He tried to flag down a taxi. First an empty one passed, then another ignored him. Recalling his disheveled appearance, he removed his pack and reached inside, once more for bills. He zipped the backpack closed and clenched the wad in his hand, looking around to ensure no one snatched it away. When a taxi appeared perhaps twenty meters away, he raised the wad in his hand and gave it a slight wave. The taxi seemed to accelerate. Then it slowed, and pulled up alongside him.

Just as he had always heard. In America, money mattered most.

"Sir," Nicolás said as he opened the door. "Please take me to the largest truck stop nearby."

14

As the elevator doors parted, Pantano saw before him a figure he had not glimpsed in decades. In fact, few in Veracruz had, she was such a recluse. Inmaculada Covarrubias Méndez, longtime wife of Arturo. The unseen matriarch. And Pantano's first love…they had dated just under a year. Up until he met Raquel.

"Inma?" he said as a hundred emotions collided within him. "I mean, hello, *Señora* Méndez."

"Hello, Chief Pantano," she said with a formal nod, quelling any expectation he had of an embrace. "Come quickly. We may not have much time."

Her small, delicate face still retained much of the freshness of her youth, despite the passage of time and constant worries, and surely the reminders of her husband's dalliances and full-fledged affairs. Or perhaps she had avoided discovering any sign of them. Perhaps that was her secret.

The steps of Gustavo and his three other men sounded close behind him as he trailed her into the room.

The cluster of lieutenants, guards, and family parted, then broke up. Sprawled on the bed was the man who was once his best friend, his once athletic figure now lost to fat. His two sons guarded him like sentinels on opposite sides.

Arturo was paler than he had ever seen, as if half of the blood had been drawn from his body. His face was also fuller than in the surveillance photos.

"Inma, and you men, leave us be," Arturo said in a voice weakened but still heavy with the weight of authority, as he stared straight above him at the ceiling. "Hector, Ivan, Jaime, you can stay."

The sound of feet filing out of the room filled Pantano's ears, but he kept his eyes riveted on Arturo. Then he turned around. Gustavo, Grijalva, Briones, and Escudero stared at him as they headed for the door. Gustavo nodded with a faint smile. Pantano swiveled his gaze back to Arturo. The moment of silence lengthened into five seconds, ten seconds. He might as well be the one to break it.

"Arturo," Pantano said. "It's been so long."

"Hasn't it?" Arturo said. "Probably too long. We delay... procrastinate. Years, decades fly by. Then situations like this arise and it forces everything."

"It's true," Pantano said. "So why...why did you want to meet?"

Another stretch of silence. Arturo turned his head his way. The eyes were fatigued, yet lucid.

"Well, Hector," Arturo said, "I had you contacted for two reasons. I want us to come to an agreement, between both of our forces. Also, something about the past. I wanted to do this now. Don't know if my heart will hold out longer."

Ivan's bloodshot glassy eyes darted about, as he tapped his food in a repeated motion. Pantano wondered if the rumors were true, that these days his godson soared on a perpetual cocaine high.

"After all," Arturo said. "The doctors say my heart is very

damaged. The first was a massive heart attack. The one yesterday was mild, but still."

Would Arturo mention the arson that precipitated this cardiac arrest? Would he mention Nicolás Nolano, Ivan's childhood friend? Or the attorney Nolano, or the murdered *curandera* and priest?

"I want your men to stop tailing mine, investigating mine in any way," Arturo said. "We both know you've been doing this more by the week. I know you might unite your force with the *federales* against mine. Know that I have men inside on the federal forces too. And many on your force. If you do end this, I promise you will have no violence in the entire city from my men. I want a new truce between us. We were friends once. And despite how the force treated me, you and I can at least look out for each other again."

Could he refuse Arturo, who very well might be on his deathbed?

"If I agree," Pantano said, "and let us be frank, if you then pass away, what happens to the truce? I assume Ivan will be chief. Will you honor these terms, Ivan?"

"Of course," Ivan said, staring him hard in the eyes, then dropping his gaze.

Within Pantano, memories of those days when Arturo was his best friend clashed with the bad blood and animosity in the decades since. Shouldn't he just agree to the truce? He probably could not trust the *federales* to reinforce his efforts. And at least one cartel would always be in force. If they did not harm the citizenry, should they just be left alone? And could he refuse Arturo's request? Something told him Arturo did not have much time...

He looked back toward the bed. Arturo was watching him. No iron stare or smiling eyes, as in years past. Just a frail, tired gaze.

"No more hits on citizens," Pantano said. "Not even laying a hand on them. And absolutely no more bribes to my men. You do this, Arturo, and you have my word."

"I swear to it, Hector," Arturo said.

Pantano glanced at Ivan. His arms were folded, his gaze fixed on his own shoes, as if in another world.

"Well, I guess this is very good development," Pantano said. "Arturo, what was the other reason you wanted to meet?"

Arturo shifted on the bed as he struggled to turn his body toward Pantano.

"Stay on your back, *Papá*," said the other son, Jaime.

"*Pues*," Arturo said, "this might be much more difficult for us to…address."

A moment of silence ensued, save for the deep breathing and faint wheezing of Arturo.

"*Papá?*" Ivan said. "Just relax. Don't move in the bed."

"It's fine," Arturo said. "Hector, this may surprise you. I have many regrets. I regret scapegoating you, all of these years. And I regret creating Segundo Cortez."

Both brothers erupted into a stir of whispers and grunts.

"*Papá*," Ivan said.

"*Cállate, hijo*," Arturo said, then paused. "I should have stayed on at the force. Despite them not promoting me. And promoting you and others over me. I should have held on and fought for the next position."

"You can always walk away from Segundo Cortez, Arturo," Pantano said.

"But I can't. Too old. And I've got too much invested. And once Ivan or I steps away, others in the cartel will just kill us. But it doesn't mean that I don't realize now that it was the wrong decision."

"It takes much courage to admit, Arturo," Pantano said.

"Hector," Arturo said. "then again, it's better that I hold Veracruz than the Xalapa Cartel."

Pantano said nothing. Perhaps Arturo was correct.

"But I became so bitter after you and Ruiz were promoted, and not me. I was angry with the chief and others. But I never should have been upset with you, too. But I was, and that was foolish. I lost a great friendship. But after I got in too deep with my new business, I could not—I figured I should not—continue our friendship anyway."

Pantano shook his head. "Yes. It's just so sad. It's so sad it turned out that way."

Arturo turned his head away, facing the wall.

"Pantano," called a voice across the room. Ivan was staring at him again. "My father did what he had to do. He just says this now because he feels vulnerable and—"

"Ivan!" Arturo yelled at the wall. He writhed, shook, and released a moan. Ivan darted across the room to his father, placing a hand on his shoulder. "Nurse! Nurse!" Ivan screamed. Jaime shot out of the room into the hall. Pantano surged forward toward the bed, his hand outstretched for Arturo's.

"Stay back, Pantano," Ivan spat.

Pantano stopped cold. It had been an involuntary gesture, after all. He must control himself.

"I'm going. Now, right now," Arturo stammered through clenched teeth into Ivan's face. "It's here. Make me proud. Make me proud, *mijo*."

15

Nicolás shuddered with both fear and excitement as the semi turned and slowed, then ground to a halt. An hour earlier, the driver had said that his next stop would be the one.

And sure enough, there it was again, on the pavement outside the truck: that same leisurely gait, and someone whistling a tune. He longed to be free again, out in the cool night air. If only this would be his last time in a truck's cargo hold. But he knew there would be more.

The bolt screeched as it turned, and the massive door opened.

He could discern the trucker's silhouette: the two meters in height, the puff of hair atop the high brow, the protruding belly and stout frame. He liked the man enough to trust him. Like him, an outsider. A Georgia boy so very far from his home.

"You still livin', buuud?" the man said, and then cackled. "Or maybe my smooth drivin' hypnotized you."

"Bobby?" Nicolás said. "Is it Albuquerque?"

"Yes indeedy," the trucker said. "Your time has come. You in the Land of Enchantment now."

"What time is it?" Nicolás said.

"Way past your bedtime. But time to tighten up the belt and

walk. Or you gonna be waaay far east of here next time this door opens."

"I understand." He stood and grabbed the pack he had used as a pillow and stepped toward the door. He sat down at the edge, and then lowered himself onto the asphalt. In the streetlight he saw the trucker, the fleshy, ruddy cheeks, the kind, squinting eyes. The thick salt-and-pepper hair and the trimmed gray goatee and moustache. Nicolás caught the scent of coffee and cologne.

He handed Bobby the two bills.

"That's the rest of it."

"Mighty 'bliged, *Señor*," the man said, shutting and bolting the door. "Be safe now. Downtown's thataway." He pointed one of his thick fingers toward the lights.

In a moment, Bobby had disappeared around the left side of the truck. Nicolás heard the cab door shut. The engine grumbled, then roared to life.

Once again he was alone in this strange new land. The feeling pervaded him: In this country, anything could happen, whether for good or ill.

He thought of Bobby. How fortunate he was to have met him when he did. And his manner of speaking—such an intriguing accent of American English. The soft vowels, the syllables drawn out and almost sung, like Italian. How did this accent ever descend from the British Isles?

Nicolás walked toward the distant lights until cramps shot through his legs. Should he rest? What if he encountered the police?

Just ahead and to his right—past the stores with their dark windows—the gas station glowed like a beacon of hope. Water, snacks, an actual bathroom, complete with toilet and sink. A respite from his trek, where he could at least run cold water over his face.

Inside it was deserted, save for the attendant. He was

Hispanic, most surely Mexican. Nicolás must ask now, before anyone entered.

"*Señor*," he said. "Any idea when and where I need to be to find roofing work around here? And to finally get a meal?"

His new reality had grown more real. Roofing work was as new to him as New Mexico itself. Could he even be hired in this work?

"*Claro*," the man said with confidence, pointing behind Nicolás. "Continue on this road here, in that direction, north. When you see the Shell station across from The Frontier diner, behind that station is where you want to be before dawn. Crew leaders will drive in, and add to their teams. Sometimes replace half their teams. Many roofers get breakfast there in The Frontier before the crew vans show, across the street. You'll find them easily in The Frontier."

"Thank you so much, friend," Nicolás said and nodded, then went for a jug of spring water and a few bags of peanuts and chips. He returned and placed them on the counter.

"It's hard work, *guey*, if you haven't done it," the attendant said. "You don't look like the type. Not that you can't do it."

"Well, honestly, I haven't attempted it."

"You know your bones will be cursing you an hour into it."

Nicolás thought of the thousands of crossers who took those jobs. All his life they seemed like passing thoughts, desperate men who happened to originate from his homeland. He had never felt their vulnerability or their resolve—until now.

"Some of us have no choice," Nicolás said, and handed him the bills. The attendant laughed and counted out his change. "I know exactly what you mean. I did it for a couple weeks. Two years ago, after I crossed."

"Thanks again," Nicolás said, shoving the peanuts into his pants pocket. Jug and chips in hand, he stepped out into the night.

Besides roofing, perhaps that is what he could aspire to: gas station attendant. Soon, or even many months from now, if he survived his assault on Segundo Cortez, and returned to America. Which reminded him—he must spend time plotting it, after he found work, shelter.

Farther down the street, on the corner of Cornell Drive and Central Avenue, he found the diner. The Frontier Restaurant, the sign read. It was a curious structure, erected in some kitschy 1970s western style, made to look like a painted brick barn with a bright-yellow mansard roof.

Nicolás pushed open the glass door. Several people sat throughout the diner, Hispanic, black and white. Uninspiring paintings and drawings—their price tags placed just below them —punctuated the walls. Nicolás headed for the empty counter. Just behind it stood a middle-aged man with freckles, small, shifty green eyes, and red hair combed down and sideways. He eyed Nicolás with seeming distrust. Did all Americans assume he was undocumented? Were they shocked by his disheveled appearance? Or maybe it was something else. He knew he was in grave need of a shower.

Nicolás glanced upward at the marquee showing the menu. He placed his order, took his number, and handed the man a few bills. Damn, he needed to find work soon. And some place to stay, hopefully under a roof. While he plotted...

He slid into a booth, and then leaned against the window.

A young white man in his early thirties sat down in the booth just across the aisle. A faint scent of sweat and marijuana followed him. His chestnut hair grew wavy and slightly unkempt nearly to his shoulders. His cargo shorts and his T-shirt reading "Crested Butte, '14ers Mountain Climbing Club" were faded and frayed, and his feet were encased in worn sneakers.

"How are ya?" the man said with a peaceful smile. His cheeks and neck were tight with youth, but the warm eyes crinkled with premature wrinkles, hinting at years spent in the sun.

Nicolás smiled and nodded. There was something genuine about this stranger. Though he no longer truly believed, he recalled a line from the *Book of John* that Padre Manolo once read to him and Esteban. Christ's words when he first spotted his future apostle Nathaniel. How did it read exactly? Yes, he had it.

"Look! Here is a true son of Israel, in whom there is no deceit." And though it was a Protestant Bible, Padre Manolo especially loved the old King James Version in English. "Jesus saw Nathanael coming to him, and said of him, Behold an Israelite indeed, in whom is no guile!"

"Fair, I guess," Nicolás said. Perhaps he should say little, reveal little. He looked out the window and across the street. Dawn had come. Atop a hill, amidst the trees, stood a ridge of brick buildings. A sign revealed it was the University of New Mexico. Behind its rooftops, mountains loomed. He was astonished to see them so green, even lush, carpeted with what looked like spruce trees.

Nicolás turned. The stranger was smiling.

"The Sandia Mountains," the man said in Spanish, with a Castilian accent. "Beautiful this time of year. I'm Case. Real name's Casey Logan. How are you, man? What's your name? Where are you from?"

"My friends call me Pato," Nicolás said, choosing to supply his nickname instead.

"Well, my friends usually call me Freedom," Case said in that Spanish more Madrid than Monterrey.

"Good name, better than being called 'Duck,'" Nicolás said as he shifted in his seat. Should he disclose the name of his homeland? This man surely can guess anyway.

"And I am from the interior of Mexico. Now just looking for work in the States."

"I hear ya," Case said. "What city ya hail from?"

Now I've caught it. An accent from the northeast of America.

"A place I am trying to forget," Nicolás said and turned to the window. My, this gringo asks so many questions, but I like him. He turned back toward Case. "Your Spanish sounds very —Spanish."

"Lived in Spain for a while," Case said, switching to English. "All over Europe, for that matter."

"How many languages do you speak?" Nicolás said.

"Seven. Spanish, English, German, Polish, Slovak, Hungarian, Czech. Then I guess I could include a little French and Italian."

"Impressive. Most Americans seem to only speak English."

"So you here for work?" Case said.

Nicolás hesitated.

Case said, "I mean, at this hour, most of the people around here are UNM students. Or men looking for work, where those crews meet across the street."

"I am actually looking for work," Nicolás said, then began to worry if he seemed undocumented.

"I'm looking for work while I work on a book, actually," Nicolás said. "But thought I'd get some breakfast before I cross the street. To see what employment I might find."

"You'll find it. I've been part of a roofing crew for four days straight. Staying with an old friend, stacking cash for a summer trip."

"I've never roofed before," Nicolás said.

"I'm sure you'll find work with a crew. You'll learn it there. Or you can do cleanup."

Nicolás heard someone call his number, and excused himself. Maybe he would make it. And find good work, and a room to rent.

He took his tray of coffee and food, and returned to his booth.

"So do you live in Albuquerque?" Nicolás said.

"I live in Crested Butte, Colorado. CB. Headin' there tomorrow morning, north. Stoppin' in Santa Fe on the way."

Santa Fe…holy faith? That sounded peaceful, wholesome. He recalled the city from history books—the name was reminiscent of Veracruz, another colonial city of New Spain.

"Santa Fe," Nicolás said. "I wonder if there is some work there."

"There always will be. It's a rich town. There's no place quite like it. People come to Santa Fe from all over the world. Many of them are damaged in some way—and they're lookin' to be healed. Some end up in Taos, north of there. With that incredible light up there, and its pueblo. Where you can enjoy the music of the mountains."

"*The music of the mountains.* I like that," Nicolás said, chuckling. "This is better than usual diner conversation, Freedom."

"Your English is very good, Pato," Case said. "Where'd you learn it?"

"In Mexico I've taught English. And American literature, for years." Nicolás felt his spirit sink. Those were great years, in retrospect. Perhaps he would never teach again.

"Speak of the devil," Case said. "What do you think I did for pay in Europe? Teaching English. Except I was more of a tutor. So you teach in a university?"

"No, in a *colegio*…I teach children in their early teens," he stammered. Damn, he was a horrible liar. He hated doing it.

"Anyway, speakin' of Mexico," Case said. "Just about every other summer I leave Colorado and head to southern California. Pick up some old friends and we roll down to Baja. Surf and grill out and sleep on the beach for a couple weeks. It's almost heaven."

"I've never been to Baja California," Nicolás said.

"But I want to always be based in the Rockies," Case said. "Well, just remember to check out the nearest range wherever you travel out west. Remember this pearl of wisdom: 'A true seeker is extremely unsettled living in flat locations. He gravitates toward high places because he wants something to look up to, a state of higher being.'"

"Your creation?"

"No, John Muir's." Case released a staccato laugh and patted his shoulder. He was a warm one, more like a Latin. And he resided on a different wavelength, or rather, a different planet. Even so, he liked Case just fine.

Perhaps in a few days he should head for Santa Fe, rather than stay in Albuquerque. Santa Fe was farther from Mexico. Farther from his enemies, outside their orbit, a place where he could plan his attack. Farther from the graves of the only family he ever had. His gut began to hurt and tears began to well in his eyes.

"You feelin' okay?" Case said, tossing his crumpled napkin into his empty plate. "Food okay?"

"Allergies. As for the food, it is not Mexican. But it's not bad, like what I have bought at gas stations in Arizona."

Case laughed. "It isn't trying to be Mexican. It's New Mexican. And it's not a gourmet New Mexican joint. But it's no Shell station either. Well, I guess I'll see you over there? Don't wait too long, if you want work today."

"I'll be over in a few minutes," Nicolás said, and dug back into his meal.

Case rose, and with a twitch of his head swept his long hair off of his face.

"If you get second thoughts, *vaya con Dios*, brother," Case said as he reached out and slapped hands with Nicolás. It was one of those strange new American handshakes. As young and as unconventional as Case himself.

"You'll see me over there," Nicolás said. Case walked away with his tray, emptied his trash, and disappeared out of the door.

Minutes later, when Nicolás rounded the corner of the Shell station, he was surprised to see about twenty men waiting.

His senses were met with a strange vibe. Was it animosity? Discomfort? Off to the side stood Case and a burly white man with a grizzled beard, somewhere in his late forties. They were the only light-skinned ones among them. A group of men regarded them with distrustful, and almost incredulous stares.

Nicolás saw and felt the eyes on him, too, though not as harsh. He scoured the crowd and recalled those first stares in that Phoenix park, the day before.

"Buenos días, Señores," Nicolás said. "Yo sé, son gringos."

Nicolás laughed, forcing it out to where it did not seem nervous. A couple of the workers followed suit.

He heard steps behind him. A middle-aged Mexican man appeared, dressed in a Carhartt shirt and pants. "Bueno, I need two crews, each of eleven men. One roof's a little steep."

A grumbling arose from a few of the men.

"If you want the work, come with me," he said in what was more of a bark. "Want roofs that aren't so steep, just hold out."

"I would like the job today," Nicolás said.

"A new one," the crew leader said. "Ever roofed before, chico?"

"No, but I learn very fast," Nicolás said. "And I'm in good shape."

Several of the men laughed.

"Seventy-five dollars for you," the crew leader said. "For today's job. I'll put you mainly on tear-off. And trash pickup. Deal?"

16

The hiss and stamp of the nail guns echoed all around the roofing site. Men stomped up and down the ladder, hauling more and more plastic bundles of shingles to stack on the roof. Atop one elevation, Nicolás stood, a couple of meters from Case. For several hours, in one rhythmic motion after another, they bent down and tore off sheets of shingles with pitchforks, tossing them over the gutter.

"Big roof," Case said. "Big tear-off, too."

"At least you're earning a hundred today," Nicolás mumbled, his knapsack still across his back.

"Yep, seventy-five is rough, man," Case said.

"Even without a minute of experience," Nicolás said, "they pay me as much as a Salvadoran with months of experience."

"Messed up, isn't it?" Case said. "Now you're seein' it. So Pato —what's your real name?"

Nicolás felt the blood surge in his cheeks and forehead.

"Actually, my real name…" Nicolás said, then drew in a steady breath. "…my real name is Aurelio."

Lying—how nervous it made him.

Again he spotted the burly white man across the roof, staring at them with a hostile expression.

"Who's the big white man who keeps staring at me?" Nicolás said.

"Dawkins," Case said. "The men call him *El Monstruo*. Avoid him, man. He hates Mexicans, and he—"

"Hey, red shirt up there," a voice called over the side of the gutter, somewhere below. Yes, the crew leader. "New guy. I need you down here with the boy doing some cleanup. Gather all the tear-off, and put it in the dumpster."

This is how he must adjust, within his transformation from venerable professor to unskilled laborer, unqualified to roof or install siding. Strange to say, this role might prove as challenging as finding his way through that Arizona desert.

He nodded at Case. "See you in a bit, I suppose."

At the foot of the ladder, he saw the boy several meters away. No more than fifteen years old, the slight boy carried a hardened, flinty expression as he grabbed the shingles and tar paper in his hands and brought them to the dumpster. Was it his first roofing job, as well? Regardless, his short life had surely not proven easy.

Nicolás noticed many rusty nails jutting from the shingles, but there were no gloves around.

Tetanus, he thought.

He glanced again at the boy, who seemed to pay no mind to this risk.

Nicolás proceeded to fetch handfuls of shingles and tar paper, bringing them to the dumpster resting in the driveway, while looking upward for the flying masses of shingles and nails.

"Why don't you put down your backpack?" the boy said.

"Long story," Nicolás said, remembering the cash and coat bundled within.

A strange thudding sound arose across the yard—it was above

them on the roof. And was there not an argument? He heard another thud, and then men speaking in Spanish.

The boy turned to him with an irritated expression.

"What's going on?" Nicolás said. "Sounds like—like a fight."

"I think I know what it is," the boy said.

Squinting and shielding his face with a hand against any nails or shingles that might come his way, Nicolás approached the ladder. He plodded up the rungs, and once he stepped onto the roof, saw that the men were nowhere to be seen.

That sound again. This time a human voice, but without words. Guttural, from deep in the throat, almost like a beast's growl. Followed by unintelligible Spanish words, uttered in Mexican accents, but in a tone of urgency. It came from the nearly flat elevation of the roof, just across the gable. Nicolás crossed the plywood decking, bare of all paper and shingles, and stepped up the gable and peered over.

He sighed in disbelief. Case lay on his back, crimson-faced. Dawkins was on top of him, his hands wrapped around Case's throat. The men watched from several meters away, arguing amongst themselves.

It was as if he was witnessing his brother's imminent murder, there in the Veracruz living room. He could not allow this. As he lunged across the bare plywood slope, his backpack still strapped across his back, he knew his days were gone as a passive observer on the sidelines. First, the arson, then the stabbing in the coyotes' semi, and then what awaited, moments ahead.

A young Mexican man in a flat-billed baseball cap broke from the group of roofers, traversing the half of the roof still covered with shingles. The man reached Dawkins just ahead of Nicolás, and tried in vain to pull him off of Case.

Dawkins swung hard at the young man's leg, knocking it out from under him, sending him crashing onto his side.

Nicolás reached the prostrate mass a moment later. With all

of the strength he could muster and his leg extended, he stomped as hard as he could onto the attacker's head in a fierce diagonal thrust.

Dawkins jerked wildly to the side, off of Case, then rolled onto his back. The young man in the flat-billed cap shot to his feet.

Once again Dawkins swung his stocky arm, sweeping Nicolás's leg out from under him. He crashed onto his side and off came his newsboy hat.

The impact of Nicolás's torso, elbow and thigh onto the shingles cast a painful memory into his mind. Perhaps it stemmed from seeing a body stretched out beside his. Again his mind replayed that first glimpse of those three bloody bodies on the tile floor of the Veracruz home. The moment he realized the cartel was truly winning, even in his own life. The shock shot through him like electrocution, or like a body plunging into icy waters, and he swung in a wild frenzy, landing blow after blow with his right fist, three times onto the man's temple and jaw.

Case kicked the man hard in the gut. The young Mexican followed suit, until Dawkins lay on his back, squinting against the sun, gasping between every few breaths. The crew had pressed closer to where it surrounded the brawl.

Nicolás rose to his feet. "Stay on the ground," he said in English. "Get up, and you'll regret it. Just stay down."

He became aware of his own disheveled hair, hanging into his eyes and along his cheekbones. He recovered his hat, and slapped it on top of his head. With his hands on his hips as he regained his breath, he stared hard at the men, from face to face. Some nodded, some smiled and even laughed, but all eyes were fixed on him.

Brakes squeaked in the driveway below. Nicolás recognized the sound of a diesel engine.

"Hey now," Nicolás heard the voice call out below. "What's going on? Taking a break?"

The young Mexican in the flat-billed cap stepped with caution across the roof's bare section, and stood just beside the gutter.

"This tall psycho you hired again, *El Monstruo*" the man said in Spanish, "he attacked the white kid. He was mouthing off about *mojados* stealing all the jobs, and the kid intervened. *El Monstruo* tried to strangle him. I tried to pull the guy off but I couldn't, and he caught my leg, knocked me down."

"This beanpole hippie needed a lesson," Dawkins bellowed in English, while getting to his feet.

"The fancy Mexican here in the red shirt got him to stop," the young man said. "Just a minute ago. Then we made sure this *pendejo* wouldn't try it again."

"Get down off the roof, Dawkins," the crew leader said. "I'll pay you what cash you've earned this far. You're done."

Dawkins stared at him and then at Case, then at the group of roofers, with the most scalding rage. He stepped toward the edge of the crowd, which parted. When he reached the edge of the roof, the teenager had stepped several meters away with caution.

"Now come down here, Dawkins," the crew leader called out. "Before you get arrested. You know how lucky we are that the homeowners aren't inside?"

"Why was that guy hired again?" Nicolás said.

Dawkins drew in a profound breath and paused, as if gathering a thought and spat toward the teenager. He turned and spat toward Nicolás, and missed.

"Have fun in the sun, little bastards," he growled, disappearing down the ladder.

"Because he's done this a long time," Case said, still winded. "He's the best at doing flashing, and replacing skylights. And handling the steep parts. Well, now we need to work steady 'til evening. And stay out of trouble. Then we'll both have a little cash. I'm heading north after this. My girlfriend's waiting on me."

"Hopefully there are no more surprises today," Nicolás said. "I'd thank the young guy for trying to intervene."

"I will when I gain my breath," Case said. "Hey, I owe you, man. My friend Pato. Hey, call me Freedom. You saved my life."

Nicolás stared up into the sky, its brightness and vast blue depths filling his heart with promise. An idea surfaced in his mind. He seized it and held on tight.

"Just get me out of here," Nicolás said.

"What's that?" Freedom said.

"Don't you have a car?" Nicolás said, turning to meet his gaze.

"Well—yes." Those innocent eyes and expression again.

Nicolás drew in a deep breath and said, "I want to join you. On your trip."

17

Make me proud.

Over and over in his mind, as he sat in the seaside café, Pantano replayed Arturo's last three words on earth.

Surely Arturo was ordering Ivan to expand the reach of the cartel—without crossing certain lines. Like the murder of the priest, and the old *curandera*. The blinding and stabbing of that boy rescued by the Nolanos.

This was an opportune time to reconnect with Ivan as the chieftain of Segundo Cortez, a man newly untempered and unfettered by his father's orders. Pantano reminded himself of today's goal: to probe and assess Ivan's interpretation of his father's last words. And if that interpretation was what he suspected, he must issue a warning.

The floorboards creaked in the otherwise-empty dining room.

Ivan entered, followed by his brother and two other men he recognized from the hospital room, days before. Pantano rose and shook Ivan's hand, noting its ever-firm grip.

"Godson," Pantano said.

"Remember my younger brother, Jaime?" Ivan said, nodding to his side. Pantano shook his hand. The resemblance was there, that keen hungry look seen in the Méndez men. But the aura of a killer was nowhere evident.

"And yes," Ivan said, "I'm training him in the family business. Not now. But soon, I will integrate Jaime into them. We will all three be in communication."

Jaime smirked, but there was still a hint of goodness behind his eyes. Perhaps it would soon vanish.

"My mother does not, and will not, approve. I didn't want Jaime in this business either, but I changed my mind. He will still live in the hacienda, but I won't involve him for a while. He's totally green. All he knows is *fútbol*. I almost want to keep it that way. But I could use him. I can trust him. Can I always trust you, Pantano?"

Ivan laughed, and then gestured to the two men beside him, "And these are some of my top lieutenants. Raúl here and Eduardo in the black shirt."

Pantano nodded at them. He did not recognize Eduardo, but the department knew of Raúl. Somewhere in his early forties, Raúl sported a muscular physique, clad in a green Army T-shirt and black cargo pants and combat boots. His hair was sheared close on the sides and back, while salt-and-pepper spikes reached up from his brow, like a porcupine's.

From espionage and surveillance, Pantano knew Raúl was the only one in the organization allowed to address Ivan by his first name, and had done so since he first met the teenage Ivan. Raúl was the top lieutenant in Segundo Cortez, and its most skilled and experienced hitman, or *sicario*. Years in the Mexican Special Forces had certainly honed his skills.

"*Señores*," Pantano said. "I saw you men the other day at the hospital. It was surely a hard day for all of us. For me, those old feelings for Arturo—they're still there."

"I actually believe you," Ivan said.

"Shall we sit?" Pantano said.

The five men took their seats at the table.

"Where's that hulking sidekick of yours?" Ivan said, smiling.

"I didn't bring him this time," Pantano said, remembering how he had not mentioned this rendezvous to Gustavo. "I don't want to involve him in this discussion."

"Very well," Ivan said.

The waiter approached the table, and the conversation ceased as he took the order for coffee, and departed.

"You look like you're doing well, Ivan," said Pantano. "Despite the circumstances."

"I realize I have so much to do. Plan the funeral with my mother. And business matters, goals I had not expected to chase for many more years. You know, I returned from that hospital that night. I stand there behind my father's desk, and you know what I think? How I will now run things much differently."

"How so?" Pantano said. The small talk had ceased.

"I hate how my father had been angry with me those last days, Pantano. That I had that boy blinded and stabbed before his release. And that hit on the priest, the healer woman, and Esteban Nolano. That sent him into a rage. Despite that Esteban actually filed suit on him. Well, my father was from a different time. And a different generation. There was that restraint in him, and that submission to boundaries and rules. And an outmoded code. I could have taught my father a thing or two, had he been willing to learn. My methods will be different, but my achievements will be greater."

Good Lord, what arrogance.

"But Nicolás Nolano, not me—he gave my father the monster heart attack."

Pantano envisioned the Nicolás of decades before at Arturo's home, the house before the hacienda. The retiring schoolboy lost in many books—real literature—he read for pleasure. Arturo once shared what transpired one summer day. The boys were fourteen, fifteen. Ivan had Nicolás over to play video games. As Nicolás perused the family bookshelves, he became obsessed with this one fancy book. Ivan's own father had laughed and hugged Nicolás, and gave him the book as a gift. Ivan hurled a *fútbol* into the shelf. And vowed to always speak nothing but harsh words to Nicolás. And to never impress his father with reading for pleasure, ever again.

And that was not all. He wagered Ivan still felt jealousy to this day. Years ago he observed the beautiful foster family the *curandera* had formed with Nicolás and Esteban, with the priest there for guidance.

Lucky damned Nicolás Nolano, Ivan must have always thought. What was it like to not have a tyrannical, criminal father and a detached, avoidant mother? Even if they were your parents by blood?

Ivan shook his head, closed his eyes, as if weary. "So the inevitable question: Still no word on Nolano?"

"His trail has gone cold," Pantano said. "Nothing has changed since you and I last spoke at the hacienda. It embarrasses me like it frustrates you. But I sense we will find him."

"Somehow," Ivan said, "I'm not convinced. You find him soon, and your next payment will be much more."

"Ivan, what kinds of rules and boundaries were you referring to a minute ago?" Pantano asked.

"Everything is on the table, Pantano. Priests, women, the old, any who oppose me, even if they are police and they interfere with any of my work. Any dissident, and any member of his family. The shackles are off."

"This cannot be," Pantano said. "Arturo knew this. There must be boundaries. Or the *federales* will insert themselves into the situation and you will regret it. It will make both of our lives hell."

Ivan remained silent for several seconds. Perhaps a modicum of logic still remained within him.

"The *federales* will involve themselves anyway, now or in time. If I go to war with the Xalapa, and don't finish them off quickly, the *federales* will jump in. But at least Xalapa's a baby cartel. About a hundred men. But bigger than I thought. Anyway, I must eliminate them. And soon. My father let them go on far too long. And they were easy to crush, this entire time. If not, in one year, they will be a threat."

"If you choose to fight them, and I cannot change your mind, then you will fight them. Though the *federales* will come. But your father, rest his soul—he did not see them as so much a threat. Segundo Cortez is not yet in Xalapa. You know that your father was more concerned with moving your territory southward. Closer and closer to Guatemala. Entry points."

"That's fine and good," Ivan said. "But I also want Xapala. It's a growing threat. And it's a feather in our cap. It's the capital of the state, after all."

"But," Pantano said, "you killing women and children and clergy, I cannot accept. You touching any of those on my force, I will not permit."

"Our payments to you will cease," Ivan said. "Think about that."

Pantano remembered his wife and her medical bills, their son and daughter, and their special-needs grandson...how that money had helped them all.

"That is not all," Ivan said, sitting further upright in his chair and puffing out his chest. No doubt he must continue to project this image, especially this early on—especially to his two lieutenants and, above all, to the police chief. "Pantano, you and perhaps even your family will then become our all-out enemy. There will be no quarter. And I don't want that. So I ask you to reconsider."

Pantano stared deep into the soulless eyes of Ivan Méndez Covarrubias. What should he do, or say about this insulting threat?

His heart raced as he cleared his throat. His finger came to rest against his hip holster. He imagined a flurry of bullets slamming into his forehead and chest, but not after he uttered what he must.

"No. You do not touch children or those on my force. In return, my cops will never pursue your men. If one does, call me. I will always answer. At the site of your kills, leave one of your *narcomantas*. But you killing my cops or children, you might as well draw on me now, while I'll draw on you. We'll probably kill each other."

"Damn, old man," Ivan said with surprise. "Actually, I like it. A bit unexpected, but oh well."

Pantano said, "You threatened me and my family, so I threatened you. It was far better when we were cordial."

"I agree to what you propose," Ivan said. "I'll honor this. My men will, too. Your force not pursuing any of my men, especially after we mark our territory after a hit, by that I can abide. That was my biggest issue. Your men interfering."

Ivan stared at him with surprise, respect, and a bit of frustration. But in the eyes, it was unmistakable—there was madness, a mind like a ship tossed on violent seas.

18

In the streetlight's glow cutting through the dusk, Nicolás spotted a chapel, bounded by an adobe fence, about one and a half meters in height. Freedom threw himself over it. Nicolás followed suit, backpack and all. Crawling under a pine just inside the wall, he propped his knapsack under his head and threw his coat over himself as a blanket. Freedom lay a few meters away.

"I guess it's a free hotel suite?" Nicolás said, peering up through the limbs.

"Exactly," Freedom said. "We're in contact with the earth. Pleasant dreams. See you *mañana* in the land of the living."

Nicolás hoped this new spot would buy him a few hours of peace and invisibility before dawn. Sleeping on a hard surface, far from any bed, for the fifth or sixth night. It was no longer a new situation, bringing a novel sensation. Was this his new normal? He felt his face and limbs loosen as he shut his eyes to the night.

The resounding toll of bells rang out above him, causing his limbs to jerk. It was a welcome disturbance, freeing him from yet another nightmare. He blinked open his sleep-crusted eyelids to an explosion of morning light.

A light breeze tousled his hair. A dog barked. His nose caught the familiar aroma of corn tortillas heating on a griddle as he raised his head from the backpack. Sitting upright, he swept his hair back and took in his surroundings, this time in the light.

Nearby stood a wooden sign. The Loretto Chapel, operated by the Sisters of Loretto? Where had he heard of this chapel? French Gothic-Revival style, right in the middle of the American state of New Mexico? He had read of it in some fantastical story he could no longer recall. It was something beautiful, odd, and mystical all at the same time. He gazed up through the branches of the ponderosa pine. Inside, unseen birds chirped away in their indiscernible language.

The dome of the sky above stretched wide and royal blue, with the scantest trace of white cumulus clouds.

It was hard to imagine that he could feel such peace and in such beautiful surroundings, while mere days ago he knelt amid his family's bloodied corpses. It was the most fearful moment of his life. That, and hurling the Molotov cocktails and speeding away.

Pushing the thoughts from his mind, he pulled his weary frame to his feet.

"Heading north, *amigo?*" he said.

"Come on, man," Freedom said, turning in his sleeping bag. "Know where we are?"

He followed with that carefree tone he had already grown accustomed to.

"You're not just in the Land of Enchantment. You're in its capital. You're in one of the oldest, most unique cities in America. This whole area's a magical place. Just let me show you around a bit. Before we head out."

Freedom stood, collected his sleeping bag, and they climbed into the 4Runner nearby. They turned around, away from the few tourists near the corner just to the north, and hooked left down the next street. A stream coursed along to their right, parallel to the street—Calle de la Alameda. A street with a Spanish name. What a welcome sight.

Soon the road cut a slight left, at an angle. Canyon Road, now a street name in English.

Quaint art galleries, upmarket restaurants, and yoga studios lined each side of the narrow road. This was no Sonoyta. It reminded him of San Miguel Allende, but then again it was completely different. The squat, flat-roofed, sandstone-colored houses, their adobe fashioned somehow from the earth that they stood on, how exotic and intriguing they were. And their turquoise door frames and windowpanes. He had seen this architecture before only in photographs. In a way, some buildings seemed like miniature Native American pueblos.

What were these trees arching over the sidewalks, gracing front lawns devoid of grass but peppered by sculptures? These great oak-like trees with coarse, wrinkled, and prominent bark, with leaves shaped like wide spades? He swore he had seen them before in Puebla, and in Mexico City.

"What kind of trees are those there?" Nicolás said, pointing. "With the wrinkled bark?"

"Fremont cottonwoods," Freedom said, rolling down the windows. "That's a true southwestern tree there. Lots in California all the way to Texas. Parts of Mexico, too."

A scent wafted past Nicolás. It was surely from coffee, but there was something to the scent totally unfamiliar.

Once again he felt what he had experienced minutes before, upon waking. Much like he had felt after first stepping out of Bobby's semi into the Albuquerque night. The sense that a new morning had dawned, that he was free—though a bit handicapped—to reconstruct his life, and a home base, as he wished. He even could stay in Santa Fe, though Freedom would continue northward. But his instinct pushed him to accompany Freedom all of the way to Colorado, even to Montana. So far from Mexico, he would be nestled in a safe refuge from any enemy in pursuit. In Montana he would acquire some weapons and training, somehow. Then soon after, he would return to Veracruz, and come for Arturo Méndez. And his vile son. However, Nicolás needed a plan in case the American police apprehended him. He did carry his identification and passport, although the name might be matched up with a fugitive arsonist. And carrying thousands of newly exchanged American dollars, crammed into a backpack, required one good background story. He needed somewhere to stash them, and an American bank account was far too risky. And then there was the hunting knife in the knapsack. Perhaps that was enough to trap him in an American jail.

Already the road had made him weary. He longed for another spot to rest, and recalibrate. A gallery appeared to their right, behind an open fence of piñon saplings. He imagined them entering the carved wooden door, crowned with a threshold painted turquoise. How he already missed those sweet moments in his old life, the one forever gone, when he would discuss great literature and view fine paintings, sculpture.

Freedom turned the car around. After a few minutes, they had returned downtown.

Once again, that architecture so foreign and beautiful surrounded him, the windows with painted turquoise panes cut into the reddish-brown adobe, the porches often buttressed by very baroque wooden pillars.

"Here's a nice spot," Freedom said, pointing out of his window. "A really popular one, Tia Sophia's. It's got one of the best breakfasts around. And that building beside it, on the left there, was an old jail. Billy the Kid was once a prisoner there. You know him?"

"Not personally, but yes," Nicolás said. "Some in my home country, they are twisted for writing narco ballads about cartel leaders. Then I remember all the romanticizing here of that man. He really was just a murderer, a thief."

"I guess you're right," Freedom said.

"Here, Café Pasqual's, The Tune-Up Café, and Maria's... those are the ones to go with for breakfast."

"You have separate lists for lunch and dinner?"

"I do. For when I have money. Hey, tell me more about this book."

Think fast, Nicolás.

"It began as an actual memoir of my travels. A discovery of the present-day American West, by a Mexican national. But I am leaning toward making it into a novel...with an undocumented immigrant as the protagonist."

The last week shot through his mind like a horror film on fast-forward. The discovery of the bodies. Hurling the Molotov cocktails and speeding away. Lying in the dark cavity inside the semi, unsure of his fate. Leaping from the border fence onto American soil. The stabbings, then the brush with death in the Arizona desert. The face of Kwewu and the Georgia trucker as they said farewell. What would the next chapter be? When would he return to Veracruz? When would he be strong enough to attack?

"Don't you just love this town?" Freedom said. "It really is more of a town. Only forty-thousand or so people. But it's totally unique."

"I do love it," Nicolás said.

"It's a Spanish colonial city that predates Boston, New York, New Orleans," Freedom said. "It was reborn decades ago as an art center, but more for the visual arts. I love it. Hard to buy a home or land a good job here, though."

They rolled toward the old city plaza, the art galleries of San Francisco Street to their right, the bars to their left, on the plaza's western side. An obelisk-like monument stood in the square's center. Nicolás pointed just beyond it, toward a rectangular edifice.

"That's the Palace of the Governors," Freedom said. Dark-skinned figures sat or crouched under its overhang, with baskets and silver jewelry displayed on blankets before them.

"Freedom, a question," Nicolás said as they continued eastward down the street. "Why are many of the thresholds and doorframes and windowpanes painted *turquesa*—turquoise?"

"It's a tradition from the Pueblo natives," Freedom said as they turned south off the plaza. "It gives good luck. It can also refer to a specific tribe. Sometimes a design from a certain pueblo is painted into the turquoise. Anyway, just one more stop on the way. Unforgettable."

Freedom parked on the street, and the two men stepped out onto the pavement.

The Loretto Chapel rose before them, stately and elegant but not imposing. Birds flitted about its spires, some landing on its slate roof. With its French Gothic Revival style, it did seem a bit misplaced, or curious, at the very least.

"You've gotta see this," Freedom said as they entered the small courtyard. To their right was that spot where Nicolás slept the night before, under the small pine.

They passed the wooden sign advertising the chapel and its miraculous stairs. After Freedom paid the woman at the front desk two dollars for both of them, they entered the chapel's side door. Freedom pointed to their left, toward the main entrance. To the left of the front door rose a dark-brown wooden stairwell.

Spiral, with no center. Strange.

Nicolás began to recall fragments of the story he read years ago of this place. Something about a miracle not of healing, but instead of architecture, engineering.

"Pato, the Loretto nuns who had this chapel built...they had no way to get up to that loft there. Architect forgot to build it into the chapel's original design. So they prayed a novena, for nine days straight. That they'd find someone with the skills to build a stairwell in such a confined place."

"What happened?"

"This disheveled man stops in, soon after that novena. No one knew who this guy was, but he had these simple tools with him. He insisted on buying the materials. Said he needed total privacy inside here. He built this in three months, by himself. Didn't use one nail in the job. There's nothing metal in those stairs. They're connected by wooden pegs. No one can confirm the type of wood he used. It definitely isn't native to this area. And there's no center, no post, no buttress. No one knows how it withstood the weight of thirty-three nuns, on its thirty-three steps. Look at that photo!"

Freedom pointed to an old black-and-white photo on the wall. A nun stood on each step, clothed in early-twentieth-century habits, and wearing those odd hats that looked like they had sprouted wings.

"How did it not collapse?" Nicolás whispered.

"That's part of the mystery. It was either a divine miracle, an answer by God or the universe to their prayers, or it was some great architectural feat. Whatever it was, it's always made me feel humbled. But I would say it was a miracle. Do you believe in miracles, Pato?"

"I have to," Nicolás said, staring at the stairwell, contemplating that day in his future, when he would come for Arturo and Ivan Méndez.

"Good," Freedom said. "Because in life, that helps."

Nicolás felt the impulse to pull out his phone, as was his longtime custom, and tell his mother or brother or Padre Manolo what he had just encountered. For the first time since their death, he realized he could no longer share with them his discoveries and spontaneous ideas.

Yes, that phone. Perhaps Segundo Cortez could have detected his location, if he had not hurled it into the surf, days ago, on his way to purchase the ingredients for the Molotov cocktails. He had heard that even if a phone was turned off, it could be traced —as long as a battery was within it.

Whatever the truth was, he distrusted technology. He did not want to risk Segundo Cortez hacking into his phone. Or bribing, coercing, or threatening his phone carrier to determine his location.

And for these same reasons, he dared not check his email. Though no doubt some of his friends, students, and the university Vice Chancellor had emailed him, expressing their condolences, asking as to his whereabouts.

As they walked toward the 4Runner, a black SUV with tinted windows rolled toward them. It slowed. His heart quickened until it sprinted within his ribs. He froze. Had Segundo Cortez found him at last?

"You okay?" Freedom said, looking back at him.

The vehicle stopped, and then proceeded up the street.

"I am fine. Now, shall we get on the road?" Nicolás said with impatience.

"Sure thing," Freedom said, and then laughed. "Calm down, man."

Soon the 4Runner coursed north up the interstate, Santa Fe many miles behind them. Nicolás checked the side mirror, and then turned in his seat. The black SUV was nowhere in sight.

Through the dusty windshield the bridge approached, decorated with a word and symbols he did not know, surely from the Aztecs' and Mayans' cousins to the north.

This New Mexico was a strange and beautiful land. But perhaps not too foreign and strange to be outside the reach of Segundo Cortez.

They passed a sign for Española. He liked the town's name, and wondered as to its history.

"Starving," Freedom said. "You, too?"

"Oh yes."

"Well then, I know a place where we can grab lunch. It's a bit off the road but worth it. I'll buy. I still owe you, remember?"

"I remember that scene all too well."

"*El Monstruo*, all right," Freedom said, shaking his head. He turned off an exit and headed eastward. Badlands appeared around them: arroyos, bone-dry washes, and tall, rocky dunes spotted with scrub grass and bushes. After twenty minutes, a sign appeared.

"Chimayó," Nicolás mouthed the word.

"You're about to experience a special place, Pato. Ever heard of the holy dirt of Chimayó?"

"I can't say I have," Nicolás said with a chuckle.

"Well, after we eat, there's a church you should see here. From the 1600s. There's a tiny room in the rear where you can scoop up this reddish-brown dirt. It's got healing properties, man. Then there's a hallway attached to this room covered with photos and testimonial letters from people who claim the dirt healed them. Paraplegics, people with stage-four brain cancer... you name it."

"That sounds fascinating," Nicolás said.

For the first half-hour that they sat in Casa Chimayó Restaurant, Nicolás studied the map splayed out before him. He tried to ignore how unkempt and soiled he felt. At least he had showered the evening before in the apartment of Freedom's Albuquerque friend.

The waiter returned, placed the two plates and a bowl before them on the table, and left.

"What is this one here?" Nicolás said, pointing to his plate.

"That would be a chicken enchilada, Christmas style," Freedom said. "Because it's done in two of the big Christmas colors, red and green. That's your red chile there and your green chile over there. And enchiladas in New Mexico aren't like the ones in Mexico or Texas. Here they're flat, not rolled. I used to opt for the green chile. Now I appreciate the red more. I think those born here, at least those of Hispanic background, go more for the red. It's smokier, a little more complex. The green's a little sharper."

He savored a sample of each chile but could not determine his preference.

"On Canyon Road, Freedom, I've smelled coffee brewing. But it had a scent I have never before encountered. I smell it right—"

"Piñon coffee. That's what you're smelling now. Brewed with piñon nuts mixed in with the coffee grounds. In New Mexico they make the most of the piñon. It's a tree that looks like a cedar, a juniper."

"And what is this soup here?" he pointed at the bowl between them.

"Green chile stew. With hominy and pork. It's a big thing around here. Enjoy it. Theirs is really good."

Nicolás sampled it. Simply delicious. The flavors were not quite Mexican, rather, they must have been New Mexican. But they were close enough to the cuisine of his homeland to give him comfort. For just a moment, he imagined he was eating in a Veracruz café.

Something moved in his peripheral vision. The five men at the corner table were *mestizos*, two blinged-out in gangster attire, three decked out in guayaberas and bowling shirts, open at the necks to brandish gold chains. Some wore their sunglasses inside. One held a cell phone to his ear, his hand festooned with a large sparkling ring. In this setting their aura was strange, and not benevolent. Could they be cartel men? Perhaps the impression was all in his imagination.

His plate and bowl were empty when Nicolás let his eyes sweep the dining room and just for a second, come to rest again on the corner table. One of the men stared straight at him.

Something told Nicolás to look away, as if he had seen nothing out of the ordinary, and to take in the rest of the diners at the tables. A minute later, he cleared his throat.

"What's with those five men seated in the corner over there?" he said in a hushed voice. "To my back right?"

Freedom paused. "Well now. Have I mentioned Española?"

"The town we just passed? On the way here?"

"Yep," Freedom said. "It's a poor town but a few of its residents are…pretty well off. Española's actually the center for smuggling drugs from Mexico and dispersing them all through the Southwest. Don't look at them again. Those might be cartel guys. Some live in Española… most only live there part-time. I used to be creeped out by it. But here they avoid trouble. Everyone here knows about them. And people have learned to live with it."

"Mother of God," Nicolás said.

Damn it all. When will I be free of all of them? How far north do I have to go?

He studied Freedom, whose eyes moved back and forth, as if out of confusion.

"We need to go, Freedom," Nicolás said.

"But Pato, you're just—"

"We need to leave now," Nicolás said. "I am walking out front."

"Fine, and I'd told you I've got this," Freedom said, opening his wallet. Nicolás stood, placing his napkin on the table. He pulled his chair back and walked in a steady pace across the dining room, into the foyer, past the hostess's podium, and out of the restaurant.

"Damn, Pato," he heard Freedom call out, a few steps behind. "Slow down, man. What's the matter?"

"Long story," Nicolás said, his heart thumping so hard that he thought he felt its beat in his neck. "But I told you, we need to leave this moment."

A vision of the cartel men bursting through the door after them spurred him to quicken his pace. When he reached the 4Runner, he turned. Freedom was a few steps behind. Solemnity weighed down his face, as if its brow held some grave thought. Freedom clicked his keychain fob and they piled into the SUV.

Nicolás kept his gaze riveted to the restaurant's front door as the 4Runner reversed from its space and crossed the parking lot. As Freedom drove toward the interstate, he broke the silence.

"You must have seen the cartels do horrible things, back in Veracruz. To react like that."

Nicolás said nothing. How could cartel men be this far north? Even dining at a restaurant in a rural hamlet. When could he be free of them? When could he find that remote refuge where he could prepare, before he sought them out? He must continue northward, and fast. But something compelled him to reveal a morsel of truth. He did not see any risk in doing so. Then perhaps Freedom would begin to understand.

"A cartel," Nicolás said, "took my brother's life. And the lives of my parents."

"I—I'm sorry, Pato."

More silence. The 4Runner veered right onto Highway 68. The terrain grew less dry until on either side rolled hills of stubby grass, punctuated by roundish, dark-green bushes one to two meters high. A river appeared to their left, its rapids rushing over rocks and past a bank thick with trees.

"That's the Rio Grande there," Freedom said. "Flowin' down

from Colorado. Past here, then all the way down along the Texas border."

They passed one small winery after another. Within an hour, the meandering and rising road leveled off. A new town surrounded them.

"Well, Pato, here we are in Taos. We really should stop at the famous pueblo here. How many three-thousand, six-thousand, ten-thousand-year-old buildings can you see in America? Built long before Columbus's great-great-great grandfather was born. You know UNESCO?"

"Yes," Nicolás mumbled. "I am familiar with that organization. Part of the United Nations."

"UNESCO named the Taos Pueblo one of the most unique places on earth."

Mountains loomed ahead and to their right, some illuminated by the sunlight, some cloaked by the shade of passing white cumulus clouds. Craft shops and restaurants lined both sides of the main drag. They passed the Taos Inn on their right, Michael's Diner on their left, a Kachina Lodge hotel on their right, and a Phillips 66 gas station sat ahead.

"The pueblo's just a few minutes away, to the right," Freedom said with excitement.

"Freedom, please. We should stay on the road. And leave New Mexico. And be in Colorado by sundown."

Freedom grunted almost as if hurt, but said nothing. Perhaps he remembered being saved on the Albuquerque roof.

He jerked the steering wheel, sending them barreling down the leftward road.

19

Nicolás stirred awake. Someone was saying his name.

"Pato, whadaya say? You've been comatose the last few hours," Freedom said, smiling as he gripped the steering wheel. Crowning his longhaired head was one of those traditional Austrian, Tyrolean, or Bavarian hats—almost like a round-topped wool fedora—with a small feather fixed under the band. What an image—it captured both Freedom's carefree nature and his eccentricity.

A sign appeared at the side of the road. Route 135.

"Where, where are we?" Nicolás said in a stammer, his mind still foggy.

"Close to my place."

Nicolás felt his mood lift.

"So," said Freedom, "what do you think of this panorama? The Gunnison Valley, in western Colorado. Land of the Utes. Just look at that range ahead. Those are the West Elks. Not the tallest around here but still impressive. Might have told you, I gave up living in Europe for the Rockies. Loved 'em too much."

Nicolás rolled down his window and draped his arm outside against the door. The mountains were the tallest, whitest, and most jagged he had ever glimpsed. Some of his worries left him, and he imagined breathing them out in a fog, then seeing the vapors flit away through the open window.

He caught Freedom's voice as he was saying, "…only in the West that you can truly be free. John Muir, Edward Abbey, Jack Kerouac and the Beats, Hunter S. Thompson, they all knew this. And now you and I do. And Stasia, up ahead."

The road wound north, and then crossed a bridge over a creek.

"That's the Taylor River," Freedom said. "It's always been legal for anyone to float it. Rich Texans moved there recently, bought some camps along the banks. They even set up a barbed-wire fence across it. My buddy Ben and I got sliced up last summer. Had to get tetanus shots, even stitches. Over a hundred of us protested, even had bumper stickers made. Cops made 'em take down that fence."

Nicolás made a barely audible *hmph* sound. The fatigue weighing down his limbs and torso was now in his head. He rolled up his window, rested his neck against the seat, shut his eyes, and ceased to fight it. Sleep descended upon him like a heavy blanket.

Nicolás blinked his eyes open to Freedom's laughter and the giggles of a woman nearby.

"This is your new friend you told me about!" the tall, attractive blonde in a baseball cap said in her thick Slavic accent, as she stood outside his passenger door. Freedom lowered the window.

"He is sleepy, I see," she said, waving a long arm and giving him a kind, innocent smile. Nicolás imagined her as a kindergarten teacher or a nurse.

"Pato," Freedom said. "Welcome to Crested Butte. Or The Butte, or CB. And meet my girlfriend Stasia, from Slovakia."

"Nice to meet you, Stasia," Nicolás said with a nod.

Freedom said, "Let's get unpacked and head up into my place."

Nicolás unbuckled his seatbelt and they headed into the lodge.

"All right, *Señor*," Freedom said as they stood in the dimly lit apartment behind the front desk of the ski lodge. "Tonight you can take my couch here."

"Well, thank you, Freedom," Nicolás said.

"Pato, set that pack down, finally, if you want. You've been haulin' that since I met you."

"Ah, it's fine," Nicolás said.

He turned on his feet as his eyes combed the walls of the small living room. His new friend was an intriguing one, indeed. Nearly every centimeter of the walls featured some odd object or other, or at least odd in that it was not typical wall decor. Stuffed animals, a snake and a monkey, hung in the corner above a surfboard, and next to an array of license plates from various American states and Canadian provinces. The wall nearby was decorated with Polaroids of Freedom climbing various rock formations, and in various European cities. The cover of a *Mountain Gazette* magazine was taped to the wall, showing a Pueblo dancer in full dress in an arid mountain scene, above the inscription, "When in doubt, go higher." Tacked into the drywall beside this was a *National Geographic* map of the United States with the locations of its various indigenous tribes. Along with this were tickets and currency from around the world, Boston Bruins ticket stubs, and Mount Crested Butte ski instructor badges from various years. The urge surfaced to venture a joke at his host's expense.

"It does look like a college dorm room and a preteen boy's bedroom got together and had a child. But I like the place!"

Stasia laughed, covering her mouth with her hand. Freedom

grinned, keeping his mouth closed in a sort of embarrassed nod at his humor.

"Point taken, Pato. I've gotta express my personality a bit, you know. Make it feel like I'm coming back to my true home when the day's done. And I can't let this place be too serious."

"What is this place? Beautiful," Nicolás said, pointing at a poster. It featured three campers beside a rushing stream, sitting around a campfire that illuminated the orange and reddish canyon walls in the coming twilight.

"Moab," Stasia said. "In Utah."

"Just due southwest of here," Freedom said. "Not the worst first stop on a trip, I will say that. It's easy on the eyes. I don't know if there's anything quite like it outside of Utah. A little bit of Mars in the States."

"That is what I thought when I first saw it," Stasia said. "You should see Arches National Park, near there. The Devil's Garden section—it's amazing."

"We thought of living in the Beehive State. Well, over in St. George," Freedom said. "I miss looking for petroglyphs. So many out there."

"Petroglyphs?" Nicolás said.

"Ancient carvings," Freedom said, "or inscriptions on cliff walls, by the native tribes."

"I see your surfboard," Nicolás said, pointing toward the corner.

"That's what I use in California," Freedom said. "Then down in Baja."

"So, why doesn't he join us in Kochevar's?" Stasia said.

"Yes, Stasia. Pato, why don't you, man?" Freedom said in a playful tone.

"Kochevar's?" Nicolás said.

"You'll see. Comin' to the Butte, it's an essential stop. Stasia and I are meeting some friends there."

They walked out of the lodge toward the 4Runner.

"Kochevar's!" Stasia said.

"A decision for Kochevar's," Freedom said, raising his eyebrows at Nicolás, "is a decision well made. I may not be an *achiever*. But I still can hit up ol' *Ko-chee-ver*."

"Brilliant verse, there, Freedom," Nicolás said and laughed.

When they were all three inside the 4Runner, Freedom hooked right onto Gothic Road.

"But Freedom!" Stasia said.

"First I want to show Pato here the valley," Freedom said. "Just for a minute."

In the canyon between the condo units and ski lodges, the road leveled off. The vista that stretched before Nicolás astounded him. The mountains stood taller and were more jagged and coated with snow than the ones he saw on the drive north from Gunnison. All around him—before, between, and behind the chalet-style vacation homes—stretched thick meadows of a bright green grass, punctuated here and there by white piles and slivers of melting snow.

The paved street segued into a road of large gravel, which soon narrowed into a winding lane hugging the eastern side of a bluff. To the right was a drop off of a couple hundred meters.

Freedom slowed to a halt, and then put the vehicle into reverse.

"What are you doing?" Stasia asked.

"You remember," Freedom said. "There's nowhere to turn around for a good while. Hold on for about thirty seconds."

Stasia shifted in her seat, her light blue eyes darting all over Freedom.

Moments later, they returned to the two-lane road. Freedom spun around in a doughnut and headed back toward the cluster of buildings ahead in the distance.

From the castle of tony metal-roofed lodges that was Mount

Crested Butte, Freedom steered the 4Runner down the meandering Gothic Road lined with aspens and grassy meadows, coasting nearly the entire way. He seemed to apply the brakes only at those sparse points when the gradient turned too steep. They passed the old Crested Butte Cemetery on their left. Soon they entered the town of Crested Butte, coursing past a general store and gas station to their left, and quaint shops to their right. After a few blocks, Freedom turned right.

All around stood houses with wooden shingled roofs and facades, one and two stories tall. They brought to mind photographs Nicolás had seen of a region he always longed to visit: northern New England. Crested Butte seemed like towns in Maine, New Hampshire, Vermont, sans the eighteenth-century edifices.

Spruce and fir trees punctuated grassy lawns and lined streets. Every other vehicle seemed to be an SUV, Jeep, or four-by-four truck, most spotted by dust or dried mud. Many featured racks for skis, snowboards, or bicycles, or at least bumper stickers or decals referencing the outdoors or some outdoor activity. Indeed, this town was something altogether unfamiliar.

"Behold your first dispensary, Pato. Bet you ain't seen one of these before! If you get tired of your beer today, you can make a purchase even with a foreign ID."

Nicolás sniffled a laugh as they passed the building. Through the glass front door a group of perhaps ten customers stood, shopping.

"And the dispensaries, Pato, or as I like to call them, the *refineries*, they're all on these streets around here."

They passed a young man in his early twenties throwing what appeared to be a lit hand-rolled cigarette onto the sidewalk. Exhaling a plume of smoke, he stomped it out with a sort of dance of his hiking boot.

"And that was no mere cigarette," Freedom said, turning to

Nicolás. "*No estuvo un Marlboro, a lo menos yo sé esto.* He's exercising the new liberty. Welcome to the highest state in America."

"Careful, *Señor*," Stasia said. "He'll say that every hour or two."

Freedom hooked left onto Elk Avenue. On their right, they passed the post office, a nondescript, square single-story. But surely, Nicolás assumed, a relic of the nineteenth century.

"This is the main strip downtown," Freedom said. "Most of what you would want to find in this town as a visitor, you'll find on this street, or close by."

"You mean all of the suitable watering holes," Nicolás said with a sly wink.

"That's all part of it," Freedom said.

Freedom parallel-parked, and they walked westward down the sidewalk. They threaded their way through an opposing stream of skiers, tourists, and townspeople, many dressed in upscale outdoors garb Nicolás recognized from American expatriates in San Miguel Allende and Cuernavaca. There were the same brands: The North Face, Patagonia, Birkenstocks and Ugg boots. After all, this was an American skiing town, with its share of hippies of all ages.

The surge of pedestrians abated. A weathered wooden sign came into view, jutting out of the three-story Victorian building ahead on their right. "Kochevar's Saloon and Gaming Hall," it read. Before the building, a trio of bikers loitered, talking to a young man in a North Face jacket. They were older, heavy, and shaking with good-natured laughter.

"We have arrived," Freedom said, as he opened the door for them.

Nicolás led the train about six meters inside and then stopped. He turned, glancing about the bar. This was no Loretto Stairwell, but for him it was a first. Above the front entrance was the first taxidermied buffalo head he had ever seen. Fastened to the clapboard walls were logging and woodsmith saws of various sizes and shapes, mining pickaxes, hatchets, logging axes, farm tools, an old pair of wooden skis forming an X over which loomed the taxidermied head, neck, and breast of a bull elk, a shelf supporting a line of old tonic and medicine bottles, and more than a few framed photographs of some bygone era. In one corner, near the ceiling, rested a large roulette wheel set into a wooden board, bearing the inscription underneath: "Original Kochevar Roulette Wheel, circa 1899." Large interlocking squares of sheet metal composed the ceiling, with a large wooden wagon wheel marking its center. With the exception of the sheet metal and flat screens on two different walls, the bar seemed unchanged for a century or more. The venue seemed thoroughly American, but too rugged and western to be a dive bar.

"Heyo!" Freedom called as he slapped Nicolás on his back. "Time to wet whistles."

Despite his studies, Nicolás did not recognize this expression. But he could guess its meaning. He edged closer to the shiny, wooden bar top.

"What will you enjoy, guys?" Stasia said.

Freedom nodded at him. "*Usted primero.*" How courteous.

Nicolás leaned over the bar and took in the American flag under the mounted head of a buck. He thought of his own homeland, so wounded and so threatened, so far away.

"I will take a bit of Don Julio tequila that you have right there," Nicolás said as he spotted the bottle. "A double."

Freedom howled with surprise, a doglike sound, and slapped him across the back. Stasia, then Freedom, ordered their draft beers. Nicolás took his glass and closed his eyes as he savored the first sip. He liked that this was one of those bars where one need not pay right upon service.

Freedom cleared his throat. "Now shall we be seated?"

"So, what brings you to Crested Butte?" Stasia said. "And the U.S.?"

"Well, work. And I—I am writing a book on my travels through the American West. From a unique viewpoint. My observations and experiences as a Mexican national. So far I've traveled through Arizona, New Mexico, and now Colorado."

Nicolás hated the lie the more it spewed from his lips. Stasia watched him with a strange expression. A shudder rippled down the nape of his neck. Could she detect his lie about the book?

Everyone seated themselves at a table by the window. For hours they chatted on, as the sun made its descent.

An iPad protruded from Stasia's purse atop the table.

It was gnawing at him, more and more. What had changed in the last week in Veracruz? He hoped at least Carla and Juan had survived...

Feeling emboldened by Madre Tequila, Nicolás asked, "Stasia, would you mind if I checked the Internet for something?"

"Not at all," Stasia said, typing something into the keyboard.

"There's a wireless connection here," Freedom said. "Even in a joint this old. Just promise me you won't look at any dirty sites, Pato."

Freedom let rip a mischievous laugh. Stasia handed the iPad to Nicolás. He began to search the Internet for news of Veracruz and Segundo Cortez.

Come on, damn it. Hurry. Where is the news? His eyes darted about the small screen as he devoured bits of articles and captions of photos.

As he read, his heart leapt with elation. And then his stomach dropped, further and further by the minute. Arturo Méndez dying of a heart attack the day after the arson and his flight from Veracruz in the semi. Ivan seizing the helm of Segundo Cortez. The attack on the Xalapa cartel. The assassination of the vice chancellor, his mentor at the university.

Ivan had gone mad, drunk with his newfound power, ravenous for blood. Had Nicolás expected anything less? He was foolish to feel surprise.

Then Nicolás encountered the news video of Carla, only a day old, showing her smiling and laughing as she interviewed the mayor. Odd—after all of that recent tragedy and bloodshed. And her lover's murder.

Next he must search for news of Juan.

A deeper shock. Juan...murdered? Poisoned in his own house? Something was afoot—even darker and sicker than he expected.

He happened upon a photo of Pantano seated at his desk, looking upward. With the melancholy of his drooping eyes, his white hair and his upward glance, Nicolás recalled El Greco's *The Repentent Peter*. Except with Pantano, there surely was no remorse.

Nicolás became aware that outside of his new cocoon, there at his table, a tense scene was unfolding.

"You did not tell me this, Freedom," Stasia said in shock. She stared down at the table.

"Well, Stasia," Freedom said, shrugging. "I'd floated the idea of a trip weeks ago. We need one anyway. Come on."

What had he missed? Nicolás had lost his bearings with what had appeared before him on the screen. Did Stasia not know of the trip to Montana?

"Why now?" Stasia said, her arms crossed over her chest.

"Well...like I said," Freedom stammered. "I need...we need a break, a trip. And Pato here...well, I hate admitting this but he saved my life. Pulled me out of a life-or-death situation in ABQ. This hulking psycho was choking me. Pato intervened in the nick of time."

Stasia looked at Nicolás, her face a mixture of shock, frustration, and gratitude.

"I want to make Montana," Freedom said. "And Pato really wants to go there. It was his only request. Come on, Stasia."

She remained silent, her gaze softening to one of kindness, even affection.

"All right then," she said. "But it needs to be short. And Freedom, after we get back—the move. Remember?"

"This early?" Freedom said, holding his palms out and upward.

"We need to," she said.

Freedom turned to Nicolás. "You know, it's been a long time coming, guy. After our trip, Stasia and I will probably make the move down to Durango. Our time in CB's done, anyway."

Freedom shook his head, took a deep gulp of his beer and said, "We used to love it. But it's changed so much. It's pricing us out, with all the wealthy retiring here. Even the vacationers building second homes. So we planned on Durango."

"We can move back, one day," Stasia said. "To live here again."

"What will you do for work there?" Nicolás said.

"First I need to set up the pre-school and the day-care for Stasia," Freedom said. "Her business ideas, Pato, and good ones. And then we need to work and save like hell if we want to ever live again in this town."

Nicolás felt their tension ebb, but still he sensed discomfort. Had he hastened their move?

"So who will we see in Montana? Mitch? Gabe? Dennis?" Stasia said, looking sideways into Freedom's eyes. He gave a single slow nod.

"Pato," Freedom said, "my friend Dennis is a big fisherman who lives in Bozeman. He's a great guy, and it's a nice college town. Now Missoula—Stasia and I have two good friends that live in northwest Montana. Mitch and Gabe. They used to live in Missoula, but now they live north of there. Beside Flathead Lake, near the Flathead reservation. Just south of Glacier National Park, maybe thirty miles south of Canada."

"Mitch and Gabe are great people," Stasia said. "And Flathead Lake's a great place."

"Mitch is an ex-Army Ranger, did two tours overseas," Freedom said. "She's an Army vet, too. Now she's a veterinarian's assistant. He's an outdoors tour guide."

Yes, that was it. Mitch, Gabe, veterans? They could help him prepare for his return to Veracruz.

"I am hoping to find work very soon," Nicolás said. "I need money."

"Well, you'll find something up there," Freedom said. "So we should leave crack of dawn *mañana.* Hell, when you see this place, you might even decide to put your stake in the ground. Or in Missoula. Or in Durango, down in the Four Corners with us. But for now, we can all head up towards Dennis. And then Mitch and Gabe. Cut through Jackson Hole, eastern Idaho on the way."

Nicolás sensed his future brightening. "This is a great idea."

Freedom paused, then resumed. "It is great. What's great is that at least we're all here together. In the West—the true West. Nothing planned. And we can still get close to nature."

"Yes, just maybe this was all meant to be," Nicolás said. "Everything leading to this journey. I would at least like to think so."

20

P antano sat alone in the nearly empty café, sipping his *agua fresca*, when she arrived—in a formfitting black dress that bared her arms and calves. He rose to his feet.

It was apparent—how she could enjoy a hold over both Esteban and Ivan.

As she approached his table, she ran her gaze above his eyes and all over his head. It must be at his thick white tuft of hair.

"*Señorita*," Pantano said, pulling out a chair just perpendicular to his.

"*Buenos tardes*," she said, studying his clothes for a moment before taking her seat. Had she not expected him to be in his uniform? And she did not address him by his title or his name.

A waiter appeared.

"*Café helado, por favor*," Carla said, and the waiter vanished.

She turned her eyes to face his.

Such a scheming one. It's all there in her eyes. Be ready for her.

"So why did you want to meet?" she asked, her head tilting to the side as she peered hard into his eyes.

Surely she had to have some idea.

"Well, glad you could join me," he said. "There are some things...we should address."

He leaned toward her and lowered his voice a couple of octaves.

"First, I know your ways quite well. Spying your little heart out for Ivan Méndez. And I learned you are involved with him. Romantically. Fine, but you need to keep your distance from my force. And you can't pull with them what you pulled with Esteban Nolano and the *curandera* and the priest. And even your own news partner, Juan—who was clearly set up. If I find out you're tailing my men again, investigating them in the slightest... well, no longer will I feed you anything for your reporting. I will shut off the tap. Immediately."

Pantano slapped his hand onto the white tablecloth. Then he noticed the smirk.

"You know," she said, "your surname is very fitting. Swamp. After all, where your loyalties lie is very murky, *Señor*. With Segundo Cortez? Or with those who resist it? And you know most of those are dead."

"You mean your dead lover you betrayed, Esteban Nolano? And the old Father and the *curandera* who looked at you as a friend? And what about your reporter partner, Juan—"

"We digress," she said. "Look, I will tell you this. If I cannot photograph what I want or talk to whom I want for a story, I have it in my power to expose you. And men on your force. For things you have done."

"Like?" he said as he leaned forward. Damn, she was unnerving. Sitting there with that complacent smirk.

"Bribes you've taken. Not even investigating the deaths of those you just mentioned. Never arresting one *capo* in Segundo Cortez. And never holding a Segundo Cortez member without releasing him in a matter of days."

Her sheer defiance sent him to his feet. He felt the blood, the heat in his face.

"You're such a whore. An expensive one but a harlot, nonetheless. I know you know this."

"You will pay for that." The words came from her clenched teeth as she shot to her feet.

"I know you better than you think I do," Pantano said in a snarl, jutting his face toward her from across the table. "Your childhood in a Mexico City slum. Your time as a runaway. You trollop. No wonder you will do anything to fill your purse, to bring you farther away from …those days."

"How," she said, her voice choking with outrage. "How did you find—"

"All right, De Echegaray. I hate saying all of that, but you have shown me such disrespect. You will do what you will do. And I will do what I will do," he said, holding up his hands, their palms facing her.

Would any of his threats and warnings take hold? Were they wasted into the air?

He began to walk away. A few meters from the table, he turned back to face her.

"Also," he said, "watch your back. And I'm not talking about me or the law."

Pantano felt her eyes on his back as he walked away. As he disappeared into the street, he imagined her scrutinizing his old quasi-military gait.

Yes, he knew. Her world had grown haunted. Perhaps she too would soon be dead by Ivan's orders. Even his lovers weren't safe.

No doubt Ivan had sworn wealth would be hers. She most likely imagined dwelling in her own estate. Even more, in Ivan's hacienda, there by his side as his queen. A world away from that Mexico City slum.

He snuck a look back across the café as he stepped away. She was speaking with passion into her phone, gesticulating in a sweeping expression with her free hand.

Most likely, Ivan Méndez was on the opposite end of that call. Ha. She loved him, envied him, lusted after him, feared him.

Yes, he must be extra vigilant against both Ivan and her.

And yet—was he himself not like Carla de Echegaray in one notable way? Did they both not present the mask of a soldier of virtue to the public, yet conspire in private with the forces of darkness?

After kicking a tin can into the gutter, Pantano quickened his pace. His wife Raquel expected him for dinner. And he wanted to get as close to her, and as far from the witch behind him, as soon as possible.

21

Such a barren landscape. Nicolás stared from the back seat and beyond Freedom, through the windshield. The terrain around Moab—with its orange and reddish-hued canyons, bluffs, and natural arches, often etched with ancient petroglyphs—did possess an unearthly beauty foreign to anything he had ever glimpsed. But this new land, several hours north of Moab, just due north of Price in northeastern Utah, near the town of Vernal —this all seemed so ugly, so rough to the eyes, with its occasional mining towns and rocky plains revealing scant vegetation. And Vernal, did it not mean springtime? *Primavera?* Where had the beauty gone? Freedom did say that the land in all of the other parts of the state was remarkably beautiful. Especially around Zion. And that the state held five or more national parks. Freedom did mention there would be a surprise in store in far northeastern Utah.

Along the entire route through the state, Nicolás had struggled to escape the memories of his dead family and the utter silence hanging within the 4Runner by imagining a sixty-something Ernest Hemingway somewhere to the northwest, in the early 1960s, living amidst the beautiful Sawtooth Mountains of Idaho. Yet it was not a good choice for a daydream, Nicolás realized. Papa had suffered from debilitating depression, alcoholism, self-doubt, and one morning had dispatched himself with his favorite shotgun to the roof of his mouth.

As Nicolás recalled his family, he reeled inside, casting his thoughts toward other things...anything.

So he tried to think of the beautiful fish that Freedom said abounded in the region: brown trout, salmon, speckled river trout, and so many others. He forced himself to envision, over and over, their sleek shiny bodies, their fine scaly skin, dripping with pristine mountain water from a blue-ribbon stream as some lucky fisherman held them aloft, one by one.

Nicolás remembered waking at the campsite that dawn. The sound of boots crunching into the sandy dirt brought Nicolás back from the land of dreams—and nightmares. His friend was pacing around like a wild man, his hair disheveled after the argument, his eyes bleary and downcast. Past the dangling open flap of her tent, Stasia laid on her side in the fetal position, sobbing.

In a couple hours they could check into a motel and wash their clothes—if his two friends could stop their feud.

Perhaps Freedom really did have some sort of obsessive-compulsive disorder. As Freedom drove, Nicolás heard him several times make a faint sound, as if he was going to begin a word, but Freedom never completely enunciated the first syllable. Nicolás and Stasia had made eye contact during one of those moments. He remembered Stasia's words back in Moab, that Freedom had been diagnosed years ago in Europe with that condition. He had been surprised. Freedom did not seem like the type.

While Nicolás kept his eyes closed, Freedom and Stasia began to argue in quiet tones, in some unknown tongue. Surely it was Slovak. Minutes later, silence.

"Pato's in a coma," Stasia said in English.

"He's sojourning in the land of dreams," Freedom said.

"It is because," Stasia said, "he could not sleep much last night. He was very restless."

Nicolás opened his eyes. He cleared his throat and bit by bit righted himself on the backseat.

"Well there you are, Pato," Freedom said.

"Last night you talked a lot in your sleep," Freedom said. "You were a bit upset about something."

Nicolás felt his face flush. "Um…what exactly did I say?"

"Well, you, well—you got very sad about losin' your parents and your brother in Mexico. But you were still out. Like a log."

The sign for Vernal appeared.

"All right," Freedom mumbled, wiping his eyes and cheeks. "What we're going to do now is turn left, turn north on this highway. This may be a highway, but it's the backroads. The road less traveled, the better route."

Nicolás felt a desire build within him to seize the wheel from Freedom, to speed them faster, northward. He could hardly wait for Montana. And it agonized him that he could not explain his mission of vengeance, justice. It would be better that they not know—at least for the time being. He must force his mind to drift. Somehow.

The 4Runner turned onto the two-lane highway. Soon, ever so slowly, the terrain began to change. The dry earth rose up from the flat, boulder-strewn plain and once again, as in southeastern Utah, it began to form bluffs and hills and canyons, though not as orange-red in color. The rocks possessed more of a brownish hue, both light- and dark-brown tones. Trees appeared, mostly short conifers. The road began to wind. There was no guardrail, and often the cliff loomed directly over him. Could boulders break loose overhead and crush their vehicle? Nicolás gritted his teeth.

Signs advertising mining companies emerged every few minutes on his left, as the road snaked wildly around rock outcrops, buttes, and bluffs. Bulldozers appeared, trucks of various sizes, and certain industrial vehicles he had never seen before. After thirty minutes, the road straightened. The pines became thicker and more numerous. He spotted that other species of tree Freedom showed him days before: birch trees. Thousands of them, along with the pines, bounded the road on both sides.

Oddly enough, Nicolás's surroundings were now alpine. He rolled down the windows, as Freedom was fond of doing. The wind that coursed all around them was cool and sharp with a distinct, clean pine scent.

"There ya go," Freedom said, and then released one of his celebratory howls. "Welcome to the Uinta Mountains. The only range in the Rockies that goes from west to east, not north to south. Look at all the pines. Douglas firs, spruces, lodgepole pines. Ponderosa pines."

"Stunning," Nicolás said. "This was your surprise you had mentioned."

Dense coniferous forests stretched on either size. This looked nothing like the Utah he had seen and heard of. It seemed indistinguishable from the alpine forests in western Colorado.

Occasional droplets began to splatter on the faintly dusty windshield. Freedom activated the wiper.

"Well, the heavens aren't the only thing needing to urinate right about now," Nicolás said. "Let's pull over for a minute."

"Good timing," Freedom said. "There's a public restroom up ahead, on our left."

He turned and parked in the small gravel lot between a water-lily-covered pond and a small wooden building.

Outside, Nicolás lit a cigarette.

"Here we are," Freedom said. "Bathroom's in that hut. Release it to all of your hearts' content."

Minutes later, as they returned to the car, Nicolás spotted a large brown blot against the light-green meadow abutting the pond's opposite shore. He thought he recognized it from photographs.

"What—"

"Don't you see it?" Stasia said.

"Behold, Pato," Freedom said. "Your first moose sighting."

The beast, far larger than a horse, was one of the strangest he had ever seen. Its broad, concave antlers stretched sideways and upwards like some odd bowl. It eyed them momentarily, before drooping its head toward the water to drink.

"That won't be the last you'll see, *Señor*," Freedom said. "Now you just need to see your first live elk, buffalo, bighorn sheep, and mountain goat. And if you get lucky, once we get into Montana, maybe your first grizzly and wolverine."

"This place is wilder than wild," Nicolás said.

"Now for the last leg of today's drive," Freedom said. "This road gets dangerous. Almost as deep a drop-off as the Million Dollar Highway, down near Durango and Ouray, Silverton."

They piled into the 4Runner, stuffed with their camping gear, toiletries, most of their clothes, the contents of their pantry, and Nicolás' backpack.

"Take the passenger's seat up front," Freedom said.

"No, Stasia should sit there," Nicolás said.

"No, we want you to see it, Pato," she said as she slid into the back seat. "Your first time in Utah."

Freedom turned left onto the mountain road and accelerated. Nicolás recalled that certain recklessness, that fearlessness in his friend. Case, or Casey Logan. Freedom Logan. What a character, a distinctly American original.

The drops fell with building frequency, and Freedom raised

all four windows. The road began to wind again. A vast, deep gorge appeared, plunging downward from their right. To their left loomed a charcoal-gray, nearly smooth rock face, crowned by a great bush-like carpet of dense pines.

Nicolás's stomach contracted, but he was surprised he did not feel more fear. Perhaps it was because he felt more reckless after hurling that first Molotov cocktail. And besides, his friend had driven this road before.

Freedom slowed, and then parked at the side of the road. He connected his smartphone by a cord to the dashboard panel, typed on the screen with his thumbs in a frenzy, and then eased once again onto the accelerator.

A beautiful instrumental song opened up all around Nicolás, with its thundering percussion, ambient synth, and guitars. The moment was a perfect blend of art and nature, with gray clouds parting across the gorge to the right, revealing a bright patch of sky. He imagined, as he had the morning before, that a new life stretched wide and sublime before him. New dimensions of living that were for him, hitherto, unglimpsed and untrodden. That just perhaps, there could be, or there had been, a Creator.

"My gooosssh, it is so byooo-tee-fuulll!" exclaimed Stasia.

The rain began to slack off to occasional droplets. Freedom jammed his door panel with his finger, and all four windows came completely down. Nicolás leaned his head and shoulders out of the window and turned around to look out to his back right across the gorge, into the sky's opening. The largest, most magnificent rainbow he had ever seen arched over the dark, seemingly bottomless gorge. The symbol of promise. The carnage and death of his recent past seemed to fade. Those nightmares seemed entombed far behind, across the mountain ranges he had traversed. Nicolás became aware of three drives battling each other within him. There was his longing for his homeland, to return and battle for justice. Out of this sprang the desire to head north, to prepare the means to head south for that same confrontation. And though it was far less potent, he sensed a dark, third drive within him—the desire to simply perish after attacking Segundo Cortez, and pass into oblivion.

But he knew which side held sway. Montana—from the atlas he knew it was just north of Wyoming.

He swung his head around to look alongside the vehicle's hood.

They had reached the opposite, northernmost side of the gorge. A blue sign approached.

Nicolás's whisper disappeared into the cool whipping winds. "Wyoming."

When he raised the window, Freedom's voice emerged from behind the steering wheel.

"Hey, man. I remember what I wanted to tell you. Last night, you kept mentioning someone over and over in your sleep. Who is Ivan?"

22

Gustavo steered the patrol car through the market. Beside him, Pantano stared out the window at the stalls with vendors selling fruit, fresh tortillas, tacos, quesadillas, and all matter of food. He concentrated on the rich aroma of tortillas penetrating the car windows, hoping it would drive his worries from his mind.

But it was to no avail. Ivan Méndez amounted to one problem that just would not disappear, even for a moment. At various points in each day, it would fade, and then come rushing back without warning.

That's right. Breathe deeply through your nose. There, now again. The aroma did comfort him. His peace dispersed with the ringing of his cell.

"It's Ribera," Pantano said, glancing at his nephew.

"We never get an evening off," Gustavo said, shaking his head.

"Yes?" Pantano said into the phone.

He heard a throat clearing itself, and then one of his top lieutenants say, "*Jefe*...it's been quite a night for Veracruz. Valles was shot dead. He was responding to a robbery in a daycare. Along with the daycare manager—a woman. Eyewitnesses saying the assailants had AKs. Segundo Cortez, *Señor.*"

"Damn it," Pantano said.

"There's more. They killed another professor from the university. Strung him up in Speech Alley on campus. The *narcomanta* pinned on the body mentioned the protests. And they did the same to Deacon Amaya. Padre Manolo Huerta's deacon. He was found in the sanctuary of the church even. And missing his head."

Pantano paused. Ivan had breached the agreement. He had snuffed out the life of one of his men. And then the professor and the deacon. He hated it, but he knew why Ivan had struck—the entire university allowed the protests in Speech Alley and on its streets. Amaya voiced his own protests to his own congregation. But Valles—for him it was just wrong place, wrong time.

"Ribera, that was expected with the professor and the deacon," Pantano said. "But Valles? Damn them all."

Pantano glanced over at Gustavo, who was staring straight at him.

"Our Valles?" his nephew whispered.

"Where is the body?" Pantano said into the phone. "Where is Valles?"

"He's already on his way to the morgue, *Jefe,*" Ribera said in an assuaging tone. "No need to come to the scene."

"I will see you in the morning, Ribera. Keep the team strong. See you at the station very early tomorrow."

Pantano placed the phone back in his pocket.

"How did they get Valles?" Gustavo said. "Segundo Cortez, wasn't it?"

"Yes. As he responded to a burglary…of a daycare center."

"*Dios mio,*" Gustavo said. "They are risking a war with us. They will get it."

As if it was so simple. That was Gustavo's youth talking.

"I'm making a call," Pantano said. "Keep driving toward Rodolfo's."

As the car rolled through the last of the market and onto the avenue toward his son's house, Pantano fished the phone again from his pocket.

He inhaled once, a profound breath. He must control himself, but be both firm and judicious.

"Ivan Méndez," Pantano said when the call connected.

"You're probably calling about your guy that got himself killed tonight." The voice was confident but without its usual arrogance.

"We had an agreement," Pantano said.

"We still do, *Señor* Pantano," Ivan said. "He entered the place, and they told him to leave. He shot first."

Strange. The kid sounded so very respectful and composed. Damned sociopath.

"My force will always respond to a burglary. Or a shooting."

"I can't ensure the safety of your men if they get themselves caught in the middle. These aren't errors committed in the fog of war. Your men are responding far too fast to calls. They are inserting themselves. Then they make mistakes. Please, order them to wait twenty minutes before responding. And if they see cartel SUVs on the scene, take a few drives around the block."

"This will just keep happening. I understand you whacking the deacon with the big mouth. But the owner of a daycare? Really?"

"He refused to pay his due," Ivan said, with the hint of a laugh. "Racketeering is no small part of my business, Pantano. Like I said, twenty minutes from now on. Anyway, I still have a payment for you. All is fine, *Señor*. *Tranquilo*."

He could swear he felt his thundering heart slow in his chest.

Twenty minutes? He could put out the new rule on the force. But no doubt it would raise some eyebrows.

"No more of this business until I return to the station tomorrow morning."

"You have my word," Ivan said. "Relax, get some sleep. Call me tomorrow for the payment."

Silence ensued on the other line. Pantano looked at the screen. Ivan had hung up.

The patrol car continued through the night, turning from the avenue into the neighborhood.

"Uncle?" Gustavo finally said.

"Tomorrow morning I am addressing—in some way or another—the entire force again. We get word of a robbery, a killing? We wait twenty minutes. Even thirty."

Ivan had won. Again. Another devil's agreement, forged by yet another bribe. And by an unspoken truth: The Veracruz police force was probably helpless in challenging Segundo Cortez.

Gustavo pulled the vehicle into the drive, and they walked toward the front door. A solid house, a safe neighborhood, an unlisted phone number and address. As safe as he could afford for his son, who at thirty-four seemed unable to support himself, much less his wife and child.

At least Rodolfo always was employed somewhere. Just not at a decent job or for long. Maybe this was his cross for not promoting Arturo. Or for some long-forgotten sin in his past. He jammed his finger onto the doorbell.

Steps approached, and the door swung open.

His son was smiling. The son he could never abandon or even neglect in any situation, who despite his lack of success, his intemperance, and his mismanagement of money…his whole life, he considered his father his very best friend and hero.

"*Papá*, Gustavo, I am so glad to see you," he said. "Come in, come in. Have you seen the news?"

"We heard it firsthand, *mijo*," Pantano said. "We could use a break from it."

His son opened the door wider. Just inside the foyer stood his special-needs grandson, diminutive even for a six-year-old, the one pure being in his life smiling up at him with an unmistakable expression of joy and surprise.

23

Western Montana. Certainly it looked different from all that had come before. Nicolás recalled that sign as they had crossed over from Idaho. "Montana: Big Sky Country" it read.

The evidence was all around him. What had started as thick pine forests just north of the Centennial Mountains at the Idaho border had segued into undulating hills and bald, roundish mountains coated with grass, with only the occasional tree or shrub. The azure sky yawned broad and wide. Indeed, it seemed almost boundless.

A sign materialized in the distance. Butte. Nicolás remembered what Freedom had said back in Moab. This city had the largest open-air mine in the nation, or the world, he couldn't remember which.

He felt compelled to speak up. Freedom had driven for so very long. "Would you like me to drive for a while?"

"No thanks," Freedom said. "I got good rest last night."

"What—what is that smell?" Stasia said.

"Well," Nicolás said. "Perhaps this is a wake-up call. Calling us to take showers."

Freedom said, "It's this city here. The mining and all that. Between Bozeman and Missoula— which are really, really nice— you've got this industrial copper-mining city. And you don't want to touch their tap water. I've smelled it, man. Good thing, though, is Butte hosts Evel Knievel Days every year. Pro stuntmen from all over the world come here to compete. It's a wild time. Saw it one year with Mitchell and Gabriella."

"Are they a couple?" Nicolás said. "Mitch and Gabe?"

"No, they're no couple," Freedom said and laughed. "Some tease 'em about that. But they're best friends. Great people, man. You'll love 'em. Always there for ya in the clutch."

They swung in the turn. Nicolás found himself heading west, then northwest, on Interstate 90. He took up the atlas that lay on the back seat beside him. Soon they would be in a town named Deer Lodge, then Bearmouth. But first they would pass near a town named Opportunity. Opportunity, Montana. He loved the sound of that. Montana seemed like his best opportunity to get settled, and then prepare for his mission to the south. And if he survived the clash, perhaps to return to this land of opportunity and rebuild a safe, full life.

As his lids grew heavier, his jowls grew slack. Nicolás allowed his eyes to close, yet he forced himself to stay awake, this time by recalling that scene from yesterday, late afternoon.

After parking at the Curtis Canyon campgrounds, they walked forward for a few seconds, pausing each beside the other on the bluff. Before them stretched an unforgettable panorama, perhaps the most beautiful, Nicolás thought, he had seen in America.

Hundreds of feet below them lay the flat grassy floor of the National Elk Refuge. Just beyond, Nicolás counted the seven tall, jagged mountains, capped with snow.

"The Grand Tetons of Wyoming," Freedom said. "You've finally seen them."

Freedom raised his hands high over his head and released two long whoops.

"*Gran Teton!*" he cried in a French accent.

"Let's see if he can resist a breast joke," Nicolás muttered to Stasia. "I wager he cannot."

Freedom mumbled something inaudible and laughed. Stasia slapped his shoulder hard.

They hiked, and afterward, sat in a semicircle in the canvas foldout chairs, warming themselves by the stone-encircled fire. The two tents stood just behind them. Through the glare of the hovering sun ahead, they squinted at the mountains, westward.

"We really lucked out," Freedom said. "Okay, let's gather round."

Freedom stood along with Stasia. "Group hug."

The three stood beside the fire in a semicircle, their arms draping each other's shoulders.

"Great Spirit above," Freedom said. "We pray that you keep us safe. Remind us how lucky we are to have life. Protect us from evil. Guide us where to go on our paths. And each day bring us closer to your beautiful creation, oh Divine Spirit."

Opening his eyes to see the ceiling of the 4Runner, Nicolás knew he had lost the battle to stay awake. How long had he slept? Regardless, that evening and night camping in Wyoming was already a great memory.

Nicolás cleared his throat, and then said, "I was contemplating our time last night and fell asleep. I was thinking...there's one thing above all I like about the West. People keep pushing forward in life, rebuilding, starting anew, and reinventing themselves. Yet Fitzgerald said there are no second acts in American lives."

"So untrue," Freedom said. "Look at me and Stasia. Reinventing ourselves after our time in Europe, rebuilding our lives. Mitch and Gabe both did...here out West."

Nicolás thought of Freedom and Stasia meeting and falling in love in Europe, then scraping together enough money to fly to Boston, and after working there a few months, to move to Colorado. Something about that tale smacked of American-ness. Optimism, hope, going West, second chances, persistence. Winning in the end, the triumphant ending. His new friends did seem to lead happy, peaceful lives, with much adventure.

The road north, Route 93, passed small town after small town. The signs showed that as they passed through towns, all the while they traversed the Flathead Indian Reservation. *Flatheads*. Not the most flattering name, but easy to remember.

All around them stretched something heavenly. They came upon a vast lake, bounded by distant mountains on the western and eastern horizon. A thick layer of pines bordered its eastern shore. He had never seen a body of water quite like this one. It was as turquoise as the waters of the Yucatan, but the lake was freshwater.

"I know what you're thinking, Pato," Freedom said. "Flathead Lake. It's this color 'cause of all the limestone particles flittering around in there. Light reflects off 'em. Looks to the naked eye like turquoise. Much prettier lake than even Lake Jackson back in Wyoming. At the shore you can see ten feet into the bottom, maybe more. Great fishing and boating and swimming, too. Chilly, though."

They turned right, skirting the south shore, and then followed the curve of the lake until they rolled northward, up the eastern shore. To the left, across the opposing lane, stretched several meters of forest, sloping downward into the rocks and lapping waters. To their right rose a wooded bluff, several meters tall. Every few seconds they passed a mailbox, and a driveway cut through the bluff to some invisible house farther beyond. A sign showed they had reached the town of Finley Point. Another showed they were crossing through the town of Yellow Bay. At last one informed them that they had arrived in Bigfork. Freedom swung right, into a gravel parking lot, and eased up to a small, quaint wooden house decorated with gingerbread molding. A wooden sign read "Dr. Cassandra Waters, Veterinarian."

"Meet a friend of mine, Pato," Freedom said.

Nicolás noticed the red Yamaha motorcycle parked out front.

"She's here," Stasia said, pointing at it. "Do you see Gabe's toy?"

"Really?" Nicolás said, as they stepped out onto the gravel. The mountain air was very cool—even cold—on his face. Was this April in northwestern Montana?

"Absolutely," Freedom said. "She's an enthusiast. Owns another bike, too."

Inside the clinic, an old man sat in one of the waiting chairs, clutching the leash of the Labrador that sat between his feet. Behind the counter in blue scrubs stood two women. One was somewhere in her mid-twenties, her porcelain face accented by doll-like features, conspicuous makeup and very long eyelashes, yet producing a decidedly vapid expression. She had straight brown hair down to her jaw, with a barrette holding back her bangs.

Beside her stood an athletic woman in her late thirties, her light chestnut hair cut short and combed upward like a boy's, with no makeup on her freckled skin. Highlighting her smiling face, as her chin was slightly raised, was an expression of both warmth and stalwart strength.

"Freedom? Freedom, Stasia?" she said, halfway in disbelief. She walked around and hugged the couple. "You made it sooner than expected."

"Great to see you," Stasia said as she and Freedom embraced Gabe.

Freedom said, "Gabe, meet Pato. Professor of Literature."

"I've heard about you," she said.

"*Ga-bree-ell-la*," Nicolás drew out the syllables as he shook her hand. "From Gabriel. Archangel and guardian."

24

"*Kootenai* is the name they used, their true name," Freedom said as they drove down the main strip. "But it's Flathead in the English translation."

He pulled the 4Runner into another gravel drive while Gabe pulled her Yamaha motorcycle alongside it.

"It's happy hour today and I know they'll all be in there," Gabe said, pulling off her helmet.

They trudged up the two steps toward the door. "José's Flathead Café" read the design on its glass panel.

"Isn't mixing natives and beer not the safest combination?" Freedom said as he opened the door, waiting until all three passed within.

Two aromas reached his nostrils—fried pickles and deviled eggs. Several middle-aged and older men sat at a table, drinking beer and playing cards.

"Logan!" one of the men said as he rose to his feet. "Case Logan, get over here, you gypsy bastard!" He appeared younger than the others, in his late thirties, and of medium height but solidly built. The man had light-blue eyes, a square jaw, a small nose, long sideburns, and a five-day beard. He wore his hair, dark brown and touched with gray, very short on the sides, the bangs slicked back onto his head. His right forearm was covered with tattoos.

"Mitchell. Long time," Freedom said, stepping forward and clasping his hand in one of those American male handshakes.

Mitch then hugged Stasia, made a few pleasantries, then turned his way. "Would this be the wandering professor? The gent with the beard?"

"That's me, yes," Nicolás said, as his new acquaintance sized him up.

"Welcome to Bigfork, bud," he said, offering Nicolás his hand. "I'm Mitch."

"Pato," Nicolás said, giving the hand a shake. He spotted a man sitting at the table in a cowboy hat, staring at him with flinty, cynical look.

"You're writin' a book, I hear," Mitch said.

"I am. My experiences of the West. A memoir."

"Well, you've come to one of the best places. We can show you some good stuff around here."

"That would be much appreciated, sir," Nicolás said. He noticed a short, swarthy, barrel-chested Hispanic man, his arms crossed, eyeing him from the kitchen doorway across the room.

Something pulled his gaze once more toward the rectangular table beside Mitch. Sitting at one head was that grim-looking man in his late fifties, wearing a gray felt cowboy hat and gray police officer's uniform.

Opposing him across the table sat a man somewhere in his mid-forties, tall and lean, in a white pearl-snap western shirt, dark-blue jeans, and cowhide western boots. He sat just a couple of meters away from Nicolás, staring up at him with half-closed eyes. His youthful dirty blond hair hung down nearly into his eyebrows.

At the table's sides sat two men, one with his back to Nicolás, and one facing him on the opposite side. All about this second man's face was something extraordinarily soft. It simply possessed a kindness, a gentleness—it resembled the face one would expect in a country doctor or a minister. The man wore spectacles, the oval lens slightly clouded as if by steam.

"Well, let me introduce you, *Señor*, to my fellow poker players here," Mitch said. "At the head of the table there, in the old-school lawman's Stetson hat, is Sheriff Will Press. Sheriff of Flathead County."

The man was already watching him with beady eyes, a hint of a smirk playing at the side of his mouth.

A policeman, even a sheriff! Please God, let this one not be like those in Veracruz. He had come so very far through a land with such a vastly different culture. Surely things would be very different…

"Next to him," Mitch said, "yes, fittingly with the face of an angel, you have Pastor Cole Wachter, pastor of the Grace Covenant Church. And across the table from the good pastor, in the red shirt, is Burning Elk. Tribal name. But his legal name's Parker Wade. Damn fine gentleman. Then at the end of the table we have Jake. He's a mover and shaker in this area, one handsome devil, but full of piss and vinegar. Jake's surely the meanest fella in all of Flathead County."

Jake shot Mitch a cold, irritated look, which was not without a touch of amusement.

"Now boys, let's all retire to The Raven," Gabe said, stepping forward and grabbing Mitch by the hands as if expecting a dance. He twirled her once, twice, then dipped her and pulled her back upright.

"Yes, let's do that," Mitch said. "Gents? Who'll accompany me? Isn't it our tradition? First here, then there. Or to The Pearl, then maybe The Sitting Duck. It's Friday evening, for God's sake."

As the men at the table debated amongst themselves, Nicolás shifted from one foot to another and cleared his throat. Impatience burned within him like a fever. At last, he had found Mitch and Gabe, the very people who could teach him firearms and marksmanship. And now he could sense there was, instead, a night of revelry ahead.

"Mitch," Jake said, standing up. "I've gotta speak with you, man."

"Okay, bud," Mitch said. "Everything okay?"

"Long story," Jake said. "Long story."

Nicolás and the others shot a glance from Jake to Mitch, then back to Jake, and then to Mitch.

Could they have been discussing him? Could he not trust Freedom? Or did Jake object to their new visitor?

"Ladies and gentlemen, and superwomen," Mitch said, turning toward Gabe. "Please excuse us both."

Jake and Mitch disappeared out of the front door. The men resumed their discussion. As Gabe asked Stasia about her Durango plans, Nicolás stared at his feet.

Minutes later, Mitch opened the door and stepped inside. Jake followed, a moment behind, and headed for his seat with a bothered expression. Mitch's eyes swept the room, and for a moment, fell on Nicolás. The sour face was something new altogether: frustration, anger, and a measure of something less defined. Sure enough, he had witnessed it in Freedom, days ago. It was a mood ruined by conflict, playing out upon a face struggling to suppress it.

25

D amn it, Pantano thought. We're interrupted again.

"*Bueno*, Raúl," Ivan said across their table, answering his phone as he leaned back in his chair in his mirrored aviator sunglasses. "You're coming now? I will be here."

Pantano was surprised that Raúl had returned so quickly. He hated that the *sicario* would arrive during his lunch. Perhaps Raúl should have erred on the side of courtesy and prudence and debriefed with his boss when he returned to the hacienda.

An idea had come to him. Though it would be not without danger, it would further project an image of normalcy and power for Ivan to meet with his most senior *sicario* in broad daylight at that very open-air café. The café he knew Ivan and Raúl often patronized together: the Café Cristal. It seemed like a worthwhile move, especially after Segundo Cortez had seen more rebellion, in acts and in dialogue, as of late.

Ivan spooned the last of his *huevos motulenos* into his mouth, and then washed it down with his pisco sour. A welcome beverage, he imagined. No doubt he fashioned himself as some sort of king, and on that first day of his reign, Nolano had thrown up the first challenge, the first affront. Simply by swinging at him, landing a weak blow, and getting away with it. Ivan was not used to being challenged or bested in any way. And every day in the weeks since, as Ivan had said, the law, the Church, the press, the students, and especially, the other cartels surely were laughing at him. He was their new clown.

Un payaso verde, a green clown—that is how they all saw the young upstart. He was a flawed fortress, hastily constructed and already besieged.

Pantano saw a movement to his right. The waiter motioned Raúl toward them and followed just a step behind. For the first time that he could recall, Ivan rose to his feet at the head of the table to greet Raúl, and then motioned for the *sicario* to sit to his immediate right. He wanted any passing on foot or by car to see and recognize them...that they dined in the open at that very café and that they still maintained control.

They lowered themselves into their seats. Raúl was eyeing him. No doubt wondering if he should speak freely in front of a police chief.

"*Dígame*," Ivan said, throwing his napkin onto the table. "It's fine, Pantano is okay."

"The head of the Xalapa cartel, Marcos," Raúl said, "...well, he is no more. I took him alive. Eventually—I finished him off. I brought the photos, videos, on my phone."

"*Bueno*, Raúl. Good work. And how many of them did we get? And how many did we lose, on our side?"

"We only lost twelve. But we wiped out over a hundred and twenty of theirs. They're finished."

"*Hombre*," Ivan said. "I will be paying you handsomely for this."

"Well, I'm still the best you've got," Raúl said and grinned. "Just not quite as good as I used to be. Inevitable, I guess. Time."

"Now I just need you to turn your talents and skills northward. And get Nolano."

"*Señor*," Raúl said. "You know I am the best at what I do. You know if it can be done, I will do it. I never failed your father, and I never failed you, unless the task was already impossible. And you know I cannot speak the language well and have no idea where Nolano is. The trail is cold. Unless you can get De Echegaray or someone else up there."

Raúl turned his way. "Or unless the chief can help us."

"Damn it, damn it all," Ivan said, pounding the table once with his fist. Several diners at other tables looked over at them, but immediately diverted their eyes.

"I must think of something," Ivan lowered his voice to a baritone whisper. "That was what *Papá* was always so good at. That's how he founded and grew the cartel, after all."

"I know, *Señor*. His strategy…that was his great faculty."

"And Raúl?" Ivan said.

"*Señor?*"

"At least show me the damned photos," Ivan said, pushing his plate forward. "Of Marcos."

Raúl looked at Ivan for a few moments with a vacant stare, which broke into a slow blink. He fished his smartphone out of his sports coat. He made a sucking sound with his tongue and upper teeth, while he made a few spastic motions on the screen with his thumbs. Then he turned the phone around and slowly slid it across the tablecloth to Ivan.

Ivan must love it. The carnage. He was drunk with it.

Removing his sunglasses, Ivan took up the device and flipped through it for several seconds. He placed the phone back onto the table and slid it back, almost in a shove, toward the *sicario*.

"Why did I ever ask to look?" Ivan mumbled, putting on his sunglasses. "Absolutely revolting."

26

"Fancy this scene much, Pato?" Mitch said, placing his pint glass on the bar between them.

"I like it," Nicolás said as he sipped his tequila, peering through the dim light out at the dance floor. The men from the poker table danced with their wives, while Gabe danced with Freedom and Stasia. "Many different types of people congregating over there, enjoying the night."

Nicolás turned, and they looked at each other for several seconds. He was poised to speak, but Mitch cleared his throat.

"I can read you well. You're all right, man. I like you. You're one of the good ones. As Freedom is. And you're his friend."

Mitch stared far into his eyes to the point of discomfort.

"Freedom passed on to me some things that happened to you in Veracruz," Mitch said, shaking his head.

What in the hell had Freedom disclosed? Then again, he'd only confided in Freedom that a cartel murdered his brother and parents. No details.

"We all got ghosts, tragedies we carry with us," Mitch said. "But damn, bud. You've got the heaviest cross to bear. You'll just have to learn to live with it somehow. Heaven knows I will have to do the same, with my own demons."

Such directness. Mitch seemed like he wanted to elaborate, that he held in some gripping story.

"Enjoy yourself here," Mitch said, slapping his shoulder. "I'm heading back out there."

Mitch found his way back into the crowd, and then resumed dancing with the young veterinary assistant from earlier in the evening. What was her name? Surely Mitch and Gabe were both after her.

Through the pounding music, Nicolás heard the bells clanging behind him. Just as he turned, the front door swung closed. A silhouetted figure entered, stopping just inside the faint glow of the overhead dance-floor lights.

She was new to him, perhaps in her early forties. Just a couple centimeters shorter than himself, fair-skinned and with light auburn hair, she possessed a curvy build that was flirting with a matronliness within her blue medical scrubs. Her face was more pleasant than pretty, but there was something about it, something about this woman, in general, that kept his eyes riveted. As she neared the bar, he drew in a deep breath, and turned back to face the mirror-covered wall behind the bottles of gin and whiskey.

He glanced down into his glass at the nectar of amber Extra Añejo, and tried to let his mind drift. Then it caught his nostrils, just a trace of it. Fresh female sweat—one of his favorite scents in the world. Not robust, but that sort that barely possessed enough muskiness to register as sweat. He slowly turned his head to the left. She was ordering from the bartender.

God, he wished he had showered.

When she finished speaking, he could not recall what she had ordered. He had been concentrating on the beauty of her voice: the sonorous rise and fall of its pitch, the well-modulated, musical tone. A mezzo-soprano, he would guess. And most likely the product of a good education and upbringing.

He could feel it—his pull toward her. She could prove to be good company. He could see her as his new object of pursuit—if it were not for his sworn mission.

"Well, you are new to these parts, mister," the voice said, playful but assured.

"Yes," he lifted his gaze up and to the side. She was turning ever so slightly toward him, the corner of her mouth raised in a smile. "It is my first night here in…Bigfork, Montana?"

"That's us," she said. "The pride of Flathead County. What brings you here, to the ends of the earth?"

"Doing some travel research for a book I'm writing."

Damn, the lie turned his stomach. Any lie, even.

"My friends Freedom and Stasia, the ones dancing over there, they brought me. We've been doing some camping. You know them?"

"I do not, actually."

"My name is Pato," he said, holding out his hand.

"Cassie," she said as she shook his hand and smiled broadly, revealing a set of beautiful teeth that gleamed white despite the dance-floor lighting. "Cassie Rivers. A pleasure."

"Wait, I recall the name," he said.

"Ah?" One of her eyebrows lifted, and she made a slight bob with her head. "Did we know each other in a past life? You're confusing me with someone else."

"No, I have it. I saw your name on the clinic where we stopped earlier this evening. You are the veterinarian."

"Good memory," she said. "I've had that practice for several years. What better way for someone who loves animals much more than people to make a living. Right?"

He chuckled. The bartender set a glass of white wine in front of her. She smiled and thanked him by name.

"So, Pato, where are you from? And tell me about your book."

"I am from Mexico. I am chronicling my travels in the west of America."

As much as he detested this fiction, he must force it a bit longer, make it more believable.

"Before it disappears," he said. "Well, in many ways, it has disappeared. But in some ways, I see it as still wild, in pockets."

"Like northwestern Montana?"

"Most likely, yes. And I think the West is the region most representative of your nation. Its spirit...personality."

"I would like to think that, as well," she said. "But you know, in a way, you could say the same thing about Los Angeles or New York City."

"How so?"

"Well." She tasted her wine. "In Los Angeles you have people from so many different cultures and backgrounds living together, many of them moving there to achieve their dreams. It's a city of dreams, in a way. And all those trying to make it in films, in music. I think that is a very American thing. Migrating there from somewhere else, sometimes from outside the country, often from states away, in pursuit of an ideal future. While risking it all, or close to it. And in New York City, the same. But doing everything on the largest scale. With great energy. That's very American, as well."

"I completely agree. So I must ask you," he said, feeling suddenly emboldened. He pointed toward her left hand. "An intelligent, educated, attractive woman like yourself, and you are single?"

"Ah," she said, her greenish eyes falling toward the bar top. "Well, I was married, once upon a time. In fact, a couple years ago. How come you are single? Well, you are still young. Thirty?"

"Thirty-two," he said.

She had a point. Why was he still single? Still sniffing the rosebuds of life, pursuing his whims, until his old life had ended, weeks ago, in his mother's living room.

"And in the States," she said, "it's not customary for a woman to reveal her age, up front. Suffice it to say I have a few years on you." She patted his forearm that rested on the bar top, then held it. A warm glow suffused his body, from cell to cell, and his senses stirred further alive.

"It doesn't matter," he said with a smile.

"Oooh, really?" she said.

Something pulled his gaze from her face and down the length of the bar. It was one of the men from the café, the figure in pearl snaps and denim who sat at the head of the table. Jake—he believed the name was—leaned slightly over the bar, his fierce stare not leaving them.

"Who is that cowboy type who never stops staring with such aggression?" he said to her. "Down at the end of the bar. I remember him, going outside with Mitch."

She turned to face the opposite direction, and then craned her neck.

"Ah, damn it," she said, turning back to Nicolás. "Jake again. Speak of the devil. My ex-husband. I was hoping he wouldn't be in here. But we don't have many choices for nightlife, and neither of us wants to give up anyplace. Or drive to Missoula every weekend. He likes to intimidate any man that I'm seen with."

"Perhaps that is why he looks so angry. He lost you."

She looked down toward her feet, her mouth morphing into a coy smile.

"So what does this man do?" Nicolás said. "His profession."

"Jake's a builder. His family owned a lot of the land here… and some of the businesses. He's crowned himself king of Bigfork in his own mind. He's walking over now. Don't fall for his macho bullshit."

"You sure know how to pick 'em, Cass," Nicolás heard a voice growl at his side, and he turned. The furious face glared down at him, all squinting eyes and drooping frown.

"Jake," Cassie said, "I'm just having basic conversation with a visitor. A writer doing research for his book. Is that any way to treat a guest here?"

"He's no writer, no damn tourist," Jake laughed. "Free-loadin' wetback vagabond's more like it."

Nicolás could feel his face flush. Besides being arrested, this was his other fear in going into a small American town. Being attacked out of prejudice. But both fates might be in store for him, this night…

"You always were a horrible judge of character, Jake," Cassie said. "Now, leave me in peace. You can have that whole half of the bar. You know, I should have gotten a restraining order on you ages ago."

Jake drew closer to Nicolás and stared down into his eyes. He felt his heartbeat quicken within his chest as he felt he must react, in some way. Against his better discretion, the words coalesced in his mind.

"So do you always have that ugly, unhappy, angry expression on your face?" Nicolás said.

The man's arms pushed outward in a powerful shove. His hip banged against the side of the bar.

"You aren't welcome in my town," Jake barked. "Your hippie friend better drive your ass outta here. Or you ain't gonna see the sun come up. *Hijo de puta.* I know you know what that means."

He felt his eyes water as he remembered Lucinda. This filth had even insulted his mother.

"Damn it!" Cassie shrieked, trying to push Jake away. "Sheriff Press is in here. I could get you locked up tonight."

Yes, this is why he could not strike first. Stay calm, Nicolás.

Reason told him he should even say nothing. But what if the man took a swing?

"Hey, settle down, Jake," the bartender said, reaching across the bar to touch Jake's shoulder. "Leave 'em alone."

But he had to at least say something. Jake had brought Lucinda into the fray. His saintly mother, who had received nothing but violence and insults in those last few weeks. Besides, Cassie was listening, watching. Jake was humiliating him before her. At least if Jake swung first, the sheriff was not far off...

Nicolás smiled. Jake, who had backed off a bit, now stood less than a meter away. "So I suppose you are an example of one of those men. The 'ugly American.' The world revolves around you, does it not?"

Nicolás saw the large fist break free like a wild horse and hurtle toward him. His right hand in turn clenched into a fist, and he brought his left forearm up to block the blow. Cassie shrieked in terror as he felt the weight of the world directed upon his left cheekbone. He felt himself jerking backward, then falling.

27

L ight. Ever so slightly, just a bit more by the second, light. Nicolás opened, and then shut his eyes. The clanging of a pot or pan. A welcoming, warmhearted smell.

Tocino, huevos, café. That familiar swirl of morning aromas. Was he in his mother's house again?

A footfall sounded—it was approaching. He blinked the last traces of slumber from his eyes. A den decorated in rustic notes. A hearth almost two meters beside him, warming him. He shook the animal hide blankets off, and struggled to sit upright. The head of a bull elk high above him, affixed to the chimney facade of large black stones. Not far away on a wall was the head of a bison.

There it was—a shooting pain in his left cheekbone. And he remembered.

"And he's up! Our fearless professor," a voice cried just behind him. Mitch.

Nicolás turned.

Mitch smiled, one hand on his hip, the other holding out a coffee mug down toward him. Freedom and Stasia sat on the couch nearby. She wore an expression of concern, while Freedom grinned with amusement. Nicolás took the mug and drank deeply. Coffee laced with whiskey.

"You may not have the luck of the Irish," Mitch said. "But it doesn't mean you can't enjoy some of their coffee, right?"

"There's my buddy Pato, always getting into trouble," Freedom said. "You just might be safer coming with me next year to surf and fish and camp down on the beach in Baja, rather than stay in Bigfork."

As Nicolás brought himself into the lotus position, he placed his hand to his temple and cheekbone.

"How do you feel?" Stasia asked.

"Like a million…pesos," Nicolás said.

They all laughed. He started to join in, but his face began to smart again.

"Quite an eventful night we had," Mitch said. "Don Juan breezes into town, and within an hour or two there's an all-out brawl. Haven't seen one like that since I was out on leave years ago. Back in a bar near base."

"He…" Nicolás said, closing his eyes, struggling to remember. "Jake—he knocked me unconscious."

"Well, that's just how it all began," Mitch said. "You took your snooze right before it got interesting."

"I'm glad it was entertaining," Nicolás said.

"Mister Old Skin and Bones here on the couch flew over like a banshee. Cassie Rivers slaps Jake across the face while Freedom hits him with his fist, however mild that must have been. Big Jake pushes Freedom near clean across the room. Lucky he didn't hit you back with his fist."

"Damn," Nicolás said, rubbing the back of his head. "Thank you, Freedom."

"Head's achin', isn't it?" Mitch asked. "You're bound to have at least a mild concussion, so you need to take it easy. And not get hit in any way for a good while. I should know. I've had many of 'em, of varying degrees of severity, in Iraq. Big part of the reason my life went to hell."

"But at least you fight well," Freedom said. "I didn't have to charge back in."

Mitch resumed, "Yeah, so I hear Rivers screaming. And I see Freedom wallerin' on the ground like a fish. Then I see you laying on the ground at her feet, and Jake in her face."

"Then you went in," Stasia said.

"I ran in and got him. Gabe saw Freedom go down, and Jake get in her boss's face, so she was in there and stunned Jake with a body blow to the gut. Almost the same second, I got his left cheek, knocked him down. Then, Sheriff Press was right up in there, broke it all up."

"I'm glad to see I helped the night become so memorable," Nicolás said. "So what became of Cassie? And Gabe? And your town bully?"

"Cassie headed home. Gabe went home. Jake went to jail. For a night. Not his first time. Big reason was Cassie and the bartender, Peters. They witnessed it all, and told the sheriff everything. He was across the room."

"You like her, don't you?" Freedom said.

Nicolás gave a lopsided grin. Damn, that cheekbone.

"I'm starting to know you better," Freedom said.

"You're lucky you didn't get arrested, though, looking back," Mitch said. "The sheriff ain't too high on Mexicans. He does tolerate the Flatheads. Next to Jake, Press might be the most bigoted guy in town. Ol' José knows all about that. I tease that I know he must have spit in Jake's food a thousand times over. José just smiles and winks."

"José?" Stasia said.

"He's the chef over at that café from yesterday. Owns it, too. He's lived here for over a decade, seen it all. Longer than me and Gabe."

"I need to find work here," Nicolás said. "I would like to talk with José. I love to cook."

"Yep, Pato," Mitch said. "You'll find work around here, no doubt. Hey, I'll drive you out to the café later today, if you're up for it. José would probably give you a job cooking, washing dishes. Well, that's if—"

"That's if you decide to stay," Stasia said.

"Yes," Mitch said.

A lone ray of light entered his world. Could it be? He turned toward Mitch, who plopped down on the couch perpendicular to the one holding Freedom and Stasia.

"I'd prefer to stay somewhere in this area," Nicolás said. "Do you know someone in town renting out a room? I'll pay rent. With what I have, and what I'll make."

"I'll charge you four hundred dollars a month. Not too bad. Includes utilities. I got that guest cottage back behind this house," Mitch said, pointing out of the window. "I used it back when I had my bed and breakfast. While I get it cleaned up, you can crash in my guest bedroom, right there."

Mitch pointed at the hallway.

Nicolás nodded. Another turn of good fortune. Feeling both grateful and guilty, he said, "That does sound like a good deal, Mitch."

He lowered his head back down onto the rug and let his eyes roam around the taxidermied elk, the bison head, the bear head, the antique rifles, shotguns, and snowshoes.

"I do need a new ID," Nicolás said. "Because I was robbed in Arizona...remember?" Another lie he had to force. He wished it would be the last.

"I can hook you up with this cat in Polson who does IDs," Mitch said.

"Now," Freedom said, "shall we eat? The smell's driving me insane."

Everyone stood, except for Nicolás.

"Great that you will stay around Mitch and Gabe," Stasia said. "You can trust them."

Nicolás swiveled his gaze over to his host. Was she right?

Mitch smirked, and then tossed back the dregs from his mug, as if it was pure whiskey.

28

"So," Mitch said, clapping his hands once and leaning against the kitchen wall. "What do you think? No way José?"

"I could use one more worker here," said José. "It is true. But how do I know he'll be good enough? And not leave me soon for another business around the lake?"

"Because," Mitch said, and clapped a hand onto Nicolás's shoulder. "He knows I would find him and murder him."

"Cooking is one of my skills," Nicolás said. "I surmise there are not many jobs available in this area. If you give me a chance, I will remember it. And make it worthwhile for you."

José paused for several seconds. He looked at the ceiling, then down at his feet, with a finger over his lips. "*Muy bien*. He starts tomorrow then. Eight in the morning. I can supply his lunch. And I'll need him in training all day. We'll wrap up at midnight, after closing."

"And he needs a Mexican ID made," Mitch said, leaning forward, his voice lowered. "And no American ID, because several people he met here know he left Mexico recently and is just traveling. But his wallet was stolen in Arizona."

"Right," José said, after releasing a loud belly laugh. "I can hook him up now with Tomás, for the ID card. I'll text him when you're on your way over."

"Much appreciated, José," Mitch said.

"*Gracias, Señor*," Nicolás said, closing his eyes as he nodded.

"*De nada, chico*," José said. "Just follow me closely during your training. Pay attention. You should make the cut. You wrote *novelas*, right? Taught classes?"

Nicolás cleared his throat. "I have taught, yes. But I am a writer of scholarly articles. Not novels, *Señor*."

"I hear you are writing a book about your journey through the United States," José said. "What is it called?"

"Em," Nicolás said. Think of something. And fast. "*Northern Passage* is the title, *Señor*."

"*Interesante*," said José.

"Northern passage, all right. That's what I'm waitin' for," Mitch said, and clapped his hands once. "To be put out of my misery. And then my passage northward. Up into the hereafter."

José eyed Mitch with an odd expression, a mixture of irritation and concern. He then turned to Nicolás.

"All right, Cervantes," said José. "See you here tomorrow at eight. And I will text Tomás now. He will need a little cash for the ID. Like one-hundred."

Nicolás gritted his teeth. More money. He had enough to cover this, and more. But the new job could not come soon enough.

They thanked José again and headed into the parking lot for Mitch's large Ford truck, where Freedom and Stasia were waiting.

"You were pretty good back there," Mitch said, as he pressed the accelerator. "Now to Polson."

"And you were, as well. I thank you."

"A lot of it's because of the small fortune I've spent in there over the years," Mitch said. "Food and libations. And José's such a good guy. He's probably glad to see you. Not many from your land around this lake."

Nicolás felt his spirit smile within him.

"Casey," Stasia said. She and Freedom began to discuss something in Slovak.

"Mitch, Pato," Freedom said, with a trace of reluctance. "New development here, gentlemen. We've decided to cut our trip short."

"What?" Mitch said. "Wow. Why? Hey, you're not thinking of heading back to Crest—"

"Well, Crested Butte for a little while," Freedom said. "As we lock down a spot in Durango. Then we start moving our things down."

"It is where Casey always wanted to go," Stasia said.

"And you, too, Stasia," Freedom said. "Well, next to your first choice, which was CB. And that's out of the picture."

"I thought you might choose Durango," Nicolás said.

"You're welcome to join us, man," Freedom said.

"When are you two leaving me?" Mitch said.

"Well…tomorrow or so," Freedom said.

"It's because of the money," Stasia said. "That is how it is so many times with the couples."

"Honestly," Freedom said, "our money's running out. In Durango I know a guy who can hook me up with a job. This is why I returned from Europe. For the heart of the Rockies. Colorado, man. The highest state. And Durango and the Animus River, that's what Stasia and I have been waiting for. It's just coming a year or so earlier than she wanted."

They began to speak again in Slovak, but this time it was more of an argument. Nicolás felt his heart sink as he looked out of the front passenger window at the lake. The waves danced and swayed and crashed against each other in the midafternoon sun. That is how my life has become, Nicolás thought. Tumultuous, lively and, in a way, full of a new beauty—but tumultuous, nonetheless. What surprise awaits? Hopefully, nothing like what I encountered in my mother's den...

29

"Aurelio Ermenegildo Esparza," Mitch said, slapping his hands onto the café's table. "Could any name be more Spanish? I like it, I like it."

Nicolás grinned as his gaze fell downward onto the table. He recalled how he had strung together his pseudonym.

Aurelio was the first name of a newscaster in Veracruz. Esparza was the surname of his car mechanic. And who would guess that Ermenegildo was a minor character in an eighteenth-century novel, published in Spain?

"And where are you from?" asked Stasia.

"Veracruz, of course," Nicolás said.

"No," Mitch said. "I think she means, on your ID."

"Why, San Miguel Allende."

"That must be part of a wish fulfillment dream of his, or something," Freedom said. "I've heard about that town. Sounds like a place you would really like."

"It's one of my favorite places, yes. I have spent much time there. How do you say it in America? Yes, a home away from home."

"I have heard that it's a great place for artists, intellectuals..."

Freedom said. "Especially painters. So it's probably a lot like Santa Fe."

"I thought the same when I was there weeks ago," said Nicolás. "Before our lunch in Chimayó, that is."

He paused. Would he be so bold as to ask this early?

"Mitch," Nicolás said, "I hear you are a survivalist. And that you are skilled at firearms."

"You could say that," Mitch said, his eyes studying him.

"Firearms comprise an important part of my book on the West. And I have always wanted to learn to shoot," Nicolás said. "Could you teach me?"

"So *Señor* Esparza," Freedom said, "you want to try Mitch's Intensive Training 101?"

Nicolás laughed, trying to calm his nerves. What if Mitch refused?

"The class has a name?" Stasia said.

"It's something I only invite certain folks to," Mitch said. "And it has to be by my personal invitation, Pato."

"How long does this…this class last?" Nicolás said.

"Depends," Mitch said. "Three weeks. Maybe four."

A moment of silence ensued. Freedom and Stasia looked at Mitch, then at Nicolás, then back at Mitch.

"Very well," Mitch said. "It ain't for the faint of heart."

Had Mitch accepted?

"But weeks, months, years from now," Mitch said, "you will thank me. If I'm still here, that is."

"Now Mitch," Freedom said. "Why would you say a thing like that?"

"Well," Mitch said, searching the ceiling with narrowed eyes. "What did Chaucer write? 'So long the life, the struggle so hard' or something to that effect. Except that he wrote it in Middle English."

"I did not know you were so literary," Nicolás said. "A very good thing."

"English was my major at West Point," Mitch said. "I loved it. Anyway, if you are seeking some feedback, *Señor*, on that MIT class, you might want to interview my teaching partner. She's as good as me. Never saw action, but she's no wilting flower, man. I never trained her, because I didn't have to."

Mitch nodded toward the front door. A figure stood behind its glass panel. The door jerked open. It was Gabe, who held the door open for the younger veterinary assistant. Third into the room was none other than Cassie Rivers. Nicolás felt his heart quicken inside his ribs. The day, overcast by the unexpected news of his friends' impending departure, had just grown brighter.

Her face illuminated when her eyes found his.

"Dr. Rivers!" exclaimed Mitch. "Miss Keyes! Corporal Gabe! What a fine addition to our dinner party."

"Look what the cat dragged in," Gabe said. "If it isn't Pato. Stood up to Jackass Jake, and took that punch like a true boss."

Nicolás felt new heat in his cheeks.

"It felt worse than it looked, I would guess," Mitch said.

"Don't believe anything this guy here tells you," Gabe said with a mock sigh.

"Even about your Mitch Intensive Training 101 class?" Nicolás said.

"He told you about that?" Gabe said, a smile playing at the edge of her mouth. "I thought that was proprietary. Some of that could get us investigated."

Everyone except Gabe looked at Mitch, puzzled.

"So ladies," Mitch said, "feel free to join us. Take your seats. It's Saturday evening anyway."

Gabe, Cassie and Kat seated themselves at the table.

"How are you feeling, Pato?" Cassie said. Her eyebrows straightened with concern while the eyes flashed with attraction.

"Better than this morning, Dr. Rivers," Nicolás said. "I do know that much."

"I apologize for Jake. But at the same time, I'm not accountable for his actions. There's a reason—reasons—why he's my ex-husband. But he's so much worse now than he was years ago. When he was with me."

"I can testify to the truth of that statement," Mitch said, and shot a furtive glance at Gabe's veterinary assistant. Gabe caught on and flared her eyes at him, then rolled them.

"So I have been hearing you're a writer, Pato," the younger veterinary assistant said. "Tell me all about what you're writing."

Nicolás looked down at his forearm resting atop the table. That lie again. Did he really have to use it in the first place? He looked up and cleared his throat.

"Well, uh, now Kat," Mitch said, "you know any writer worth his salt keeps those details secret until the time's right."

"He's writing a memoir of his experiences traveling the modern-day American West," Cassie said. "As we were discussing last night. Last fun-filled, unprecedented night. Isn't that right?"

"We were, yes," Nicolás said. "Before we were rudely interrupted."

"And the world came down," Freedom said, and laughed.

"By the way, great stunner shot, bud," Mitch said, looking at Gabe.

"You remember we've practiced that," Gabe said.

"So anyway, gentlemen," Cassie said, her chin poised high. "I do have a request."

"And what would that be?" Mitch said.

"I need a lot of firewood chopped. And I need someone to landscape my lawn. It's growing a bit wild. And I've been too zapped from the clinic to take care of it."

"You need your lawn groomed?" Gabe said, and then laughed. "It's growing wild?"

"Make that joke again, Gabriella, and I'll make you work the next Saturday shift," Cassie said, chuckling.

"Sure, I can do it," Mitch said. "I know our man here is up for it, too."

"I will help. No problem," Nicolás said.

"I'll pay you handsomely," said Cassie. "And I'll cook you men a meal or two so you won't have to leave during the day. But I would need you tomorrow, say, at nine."

"We'll be there," Nicolás said.

"Yes indeed," Mitch said.

Once again the door opened wide, its bells jingling.

Amid an awkward silence, Jake stood, eyeing everyone at the table, one after the other.

"Howdy bud," Mitch said with cheer. "Guess you wanted to get out a bit?"

"You're pretty upbeat considerin' your circumstances," Jake said. "You goddamned alcoholic. Drug addict. Dishonorably discharged loser."

Nicolás straightened in his chair. Such venom. Spoken the night before and now again. Somewhere inside this cowboy is a red-hot cinder of hate.

"Now Jake," Mitch said. "That's not a very polite thing to say in such pleasant company."

"Get the hell outta here, Jake!" Gabe said. "You start something, you'll get jailed again. This time, a felony assault."

"Time to leave, man," Freedom said, drawing his words out in a weary tone.

"You know, the eight-hundred-pound gorilla in the room ain't exactly me. Or that hippie boy or the lesbian or even my bitchy ex-wife," Jake said, pointing toward Nicolás. "He legal?"

"Of course he is," Cassie shot back.

"Sure?" Jake said, smiling while bobbing his head once.

"I have identification," said Nicolás. "All legal."

"He's just visiting anyway," Cassie said. "He's an academic, conducting research. He's the opposite of everything you are. You know, a tourist can visit…last time I checked."

"Oh, his stay here'll be pretty temporary," Jake said. "You'll see."

"Excuse yourself, Jake," Cassie said. "Just leave us in peace."

"Can't stand the sight of the lot of you, anyway," Jake said, opening the door. "Makes my gut turn."

Jake slithered out of the door and down the steps.

"Sorry, everyone," Cassie said. Her eyes were bloodshot, her cheeks flushed red.

Nicolás glanced beside him. Mitch's right forearm shook with fury as he moved to hide it beneath the table.

30

"Are you sure you want to do this?" Nicolás said, placing a hand on each of Freedom's shoulders. "So soon?"

"Is Stasia down with this, too?" said Mitch, his arms folded across his chest. "This is a big move you're making."

Stasia said nothing as she glanced eastward at the Mission Mountains. Her nostrils flared, her lower lip drawn inward, almost as if she was nauseous or stifling a scream.

"She's with me, Mitch," Freedom said with a dismissive air. "It's all right. I know you care about us. But it's been our plan for a while now. It's been my plan for years."

"Well, if you two reconsider," Mitch said with a slight sigh. "And ever want to relocate up this way, offer's always been there."

"Of course," Freedom said with a cheerful lilt.

"*Vaya con Dios*, Don Ermenegildo," Freedom said, leaning forward and hugging Nicolás. "Or rather, my brother Pato Esparza."

Stasia leaned in and hugged them both, and then Mitch joined in.

"We will miss you," Stasia said. "We will come back to see you."

Then the hug broke apart, and Freedom and Stasia settled into their seats.

"And Pato," Freedom said. "Good luck with the MIT 101."

"In a few weeks, you won't recognize him," Mitch said, grinning.

It was final. Mitch had accepted his proposal after all.

"I've got the Great Spirit with me on my drive," Freedom said, winking once and making a clicking sound. "See you all down the line."

The 4Runner's engine stirred alive. Freedom and Stasia rolled down the long gravel drive and around the bend, thick with mountain pines.

"Now you're stuck with me, *amigo*," Mitch said. "Two savage bachelors left to their devices. Me with Kat—if she'll have me—and you with the good Dr. Rivers. Hey, speaking of…we should get going to her house. She's got a day of work in store for us. Will earn you a little cash."

They grabbed the bottled water from inside, and then they were off in Mitch's truck.

The house of Dr. Cassie Rivers was impressive indeed, and something he had never before seen: a broad, two-story log cabin.

"Welcome to my abode this fine Sunday morning," she said, outstretching her hands high above her head in a V-formation, as if making a happy announcement. "Can I get anyone a coffee?"

The men declined, and Cassie led them around the side of the house.

"Mitch, if you could gather this wood I've brought from different parts of the property, all lying around that general area there," she said. "Cut it up into firewood segments with the chainsaw in the garage. It's open. And you, *Señor* Pato. If you could help Mitch stack the wood against the side of the house. He'll show you where. Also, if you could put the smaller branches into the wood chipper. Mitch will bring it out from the garage.

Then I need the chips spread out evenly in the shrub beds alongside the house. Just ring the doorbell should you need water or the bathroom."

They worked for more than two hours. As the lunch hour neared, Nicolás became aware that his bladder was full, and he contemplated walking off just outside her line of sight and watering the bushes. But he wanted any excuse to lay his eyes upon her, to talk with her. He excused himself to Mitch.

"Wait," Mitch said, holding up an index finger. "Pato. I've done work here before and it was never like this. She normally does all this stuff herself, with ease. And I think these jobs are a little ill timed. Maybe even unnecessary this early in the year. So I think she wants to check you out some, to have a little more privacy with you. Of course, with me watching out for any rash moves of yours."

Mitch winked.

Nicolás laughed. He believed it. Attraction had made itself evident in her face and words from the start. And from that first moment she had no doubt seen his affection for her. Yet this is something he must resist. Weeks, perhaps a couple of months— he could not stay long in this town. That monumental task awaited him, looming in his future like a dark tower, thousands of kilometers to the south...

He walked up the cobblestone path to the wooden front steps. Seconds after his first ring of the doorbell, she appeared at the door. Had she been watching them from a nearby window?

"Well, come in, mister," she said, pulling the door open and gesturing inside. "You've gotten a lot done. Need the bathroom? Something to drink?"

She was wearing a long red and purple paisley dress with green canvas slip-on shoes. A pink bandana headband held back her hair.

"The bathroom would be nice," Nicolás said. As he followed

her into the foyer, he breathed in through his nostrils. For the first time since he'd been around her, she was wearing perfume, an alluring scent.

She led him to the foyer bathroom, just underneath the stairwell.

When he emerged a few moments later, his ears caught her footfall on the wooden boards in the next room. Probably her den. She rounded the corner with a teacup in her hand. "Like some? English darjeeling?"

"Please, yes," he said, and she led him down the hall and left into the kitchen, a spacious kitchen with dark wooden ceiling beams and walls replete with framed photographs.

"I'd like to continue our conversation sometime," she said. "About your book and everything. Jake had to rudely cut it short."

"This was the house you had together?" he said.

"It was."

"Much house for two people," he said.

She sipped her tea, looking down at her feet. Had he insulted her?

"I wish I could see Mexico again," she said. "It's been many years since I went."

"I could be a great guide. But now is not the time for you to go. One should wait many years. I really desire to return, and at the same time, I want to never do so."

As he spoke a memory surfaced, until it collided with a very different one. He was a young boy at the annual Easter festival by the Veracruz seashore. The ocean breeze wafted through the plaza's teeming, smiling crowds as the *danzón* and *son jarocho* music and delicious aromas from food stalls filled the air. His mother led him and his brother each by a hand through the celebration. The sunlight was so bright that at times he had to squint, and even close his eyes completely. Then his ears would find the chords from his favorite musical instrument: the *jarana*, that small eight-string guitar of *son jarocho* music. And he could hear his mother singing, and his brother giggling. Interrupting this blissful remembrance—he knew not why— was that image of the bloodied bodies of his mother and brother on the floor of that dimly-lit living room, mere weeks before.

"You must tell me more about Mexico sometime," she said. "I was wondering—do you like Montana? The Flathead Lake region? Out west in general?"

"I really do like it," he said. "More and more. I like Montana very much, and of course I like northern New Mexico. Overall, I believe there is a freedom in the West of America. At least a *feeling* of freedom, that one cannot find in many places."

"I'd tend to agree with you on that. Think you might stay? Find work?"

"I'd like to teach Spanish in the local schools." Well, not after being a fugitive from the law. He remembered the Molotov cocktails and the stabbings in the Arizona semi. If she only knew...

"I'd also like to train as a chef though," he said. "I have always loved food."

"Well, it's in your blood. Look where you come from."

"Thank you," he said. "You know, José at the café gave me a job. Part of it involves him training me. As a chef."

"Oh, that's wonderful!" she said. "Another excuse for me to come in there more often."

He smiled along with her. She brought her gaze down, as if her candor embarrassed her. Was she regretting her flirtation?

"I would like you to come in more often, too," he said, and smiled, and then took another slow sip of his tea.

"You know, after we spoke in The Raven Friday night," she said, "I haven't really stopped thinking about you."

Heat built within his face and neck. Her words were even better than he longed to hear.

"I have been the same, Dr. Rivers."

He took a step forward and, holding his tea away from his body, held her close. His lips found hers. She responded with such immediacy and passion that he knew her words to be true. Her open hands swept across his shoulder blades as her mouth pressed hard onto his. He concentrated on tasting her lower lip, then her upper lip, both somewhat full but both surely divine. His tongue plunged into her mouth. Eventually, they pulled their faces apart, dizzy and drawing in deep breaths.

"That was magnificent," she said. "I've wanted that."

"Really? I did as well."

"But you're definitely a cigarette smoker," she said.

Damn. Perhaps this was what he needed to hear to finally quit.

"So what are you looking at?" she said. "On the wall."

He took a step backward.

"Tell me about these photographs," he said, lifting his chin in a gesture at the framed pictures several feet behind her on the wall.

"Well, these are my memories. And people I hold near and dear to the heart. Some are moments from my youth," she said with half a sort of playfulness, and half a sort of mourning, "I guess the last traces of it are escaping me now."

"Not true. So who is this?" He pointed at a photo of an older couple.

"Those are my parents. They live in Boise."

"And who is this?" The photo was of a lanky man in his thirties.

"That's my younger brother. Lives in Portland, Oregon. So," she said abruptly, her voice raised an octave, "how about some more tea? I sure want some."

"No thank you. And this?" he said, gesturing toward a slightly larger photograph of a smiling boy of perhaps five or six, standing in a sweater. The blonde bowl-cut hair, the soft features —the child could have been in Hollywood films. "The boy?"

She froze in her path toward the teapot, her back facing him. "You just had to ask," she said, looking downward, then at the ceiling, her hands suddenly on her hips. Then she turned toward him. Her eyes were moist. "That was all an example of life's cruelty, unpredictability. And why I love God, I fear Him, and to some degree, I hate Him."

Damn his curiosity. Why had he asked? She had lost a child...

"I—I am very sorry, Cassie. I should not have—"

"Sean. He was my only child. Jake's and mine. He was killed. An accident, three years ago."

He moved to embrace her, again. She let him wrap his arms around her, and her arms squeezed back. For a moment, she laid her head on his shoulder, and it seemed he was forgiven his prying, that she could even take comfort in his arms.

Then she broke away, stepping with resolution across the hardwood floor of the kitchen and foyer into the bathroom.

31

Outside José's kitchen it may have been all English, but only their native tongue was spoken inside its walls, and he liked that. Just José and himself and the Salvadoran.

Oscar, perhaps only nineteen or twenty, did not like him. Perhaps in another life or in another situation they would have been friends. But the simmering was apparent in the glances from the very swarthy face and its obsidian-dark eyes. Surely Oscar coveted Nicolás's primary role as the new sous chef. Instead he still swept, washed dishes, cleaned off countertops and took out the trash.

After all, Freedom told him it often was that way with the Central American crossers. Regarded as the bottom of the heap. Paid less than those from Mexico by the hour or the day, it did not matter. Nicolás knew he was fortunate. And with he himself being a Mexican national of European descent, he could only imagine the resentment burning inside the skull of the young worker, who looked even more native than Kwewu.

"Smaller cubes, son," José said, pointing at the cutting board piled with small strips of green poblano pepper. "I need them just a little smaller."

"Yes, sir," Nicolás said as he proceeded to cut the strips in smaller dimensions.

"After you are done with that, we will store the pepper in a plastic container in one of the fridges. And then we will start on the salsa. All three of them. You are moving a bit slowly but you're not that bad, I see. It's just prep work. And it's only Monday morning, right?"

"Oh yes," Nicolás said.

Yet as the lunch hour neared its end, he could feel the fatigue. Except for the day before at Cassie's, he had not worked in some time. He could also feel Oscar's eyes searing into the back of his head.

"Now run these out to table six," José said. "Remember the numbers. Six is the one against that front window by the big tree. Pastor Wachter gets the *pollo al pipián*. His friend gets the *caldo de res*. You know, Burning Hawk, the Indian."

Nicolás grabbed the bowl and the plate and headed out into the dining room, now only a third full.

The minister awaited his arrival with a mild, kind smile, not showing teeth. He made a humming sound, signaling his pleasure with the dish Nicolás placed before him.

"Two days later and I see you are learning from the master," Pastor Wachter said. "He's the best cook in town."

Nicolás smiled back and placed the *caldo* before Burning Hawk.

"I count my blessings. And they are many," Nicolás said, then regretted the expression. For some years, he had not believed.

"Your English is very good," Burning Hawk said.

"Why thank you, sir," Nicolás said.

Then it came to him—how he could feel closer to Padre Manolo, and even to his mother and brother, to some extent.

"You know," Nicolás said, "I would like to attend both of your worship services. Gabe told me how much she liked them."

"Really?" Pastor Wachter said. "Well, that's great. We'd love to have you."

"Hey, Cole," Burning Hawk said. "This young man may find an interest in our worship event. The conference. For his book."

"Good idea, sir!" the pastor said. "We're hosting this intercommunal spiritual study and worship service in a few days. People from the Flathead reservation and people here in Bigfork. Some from Yellow Bay, Polson, too. You might like it."

"That does sound intriguing," Nicolás said, glancing back at the kitchen window. José was watching him. "I'll be attending, if I'm not working."

"Yes, you should come," Burning Hawk said. "A great opportunity to learn about my people, too."

"I will call Mitchell, give him the details," Pastor Wachter said.

Nicolás thanked them and excused himself. As he beat a speedy route back toward the kitchen, he spotted a figure sitting in the far corner, against the kitchen wall. Sheriff Press was pursuing him with his stare.

Once inside the kitchen, Nicolás hooked right.

"My apologies," he said. "They wanted to tell me about an event they were inviting me to."

"That's fine, son," José said. "If you're bringing out the food, you have to be able to talk to customers if they ask you questions. The Protestant, Wachter, and Burning Hawk, I always liked them. Good people for you to know."

"I did see the Sheriff," Nicolás said in a loud whisper. "There in that corner just outside the wall from you."

"Yes, he is the one who is getting my best work," José said, handing the plate to him. "I can't say he has bad taste. But I know he despises us. Oscar and I both. And now you."

"Did you spit?" Nicolás said with a chuckle. "As Mitch alleges you do?"

"Not this time," José whispered, unable to fight his lips from pulling back into a smile. "Only once, years ago. When he humiliated me in front of several people in this town."

Nicolás headed out of the door with the plate. The Sheriff eyed him with suspicion, and merely nodded when the plate was set down before him.

"So," he said once Nicolás had started back for the kitchen. "Now you're gainfully employed."

"Oh yes," Nicolás said. "I've been lucky to meet such great people on my trip."

"Don't you cause any ripples here in my town, though. Stay away from Jake. And maybe you can keep that Mitch in line."

Nicolás smiled, gave a nod and headed for the kitchen. He was surprised, based on the harsh looks he had received from the man, and the comments from Mitch and José that he had gotten off unscathed.

As Nicolás swept through the corridor of the kitchen, Oscar raised his eyes from the dishwasher and fixed a stare harsher than the Sheriff's onto him.

Nicolás smiled and greeted him, "Oscar".

He did feel sorry for the discrimination Oscar faced, and he admired his tenacity in trekking this far north for a new life in a town and culture so far from his, in a job that was so menial. Perhaps Oscar could be his friend.

Yet Oscar looked back down toward the dishwasher, from which he pulled a full, steaming tray. And then he shook his head.

32

That night he sat before the fire, Mitch's laptop open on his tired knees, a Veracruz news site illuminating the screen.

"Yep, I know what you mean about being careful around the sheriff," Mitch said as he placed another log on the fire. "Press isn't one you want on your bad side. Especially if you got a fake ID. Or if you're a fugitive in any way."

Nicolás studied him. What did he know? What had he discovered?

Mitch turned and nodded once, his eyebrows raised. "He had to make his little comment about me. Like his buddy Jake the other day. But don't worry...Jake is more the guy to watch out for. Still, I think Jake's trying to avoid you just as much as you're staying away from him. And Press—well, let's just say I've got a little on that good ol' boy."

"I don't understand the expression," Nicolás commented. "Got a little on?"

"I have valuable information about Press that I never released, but could if I so desired. And he knows it."

Nicolás stared until Mitch continued.

"Some photos I snapped with my phone one night. In the

parking lot behind the Dairy Queen. I caught the long-married sheriff in his clearly marked patrol car, on top of the shift manager. In the photo you can see both of them in the back seat. Woman wears a beehive hairstyle."

Mitch walked back into the kitchen. Nicolás remained on the couch, replaying Jake's and the sheriff's words about Mitch being in trouble. It was apparent that Mitch wanted to steer clear of the matter. Nicolás looked down at the laptop screen glowing before him in the dark living room. Veracruz. His city was like a horrific battle on some far-flung plain. It was like some tropical land half a world away, some backwater few in rich western nations devoted one thought to. In his hometown, a dictator was executing and imprisoning his way to absolute power, day by day. Veracruz was a once-tranquil locale where even women and children suffered the unimaginable, inflicted upon them by boys and grown men. Perhaps a soon-to-be Darfur, a Rwanda.

Was he now sick? Was he a voyeur, staring at that screen? If he closed his eyes, if he never again searched for its news, his city would exist in his head only in memories.

In a sense, Nicolás was wise and prudent to flee. Yet in a sense he found himself a coward if he never returned.

The temptation was there. If he never again spoke of Veracruz, of what occurred there, perhaps the nightmare would fade. He could enjoy friendships and gainful employment, perhaps even soon as a teacher again, where he found his surroundings idyllic, majestic.

Yet he would return in the end. It was his mission. It was his unspoken pact with the dead, with one of the three. Though Lucinda and Padre Manolo would have scoffed at the idea, Esteban would have applauded his return—to avenge, to help the city and its people. His brother was a fighter, imbued with a warrior spirit.

He missed his brother so very much, and so many of his

qualities, from his bravery to that thoughtful expression often in his eyes that revealed his focus on principles and morality. Had he been jealous of Esteban, as Padre Manolo once asked? No, not at all. It was Ivan that was the object of his jealousy. Though he would never admit it, Nicolás hated how a school bully grew into such a corrupt, cruel man, all while enjoying the luxury of knowing the identity of his two blood parents. Yes, Ivan, the new chieftain. Not merely a killer but a king of killers.

Nicolás knew he must return, even if for a day. Even if it was his last act.

But while he found the right time for his return, he would prepare, train. He would somehow acquire arms. His gut told him Mitch and Gabe crossed his path for a reason. How lucky he was to have encountered Freedom, and saved him that day on that Albuquerque roof.

Nicolás missed his Colorado friends, and wondered where they were. It had been two days. Had they reached Crested Butte? He wondered when, or if ever, he would see them again.

In his mind he found himself replaying that image of Freedom in the Albuquerque diner, gesturing with passion, mouthing the words "music of the mountains."

Mitch returned from the kitchen and sunk into the couch perpendicular to his.

Nicolás raised his gaze toward the bison head on the den wall. "I love the bison, Mitch."

Mitch turned on the sofa to observe the large mass of dark brown, woolly fur. "North American buffalo. It's an American icon. Once it was the king of the plains. That baby weighed about two thousand pounds, one ton. Stood six feet tall at the shoulders."

"Really?" said Nicolás.

"Really. Back in the day they carpeted the American plains, sixty-million strong. You know they were the largest group of animals ever assembled on planet Earth? Until the white man arrived out west. Within fifteen years, by 1883, the sixty million had dwindled to under two hundred of 'em."

"*Dios mio.*"

"But now the population's greatly rebounded. It's steadily climbing."

Mitch paused.

"So Pato. I know you must miss 'em. Your family."

He knew Freedom had told Mitch. Still, if only he could have heard exactly what was said.

"More than you could imagine," Nicolás mumbled. He strained to keep his eyes from welling up. Not in front of Mitch.

"Perhaps I can," Mitch said. Nicolás turned and glanced his way.

"My parents both passed. My father ten years ago...my mother just last year. Miss them more by the day, it seems. In the winter, especially up here, it gets harder. You know, I was an only child. So like you, Pato, I no longer have anyone. What I have are some Army buddies sprinkled around the country. Some still overseas. And I have Gabe and the townspeople here, in Bigfork. And all around the lake. A couple friends in Missoula. And of course, I—we—have Freedom and Stasia. Worth their weight in gold."

"That they are," Nicolás said. "I guess you heard that I found my foster parents both dead. And my brother."

"Yes, Freedom had mentioned that. And that, the horror of it...well, I have seen many evil and horrible things. But that—I cannot imagine."

With Mitch, he could divulge some details. He was comfortable with it.

"Propped against them was one of those pieces of cardboard that cartels often leave at the scene of their hits. Handwritten in permanent marker. Warning me to not raise a finger or a voice against the Segundo Cortez cartel. Not just warning but threatening me."

Mitch said, "But first they would have to find you. And they will want you dead. There are others they want dead, probably far more than you. But especially if they ever catch you down there —well, they'll want you to suffer greatly first."

"And they will want to put one of those damned signs against me," Nicolás said, huffing air out of his mouth.

"But they won't get you. They will not win. I won't let 'em, the bastards. And you won't either." Mitch's fiery stare seared into his. Then it morphed into a wink and a grin. "Not after the training I'll give you."

"Thanks again for all this, my friend."

"No worries," Mitch said. "I enjoy it. You know, among other things, I was an instructor with the Army Rangers."

After several moments of silence, Nicolás said, "What did Jake mean when he accused you of all of those things? Before he left the café?"

"The dishonorable discharge, the drugs, alcohol, me being unemployed, all that jazz?"

Damn his curiosity. Nicolás said, "I probably should not have asked."

"No, it's fine. I went to West Point, you know. Once upon a time."

Nicolás recalled the T-shirt Mitch had worn when they had met the Friday before in José's.

"I graduated West Point like my father and grandfather. Had a promising career with the Rangers. Hell, I made my mark. In the monumental waste and lie that was the Iraq War. Bush's war. Hmmph." Mitch swigged from the longneck.

"I even earned a few medals in Afghanistan. Was over there a few years. Not as long as in my tours in Iraq, but I would have stayed on. Then—something happened."

Cradling his beer in his lap, Nicolás leaned forward.

"It wasn't just that I had lost many friends over there. I had lost many of my best friends, in Iraq. In Ramadi, in Fallujah, towns now controlled by ISIS. A total waste, it was. But seeing friends get offed in front of me, that was very hard to take. My therapist down in Missoula diagnosed me, of course. Post-traumatic stress disorder. Not like that was a groundbreaking discovery. One of my best friends, Adrian...he was firing his M-4 alongside me, in a firefight. He was Puerto-Rican, from New York. You resemble him...saw that the first time I met you. Well, he was hit in the face. Bullet went right up into his brain, right in front of me. My top wish? That had never happened. Next to that? That I hadn't witnessed it."

The words had moved Nicolás. He wished he could put his beer aside on the coaster but declined to move it from his lap. With his candor, Mitch had frozen him in place.

"I am so sorry, Mitch."

"Appreciate that, bud. Anyways, losing Adrian had nothing to do with me getting booted from the Army."

Was it drugs? Insubordination?

Mitch took another swig, a longer one, and shook his head.

"Afghanistan was—it is—a very different war from Iraq. In so many ways. At one point, we were working closely with the Afghan military brass. And we learned a disgusting, evil thing about many of them. These were the generals and colonels of the Afghan army. And each one of those bastards had a boy of no more than twelve as their concubine. These boys, it was not of their own will. Many tried to run away. Me and my men voiced our outrage to our superior officers. We had seen nothing like it, ever. It was an institutionalized thing. Totally accepted by the Afghan army evidently. And our own brass didn't want to cause waves. 'We all have to work with them,' our American superiors would say over and over."

"Good God," Nicolás said.

"Exactly," Mitch nodded his head. "One day, I heard this screaming. And this little boy was running out of one of the Afghan officer's quarters. Kid was bleeding from his nose and mouth and had a black eye. Back then I spoke decent Dari. It's an Afghan dialect of Farsi, or Persian. And this little guy was crying in Dari, telling me what this general had done to him for months. I got one of my men to secure the kid, protect him. Then this Afghan general storms by, lookin' for him. I get the boy to identify him. It was the guy. Well, I beat him pretty soundly with my fists. Kicked the hell out of him, too. Once in the face even. Last thing I did was slam him once onto the ground. That was when my commander had some of our own guys train their weapons on me. They locked me up. Eventually they released me and I headed back to Montana. Dishonorably discharged. Only thing worse, Nick, would have been serving time in Fort Leavenworth."

"That is unbelievable," Nicolás said.

"On the contrary. Believe it. I'll always love the military. But some of the upper brass will sell their men out in a heartbeat. You remember Eisenhower?"

"The American general?"

"And he was later an American president," Mitch said. "In his last speech, he warned the nation about the 'military-industrial complex' getting too much power. He invented the term. The guy that had seen more war than anyone, both world wars. So—what do you think happened with the boy?"

Mitch rose to his full height on his feet. Nicolás saw a hostile look spreading out upon his friend's face, the bugging eyes, the nostrils slightly flaring.

God, he was intense. Was he about to become violent? Was Mitch all right?

Nicolás fidgeted on the sofa and cleared his throat. Before he could answer, Mitch spoke.

"My superiors let that general regain control of that boy. That kid will be—no, he is— scarred for life."

Mitch turned and walked toward the kitchen. Nicolás let his gaze fall to the floor. A sudden nausea stirred in his stomach. There were things after all more disgusting than his people celebrating cartel leaders in song.

"I'm getting another brew," Mitch called out. "Want one?"

"Of course. Please."

Nicolás shook his head, wondering what must have happened to the boy. He scanned the room, taking in the taxidermic game and framed photos of fishing and climbing trips.

"Liking my spot here?" Mitch said, handing him a bottle.

"Oh yes," Nicolás said. "It would be the dream for most men."

"When Mom died, she left me an inheritance. And I bought this baby here. It's all paid for. I just have property taxes and all that."

"So Freedom told me you are a guide. That was your business, right?"

"Still is, Pato. I shut a lot of my activities down during the frigid Montana winters, you could imagine. I should have gotten things started by now. But I've just been so sluggish lately. Usually by May I'm a fishing guide. Hunting guide, climbing guide. The job our man Freedom always wanted in Durango. Except he will be a language teacher, too. I guess I missed the mark with my business. I've fallen into the bottle, got lost in the bottle. And a couple other things. Like Jake so publicly reminded me the other day."

"I was wondering why you didn't argue with him. Or knock him down again."

"Well," Mitch began, then took a deep draw from his bottle.

"I've got a big something on the sheriff, as you now know. But Jake, well, boy's got a little somethin' on me."

"You weren't caught behind Dairy Queen, too, were you?" Nicolás said, eyeing him and a forcing a mock-skeptical expression.

Mitch laughed in a convulsion, beer running down his chin.

"Not quite, Pato. But he loaned me some money. I have to pay him back pretty soon."

"And you fought him all for me?" Nicolás said.

"Well now. I look over and I see you down for the count. And Freedom on the ground. And Gabe running at him. I had to act. Could've been worse. Jake's a big boy, but I could've knocked him out. Remember also that the sheriff was a mere hundred-feet away."

"So tell me more about this," Nicolás said. "Your friendship with Gabriella. Gabe."

"Some wonder if we got something goin', she and I. We've been seen almost everywhere together. And you can imagine how conservative small American towns can be. Well, not as conservative as where I grew up."

"Which is?" Nicolás said.

"Lil' town by the name of Jenks, Oklahoma. Just south of Tulsa. That was before my dad moved us to Missoula. Anyway, when I returned from the Army, I met Gabe. She also served in Iraq. We've got that link, the Army, same war. And I suppose you could say we're both mavericks, not traditional Bigfork residents. She's a masculine lesbian, I'm a hard-living libertarian who speaks his mind. And I resist all invites to go to church."

"You and I share a few things in common," Nicolás said.

"She and I," Mitch said, "would do anything for each other, just about. After I lost Mom, Gabe in a way became my mother, even though she's a few years younger. Or the sister I never had. You catch my drift. She keeps an eye on me, never lets me get too far gone. You know, once upon a time, I was a guy every middle-aged mother wanted to introduce her daughter to. Now, I'm damaged goods. Ruined. But you, my friend. There's still lots of hope for you."

Mitch was indeed despairing, more than he had assumed. But both of their lives had improved since suffering their great tragedies. He and Mitch had emerged through grit, had they not?

"No, there is hope for us both, Mitch," Nicolás said. "Though we have experienced atrocity. Thanks for being so forthcoming. Even about Jake, and your habits."

Nicolás paused, clearing his throat.

"See, Mitch," Nicolás said. "Your experiences reinforce my philosophy. Life's just unfair. And unpredictable, usually. One must plow through it, by sheer force of will."

"Okay, Mr. Friedrich Nietzsche," Mitch said. "Ha. No, I'd have to say I agree. So you were telling me about Veracruz. And Padre Manolo and Doña Lucinda. And your brother—his name was—Esteban?"

"Yes, Esteban," Nicolás said, looking down across the rug into the fire. The details would be safe with Mitch. "I told you that I was an orphan. My brother and I both. He is, well, he was also my biological brother. We shared the same biological parents. I learned that they lived in Mexico City. They left us when we were mere toddlers with the parish, in Veracruz. The diocesan priest there was Padre Manolo. But of course, the church would not let him raise us. And not there on church grounds. He placed us in an orphanage and saw to it that, well, we had what we needed. And even more. One day Lucinda adopted me and Esteban. She was a healer. A *curandera.*"

"I've heard of them," Mitch nodded. "*Curanderos* and *curanderas*. Folk healers of a sort, right?"

"They at least believe they are folk healers. In Mexico, *curanderismo* preserves many Aztec beliefs, customs, and herbology, medicine. Blended with the Catholicism of the Spanish conquerors."

"Hmm," Mitch said. "Interesting stuff. I can envision you teaching one of your classes."

Nicolás smiled.

"So Lucinda, or as she was known in Veracruz, Doña Lucinda, she became my mother. And Esteban's. Our foster mother." His eyes started to well with tears, though he fought it. The beer did not help.

"I am sorry, Pato," Mitch said, looking down at his hiking boots. "Maybe we should talk about something—"

"No, it's fine. Well, that is a custom among some *curanderas.* Going back hundreds of years. To adopt vulnerable young children. And Padre Manolo was like a foster father in a way. We didn't see him every day. We lived with Luci. But we saw him often. He had us educated in the local parochial schools. Helped Esteban attend a good law school, helped me get my doctorate in literature."

"But I take it he didn't teach you to fight," Mitch said.

"No, not really," Nicolás said with a wistful smile. "But almost everything else, yes. And Lucinda taught me to cook. She also taught me much about *curanderismo.*"

"I bet she and the padre were great people. And your brother. You say he was an attorney? Spoke out more and more against the cartel?"

"Yes. It originated with Padre. In Veracruz, he was the first man of the cloth to publicly criticize the cartels. And until a few years ago, a priest could do this and not fear retaliation. He persuaded my mother to take a more active role in speaking out. She had just as much sway over the people in Veracruz as he did. Actually, even more. And Esteban was convinced. He actually filed a lawsuit against Arturo Méndez, the chief of Segundo Cortez."

"That's the man you—that cretin that was your first blood."

"First blood?" Nicolás said.

"A hunting term. Means the first animal you ever bagged. Hunted, shot, and bagged. You may not have shot him. But you gave him a fatal heart attack. Indirectly, after you lit up that warehouse, by what you read online. That's just my read on it."

"Perhaps. But I set the fire only because he had my brother and foster parents killed. I made every possible effort to keep from getting involved in their cause. Even to the point of causing great friction between me and all three of them. And anyway, it's not like I could acquire some gun to go after Arturo Méndez."

"So why did you resist getting involved?" Mitch said.

"Me, just a civilian, not in the military? Or a top politician? It would mean guaranteed, imminent death. Should I be resented for not wanting that? I just wanted to pursue what I always desired."

"And that was?" Mitch said.

"I wanted two things. To teach literature in peace. This would get my students to love literature as I love it. And—I admit that I wanted what the Italians call *la dolce vita*."

"Well, I do want that, as well, I admit," Mitch said. "Part of the reason I hit it so hard. To ease the pain, but also because I at the same time really do love life."

"Well, surely one of those two reasons is more powerful, inside you," Nicolás said. "Which one is it, the former, no? Easing the pain."

"I guess you're correct, Pato. Pato Freud!"

Nicolás laughed.

"So, update," Mitch said, looking at his phone, its screen now illuminating the dim couch perpendicular to Nicolás's sofa. "Gabe offered to take you to work from here on out. This house is on her route to work anyway. She says she wants to hang out with you."

"That sounds great," Nicolás said.

"It's also because she thinks I will corrupt you if we spend too much time together, Pato."

"Perhaps," Nicolás said.

"So not to wax serious again. But tell me about this Carla bombshell. I need to know more about her."

"Well, as the American expression goes: I never saw it coming. Her betrayal. I knew she was involved romantically in some way with Esteban. And in her journalism she had differed from most Mexican journalists. She veered into the territory of casting Segundo Cortez in a bad light. She criticized it, in her journalism. She and her reporting partner, Juan. They were not as vocal as my brother and parents, but they were vocal enough. But somewhere along the line, she was corrupted. The Méndez family got to her."

"So this is your guess?"

"It must have happened. That's how Segundo Cortez knew my brother and mother and Padre Manolo were in one place. Without Carla being there."

"Sick," Mitch said.

"Of—of course," Nicolás said. He felt a wave of grief and disgust build within him. He could not weep here in front of this rugged soldier. "One second. Bathroom break."

After he closed the door he turned on the faucet and splashed water onto his face, and onto his closed eyes. Because he did not want to see the tears that might come. The water dripped from his eyes and face, masking any trace of tears. He ran wet hands across his beard and into his hair. All the while he stared into the light brown eyes peering out from the mirror.

He became aware of that urge, a frustrated desire he had felt with greater frequency in the recent weeks, to pick up his phone and call his brother, Doña Lucinda, and Padre Manolo. But it always ended the same: against the towering wall that denied him. The wall of cold death, past which lay the unknown, and perhaps all the world's secrets.

Their funerals had come and gone without him anywhere to be seen. Somewhere—in some field, perhaps in Lucinda's family plot—stood their gravestones, bearing inscriptions he had not yet glimpsed. In his core he knew he must return. Not years from now, but sooner. Much sooner.

Pato—he disliked the name more and more. The timid duck that flew far away, into the horizon.

He ran his hands under the faucet and brought them to his face, sending twin cascades of water down his cheeks and into the sink. He blinked and focused on the countenance staring out at him from the mirror. A face youthful and serene, yet taking all of its features as a whole, a visage bearing an unmistakable edginess, a hunter quality.

Where would he be in a months' time? In a year? Instead of wondering, he must chase what he wanted.

Shame swept over him again. That they had perished, and he had lived. And another emotion, slightly different. What was it? Yes. It was guilt. That this jaded hero, this fellow tortured soul, had helped him so freely.

He shut off the faucet and ran his palms down his cheeks, staring into his own eyes. He must make this all worthwhile...

33

Pantano felt his fatigued limbs sink further into the passenger's seat as the patrol car approached his daughter's neighborhood, further from a grueling workweek and closer to two full days of rest.

Gustavo drove in silence as twilight gave way to dusk. In the dying light, Pantano could see his nephew's drooping eyelids.

"Maybe I should talk to you," Pantano said. "Keep you awake as you drive."

"I'm fine, Uncle," Gustavo said. "And we'll be there in a minute."

At least we won't have to deal with any student protests. Every damned day this week. But I'm starting to understand why. Especially with that hit on that firebrand political science professor. He was widely revered. Something would happen that night, no doubt.

Pantano closed his eyes. Just a minute…a half-minute of rest would be fine.

The speaker of the police scanner radio opened up. Static, then a hissing sound, and a pop. Then a voice, beginning with a forced composure, yielding to a passionate barking. "Officer

Miranda here. Miranda. Campus Station, Building Two now on fire. Need backup."

"And now it comes again," Pantano said. "Damn it. We should respond to this one. That station was my first post. Arturo got me to join the force and we were stationed there."

"You're the police chief, *Tio*. Are you sure you want to get that close?"

"Accelerate, Gustavo," Pantano said. "We can't let them get away with this."

Gustavo said, "Uncle, the students know we have looked the other way for months. Even longer. They despise us now."

"It is true," Pantano said. "I admit I was not expecting this level of retaliation or fury."

"I'm saying you will be a target. They've seen you on television. They'll know you're the chief."

"Do it, Gustavo," Pantano said. "We are armed. Others are responding, too."

"Si, *Tio*," Gustavo said.

Closing his eyes once again, Pantano felt the car surge beneath him. Gustavo responded on the radio that he was approaching, as did others. Miranda gave his location. As more news of vandalism and arson came through the police channel radio, Pantano kept his eyes shut.

He never envisioned the youth would become so defiant, so fast, with such ferocity. The older generations had accepted it, in many ways—the complete intertwining of organized crime and regular society. And despite the popular jokes about that youngest generation—of their sloth and their entitlement and naiveté—the youth had reacted with bravery and character he wished he still had. He had lost these attributes, as had Arturo, so far back there in his early twenties.

Pantano felt the car turn right, and a moment later, left. Then it slowed.

"*Mierda*," Gustavo said in a loud voice. Pantano opened his eyes.

"The students are in the roadway," Gustavo said. Pantano bolted upright in his seat.

"What do you want me to do?" Gustavo said. "Order them to disperse? Speed straight ahead? Turn around, and find another way toward the campus station?"

In this distance, Pantano could see the flames of the campus station. In the foreground, the wall of youth advanced toward him like a slow-moving wave. Fire and police sirens sounded in the distance in a constant cacophony. He snatched the small boxy microphone of the radio.

"Disperse now," Pantano said. "You need to disperse immediately."

Still they advanced.

"Get out of the road now," he barked. "That's an order."

Still they approached.

"Should I accelerate? Turn around?" Gustavo said, his voice now filled with anxiety.

"I don't think they'll move," Pantano said. "And they're children. Turn around. We can't—"

Pantano flinched, his words cut short by the burst of flames across the hood of his car and windshield.

"Molotov cocktail!" Gustavo yelled. He jerked the wheel and slammed his foot onto the accelerator, pushing the car forward and then spinning it around.

"I can't see, I can't see!" Gustavo said.

An object crashed onto the trunk of the car and the rear windshield was covered with flames.

"Get out of the car!" Pantano said. "Draw now and get out! That's an order! We'll get to the others on foot."

Pantano drew his pistol, followed by Gustavo. "Open the door now, Gustavo, and come over to my side. Go!"

The doors jerked open in unison. As Pantano swung out of the car, he fired once into the air. Gustavo did the same. Then as he took brisk steps away from the car, Pantano pointed at the line of students, firing once above their heads.

"Freeze now, goddamn it, or I'll start shooting you one by one," he said.

The advance ceased. He could see their sweaty faces: some angry, fearful, some shocked. Almost all were of college age.

Gustavo drew up alongside him.

"I'm here, *Tio*," he said.

"Drop the bottles now," Pantano said. "Or we will shoot them out of your hands. Some of you will be hit. We don't want that."

A bottle clanked and rolled onto the ground, and then another burst onto the ground.

"We know you're the police chief," a voice shouted. A young man took a step forward, then stopped. An inner outrage manifested itself in every centimeter of his face.

"Hector Pantano, I see you all the time on television. I've heard you on the radio. And you—"

"You do absolutely nothing," a female voice interrupted him. "You do nothing to protect us. You don't even try to appear like you're pursuing Segundo Cortez. You're letting them pick off the people. The vice chancellor...Professor Gutierrez today."

"We know what you're doing," the boy said. "You need to change this tonight."

"You can do something if you want, *Señor*," she said. "You are powerful enough. You have enough men to do this. Ivan Méndez is just an angry boy."

"Stop taking the cash he offers you," the boy said.

"Do you promise you will change things?" she said.

Pantano turned to Gustavo.

"You don't need to promise anything, *Tio*," he whispered.

"I do," Pantano said to the crowd. "You will see. I will do the best I can."

"When? You *can* solve it," the girl said. "Can we believe you?"

"You can," Pantano said. "Now you destroyed our patrol car. You need to disperse now. We need to get over to the fire you set. You children need to disappear and go home immediately, or you are all subject to arrest."

The line held, and then the boy said, "Let's get the hell out of here. We've done enough tonight."

As the line broke up and moved past them, Pantano and Gustavo held their pistols with both hands angled downward. Soon the faces were gone, and the figures shrank away from them and the distant fire, and more by the second down the street.

"*Vámonos*, Gustavo," Pantano said. "That ended better than I expected. Let's get over to the fire."

34

"Wake up, Don Aurelio de Cervantes," Nicolás heard Mitch say. Was he dreaming?

He stirred awake on the couch, then sat upright. In the meager dawn light filtering in through the windows across the guesthouse, he could see Mitch dressed in dark-green army fatigues and black combat boots.

"Still gutsy enough to accept the challenge?"

"Pardon me?"

"I want to know if you have the mettle to accept the Mitch Intensive Training 101. MIT. But a very different type of college than the one out east."

"Of course I accept," Nicolás said. "Now?"

"Now is as good a time as any," Mitch said. "It's one of your days off from the café. And the day's just starting."

"I will do it," Nicolás said, rubbing his eyes with his fists.

"But it'll be very limited at first in terms of what we can do, the training you will get," Mitch said. "Eventually you will get all of it."

"I don't understand," Nicolás said.

"You probably suffered a concussion last Friday night," Mitch said. "You need to take it easy at first."

"I think that's probably a very wise precaution," Nicolás said.

"Get some proper clothes on," Mitch said. "For outside on the property. I'll hit the bathroom over in the house. Coffee, water, and muffins are in the kitchen if you want some."

Mitch left the guesthouse. Nicolás rose and put on his jeans, flannel shirt, and coat that were lying on the rocking chair on the rug. He, too, headed for the main house.

"*Dios mio*," he said, under his breath as he entered the kitchen. He counted them. Eleven longnecks standing empty about the countertop. Big Sky Country Brewing's Moose Drool, the bottles read.

How does he have it in him? Where does he get the energy, to rise so early after this?

The clock on the kitchen wall showed seven-twelve. He had retired to bed at eleven, and Mitch had not had more than a beer or two at that point.

Floorboards creaked nearby. Mitch appeared at the kitchen's edge.

"Last night's casualties," Mitch said. "Don't mind them. Couldn't sleep again. Anyway, shall we be off? Need any water, food, coffee?"

"Coffee, please," Nicolás said.

"I'll put some in a thermos for you, too. Cream, sugar?"

"Cream, no sugar," Nicolás mumbled.

Mitch fumbled about for a thermos, which he filled with steaming coffee. After he added half-and-half from the fridge, they were out the door.

In the garage nearby, after Mitch disabled the alarm, Nicolás was surprised to see the small arsenal of rifles, semiautomatic pistols, and revolvers arranged atop a table in an unadorned, enclosed room in the corner.

Is this how it is in America's Mountain West? Or in rural Montana?

"Now your education begins," Mitch said. "Or resumes. You said you and your brother would sometimes shoot his guns. So I think you're probably at least decent with a revolver. First I'll train you to load and unload and manage a .45 semiautomatic pistol. This is a good go-to handgun. A revolver's a good backup gun. 'Cause these semiautos, they can jam. Or have an 'FTF.' Failure to feed. And you can run out of rounds, of course."

Mitch selected a pistol from the spread, then a few empty magazines, and a box of rounds from underneath the table. He showed Nicolás how to load one magazine, and then had Nicolás load a few others.

"Very good," Mitch said. "Now this is how you pop in the mag. By the way, never call it a clip. Dead giveaway that you're a novice."

Mitch pushed the magazine into the grip of the pistol until Nicolás heard the click. Then he showed him how to release the magazine.

"Now you try. Make sure you're pointing the barrel away from us both. And never let your index finger—or any other finger for that matter—get in that trigger guard there. Unless you're ready to discharge the weapon. Learning that is what is called 'trigger discipline.' You don't want an unintentional discharge. With Dr. Rivers either."

Nicolás practiced popping in magazines and then releasing them. A few minutes later, Mitch took the pistol from him.

"Nice work for your first time," he said. "Ha, not what I expected out of a literature professor, I must admit. Anyway, we'll practice this later. Way I figure it, if these ghouls come up this way, the most likely gun you will use, if need be, is this kind of gun right there. Perhaps followed by a revolver. After that, I'd say odds are you would use a long-arm. I'll wager it will be an AK-

47–style semiauto assault rifle. Over a .556, an AR-15–style rifle, as is used in our military. Well, mine. And I believe by Mexico's, as well. And Israel's. Now, you know those cartel people, they're like the damned jihadis. And like the Viet Cong were. They overwhelmingly favor using an AK-47 platform. Why? They may not be as accurate as our ARs or .556s, whatever you prefer to call them. But they jam less often and can put up with a helluva lot more abuse and grime. And humidity and harsher conditions. Given the choice, I would usually opt for the AK over the AR."

"Now we will practice loading one. It's not technically an AK-47 though, made in Russia or the Soviet Union or in China. It's a WASR. Pronounced like the German word for water. *Wasser.* A WASR is a cheaper version of the AK-47. Made in Soviet bloc countries like Romania, during our Cold War. That particular one is a WASR pistol. I know, ugly as all hell, but it's more dependable than a farm mule. But first…"

Mitch pulled another rifle from the table and placed it in Nicolás' hands.

"I like it," Nicolás said. It was heavier and longer than the WASR, and better looking. He gripped the rifle and lifted it toward his cheekbone, closing one of his eyes and aiming with the other. A vision of Segundo Cortez men falling before him filled his mind, and he inhaled deeply at the sheer force held in his hands. It was a sensation completely foreign to him.

"That's a Bulgarian one, Pato, made by Arsenal. A brand-new SAM-7. One pricey AK, about fifteen-hundred bucks. To me, as good as a Soviet or Chinese one. Definitely better than the Romanian one up there. Only gun I can think of where the receiver is forged, then milled. Imagine if you had this baby down in Veracruz that day with about five or six fully loaded mags. And see the foldable stock, for close-quarter combat? Like an Israeli Galil. Think of this as a Samurai's sword. Could be used effectively for centuries. Just gotta keep her clean."

"These are not legal to own for citizens of my country," Nicolás said.

"I know," Mitch said. "And they may not be for citizens here much longer. Another subject for another day. Well, let me ask you this. Your military and police down there in that banana republic—they doin' much to protect your people against the cartels that use these rifles?"

"The police and military often are the cartel, part of the cartel."

"I'm well aware. But the good could take out a lot of the evil by being able to properly fight back, Pato. How are the good able to have a fighting chance against evil? How can the strong protect the weak?"

"Of course I've thought the same, Mitch, quite often." Nicolás felt grateful for this training, but mildly insulted at the same time by such questions. Why else would he want to learn to shoot such rifles?

They practiced loading and unloading the WASR. Then Mitch and Nicolás did the same with the AR-15, the Marlin .45-70 lever-action, and the .308 Accuracy International sniper rifle. Each time, the act grew more enjoyable—as though he had, within himself, uncovered new potential, a power that increased by the minute.

"Enough for today," Mitch said. "I think you're a natural. Haven't seen you shoot yet, but that comes later. I'll teach you to clean each weapon, the boring part. Then comes the most exciting part."

"And that is?" Nicolás said.

"I will teach you how to fight, without weapons. And win, against a larger and more powerful opponent. I know you can't fight well now. But after this training, you'll be able to beat Jake with one hand tied behind your back."

"I look forward to it," Nicolás said, feeling both confident and skeptical.

Mitch stood looking straight into Nicolás's eyes. Then he tilted his head, pondering.

"You know what, Cervantes," Mitch said. "I think you should be good enough to shoot today. I suspected you'd have a concussion of some sort. Gotta watch out for those, reinjuring yourself, making it much worse. But Cassie thinks you checked out, you're fine. She examined you minutes after the fight, remember?"

"I wish she would examine me," Nicolás said.

"I bet she already did up in her house the other day," Mitch said and laughed, pointing at him. "While I was breakin' my spine over the wood. So do you feel any guilt over that? Somethin' better have happened."

"Well—a kiss, that's all. But a very good kiss."

"Ah-huh. Now the truth emerges." Mitch checked his watch. "Let's hit the range for a few hours. I want you to practice with all six guns, get you to where you know 'em well."

After they stopped in the kitchen to take some bananas, muffins, and bottled water, Mitch placed the handguns in range bags and the long-arms in long black plastic rectangular boxes. Then he laid them along with several cardboard boxes of ammunition in the truck bed.

"By the way, Pato, bring the cash you earned yesterday. And some of your other money. You'll see."

Nicolás headed for the guesthouse and retrieved some cash. What did Mitch have in mind? As he walked back toward the truck, he swore to himself he would spend none of his reserves, unless he encountered something necessary.

Then they zipped west along the north shore of the lake and then cut north. As a city came into view, with no tall buildings, like Santa Fe. Yet there was nothing beautiful or stately or elegant to the eye, as far as Nicolás could see. Full of squarish edifices, most of the structures were laid out in a utilitarian spirit.

"Welcome to Kalispell," a sign read. Nicolás mouthed the words in silence.

"We could've gone shooting elsewhere," Mitch said. "But the better range is up here. There's a store near the range that we can hit afterwards...get you some things."

As Mitch pulled into a large asphalt parking lot filled with all sorts of trucks and a few cars, Nicolás saw the sign and knew they were at the range.

For the next three hours, they alternated shooting one gun at a time. Mitch ensured Nicolás knew how to load and discharge each weapon, and activate its safety. Mitch held down the switch to position the target at various distances. The din was so great in the range from several other shooters that Mitch had to yell so that Nicolás could hear him through his protective earphones.

At one point, as Nicolás fired the AR-15, he caught a nearby movement in his peripheral vision. He turned. Mitch staggered backward on his heels like a man shot, his shoulders trembling, his eyes bulging behind their light-red plastic protective glasses. Mitch regained his composure and, with his hands, smoothed the front of his T-shirt from his upper chest down to his belly. He looked embarrassed, looking downward and sucking in his upper lip.

"Excellent—excellent work, Pato Cervantes!" he thundered, laughing.

They practiced again with the AR-15. Afterwards, Mitch loaded the gun cases and range bags into the truck bed while Nicolás stood guard beside it.

"In this case it would be better if we had your lady friend's 4Runner," Mitch said. "Or Freedom's."

They turned right onto the road, and then north on the highway.

"I know you saw me have one of my moments today at that range," Mitch said. "It was embarrassing. It's not my first time. It's the post-traumatic stress. But don't worry about it—it won't affect you. Well, I guess your resemblance to Adrian, and you shooting the AR, which is a lot like his M-4, it gave me a flashback. It shook me."

Mitch chose an exit and, seconds later, swung into another parking lot.

"One of the best outfitters around, bud. We're gonna get you some proper wear. Not your same threads every other day. And we'll get you some other goodies. Bring your cash, it'll be well worth it."

An hour later, they headed back south on the highway toward the lake.

"Good work today, Pato. Now I know you're a natural with firearms. Learning quickly. And we'll keep practicing. Every day we can work at our MIT 101 program. I want to get you to where you can live off the land if need be. Fish, hunt. And I want you to not just be as good as any potential attackers from that cartel. I want you to be much more skilled than them. I want to impress upon you a valuable lesson. You must learn to not hide from your enemy for long, but to turn and fight it, and then either demoralize it and break its will, or destroy it. Odds are with this situation, you want to destroy what you find. And in such a way that it demoralizes its remnants."

Did Mitch want him to return to Mexico to fight? Surely not with one of his weapons.

He recalled the YouTube videos he had seen in the last few days. The narco ballads cropping up, odes to kingpins rendered in rap form. But then there were the anti-cartel rants. Would not those few rebels, the bravest of the brave, appreciate his return to his hometown to attack the beast? Would he not inspire those few, who would then inspire more to join their ranks?

Mitch parked between his house and garage, and said, "I'll whip up some grub, bud."

Nicolás thanked him and headed for the guest-bedroom. He laid his new acquisitions on the bed: sock hat, thermal underwear, canvas jacket and pants, T-shirts, wool socks purchased on sale. Beside them he placed the SOG knife and its sheath. In the next few days, he would replenish this money at José's café.

He headed for the shower. Soon he would be in attire better suited for the season and place. But then he recalled the laptop on the couch. He sat and began to peruse the Mexican news but found he could not concentrate.

For some reason, Nicolás recalled the moment when his eyes first crawled up the dark stones of the chimney column to the head and upper chest of the bull elk. He imagined the great beast, back in the days when it roamed plains and fields, foraging on grass, free at least to some extent. Had it known it was meeting its end? Did death come swiftly, with mercy? Or was it painful?

Could his enemies somehow locate him, pursue him? Was he like the name of that restaurant and bar in Bigfork, a sitting duck? And was Mitch, here in this remote Montana outpost, at risk due to mere proximity?

He must strike, before they struck him.

35

Pantano tried to crawl away, but in his dream the kicks kept coming faster and faster, goading him farther up the hill. Pain shot through his cracked ribs. With his torn scalp stinging from the blows, he dared not even raise his head for fear of being struck in the face.

There was no hope of living. All that remained was hope for a swift death.

But then he heard that voice. A woman's, at first high with outrage and urgency, commanding the men to stop, then tender and soothing like a mother to her child as she called out to him.

He could hear the men standing over him, then shrinking away from her advance.

"Hector," she called. "Hector, dear."

He raised his face from the dust. She stood before him, several meters off, halfway up the hill. Behind her at the summit stood the place of execution, the stake looming tall where he was condemned to be burned.

"I won't let them hurt you anymore," the figure said. The accent was odd—something from some far-off land.

He focused his blurry gaze on her. Covering her head was a

thin shawl, which descended into a white linen robe from some long-gone era.

"I won't let them take you, Hector," she said.

Hers was a Middle Eastern face, more specifically a Jewish one. Its features were strong, yet framed an expression so youthful, feminine, and gentle. The widening, light-green eyes connected with his in a glance of overwhelming love.

It was unmistakable. Yes, he knew who she was.

But then the eyes morphed into a dark brown. He blinked hard. Those eyes narrowed, meeting his with a gaze full of guilt and sadness but tinged with the faintest seductiveness. The thick luxurious lips parted into a smile. His gaze sunk, and he saw the robe was now of a black linen. This was a different person altogether. Who was this?

And then the image blurred and there was a flash of light. Mist surrounded him. Once again he found himself in the humid air and scents of Veracruz. The woman in black had morphed into a different figure. He recognized clothes from mere decades before. The face he could not discern.

"It is time for you to go back, Hector," she said. "We didn't let them get you. Now go—go!"

He felt a nudge on his arm, and he blinked several times. He wiped his face with the palms of his hand. Above him was the ceiling fan in his bedroom. In his nostrils was the morning smell that greeted him every morning: Raquel's breakfast.

"I had to wake you early, Hector," his wife said. "I think you were having a nightmare. I might as well wake you."

"Raquel," he said. "I believe I was."

"Breakfast?" she said. Her face was serious. Something was weighing her down.

"Of course," he said, sitting upright.

He followed her into the kitchen. "I have some coffee made.

Let me pour you some and let's sit out on the veranda first, for a minute."

What did she want? Surely not a divorce. Decades of marriage and harmony, only a few recent arguments.

They sat on the wicker sofa outside. The humidity and heat had already started in.

"Hector," she said.

"Yes, love?"

"We received a call, a death threat this morning, while you slept," she said. "Does that surprise you?"

"What did they say?"

"That you are part of Segundo Cortez. That you might as well be one of their *sicarios*. The man promised that soon you will be dead. Then he hung up."

"How in the hell—our number is unlisted. Somehow..."

"Hector, you're overwhelmed," she said. "The new mayor of this city is Ivan Méndez. This happened so fast. He's ruining Veracruz, your life, my life, right when we should be enjoying a new time of peace. It's clear you are not willing to solve the problem. Or you just cannot."

"I—I am paralyzed," he said, surprised with his sudden candor.

"I know," she said, taking a sip from her cup. "I want you to stop taking his money. At first it wasn't so much so, but now it's obviously blood money. Blood of everyday citizens."

"Is that all that is on your mind, Raquel?" he said, leaning forward and searching her eyes.

"I want you to retire," she said. "Now."

"What? Raquel."

"You must do it very soon. Or I am moving in with our son."

"Raquel, we've been married for thirty-seven years. Happily."

"You need to do it now, Hector," she said, then rose and walked into the house.

36

"Good God," Gabe said that morning, as her hatchback accelerated down the road. "Stop him next time he's drinking that much. Didn't you see what was all over the kitchen countertop?"

"I did, yes," Nicolás said. "He must have continued after I went to bed. He's done it before. Last night we had several beers together but—"

"I saw he put a big dent in that handle of bourbon. And there had to be half a case of longnecks on that counter."

"I noticed, too," Nicolás said. He thought of Mitch's words. He could see the mother in her. A beautiful quality. "I suppose you're right."

"Gosh, I just worry myself sick about him," said Gabe. "Last year he ended up in the hospital. Did he happen to tell you that?"

"He did not."

"Mitch might seem bulletproof to you. All laughter and machismo. But the dude is fragile. He's more vulnerable than you think. He went through more over there than any of us could imagine. And then the way he was discharged. Ultimate humiliation…"

"So why was he hospitalized?"

"Well, suicidal ideation. Pastor Wachter, Parker Wade—or Burning Elk—and I convinced him to check in to a mental hospital. Down in Missoula."

"He told me about seeing his friend killed in Iraq," said Nicolás. "And then trying to defend that little boy."

"Yes, like I said. Did he tell you about the massacre?"

"Not yet," Nicolás said. "A massacre of Americans? Or of the enemy?"

She was silent for a second. Then she turned from the windshield and momentarily looked into his eyes. "Well…both."

An eerie silence pervaded the vehicle.

"Iraqi civilians?" Nicolás finally said.

"They were Afghan insurgents. They had just surrendered. After they'd wiped out a big swath of our troops with IEDs and gunfire. Mitch and a few of the men under him took no mercy. Like twenty of them. He's scarred from that though. Inside. A knife cuts both ways."

"That's horrible," Nicolás said.

"You know, I like you, Pato. You're the kind of man I like to be around."

"And what kind of man is that?" Nicolás said.

"Masculine, but not to the point where it's a mask or a bullying thing. Yet sensitive, deep. I can see how you and Freedom are friends."

"And I can see how you are his friend," Nicolás said.

"So you put the moves on my cute boss yet?" Gabe said, an eyebrow raised.

"Not quite," Nicolás said.

"You should," Gabe said. "I can tell she really likes you."

He felt himself blush. The sensation of shyness gave way to relief, then hope.

Gabe said, "I wish Kat would want me. I keep hanging on. Even though she's got that druggy past."

"Drugs?"

"Yes, the hard stuff. But she's clean now. I helped her. I tell you because she would tell you anyway."

"Well," Nicolás said. "She and Mitch... even a fool can feel their sexual tension. So why do you keep hanging on?"

"Because I am hoping against hope," Gabe answered.

"Pardon me?" Nicolás said.

"I am still holding out that I could flip her. Convert her."

Nicolás laughed, and then Gabe joined in.

"I like you, Pato. We should hang out. But do me one favor."

Nicolás turned back toward her.

"Don't let Mitch drink," she said. "At least not there at home. It brings him closer to the darkness. He's got you on that training regimen, but challenge him to join in. You guys call me to join if you want. I can also keep an eye on him then. And if you want a drink, bud, call me up instead."

"I still don't have a phone," he said.

"Ah, that's right. You need to get you a burner, down in Missoula. Call from his landline. Or from the café."

"Yes. Thanks, Gabe. Gabriella!" he said as he stepped out of the car into the café's parking lot.

"Here's my number on this card," she said as she scrawled her number on a business card and handed it to him. He leaned in and took it. "And Pato, watch your back. Jake's still bitter. Keep in touch."

Nicolás eased the door shut with one hand, and waved with the other.

Inside the kitchen's rear door, a rich aroma greeted his nostrils: sautéed onions, eggs, cheese, peppers. He could pick out all of the components, and knew full well the breakfast was a Mexican one, though the café never opened until eleven.

"There you are, Pato," José said. "You and Oscar and I are about to have a nice treat."

"I can smell it. I can see it," Nicolás said. He looked down over José's shoulder into the pan. "*Ay caramba, desayuno para un rey.* Let's see: eggs, poblanos, portabellos, cheese, potatoes, avocado, tomatoes, caramelized onions. And a little escabeche."

"*Correcto, chico,*" said José. With his spatula, he transferred the magnificent amalgam onto a large platter, then shut off the burner and thrust the pan under cool water from the faucet. He pulled on a mitt and retrieved a cast-iron, lidded pan from the oven. After setting the pan onto the stovetop, he removed the lid, and placed the contents inside a covered plastic container.

"*Vámonos, hombres,*" he said, leading the men into the dining room. "Take your seats. I'll be back in a minute." Oscar and Nicolás sat at the small square table.

A scraping noise sounded all around them in the stereo system, and then a song ensued. It was a Mexican ballad from the 1970s. And all at once, the aromas of the corn tortillas, the sautéed poblanos and onions intertwining with the mushrooms, and the coffeepot between them atop the table mat, fused with the singer's soaring voice in one glorious daydream of a childhood breakfast in his mother's house. In Oscar's delighted expression— the man had surely enjoyed José's custom before—he saw his brother Esteban. He glanced at José as he sank into his seat. Nicolás saw the face of Padre Manolo, then Doña Lucinda, then once again the smiling priest on those mornings, when all was hope and comfort and love, and it was 1993 all over again. When no threat of violence or abandonment or harm hovered, just that love, rendered in the two arts of the music and the food of his homeland.

"*Una oración antes,*" José said. And he took a hand of Nicolás and of Oscar and said a blessing in Spanish.

With his eyes closed, Nicolás shuddered. He felt like he was holding the hands of his brother and the Padre once again.

"Now," José said, as he opened his eyes and released his hands. "This is our time, *caballeros*. Before the lunch-hour wave bursts through my door."

"I did not have any Salvadoran music," José added as he smiled at Oscar. Then he looked at Nicolás. "*Mijo*, why the red eyes? Did you smoke some marijuana this morning? Or does this feel like home?" The barrel-chested man laughed and smiled tenderly at him.

"Of course, reminds me of years ago. Growing up," Nicolás said. "All the more bittersweet because I no longer have my homeland." Why should he hold back? What did he have to lose by disclosing it?

"And because I will tell you," Nicolás said, "I lost my brother and foster parents to cartel bullets. It was like I was there again with them."

"I am sorry, Pato," José said. "You have a kindred soul here."

"Yes?" Nicolás said.

"Why, yes," José nodded at Oscar, as if prodding him to speak up.

"I lost my grandparents," Oscar said, "to one of the Salvadoran wars. Decades ago. I know many who lost their parents, grandparents. I would rather live as a pauper here, then as a king in my home country."

"I am sorry, Oscar," Nicolás said, reaching across the table and squeezing his shoulder.

"Well, we're doing pretty well now," said José. "Hey, it was part of my blessing, remember? And it's the truth." He rose and lifted the lid off the plastic container, and motioned for the men to commence eating.

The three prepared their tacos and coffee, and began to eat and drink.

Halfway through the meal and a few songs later, Nicolás felt compelled to speak.

"*Señor,*" Nicolás said. "I think he may be too timid, or polite, to ask. But I believe that Oscar would like to try his hand at cooking here, as well."

"*Sí?*" José said, looking at the young man, then at Nicolás, then back at the Salvadoran.

Oscar looked down at the table, smoothed a wrinkle out on the tablecloth with his hand, and gave a barely perceptible nod.

"*Es la verdad, chico?*" José said, keeping his eyes on him.

"*Pues sí,*" Oscar said. "Please. If I may."

"*Bueno,* on the days when Pato does not work, I will teach you some things. And Pato can wait tables, too. Can serve everything but *el alcohol, claro.* I can bring those out."

Nicolás searched for signs of irritation in José's fleshy, taurine face, but could find none.

"I like that, Aurelio," he said, with a wink at Nicolás. "Being the team player. Tomorrow I will start to teach Oscar."

When the lunch hour arrived, the café began to fill. José stood by the stove, preparing the food, as Oscar stood just alongside him, helping where needed. Nicolás bused tables. José's wife Lupe—who was even shorter and portlier than her husband —served as the sole waitress. Nicolás was bringing a tray of cups of coffee out to one table when he spied a face squinting at him across the room.

Sitting at a small table was Jake.

On the opposite side of the room, alone at a table, sat Cassie.

"Here we go," Nicolás muttered.

He bused a few more tables and delayed looking in the direction of either diner.

"I need some guac and chips and water on table six," Lupe told him. "And some red chile and chips and coffee on table twelve as soon as possible."

In the kitchen, Nicolás prepared the four items, and returned to the dining room with them atop his tray. He arranged the small stone *molcajete* of guacamole, a basket of chips, and the water onto Cassie's table, avoiding her gaze. Though she said nothing, he could feel her eyes on him. It hurt to ignore her in front of Jake. But he could not inflame the man. He imagined being shoved into a local jail cell, his true identity exposed. As long as he did not lose his head...

He lowered the small cup of red chile, the tortilla chip basket, and the coffee onto the other table.

"Jake," Nicolás muttered.

"Already forgot your name, partner. I see how she looks at you. She can't hide it well. But you're just her escape. Her out. A new adventure."

"I don't see how she looks at me," Nicolás said. "I'm just trying to scrape together some money to live and write my book."

"Sure," Jake said.

Nicolás turned and headed with his tray into the kitchen.

When he returned with his tray full of cups of water, he did not look at Jake. After placing the cups before a table of diners in the corner, Nicolás walked back toward the kitchen. In his peripheral vision, he saw a mass of crimson. On Jake's table was a puddle of red chile. His basket lay on the ground beside his boot, some chips on the wooden floor, some atop the table.

"Musta had a lil' accident, boy," Jake said, shaking his head with a wry smirk. "Can't fault me for that. I need you to clean this up."

"Sure," Nicolás nodded. As he leaned over to wipe the table with a rag, he chuckled, staring into Jake's beady eyes. "You know, you're as sloppy a customer as you are a fighter. Boy."

Jake gave a jolt, and sat up, ramrod straight, his nostrils flaring.

Nicolás held up an index finger, walking slowly backward toward the kitchen. "Well, let me get a cloth and my broom."

He turned right once inside the kitchen. José was stirring a small pot of mole.

"*Señor*," Nicolás said, tapping him on the shoulder. "*Señor*, we have a big problem."

"Yes, we do," said a familiar female voice behind Nicolás. He spun around.

"I saw Jake turn over the salsa and the chips," Cassie said. "He was staring at Pato while he bused my table. Pato didn't even speak to me or look my way, and once he hit the kitchen, Jake grabbed his salsa and chips and spilled them all over."

"*Dios mio*," José said, turning off the burner and moving the pot across the stove. "So who's worse, your ex-husband or the sheriff?"

"That is a mystery, José," a voice behind her said. It was Lupe, her arms crossed as she shook her head.

"Come with me, Pato," said José. "And you, Oscar. Now. Oscar, you stand behind me."

Once in the dining room, José hooked left and walked up to table twelve. Nicolás and Oscar stood just to his sides, with Lupe and Cassie just behind.

"Jake. I know what you did," José said with quiet force.

The chatter in the café fell, second by second, into silence. Nicolás could feel the eyes of the room upon him as he stared at Jake.

"Just what did I do?" Jake said, remaining seated. "Had a little accident, is all."

Cassie said, "I saw you overturn those chips and salsa on purpose, Jake."

"Jake, did you do this?" José said.

"Why don't you go back in there and just finish my meal?" Jake said, shaking his head, wincing with irritation.

"I'm sorry, Jake," said José. "You must now leave my business. You are never welcome here again."

Jake scraped his chair backward and rose to his feet. He stepped forward and stared at Nicolás.

"Look at this. Three wetbacks throwing me out. That one 'bout as legal as a bag of coke. And then a spiteful bitch who don't know what she had."

"I know what I had with you, Jake," Cassie said. "Or didn't have."

"You need to leave now," Nicolás said, hearing the diners whispering around him.

Jake stared hard into his eyes, as if sizing up the spirit within.

"*Vete de aquí*," Nicolás growled, pointing at the door.

Jake stared a moment longer, then tossed up his hands. "Awright, fine. You got me. I'll hit the road. Food was mediocre anyway."

"Get out of here now," Nicolás said, pointing at him. Louder whispers from the other patrons.

"Oh, you'll see me again, son," Jake nodded, laughing. "I assure you that."

Jake neared the front door, surely masking his humiliation with his sauntering gait, his scuffed cowhide boots falling with heavy thuds on the floorboards and down the concrete steps. The diners continued their whispering a moment longer, then resumed their chatter, eyeing their new neighbor with surprise.

Nicolás turned to his immediate left. José glared past him at the front doorway, drawing breath in and out through clenched teeth. His eyes turned in their sockets and met his, and the face softened. José nodded at him with pride.

"*Muy bueno, toro*," José said with a nod.

Toro? And not Pato? Bull, and not duck? Had he shaken off the nickname after all?

Nicolás turned. Oscar, Cassie, and Lupe farther behind were observing him with admiration and amusement.

His memory ushered into his mind a scene from that February, months before. Though Nicolás had only heard accounts of it, he imagined Padre Manolo standing, unarmed, that morning before his rectory. The Segundo Cortez henchmen Padre had just confronted broke their formation around Esteban and—staring with fury at the short, stalwart pillar of a priest—stepped back toward their parked Cadillac Escalade.

37

"So what would you have done if I hadn't left that card with my number beside my plate?" Cassie asked, cradling her Chardonnay, looking out from one of her upper deck's lounge chairs toward her expansive front lawn.

"I would have called Gabe for a ride," Nicolás said, sipping his Cabernet in the chair beside her. "Hung out with her a bit. So everyone in the kitchen guessed who I was calling on their phone. You have blown my cover."

"Oh well. It's worth it," Cassie said. "And Gabe is a great assistant. I wish she would stay for good."

"What do you mean?"

"I think I'll lose her soon. To Missoula, or Bozeman. Or Denver. Based on things she's said. It must be hell being a young lesbian in Bigfork, Montana, for God's sake."

"I can imagine," Nicolás said.

"So why were you ignoring me in the café?" she said. "Or at least pretending you hardly knew me?"

"I just—I just don't want to attract any more attention in this town than I already have."

"Nonsense," she said. "What do you have to worry about?"

His stomach grew queasy. She surely had no idea.

"I like what you've done with this big yard," he said. "All that dense grass. And that fence over there made of stacked stones."

"Why thanks. I'm going for a kind of sanctuary, I guess. You and Mitch can mow that grass and plant some flowers if you want. I'll pay you well."

"I'll do it," he said. "So I'm eager to see your home library you mentioned."

She said, "First, let's get refills. And we can play some music, dance a little."

"Now that sounds like an excellent proposition," Nicolás said.

They brought their glasses into the kitchen and she refilled them.

"I just...I just love it when you're here," she said.

That candor again. He loved it, and how it often came at random moments.

"You are so kind," he said. "I love being with you, as well."

Cassie set a glass plate on the marble counter, and upon it arranged some Havarti, Manchego, strawberries, and a dollop of honey.

"I can be myself around you," she said. "I feel free. I don't have to suppress anything. Like I had to around Jake. My education, my mind, the thoughts that hit me I'd like to express."

"With you I feel that comfort," he said. "I guess I feel that sense of kinship. You are intelligent, experienced. But you also have innocence, and that big heart. For animals, people..."

She smiled, a shy smile that lit up a blushing face, and said, "Come see the den."

Cassie set the plate down on the table between the two sofa chairs.

Something caught his eye, and he turned his head. A stretch

of bookshelves lined the wall, over five meters in height, and perhaps ten meters wide. They were bursting with paperbacks, magazines, periodicals, and hardbacks, some of them leather-bound.

"*Ay caramba,*" he said, breaking off and heading for the shelves.

"I had no idea you liked to read so much, Dr. Rivers. Or were so…literary."

"I'm sure you've noticed there's not much nightlife up here. And I've loved to read since I was a girl."

He perused the shelves. They contained much of the Western literary canon, a decent amount of contemporary fiction, many first-edition novels from the last century, much history, many biographies and autobiographies, a myriad of issues of the *New Yorker*. He pulled one from the shelf. She even had a subscription.

"You like that?" she called over to him from her sofa chair.

"I love it," Nicolás said. "Ha! You are just my type. So I see a lot of books by Jim Harrison. And about him. Who is that?"

"A good novelist to read," she said. "Especially if you're going to live out here."

Nicolás walked over and sat in the other padded chair beside the small round table, setting his wineglass down alongside the plate. Cassie took two remotes and pointed each at the large flat-screen against the wall, mashing her thumbs against the buttons.

"I knew you'd like my collection," she said, and then added with a knowing air, "But I know what you really need."

Music opened up all around them. Nicolás spotted a speaker in each of the ceiling's four corners. He recognized the song. There amidst the wilds of northwestern Montana, it was none other than—Maná. The band he had grown up to, the group that composed much of the soundtrack to his youth. At first it was the nineties, then the early two-thousands, there in that spacious den with the floors, paneled walls, and ceilings of polished, beautifully varnished wood echoing with melody.

"How's that?" she said. In her intelligent face glowed an unmistakable childlike enthusiasm.

Dancing, shimmering in his memory was a moment he had enjoyed, so long ago he had nearly forgotten it entirely. His portable stereo atop the towel on the Veracruz beach played that very song. His first girlfriend leaped to her feet and dashed giggling across the beach toward the surf and he pursued her. She sprinted into the waves, then dove and disappeared under them. He followed just behind. After a few seconds under the water his arms found and embraced her, and they rose until they reached the surface...

He looked out at the bookshelf and stood. Then Cassie stood with him. But he had already turned to her, taking in her face, and the sweet softness of its features. When she faced him in turn she brought up her hands, like she wanted to place them around his shoulders to dance. Across his shoulder blades, he could feel her palms and fingers stretching out. The moment he went for her lips, he felt those hands pushing him toward her.

On her warm lips was the faint taste of the Chardonnay, mingled with remnants of honey and strawberries. He recalled their first kiss, in that same house days before. Yet this one was different. This time her lips told him that they expected it with confidence—it was comfortable, where the first had been purely primal, a sating of a long-aching urge.

And there they were again, those tongues, warming what little coolness their mouths felt from the wine and berries. My, her taste was splendid indeed. He indulged a few moments more and then pulled his face back, just the slightest bit.

"So why did you get—why did you choose this? The music?" he said.

"I've liked it a long time. And figured you would, too."

"Many memories," he said.

"Hopefully good ones," she said as she held him, looking up with the slightest concern into his eyes.

"Yes, mostly," he said. "Joy and sadness. And comedy, but not without tragedy. The way life is, in general, I suppose."

"You should tell me about these memories," she said. "Later."

Their mouths came together fast, in almost violent kiss. And then they relaxed, enjoying each other.

He brought his hands to her jaw, cradling it with tenderness, as if he was holding some Faberge egg or crystal sculpture. It felt small in his hands. She was womanly indeed: soft and delicate yet strong in all the right places.

Almost by instinct, almost as if they shared some sort of telepathic union, they began at the very same second to shed each other's clothes. First the shirts, then everything below. Soon they stood running their eyes up and down, each enjoying with delight the unobscured vision of the other.

He knew she was taking him in, his flesh all sinew and hardness, as she looked down from his toes and up into his face. And with his gaze he aimed to absorb every bit of her, every cell. How different she was from all other women he had ever seen in the nude. The light auburn hair, somewhat wild, down to her shoulders. The eyes were a mystery: green, greenish hazel, greenish brown, he knew not which. The milky complexion, the orange freckles, few on the cheeks but spreading out in great number across the slender yet athletic shoulders. The full, round breasts with pink nipples. The thighs and calves, well defined but not quite thick, the delicate feet, slender and with green nail polish on the toes. He brought his eyes up to what he thought he had noticed: the touch of cellulite near the side of the upper left thigh, the few stretch marks about the abdomen. And running a few centimeters north from the trimmed, reddish-brown hair of the pubis, the faint yet unmistakable horizontal caesarean scar.

Yes, she was a woman beguiling to see in her most natural state, despite her flaws. The marks not of a girl but of a woman who had lived.

He drew himself nearer to her. They kissed again, caressing each other, combining the warmth of their bodies.

"I taste the cigarettes, but you're one great kisser. Hey, come with me," she said with a youthful giggle. She grabbed his hand and led him toward the stairwell, then broke free and ran up the stairs. He chased after her. The steps ended in a hallway. She burst into a room, and just upon her heels, he saw that it was her bedroom, all purple curtains and the scent of perfume. She tore off the duvet and leapt onto the bed, turning in midair and landing flat on her back. He jumped on top of her, landing on his palms, dangling just above her.

They licked, bit and tumbled across the bed—him on top, her on top, then lying on their sides facing each other, and then him laying behind her, breathing like a ravenous beast down her neck.

Eventually they lay immobile, their chests heaving, the sheets below them soaked. It seemed like no time at all had passed, but it must have been hours, as the room was now virtually pitch-black. It was the best sex he had ever had, yet they spoke not a word. Her hand found his, and he squeezed it and held it for some time, before he found himself stirring.

"Everything fine?" she said.

"I just need your bathroom."

"Down at the end of the hall, to the left."

Nicolás felt his way out the door, and hooked left. Down at the end of the hallway, in the scant light the stairwell let in from the den below, he saw a closed door on either side of him. He hesitated but opened the door on the right, stepping just inside. He felt for the light.

It was no bathroom. Cartoon drawings and Seahawks pennants covered the walls. Dressers against the walls were layered with dust.

In one corner was a small bed with a down comforter emblazoned with cartoons. The comforter and covers were torn back, as if someone had just risen from sleep.

A dust-coated rocking horse filled the opposite corner. He stood there, staring in the silence, until he heard her gasp behind him.

"No no no." He heard that whisper, both maternal and haunting at the same time, as she yanked his arm, pulling him back through the doorway. She slapped off the light switch, shut the door, then placed a hand on his shoulder and steered him back, away from the room and toward the door facing it. He imagined that this was how she would talk in her clinic to a small pet. Yet in her tone was a certain sadness.

She repeated it, twice. "No no no…no no no…."

"I—I'm sorry, Cass," Nicolás said.

"It's okay," she said, and walked back down the hall to her bedroom.

When he opened the bathroom door to leave, he saw that she had turned off the light downstairs. The hallway was completely dark. He stretched out a hand and felt his way down the corridor, then turned right into her bedroom. His hand found her bedpost. He lowered himself into the bed, and felt for her. She lay on her back. He rested his hand on her shoulder.

"Cassie—Cassie, I am sorry I…entered the wrong room."

"Don't be," she said. "You would have seen it eventually."

There was silence, for several seconds. "It happened three years ago. I was at work, and Jake took Sean in his truck, pulled up to the gas station, and went inside to get some milk. Left Sean in the truck. Locked it. I always asked Jake never to leave Sean alone in the truck."

Nicolás became aware of his front teeth pressing down on his tongue. Had the boy been abducted, murdered?

"Sean let himself out, ran across the parking lot. A bunch of UM fraternity kids—you know, University of Montana—were driving up to Glacier. And they swung around, looking to park." Cassie pronounced the last words in a whisper.

"And just as—right when Jake opened the door and stepped out of the gas station, and looked out at the parking lot, that's when their SUV, that's when it—"

Her next words were unintelligible. They were whimpers wet with tears.

And so her experience was the reverse of his. She was a parent who had lost her only child, and felt she could have prevented it. He was the child that had lost his parents, and his brother. And perhaps he could have prevented it all.

It was not solely her unpredictable candor; it was her demeanor and mannerisms, and her thirst for knowledge that caught his attention. But even more—she surely would not have guessed it, but her experiences pulled him so hard toward her. And her ensuing emotions that mirrored his: happiness, peace, defeat, loss, guilt, regret, loneliness, pain.

Yes. More than anything, he wanted to stop her pain. At least that.

He reached out and grabbed her other shoulder and turned her onto her side, facing him. Then he put his arm around her and pressed her chest into his, almost as hard as he could. Her cheek was warm and wet against his.

"Sean is gone, Cassie. That can't be changed. But I'm here, though. You have me here."

"Don't you know that—ah, I think I might love you, Aurelio."

The words spoken right up against his ear flooded him with joy and shame, all at the same time. He was so lucky and happy —and honored—to have the love of this woman. But this wounded soul risked becoming even more wounded. Once he returned to Veracruz, would he survive? And if so, would he make his way back to Bigfork?

38

The next day, after they hooked the boat into the trailer, Nicolás, Mitch and Gabe stood in the parking lot beside Flathead Lake.

"Sparrin', fishin', then shootin'. Now that's what I call an active day," Mitch said. "How do y'all feel?"

"Amazing," Gabe said. "You, Pato?"

"I will tell you how it is that I feel," Nicolás said. "I am twenty again. And my summer break from university's just begun."

"That's one helluva feeling, bud," Mitch said. "I remember that feeling."

"How's the soreness?" Gabe said, grinning and raising her eyebrows above her sunglasses, giving off an impish air.

"It's there, I can feel it," Nicolás said. "Apart from that and my lack of sleep, I feel fantastic."

"Well, look," Mitch said, "it was a hard sparring, thirty minutes of it. Not your first, but you know. With me and Gabe both tradin' off, no easy feat."

"You'll get better," Gabe said. "Just keep at it."

"We should do that every morning," Mitch said. "Or every

evening. Ever heard that line by Woody Allen? Eighty percent of success is had just by showing up every day."

"And I know why you couldn't sleep, Nick," Gabe said. "Mitch told me all about it. When did you finally get home, lover boy?"

"Around seven, eight in the morning," said Nicolás.

"Uh huh. Dr. Rivers finally finds her man," Gabe said in a disillusioned, almost defeated tone. "But I'm happy for you, bud."

"Gabriella's jealous," Mitch said. "Got her eyes on all the single women here in town, Nick. Not many of 'em here."

"Speaking of," Gabe said. "Why don't we cap off the day in Missoula? At The Rhinoceros? We've been cooped up here far too long."

"That's an idea," Mitch said.

"So why don't we go together to Glacier," Gabe said. "Pato has his new ID card. And it's just north of us. I was thinking we could go camping in a few weeks."

"Very true," Mitch said. "But how 'bout you see if you both can get off tomorrow and Saturday? We could even try to see if Cassie could come. And of course, Kat."

"Sometimes Cassie shuts the office down on Saturdays," Gabe said. "Or gets Shelda to work. Shelda's this other assistant who fills in time to time. But Mitch, I know what you are up to with Kat and your Marmot tent."

"Who, me?" Mitch said with a broad grin. "So Pato, you know this is one of the preeminent fishing lakes in the northwest? Under these waves we got whitefish, lake trout. And northern pike, bull trout. This and Lake Koocanusa to the northwest of here, by the Salish Mountain range. I like going for the kokanee salmon up there."

As Mitch spoke, Nicolás became aware of the nagging pang in his soul. He truly missed Cassie. And that was why he could not sleep much, there in the guest bedroom. In so many ways, she was so unlike the women he had gone with before in Mexico. And it was not merely physical. She was ten years older than him and had more to say than a younger woman—more memories, more experiences, more opinions. He missed the timbre of her voice, her candor and depth, her mannerisms. In his mind, he tried to replay them.

But what bothered Nicolás is what Cassie sometimes called him: Aurelio. She was one of those with whom he must live that lie. He could divulge to her his actual name, and the true reason for his arrival in their midst. He could tell her about Esteban, his parents, Juan, Carla, the Méndez clan. Or he could not, and let her fall off, and distance himself from her, which might be better for her. He did not know what the next few years held. After he returned to Veracruz, got his just revenge, and then returned to America, should he stay on the shores of this beautiful lake? Or should he leave his new friends, move west or east and melt into a vast American city and become invisible?

If he returned to America to settle, this is where it should be. It was confirmed again, far down within his core. He had not imagined a place like this as he lay in the dark cavern of the semi hurtling north and west through Mexico.

He did know something, though. By committing that arson weeks ago, he had truly crossed the Rubicon with Segundo Cortez. Nicolás loved that old expression, a reference to an ancient Roman war.

How irate Ivan Méndez must be at this hour. The class bookworm had burned one of the properties of the class bully's father. Then given him a heart attack, and then vanished. It was more than he had hoped for, when lighting that first Molotov cocktail.

Nicolás lifted his eyes from the waves dancing beside the truck, and gazed through the trees, then stared south. Far into that horizon, between the mountains and the gulf, mere kilometers from the jungle, with its crumbling Toltec and Olmec ruins, Ivan Méndez had to be writhing inside, in agony and fury, like a wounded serpent.

In this, Nicolás knew he took sick delight. Never in his life had he taken pleasure in the failure or pain of a fellow human. But Segundo Cortez had changed all of that. And soon, Esteban and his parents would achieve some of what they had hoped for, through him. He would return, if for a short while, and strike back. At least he was still in the fight, by surviving and preparing. Segundo Cortez, and its partner in the Veracruz police, would never expect the new Nicolás Nolano.

Though he knew his resolve had wavered in certain moments, he knew it was his mission, and his fate. It was fixed, it was set within him, and not just because of the murder of Esteban, his mother and Padre Manolo. The vibrant, life-celebrating city of his childhood and youth needed him. Veracruz suffered horribly under what was in effect a death cult. And like Esteban had urged him, now was the time to give back. It was her time of need.

He must cut out her cancer. Or at least slow it from metastasizing. He had to get Ivan, and even better, the top command along with him.

After they filled Mitch's truck with fishing gear, catches and all, Mitch headed north, skirting the eastern shore of the lake on Route 35.

"How about some more of the ole MIT 101?" Mitch half-said, half-sang in a folksy accent.

"The Mitch Intensive Training 101," Nicolás said. "Let's go."

"Well, it's the way to learn, bud. First let's stop at my place on the way," Gabe said. "Want to bring something."

Upon arriving in Bigfork, Mitch turned into the gravel lot of an apartment complex.

"You guys come up," she said. At her door, she giggled. "My two boys! The only men ever allowed into my place."

The walls inside were covered with license plates from various states, and two posters, one of k.d. lang, and one of Tupac Shakur. Christmas lights lined the perimeter of the ceiling, and stuffed animals lay on the couch.

"You and Freedom secretly are twins, separated at birth," Nicolás said.

She laughed. "You figured it out. Now make yourselves at home. Just gotta grab something."

She disappeared into her bedroom and returned a few seconds later toting a green canvas duffel bag.

"All right, got my range bag. Now we're talkin'."

At the house, Mitch and Nicolás placed the ice chests in the kitchen. Mitch then unlocked his garage and they loaded three rifle boxes into the truck, along with an ammo can and a range bag of loaded magazines.

They spent all afternoon at the Kalispell range. In between shooting their own WASRs, Mitch and Gabe ensured Nicolás had fully mastered loading and shooting his own, as well as the two pistols, Gabe's .40 caliber semiautomatic Glock and Mitch's .45 Colt Commander. By the end of the afternoon, Nicolás's marksmanship with all three arms had drawn many compliments.

Back in the kitchen, Gabe taught Nicolás how to gut and fillet the fish. Mitch opened the fridge, and his head disappeared behind the door. The sound of bottles clinking together filled the kitchen.

"No, hon," Gabe said with resolution, but without force. "No, Mitchell. Take a break from that, all right?"

He hesitated and then closed the door.

"Awright, Ma," Mitch said. "She mothers me, Nick."

"It's a good thing," Nicolás said. "She loves you, Mitch. And now, I insist on taking over. I have much cooking in my past. And now in my present."

"Fair enough, bud," Gabe said. "Holler if you need me." She headed into the den and joined Mitch in front of the flat-screen.

Nicolás knew where Mitch stored the relevant pans, cooking utensils, and spices. But first he would have to assess what ingredients lay in the refrigerator. He opened the door. Thankfully, many options were at hand. He rolled up his sleeves, washed his hands, and set to work. A calm, suffused with a sense of joy, settled over him. Cooking had that effect, every time.

"How's it goin' in there, Julia Child?" Mitch called from the den.

"You will see, Mitchell," Nicolás said with an air of bravado. "Just whatever you do, don't peek until I let you know it is prepared. You will spoil it."

Twenty minutes later, Nicolás shouted, *"Buen provecho!"*

Mitch and Gabe swooped into the kitchen, their faces brightened with childlike excitement. On the round kitchen table lay three settings, displaying three identical offerings of pan-fried fish fillets, squash medallions dusted with cayenne and garlic salt, and a small kale and carrot salad, dusted with blue cheese and apple cubes.

"Hot damn, look at this," Gabe said, lowering herself into a seat. "Very nice, Nick."

"If it tastes as good as it looks, we're in for some treat," Mitch said, sitting along with Nicolás. "The smell was driving us crazy."

"And now for a toast," Nicolás said. "To good friends, and to a long safe life enjoying all the West can offer."

"I'll toast to that," Mitch said, as all three clinked water glasses.

"We need a blessing," Gabe said, and they joined hands. Though he did not know the exact words in English, Nicolás recognized the Lord's Prayer, the Pater Noster. And Gabe's last lines, different in content from what he had known:

And lead us not into temptation,
But deliver us from evil.

Nicolás shivered. Where at this moment was Ivan Méndez? What was he plotting? What was he planning for him?

"You believer, you," Mitch said to Gabe. "You haven't had your faith broken. Still holdin' on to those old myths."

"Hadn't we agreed not to discuss faith, Mitch?" Gabe said.

"Opium of the masses," Mitch muttered, barely audible.

"But in the United States," Nicolás said. "Are there not centuries of tolerating various religions, kind of a gentleman's agreement? Yes, enshrined in your Constitution?"

"Ah yes, now, music to my ears," Mitch said. "Now you are referencing my Bible."

"He's probably got the entire document memorized," Gabe said.

"True, I should be more respectful," Mitch said. "It's just that I feel comfortable around my friend here, Pato. And I detest organized religion. But there are many reasons that Constitution, though it's flawed, is the longest one in effect in the world. One reason: freedom to worship as you please.

"I may be an agnostic, and may get highly annoyed at religion," Mitch said with passion. "But what I hate is when people fight over religion or one faith fights another. What a waste. So—do you believe, Pato?"

"In a personal God? In a life after death? I have before, somewhat, many years ago," answered Nicolás, staring down into his plate. He recalled glimpsing the red-tailed hawk just as he was about to surrender to death in the desert weeks before. And the red-tailed-hawk feather necklace of Kwewu, the one man who came through for him the following day. "Lately I'm growing more open-minded. In Arizona, I might have received a sign or two. But have you ever looked at religion as a sort of—artistic expression, if you will?"

"What do you mean?" Gabe said.

"An effort by a certain culture," Nicolás said, "whether they know it or not, to express themselves in an artistic way. But instead of in paint or in film or on paper, they do it with symbols. And hymns, and mythological, fantastical figures. And rituals. Whether one is a believer, agnostic, or atheist, I say religion can be a very beautiful thing."

"I suppose you're right," Mitch said. "But I ultimately believe in three things. Myself. The great friends I feel I can trust. And the U.S. Constitution. Beyond that, I'm not holding out hope in any hereafter, or forgiveness or punishment."

"Pato, I think you might feel even more enlightenment, pretty soon," Gabe said. "Pastor Wachter's worship service with Parker Wade—Burning Elk—and some of the Flatheads. In three days. I'm going."

"I'm sure not," Mitch said. "But I think it might be a good thing for you to see, though, Pato. For the native side of it."

"You have not yet tried the meal," Nicolás said. "I want your thoughts."

They all three delved in.

"Cervantes," Mitch said. "You have found your niche."

"Wow," Gabe said, her eyes closed in ecstasy. "Yep, you found your calling."

"And this fish," Mitch began. "Okay, so I'll attribute ten percent of its deliciousness to its freshness. And those pristine waters. But the other ninety is raw talent."

"Thanks, bud," Nicolás said.

"Bud! Now you're learnin'!" Mitch said, slapping Nicolás's shoulder. "Hell, I'd like to see what you do with some of the local game. It's in my freezer in the garage. I can thaw out some for you. Elk, deer, geese, duck. I hunted it all last year. Lots of salmon in there, too. Caught it myself."

They finished their meal and retired to the den. Mitch found them a film on Netflix: *Jeremiah Johnson*. An hour through it, Nicolás drifted off to sleep. When he woke, the room was dark. Mitch and Gabe were gone. And he felt in his soul a profound longing to return to his homeland.

He still recalled fragments of his dream. He was a boy and he was walking with Esteban on the beach in Veracruz. They followed Doña Lucinda, walking ahead of them in the distance. It was a summer morning, warm and brilliant. The sky darkened until a chilly, dense fog formed on the beach ahead. Phantom ships appeared offshore, nearly transparent as they moved on the horizon. Soon the fog engulfed him and Esteban and they could see nothing.

He wiped his eyes and headed over to the other sofa. He booted up the laptop, eager to read the Mexican news. Then he remembered the Segundo Cortez YouTube channel.

After ensuring the volume was not turned too high, he clicked the link. His heart thudded with violence inside his chest.

At first there was static. A figure came into view, sitting at a desk across the room. The lens zoomed in. Ivan Méndez was dressed in a black suit, and an open-necked, white button-down Oxford shirt. He was smiling, but his black eyes narrowed, flashing with menace.

"I am Ivan Méndez. You should know that if you challenge Segundo Cortez cartel, or you incite rebellion against her, you will end up a movie star of sorts. You will star in your very own video on our Segundo Cortez YouTube channel. And you'll be crying like an infant, as you're butchered like a calf."

Static filled the screen. Then it was flooded with dim light. Two dark male hands appeared. One hand ran a blade, almost a meter long, up and down a sharpening rod held in the other hand. Nicolás had never seen anything like it, a blade halfway between a knife and a sword. It was shorter than a machete, but as thick as a samurai sword. The video ended. He saw that it had more unlikes than likes, and each of the two figures numbered in the tens of thousands.

He clicked on another video. A room, a study vaguely familiar to him. Then a figure in a chair, his hands bound behind him. Nicolás could see that this man, whoever he was, was drawing and releasing heavy breaths. The camera zoomed until the captive's face came into view.

It was his vice chancellor from the university, his mouth bound with duct tape, the eyes contorting in an expression of intense fear. That same strange blade appeared before the lens. Nicolás exited out of the screen as fast as he could, feeling a wave of nausea rise and then crest within his stomach.

Mitch's house was silent, but for the wind coursing through the aspens, firs, and spruces just outside the den window. Nicolás placed the laptop on the sofa and ran in his socks into the guest bedroom, then into its bathroom. Flicking the light switch on, he fell to his knees before the toilet, heaving up his trout dinner.

39

Today had already become the worst day of his life. At least the worst that he could recall, Pantano thought, as he drove the Mercedes sedan through the late night's mist toward the Méndez hacienda.

He should call him again. At least one more time.

"Why do you call again?" Ivan answered.

"Ivan," Pantano said. "We had a pact. An agreement, of honor. Or is there no honor among thieves like us?"

"Reckless move to insult me at this point, Chucho Pantano," Ivan said.

"Ivan, just let him go. Please, man. He didn't know what he was doing."

"This one will die," Ivan said, and then laughed. "And a grim death. Unless you get over here and pull one hell of a negotiation. And maybe prove your loyalty."

"Ivan—"

"You might want to hurry. I'm feeling antsy. I just might dispatch your guy in the next thirty."

"I'm driving as fast as I can. This will all be okay again, soon. Do not touch a hair on his head."

"Well, we already have. He is still alive though."

"No more. Do you hear? I will be there," Pantano said, then ended the call.

He had to go in person. It was his youngest cop on the force. And the son of his good friend. Once upon a time, many complimented him on his skill at negotiations. Had that utterly vanished, along with his bravery and honor? Would it not be better for him to take out a larger life insurance policy and provoke Ivan enough into finishing him off? Now there was an idea...

Damn Ivan for ruining the city, and damn Nicolás Nolano for ruining his life. Would Arturo, watching from the next life, understand if he one day killed both Ivan and Nolano?

As he turned down the hacienda's lane, the caravan of cartel SUVs came into view. His heart beat even faster. Every cell within his body revolted against his actions, signaling grave danger. Truly he was descending into what might as well be the nethermost reaches of hell.

He sensed this would be his last night. But he could not abandon Morales to these devils. If Morales were to die, he would have to die alongside him. If only he had taken out a larger policy...

A squad of about eight men, rifles in hand, emerged from both sides of the road and approached. Pantano allowed the Mercedes to coast several meters toward them, and he then eased onto the brake. The squad divided and each half approached a side of his car.

"Pull over there and come with us," a man said. "*Señor* Méndez is expecting you, of course."

Pantano parked the car beside the road. The man frisked him as the others surrounded him, grinning at him in silence.

He had not even left his pistol in the car, but instead at the station, after the night's first phone conversation with Ivan. And he knew full well the risks of being without it.

As the stocky man led him up the pathway to the front of the hacienda, Pantano took in the full view of its orange-red seventeenth-century baroque façade. He hoped to live to appreciate such beauty again, in other architecture, in art, and above all, in the faces of Raquel and their children and his grandchild. Yet he knew it from his core—this night truly was his last.

The hacienda foyer was cool, a welcome comfort.

"You know the way, Pantano," the man said, pointing toward the closed door. "The study, of course."

The man opened the door and ushered him in. His heart surged into an even faster rhythm as he crossed the threshold.

At the far end of the room was something entirely new: an altar covered with lit candles. Attached to the wall beyond was a tapestry of a skeleton in woman's robes, holding a skull. *Santa Muerte*, the trendy saint of cartel leaders and foot soldiers. Saint Death. The mere look of it was evil. Absolutely disgusting—and chilling.

Ivan sat behind his antique desk, sprinkling a line of white powder onto the lacquered oak top.

"And he arrives," Ivan said, with an air of sarcasm as he pulled the thin tube from his shirt pocket.

Three meters before him, two guards were mopping up a pool of blood on the floorboards.

"I suppose you missed the show," Ivan said. "My first assassination attempt from within my own organization. Eduardo attacked me. I ended up dispatching him myself. I tested him, and he failed me. Ordered him to kill his childhood friend, and he refused, then went for me."

He snorted the line of white into his nostril. "Pantano, you know this was rolled from the first dollar I ever won in a cartel hit for my father? I never told him that. But ah, Father would be so disappointed in this. And on his desk. Damn it, *Papá*. But he will soon be proud. My methods will be different. But my achievements will be greater, Pantano."

"Ivan," Pantano said. "You must let Morales go. He's a good man. He's one of my best, and you and I did have an agreement. What did Morales do to make you do this?"

Ivan's eyes peered straight into his: a strange amalgam of fiery intensity, a certain calculating quality, and the slightest sliver of humor. That same condescending amusement.

"Bring in the cop now," Ivan said, as he continued to stare at Pantano for several more seconds. "I got tired of the agreement you created, Pantano. And an agreement is no longer needed between us."

"Why is that?" Pantano said.

"Because," said Ivan, staring hard with a perverse smile, "this is your last night alive."

A sharp chill spread through every centimeter of Pantano's body. His instinct proved correct.

Three knocks sounded at the door.

"*Entra*," Ivan said. "But first a little reunion."

In the doorway a guard appeared, then entered, followed by Morales, limping in his bloodstained uniform, his face cut and bruised, an eye black and shut. Two guards brought up the rear, one with his hand around the nape of Morales's neck. Pantano saw that the man with the hand on his neck was in fact Raúl, who pushed his captive forward until he collided with Pantano, who caught and held Morales's weak body upright.

"I'm here, Diego," Pantano whispered.

"You will pay for this," Pantano said, snarling at Ivan, "unless you let us go this minute. Then all will be forgiven. We can start over."

"Why would I do that?" Ivan said with a shrug. "Or care?

You're no longer needed. You're an impediment. Can't you comprehend that?"

"Raúl," Ivan said, gesturing with a toss of his chin toward Pantano.

Instinct urged him to turn his head toward the *sicario*. There was that face again, broad like a lion's, hair preened up off its forehead, the eyes dead and devoid of emotion except for a hint of fury. His vision went blurry, then dark, as a fierce blow collided with his cheekbone and he fell.

He came to. Morales lay somewhere close beside him, screaming in outrage, then desperation, then despair. Feet kicked Pantano from what seemed like all sides.

"Kill him!" Ivan screamed. "First kick the hell out of them, damn it!"

"You won't see the end of this year," Pantano gasped. "Little boy. With his father's gun."

The beating ceased. Sheer silence filled the room, but for the guards and Morales panting, out of breath.

"Show it to him first, Raúl," he heard Ivan say. Something cold and hard slapped his face, and he creaked open an eye. The *sicario* stood a meter from them. He leaned over with a smile, showing them the glistening blade nearly as long as a machete's.

The door burst open.

"Ivan! Ivan! Stop this minute!" a female voice shrieked.

Once again, dead silence, but for that same labored breathing.

"You touch them in any way again, and you're dead to me, Ivan," she said. "And you can go live elsewhere."

Pantano knew that voice. After decades, it remained much the same, still retaining its high, girlish register. He blinked the blood and sweat from his eyelashes and turned. Inma was standing below the threshold.

That recent dream returned to him. The Virgin Mary, then

Magdalene, then the third figure. The blurry image in the clothes from decades before. That figure had been Inma, his first flame, after all.

"Very well. Get those two to Pantano's car," Ivan said. "Now. Then let them go."

Pantano grabbed Morales around the arm and helped lift him to his feet.

"Though you don't deserve to be released," Ivan said. "Particularly you, old man."

Those two words grated in Pantano's ears. Such disrespect, so much as of late, from so many. He could not resist a retort.

"We deserve to be released, at least one time," Pantano said, lifting his chin at the man who was still his captor. "Know why?"

"Oh?" Ivan said, arching an eyebrow. "Enlighten me."

"You remember that scar around your father's right ankle," Pantano said, "God rest his soul."

"How dare you bring him up," Ivan said.

"He and I were ambushed, back when we were partners," Pantano said. "I made it out, but Arturo got his ankle caught in barbed wire. I shot my way back in and helped get him out of there. Saved his life. Ask Inma."

Ivan shot a fevered glance at his mother. "Is he lying?"

"He speaks the truth, Ivan," Inma said. "He saved your father's life."

"He was my best friend," Pantano said. "Perhaps in the next life, our sins all wiped clean—we will be best friends again."

Ivan paused. "Enough, Chucho Pantano. Sentimental fool. Get Morales and leave."

Pantano grabbed Morales again by the arm and pushed him toward the door. As they approached the threshold, Pantano's eyes found Inma's. In her gaze was both relief and what he had detected weeks before at the hospital—an unmistakable hurt that had never dissipated.

40

As they sipped coffee in the garage, Mitch watched Nicolás loading, unloading, and then cleaning a WASR rifle and WASR pistol. After Nicolás cleaned both firearms, he placed them onto the table's spread.

He would tell Mitch of the videos from the night before. Raising his eyebrows and tilting his chin downward, he cleared his throat.

"I have kept you informed," Nicolás said, "of all that is going on with Segundo Cortez and myself. Last night I checked the cartel's YouTube channel. There were two videos with many comments, likes and unlikes. One showed Ivan Méndez personally issuing threats against dissidents. It ends with someone's hands sharpening this long blade. Almost like a shorter samurai sword."

"All right," Mitch said, "I'm trackin'."

"The next one I cut off after about three seconds. It shows a hand gripping that same blade and approaching the vice chancellor of the university where I taught. In his face, you could see the greatest fear imaginable. I had to shut the video off after three seconds."

"It would have been poison, Nick," Mitch said. "Good move."

"I would enjoy seeing them suffer," Nicolás said, his arms crossed, shaking his head. "Anyway, again, if Méndez ever mentions me, I promise not to reply in any way."

"So what's the reaction in Mexico to these posts, from what you can tell?" Mitch said.

"There are tens of thousands of comments to his post. Tens of thousands of unlikes. Slightly less likes."

"Those are the very sick, you know," Mitch said.

"The Internet, social media," Nicolás said. "They're pretty complex inventions. Think about it. They provide the means—and it was impossible years ago—to give an immediate, worldwide audience to the sick, the insane, the evil and twisted. Good news is that the good can employ the same tools—for justice, for what's good, to create."

"Well, well, well," Mitch said. "Listen to you!"

"I suppose I have not yet lost the mantle of idealist," Nicolás said.

"Problem is," Mitch said, "I do think it's too risky to battle those bastards in cyberspace. To use social media against them. Somehow it would divulge your location."

Nicolás nodded.

The sound of crunching gravel under tires met his ears.

"She's here," Nicolás said. They set down their mugs and walked outside.

"Well, look who's up early again," Gabe shouted across her passenger's seat and out her rolled-down passenger window. "Doing the old MIT 101?"

"Of course," Mitch said. "We just finished. Trying to get more sessions in. I start up as a guide inside two weeks."

"So you're rejoining the proletariat," Nicolás said.

"What's that?" Gabe said.

"Ah, nothing," Nicolás said. "How are you this morning, Gabriella?"

"Not bad. It's Friday, after all. Looking forward to my last workday this week. You boys still up for Glacier tomorrow?"

"Totally," Mitch said. "Think we can get Cassie and Kat to make it, too?"

"We'll have to see what the good doc says," she said. "But she'll probably want someone to stay behind. Don't know if she has any appointments scheduled for tomorrow. Well, we have to head out or we'll be late. Will let you know what the girls say about tomorrow."

"And I'll let you two know if I can get off of work myself," Nicolás said.

As the Hyundai rolled out of the driveway and down the road, for some reason, he recalled Cassie's son.

"I know what I have wanted to tell you," Nicolás said. "About Cassie."

Gabe kept her eyes on the road but leaned toward him.

"She told me about Sean, her little boy," Nicolás said. "She told me everything."

Gabe blew air out of her lips and said, "Oh God, that. That was horrendous. I loved him very much. I babysat him a few times."

She paused for several seconds. He could hear her swallow, one time.

"Jake and Cassie were still together at that point, of course. But their marriage was already very strained. It wouldn't have lasted. You know, that little boy was everything to me."

Nicolás stared through the windshield, but could hear tears in her voice. Embarrassment crept over him.

"Thank you for sharing this, Gabe. You know that it wasn't your fault."

"That doesn't matter," she whispered after several seconds.

"Jake never could live it down. Or live easily with himself after that. And Cassie couldn't live with him. It was cooked. Hard to say, though, when I look at it and try to be objective…who takes it harder. Cassie or Jake."

Gabe pulled into the parking lot of the café, rolled along the side of the building and parked near the back door.

"Guilt and regret are the most difficult," Nicolás said. "Whoever feels them more, Cassie or Jake, is the one suffering the most."

"Not ours to know," Gabe said, looking out of her driver's window. "Pick you up right here at five."

"Thank you, Gabe," Nicolás said, as he stepped out of the car and shut the door.

In the kitchen, his stomach, still queasy from the story of Sean's death, was somewhat calmed by the sound of Mexican music. But not just ordinary music from his home country. It was *son jarocho* music, from Mexico's eastern coast. Perhaps José had chosen it just for him.

"*Te gusta?*" José asked. Nicolás smiled back, as memories rushed back inside him.

"*Claro que sí, Señor,*" Nicolás said.

"So how was yesterday? Do anything nice?" José asked.

"Mitch and Gabe took me fishing. On a boat, on Flathead Lake. Then I cooked them our catches, along with a salad and squash I prepared, in a certain style, of course."

"Ah hah," José said, his hands on his hips.

"José," said Nicolás. "Would it be possible for me to take off tomorrow and the next day. For a camping trip with Mitch and Gabe in Glacier?"

"Late notice, Nicolás," José said, and paused. "Sure. I take it you've never seen the park?"

"Never," Nicolás said.

"Well. You are in for a treat. It's like heaven. And so," José said, turning and walking farther into the kitchen. "Oscar here did well yesterday. He's learning fast. I want you to each cook a dish today. See where you both stand so far, who is the better chef. I've been investing in you guys. I know you will both be good."

"All right then," Nicolás said as he glanced at Oscar, who looked up with a shy smile as he wiped the countertop.

"Now get some of these breakfast tacos, over here," he said. "Oscar already had his."

"*Papas, tocino, machaca, huevos*," José sang in a falsetto. "Bad for the arteries. Good for that big Latin heart."

The lunch crowd flitted by, much faster than normal, with no fireworks or even mild surprises. After José locked the front door, he reappeared in the kitchen.

"*Pues, caballeros*," José called. They looked up, Nicolás from chopping onions, Oscar from the tray of dishes he was at the point of loading into the dishwasher. José pulled a cigar and clipper from a drawer near his workstation. "Come join me out back for a bit. Take a break. Relax. Grab a real cola, if you want."

Oscar withdrew a cold Mexican Coca-Cola from the refrigerator and glanced at Nicolás, who gave a polite nod of his head. Once they gathered out back, José placed the cigar between his lips and rotated it over his lighter, ensuring it was evenly lit.

"Lupe and I are about to retire, probably next year. I want to keep the restaurant open. I can replace a server easily. And find someone with papers who can serve *cerveza*. No offense meant. But I will need a full-time chef. I could really use three just in the kitchen. A dishwasher, a chef, and a sous-chef."

"*Sí, Señor*," Nicolás said.

"Well, I need to have full confidence in the person I make chef. And the sous-chef must substitute at times for the chef. So I'll be looking at you two more closely for these roles. I know you're both interested. And sometimes I think of opening up a small place in Coram or in West Glacier, right by that main entrance to the park. It would get great traffic. Maybe not as many regulars, at least at first, but lots of diners."

"I can imagine so," Nicolás said.

What a pleasant development. This might not be such a bad Montana future. If I return alive from my crucible, of course, in Veracruz.

"In which case, if you both pass the test, over the next several months, I could have one of you here, and offer the other guy the kitchen up north. But this is just a dream at this point, is still just an idea. A hope."

Oscar nodded, and continued to sip his Coca-Cola. José and Nicolás then discussed possible changes to the menu. When his cigar had burned down to a stub, José tossed it onto the asphalt. "Come with me, men. I have an idea."

Inside they paused by the front workstations.

"Aurelio, you take this position. And Oscar, you get this workstation. Do you know the specialty of the house? What is it?"

"*Pues, el bistec a la tampiqueña?*" Oscar said.

"I would say the *puerco adovado*," Nicolás said.

"I think you are equally correct. Hell, it's all good when done by our hands, no? Oscar, I want you to cook me a small portion of the *tampiqueña*. And Aurelio, you cook me the *puerco adovado*. Hard to say which one I love more. And I'll do a little taste test. Then we all eat the rest and we get us some bowls of that *caldo* in the fridge. *Bueno*, ingredients are in the usual spot, *caballeros*."

Nicolás and Oscar glanced at each other and each released a laugh, each very similar to the other, not a nervous laugh but instead of giddy amusement. It instantly struck Nicolás as both something off of a film, and as something quite unique. It was the first time he had ever heard Oscar laugh.

José retreated into the dining room to wipe down the tables

and to sweep the floors. Then he sat down at one of the tables and with a pen, ledger and calculator, he set into his bookkeeping.

Nicolás finished first. After placing a tiny portion onto a saucer and tasting it—and ensuring that the lid properly crowned the pot of seasoned pork tips—he slapped his hand onto the small kitchen bell. Three minutes later, Oscar pulled the pot from the oven and, onto a platter, he spooned the steaming contents: steak strips, caramelized onions, kosher salt, black pepper, minced garlic, bell pepper, Roma tomatoes and cilantro, all blanketed with melted cheese and green chile strips. Oscar placed a clean fork into the dish and scraped some in turn onto a saucer. He rolled around a bite of it in his mouth, and then after ten seconds, slapped his hand on the bell.

José appeared in the threshold to the kitchen. Oscar shot them both a sheepish smile, for once showing his crooked, chipped teeth, and then stared with anticipation at the stovetop where both creations lay. José pulled a plate out of the cupboard and spooned a larger portion of each dish onto opposing sides of the plate. He first tried a large bite of the *bistec a la tampiqueña*, his jaw working slowly, his eyes closed in concentration. Then he cleared his throat and ran a spoon under one of Nicolás's pork tips and its accompanying crimson sauce and brought it to his mouth. He chewed slowly, his eyes shut for several seconds.

"Very, very close between the two of you, *caballeros*. A difficult decision. I would say Oscar, yours gets an eight-point seven. Aurelio, yours gets a nine-point three."

"*Hombre*," Nicolás said, drawing out the two syllables in disbelief. José nodded at him with pride. Nicolás looked over at Oscar, and noticed that he could not raise his eyes from the floor. Oscar's shoulders slumped inward as he took two long strides, pivoted, and resumed his place behind the dishwasher. Leaning slightly forward, Oscar seemed exhausted, as if he had lost all energy and hope in one stinging defeat. He propped himself against the dishwashing station, his shoulders still sloping inward like an archer's bow. On his face was an expression of half shame, half exhaustion.

Nicolás could not contain his unexpected thought: "But wait, José. It's not completely fair. I have cooked Mexican cuisine for over a decade, since I was twenty-two or so. He just started cooking Mexican cuisine several days ago, right? Right?"

Oscar's eyes lit up and he nodded. José looked more intrigued than anything.

Nicolás said, "But no one up here is Salvadoran, am I right? No one around the lake?"

"No," Oscar said. "I have never met a Salvadoran in Montana."

"So Oscar, why don't you make us some *pupusas*. If you can somehow make those thicker tortillas, and what goes inside, you can improvise?"

Oscar again gave that shy smile as he looked down at the dishwasher tray full of plates. "*Pues...pues...está bien.*"

"So José," said Nicolás. "How about if you can pass by the grocery store soon, and Oscar can get any ingredients he would need? He may want rice flour for his tortilla. And just see what he comes up with."

"I can do that," José said. "I'm interested to see what he cooks up. Never had Salvadoran food. Only seen Salvadoran *fútbol*, their team. When I was younger, in Mexico."

And with that, Oscar looked and moved like a new person. He loaded the tray into the dishwashing machine with gusto, almost with pleasure.

José looked askance at Nicolás and gave him a warm slap on the side of the shoulder.

"Young man, you are a unique one. You're harder to figure

you out than I expected. Hey, what's wrong? What's eating at you, *mijo?*"

"You remind me of Mexico," Nicolás said. "The Mexican food here does, too. Don't mind me. I'm just missing my family. I'm missing my hometown."

José stared, nodding, his eyes searching those of Nicolás.

41

"So I am happy that I finally experienced Glacier," Nicolás said. "And now we are up to five fish."

"Well, we did make it to Logan's Pass," Mitch said. "But there's so much more to see in this park. It's so very vast. You've just glimpsed the tip of the iceberg, guy. There's Porcupine Ridge, Mount Cleveland, lot of points off the beaten path. Really wish Gabe didn't push so hard for that church event tomorrow night. We could really see this park. Then head back before dawn on Monday."

As he and Mitch stood on the ridge, Nicolás squinted through the midafternoon sunlight down at Lake McDonald below, then turned left and eyed Cassie, Gabe and Kat as they fished on the distant shore. He said, "And so—I think it's time Cassie becomes the third Bigforker to be let in on my secret."

"I think you're wise to tell her, Nick," Mitch said.

"You know she can be trusted," Nicolás said. "If I can't tell Cassie, I've got to disengage now, surrender any relationship with her. And stop sleeping with her, of course. But if I tell her now, at least she knows what she'll be getting with me. Or risking."

"I know you can trust her," Mitch said. "Gabe knows this,

too. I never was good with women, dating, love, and all that. But I do know that much."

"I will tell her today," Nicolás said. "So it seems like you and Kat are getting along nicely. Growing closer, from what I have observed today back on the trails."

Mitch laughed under his breath. "So far, so good. Don't jinx me."

He turned away from Nicolás and walked back down toward the shore. Several meters beside Cassie and Gabe stood Kat, smiling at Mitch as he approached.

Cassie turned, as if she could read her lover's thoughts, and faced him. An expression of concern surfaced in her eyes and she motioned for him to join her. He broke from his stance on the ridge and started down the hill.

Nicolás pulled up alongside her and draped his arm around her shoulder as they looked out at the waves. "Never can I recall, as an adult, Cass, feeling such peace and hope as I have on this day."

"Well," she said and giggled, "when the main roadway here is named Going-to-the-Sun Road, what should you expect?"

"I feel what I felt as a child: almost complete equilibrium."

It was not a lie. He felt it—in their union, there was balance. Though cultural opposites, they were two wounded souls who identified with each other's goodness. And to an extent, their naiveté and their past traumas.

He could hold steady in this moment, reveal nothing, and it would remain blissful. But he knew that night, or the next day, he would regret not divulging all of the truth.

"Except one thing gnaws at me, Cassie."

She turned toward him. He was already staring into her eyes.

"What, Pato? You are getting the urge again?" She cuddled up to him, pressing her breasts into his chest.

Nicolás produced a sort of sighing laugh. "Let's get over to the tent while the others are still here a while."

They turned and walked, not with a brisk pace but not with a leisurely one either, up the ridge and across Going-to-the-Sun Road. Nicolás felt his heart thudding faster at what he knew he must disclose.

At the crest of the ridge, Nicolás snuck a quick glance back down at his companions. Mitch smiled his way, while Gabe flashed a thumbs up.

Upon reaching the cluster of four tents and two vehicles, Cassie grabbed his hand and tugged. He pivoted on the balls of his feet and found her full wet lips pressing onto his. They kissed for a moment, and then he grabbed her hand in turn and gave her a slight tug toward his tent. He unzipped the front and in a flash they were inside.

"Zip it up," she said, then giggled. "Then get unzipped."

He pulled the zipper down until the tent flaps were completely closed, and then lay on his side.

"What is it, baby?" she said.

"Ah, Cassie," he said in a lamenting tone.

"Let me guess. Cold feet. I knew it. I fell in love with a Millennial," she said, her tone growing more irritated by the second. "You don't want a relationship. No, you're just passing through on your research. Or you're returning to Mexico now."

"That's not it, Cassie," he said, feeling the nausea spread inside him.

"Just tell me. You care about me, but you don't love me," she said in a soft voice, with a hint of defeat as she slapped her thigh with an open hand.

"No, Cassie." He turned his head to face hers, which lay on the pillow, facing him. For the first time, he would admit it. "I— I know for sure that I love you."

Her eyes moistened as they searched his.

"But that is not the problem," he said, exhaling hard. "I know you, but you do not yet truly know me. Promise me that you will be fair to me. Listen to what I tell you, and do not run out of this tent before thinking a long while about what I have said. Then if you want to drive off, I understand."

"Oh God," she whispered, drawing out the words.

"And promise me that what I tell you, you will keep between us. Actually, it is a secret amongst great friends. Freedom, Stasia, Mitch, Gabe, myself, and now you. This is not for Kat to know, or any others in the town."

"I promise," she whispered.

And for the next thirty minutes, he related every last detail that remained within him. From the names of his foster parents, to details about the murder of his family and the arson, to his experiences in the semi, in the Arizona desert, and in Kwewu's truck, he shared all that leapt to his mind. At the end, he pulled his eyes from hers and studied the orange canopy above them.

"I held this all back because I did not want to endanger you in any way," he whispered. "It is true that I love you. I am willing to risk telling you now, and I feel that I must. As I have said, Mitch and Gabe both agree."

"You did what I would have done, Aurelio. Or rather, Nick," she said, shaking her head while closing and opening her eyes in a slow blink. Her eyes were fully dilated, almost as if she was in fear of her life.

"You know, Cassie, I think you would have."

"I am happy that you told me, as frightening as this all is. And I understand you not telling me earlier."

"I wanted to be sure," he said. "Sure that it was real between us. Real coming from me. And from you. And I can feel it now— I know it is. I felt it that night when we were in your bedroom."

She closed her eyes and pressed her lips once more into his.

"Let's just stop talking for now," she said. "Enough's been

said. Let's just concentrate on..."

"On doing?" he said with a mischievous smile.

"Silly boy, well, yes. Let's concentrate for a bit on doing. Before the others come over."

They sat up and began to remove their clothes. Then with a grunt of frustration, Cassie began to tear hers off in a frenzy. Seeing this, he followed suit until he pulled her, as fully nude as he was, underneath him. She was as passionate as she had ever been, at one point reaching up and squeezing the hair atop his head in her fists as he strained on top of her. And then—minutes later—they panted beside each other, like two mighty engines pushed to their limits and then cooling at rest.

They lay there, their eyes closed, until long after their breath had returned to normal. Then Nicolás heard footfall and the snapping of twigs nearby. Seconds later, a woman's laughter, full and throaty. He knew that voice, a female contralto. It was Gabe.

And then a girlish giggle, surely Kat. Followed by a baritone monotone—Mitch uttering some declarative sentence.

"Are they sleeping?" Nicolás heard Kat say.

"Don't count on it," Mitch mumbled.

Nicolás whispered in Cassie's ear that he was falling asleep, and in a few minutes, they both had drifted off atop their sleeping bags.

When they woke and dressed, Nicolás brought the zipper toward the top of the tent and folded back the tent flap. Mitch was sitting on a foldout canvas chair near the blazing fire. Kat sat upon his lap, her back leaning against his chest.

Mitch made a sort of humming laugh in his throat. "Come out and enjoy the fire, guys. It's not the same until we're the Fearsome Five again."

Nicolás stepped out of the tent, followed by Cassie. Kat turned on Mitch's lap, and they drew their faces close until their lips smacked once, then twice.

"You guys are all making my tummy turn," Gabe said.

"All right, I'll start preparing the food," Mitch said. "Join me, Cervantes?"

Mitch, joined by Nicolás, walked over to his truck bed, opened the cooler and pulled out one of the fish from the ice. Then Mitch laid his cutting board flat on the bed and began to fillet the fish.

"Lil' somethin' happened while you and Cassie were frolickin' in your tent, bud," Mitch whispered.

"What was that?" Nicolás said.

"We've been flirting hard all day. And we had a good talk. And finally started kissing. But there are some college boys that came by. Camping about two-hundred feet down that path, farther into the campground. There's a young buck she's got a liking for, I can see it. Tall good-looking fella, probably no more than a couple years younger than her."

"She is in the prime of her youth, Mitch. Young in years," Nicolás said, "but also in maturity, from what you and Gabe say."

"It's showing, bud. I can tell she wants to go over there. Keeps looking over there. He gets quite loud. Center of attention. Kat came with us. She stays with us."

"Do you think you are overreacting?" Nicolás said.

"Look, we don't know those people," Mitch said. "Anyway, you have fun today?"

"I had a splendid time, Mitch. Never have I seen such sharp mountains, which looked like God had just carved them with a gigantic knife. And I saw my first glaciers, actual glaciers that remain. And cedars. I did not expect to see cedars so very far north, and inland. I can understand those sorts of trees growing on the Pacific coast, or way inland to the south, but here? The beauty was overwhelming."

"We'll come up here again soon," Mitch said. "It's always

here. One of the very best national parks. Freedom agrees. Of all people, he knows. I think he's been to all of 'em."

After Mitch had gutted and filleted the fish, Nicolás dashed olive oil into the cast-iron pan and poured onto it the vegetables he had chopped earlier that morning, then sprinkled them with cayenne pepper and garlic salt. Nicolás poured the garlic and cilantro sauce onto the fish, while Mitch brought out two baguettes.

When they returned to the campsite, they saw Gabe, Cassie, and Kat chatting in their canvas chairs around the snapping fire.

"Wow, look at all this," Cassie said, looking at the men as they carried the pans. "And it smells great. We have our own personal chefs traveling with us."

Mitch said, "That's probably the cayenne, magic garlic and cilantro, and some potion or concoction sauce our buddy had all cooked up before we left."

Mitch hooked the pans to the square arch-like cast-iron frame erected over the fire. He mumbled to Nicolás, "Show you, bud, how to cook these over a campfire."

"I'll hook up the cornbread when those are done," Gabe said.

"That's always a treat, guys," Mitch said. "Gabriella's melt-in-your-mouth cornbread."

The men joined the women in the two remaining canvas chairs.

"So you've seen many new sights today, Pato," Gabe said. "Many new experiences."

Cassie shot Nicolás a furtive glance, not without a hint of a knowing smile.

"I was telling Mitch how impressed I was," Nicolás said. "The mountains here appear different than in the lower Rockies. And the cedars growing this far north were a surprise to me. And seeing glaciers, this far south."

"They're shrinking, too," Gabe said. "Faster now. In the last few decades it's gotten really bad. See 'em while you can. Well, glad you've enjoyed the trip."

"Just how peaceful it is out here," Nicolás said. "I love it. And no pollution. No construction. Just melting into, blending into nature."

He looked around him at the others, then at the fire and the tents, at the aspens and cedars all about, and the mountains and the azure of the lake in the distance. It was quite nearly utopian, what he was seeing and feeling. Five people, so very different, in complete peace in such a blissful retreat from the world and its harried, corrupt civilization. No violence, no greed, no jealousy, just nature and peace and sublime beauty.

Mitch stood and walked over to an ice chest nearby, on the bed of pine needles. "Root beer? Blueberry cola?"

He passed a few out after removing the caps, then resumed his seat and drank deep.

"Maine Root Cola. It's good," Mitch said. "For a soda."

"He's itchin' for that beer," Gabe said.

"She's on me like a hawk," Mitch said. "Will throw a fit if I try to bring some out here."

"Looking out for you, Mitch," Gabe said, rising and walking past them to the truck.

Mitch set down his soda and rose, spatula in hand, and stepped toward the fire. "Check this out, Cervantes."

Nicolás watched while Mitch stirred the vegetables and poured in some more water. "Nothing needs to be done with the fish. Just a bit longer. We're basically doing campfire broiling. Cooking the trout and pike through from underneath. Gabe's readyin' the cornbread. She doctored up the mix before we left."

Soon they feasted on the fish and stewed vegetables, and then the cornbread, rich and slightly sweet, for a dessert.

"Cervantes is right. This really is paradise," Gabe said. "Well, close."

"Cervantes, Gabe, help me bring the cookware to my truck, please," Mitch said after they finished eating. "We've got to lock it in the tool box. Bears, you know."

When they returned to the campsite, only Cassie sat alongside the fire.

"Where'd Kat go?" Nicolás said.

"Let me guess," Gabe said. "I know her well."

"I tried to persuade her to stay," Cassie said, looking down and shaking her head. "She was obstinate. Wanted to check out what that camping party is up to."

"She wants to check out Ken Doll over there, more like," Gabe sighed.

"Well, so be it," Mitch said, tossing his water bottle onto the ground. "Damn it to hell."

"Mitchell," Gabe said. "That mouth. I'm gonna wash it out with Tabasco."

"It should be beer," Mitch said, elbowing Nicolás. "Or whiskey, better yet."

Despite the wisecrack, Nicolás could detect the pain and disappointment in his friend's face.

"So," Nicolás said. "Now that young Kat is out of—what is that word—earshot…"

"Yes," Cassie said. "Nick here told me everything."

Gabe and Mitch shot a look at Nicolás.

"Yes," Nicolás said. "Down to every detail."

"Feel better now, bud?" Gabe said, smiling.

"Of course," Nicolás said. "It's the way it should be, that you all know. And if I'd told you earlier, perhaps you would have avoided me, shunned me. At least rejected me."

Nicolás realized he had used the word *rejected*. He caught himself sneaking a look at Mitch, who sat sprawled back into his chair like a rag doll, his reddening face and sullen gaze angled downward into the fire.

42

Nicolás opened his eyes. All about him was utter darkness. He strained his ears and he could hear the fire snapping outside his tent. And then, though barely audible, a stirring.

Closing his eyes once more, he attempted to sink back into the warm ether of sleep but found it impossible. He sat up and then slowly unzipped the tent flaps and emerged, at first on his hands and knees and then on foot.

A lone figure sat by the fire. Nicolás blinked several times.

"Mitch?" Nicolás whispered. "Can't sleep?"

"Course not," Mitch said. "Thanks to our young guest. Kat never returned."

"She's probably in that guy's tent," Nicolás said, instantly regretting his words.

Mitch brought his eyes up from the fire onto his.

"Think I'm an idiot?" Mitch said. "Shouldn't we go over there? And get her back over here? She might not be safe."

"We shouldn't overreact," Nicolás said. "Let's just wait 'til daybreak at least."

"What if something happened to her? Or will happen to her?" Mitch said.

"We are not her parents," Nicolás said. "She makes her own decisions, and how do you say—she needs to own it."

"Agreed," Mitch said.

"I hope you can get some sleep," Nicolás said.

"Well, there always is that," Mitch said, drawing his stare back down into the flames. "Hope."

Nicolás returned to his tent. Once inside, he felt the weight of fatigue once again pressing upon him, and he drifted off.

The aroma of eggs, ham, and bacon shook him from his slumber. He blinked and wiped the sleep from his eyes and turned onto his side. Cassie was awake, and lay facing him.

"Hey babe. I woke but didn't want to wake you. You were making the funniest noises. Cute noises."

"Probably because I was a child again," Nicolás said. "I was feeling that way yesterday, remember? I was a child and was with my family during the first Christmas I could recall."

"The true child may be out there," Cassie said. "Did she return from that other campsite?"

"I woke in the wee hours this morning," Nicolás said. "Don't know why. Crept outside and only Mitch was out there. He was sleepless. Kat had not yet returned."

"Damn it. That girl," Cassie sighed. "What a creature of whimsy. I like free-spirited people, but not when they are to the point of—complete inconsideration for others. It affects my practice, too. Would you believe it?"

"Well, maybe she came back to her tent," Nicolás said. "I'll investigate."

Outside, Mitch and Gabe sat in the dim but growing light of dawn, sprawled in their canvas chairs. The fire danced before them with half of the fervor of the night before. As Nicolás shuffled over to them, he saw that Gabe seemed well rested. But Mitch looked like a zombie, his face drooping, his eyelids heavy, under which there were conspicuous black circles.

"*Buenos días, compañeros,*" Nicolás said.

"Good mornin', sweetie," Gabe said. "Sleep well? Poor Mitch sure didn't."

"Still not back?" Cassie said, drawing up alongside of Nicolás.

"Not quite. Well, I'll get breakfast going," Gabe said and walked over to the truck.

"I'm sorry, Mitch," Cassie said. "She's not worth the worry."

"Or the desire," Nicolás said.

"You need a woman at least a good few years older than Kat," Cassie said. "I know this. She works for me."

"She's right, Mitchell," Gabe said from the truck. "You forget you're thirty-seven."

Mitch said nothing. Nicolás took a seat beside him, while Cassie walked over to Gabe.

Mitch cleared his throat. "Kat only thinks about herself, Nick. We were having the best time here, and she ruined it. I didn't sleep a lick."

Gabe and Cassie returned with two cast-iron pans, one filled with venison sausage links, the other with the shredded hash browns that Gabe had brought.

"Well, look at this," Nicolás said as Gabe hooked the pans to the iron frame.

"Thanks, ladies," Mitch said. "So after we eat, let's strike the camp, strike the tents."

"Strike—what is the meaning of that expression?" Nicolás said.

"Means let's pack up everything and go back to Bigfork," Mitch said. "But after I make an attempt to see if she'll join."

Gabe groaned as she stood over the fire, stirring the food, mumbling something under her breath.

After they ate, they put out the fire, broke camp, and packed everything into Mitch's truck and Cassie's SUV.

"I'm headin' next door," Mitch said. "I was unable to prevent sexual abuse years ago. Not saying it happened here. But I won't let it happen again under my nose. Come with me if you want, Cervantes."

"Sexual abuse with Kat is going too far," Gabe said. "She seemed really interested in that guy. And she's an adult, Mitch. She can make her own decisions. And at least she's not still using."

Mitch said, "We don't know that. Remember, Gabe, we're what, twenty, thirty miles from the nearest town? Nothing but woodlands, all around. She's been reckless in her life, but she's our friend. We can't just leave her here and assume she'll get home safely."

Mitch started for the edge of the woods.

"I'm coming with you," Nicolás said, and joined him.

"For the love of God," Gabe said, "Really?"

Yet before they could continue, out stepped Kat from the forest's edge, and headed for her bag by the fire.

"What were you doing?" Mitch said. "What are you doing?"

"I need something from my bag," she said. "Look, I was just hanging out with these guys, all right? I like Brandon, okay, Mitch? Big crime, I know."

"Kat?" Mitch said. "You disappeared. We didn't know if you were safe. You don't know these people. Last chance if you want a ride. I'm leaving."

"Just leave, Mitch," Kat said. "Yesterday was fun, but we're not meant for each other. I'm interested in Brandon."

Then she picked up her bag and disappeared back into the forest. Nicolás glanced at Mitch. His eyes were closed as his head drooped, as if with defeat.

"Stay longer if you want, you all," he said. "I'm heading back to the house. I'm sorry."

Nicolás saw that Cassie and Gabe were staring at Mitch with both pity and surprise.

"I'm sorry," Mitch repeated.

43

As they drove back from dropping off Cassie, Gabe said, "Sure you don't want to join me at the church event? It's a special service."

"Sorry, Gabe," Nicolás said. "I'm just too tired from the trip."

"Just wanted to make sure," Gabe said.

"I feel so bad for Mitch," said Nicolás. "I think it's even brought me down somewhat."

"Ah, he'll get over it," Gabe said. "He was just so humiliated by her behavior."

He should not speak anymore of his friend's loss. He would change the subject.

"Gabriella. You and I still need to go on our little Missoula trip."

"Right on," she said. "You'll love it. We'll cruise down East Broadway Avenue, and you'll see all the dive bars, hole-in-the-wall eateries. And the organic food co-ops and vintage clothing stores. You'll like the independent bookstores."

"I miss those college towns," he said.

"It's something else. Eventually you pass this marble courthouse and you see this grassy, treeless hill," she said, "and it displays this single symbol. A gigantic peace sign. It's not done in white paint but apparently in whitish rocks."

Nicolás chuckled. He recalled such inscriptions fashioned on Mexican mountains, but they were often quotes from scripture, or the names of cities or neighborhoods.

"Anyway, Missoula's more like a large town than a city," she continued. "My kinda town, Pato. A little to the left of Bozeman. Maybe not as friendly, but a little bigger, wilder, and more free. Anyway, we can go one day and at night end up at the Rhinoceros."

"Freedom had mentioned it," Nicolás said. "A dive bar? He told me it's an essential stop."

"He's right. He knows it because I took him and Stasia there. Fifty-two beers on tap. And a good variety of people. Students, professors, hipsters, a few people in medical scrubs, some young professionals, some rancher types, lots of outdoorsy people."

"So, you were saying you lived in Missoula years ago?" Nicolás said.

"I did. I went to UM a couple years, but it couldn't hold my attention. I was passing a recruiting station one day…realized I wanted to join the Army. Did a tour overseas and when I returned, I lived in Missoula a couple years. But I craved that peace I could find around Flathead Lake. I found a job with Cassie and stayed. Came out to my family, and they basically disowned me. To this day, we rarely speak. It's a good thing, anyways. Never told you this, but my uncle molested me when I was eight. My family refuses to believe me. They defend him. I sued, but I just couldn't prove it. The townspeople like to think what he did somehow made me a lesbian. And gave me the grit to be a soldier."

Good God, even her. Gabe, Mitch, Cassie and now me—all of us on the shores of that lake are so scarred. Far more than most.

"I'm sorry, Gabe," Nicolás said. "About what he did. That is horrific."

"I appreciate that. Well, around that time I returned from my tour, I got into a relationship with the only lesbian I found up by the lake. She was a cutie, too. But things fell apart and she moved away. Haven't seen her in years. That's the short version of it."

"Do you think you will move away soon? Away from the lake, Bigfork?"

"Probably," Gabe said. "It's beautiful living up here. I've got two good friends in Cassie and Mitch, but I've become so lonely. Besides, while the place isn't very conservative, it's a tad too buttoned-up. People gossip sometimes that Mitch and I have something going on together."

"I understand," Nicolás said. "So would you move back to Missoula, or to a larger city, farther away?"

"I do love Missoula. I feel free there. But I don't know if it's big enough to hold me anymore. Maybe I'll end up in Denver. Maybe a city out farther west, where I can enjoy the outdoors, like Seattle. And it's got diversity. I've saved for this, for a while now. I knew the good Lord, the Spirit, will help me."

Her last words reminded him of Freedom.

"So, Nick, do you see yourself staying? I know you've found some good friends. And you found Cassie. But you were a college professor in Mexico, in a historic beach city."

I will stay, yes. After I return—if I survive—from Veracruz.

"I can see myself staying. Life is special here. The proximity to nature, to such a variety of nature, at that. And there's a freedom I feel, with the people, and the land, that I have found nowhere else. I believe I am in love with the West of America."

"And you are in love with Dr. Cassie Rivers." She turned his way. Her eyes were smiling at him. He looked down at his dusty boots on the floorboard, and smiled with great shyness. He imagined he must look like Oscar.

"Pato, you don't know how lucky you are. Mitch and I both like her. But she doesn't want Mitch, couldn't deal with all of his faults. And he's too intense for her. They're just good friends. What Mitch really wanted was Kat. Anyway, you think Cassie's the one? Or will you continue playing the field?"

He hesitated. Some sliver of him, deep inside, wanted to. But for the first time he realized it. His friend was right. And he had changed. The man about town, the hunter after his own fleshly whims, had melted away.

"It's Cassie, isn't it?" she said, looking at him with curiosity. "Romeo, you really are in love with her."

He felt his face flush. Gabe had caught him unawares.

"Gabe, I wish you could see your face!" he said, and then burst out laughing. "That's not all. I changed. Before, with women, I—I'm different now. Those massive life events in the last couple months. And somewhere along the line from Veracruz to here, I just changed in how I see women."

"How so?"

"I used to use women for my own pleasure. It was more of a superficial thing. I lived for myself. I didn't know love, at least romantic love. I think doing things for others changed me. Like what I did for that Salvadoran woman on the semi, for Freedom on that roof. And in my time with Cassie and Mitch and you—I changed. And I think perhaps you had an influence on things. At least with the women part."

She nodded. "I think there's some truth to that, Pato. Yes, this has all changed you forever. The things you've had to do, the friendships you made, the love you have felt for different people on your way to that lake, and since then—yes, you've changed but you are also *changing*."

"How do they say it in America? I really dig you, Gabriella. You're deep. And spiritual. I can see why you are friends with Freedom, and he is friends with—"

"And why Freedom is friends with you," Gabe said. They glanced at each other, almost by instinct, in one synchronized movement, and then laughed.

"Thank you for sharing all of that with me, Gabe," Nicolás said.

Gabe turned to him with a faint smile. She was pulling into a convenience store parking lot.

"One minute," she said. "Want anything?"

"No thanks," he said. As she shut the door and walked inside, he followed her with his eyes. The mental image he captured reminded him of what he had gathered from his bathroom mirror back in Veracruz, before his old life vanished: a strength, a spring-footed adventurousness, pervaded by an unmistakable aura of loneliness.

Nicolás allowed his eyes to close as he rewound the events of the day. From watching Mitch as he slinked into his truck to drive home, to kissing Cassie goodbye in her driveway in front of Gabe.

He realized it was holy Pentecost Sunday, Whitsunday. What did Padre Manolo say about Pentecost? It was when the Holy Spirit lets new powers, strengths, and blessings descend to those good souls who honor Him.

Nicolás first thought of Mitch, no doubt fast asleep in his house several miles away, finally at peace and rest.

Though he never regained his Christian faith after he lost it as a teenager, Nicolás prayed with fervor that his friend would find peace, love, and healing for those thoughts that still haunted him. He remembered his other close friend, the one at his side moments before, who had grown to be like a sister. Nicolás recalled the image of Gabe walking into the convenience store minutes before, how he felt loneliness hanging about her like a cloud.

He prayed she would find true love and peace, and a new job

in her new city, wherever she would soon go.

In his imagination, Cassie's smiling face replaced Gabe's. He prayed that his presence would bring no harm to Cassie, that she would heal from her loss, and that she would continue to be with him as long as he could have her.

He remembered Freedom and Stasia. How were they? He did not know. He last heard from them days ago. He prayed that his friends would find safety and fulfillment in their new town. And that Stasia could forgive him for Freedom's pledge to take him to Montana.

Nicolás thought of his warm and beautiful new family from work: José, Lupe, and Oscar. That they would live long lives of peace, joy, and health.

Kwewu next appeared in his mind. He prayed that he was safe and at peace, and that Kwewu found fulfillment in his life.

Then there was the young woman with the harelip, and the boy from the semi. He prayed that they still lived, and were at peace, somewhere.

Nicolás realized he had rewound his western saga in slow motion in his mind. Truly, he had met such interesting and usually benevolent people along the way. And in many ways, he had been fortunate that he had pulled himself away from his journey's pitfalls.

Next in his mind—it was inevitable—he thought of those foremost in his life before he crossed the desert: Esteban and Lucinda and Padre Manolo. Lucinda, his remarkable mother and friend—in two weeks she would have turned fifty-four years young. He felt his eyes water, a pang swell in his throat.

Nicolás opened his eyes as he felt a shift in his soul, a message received and accepted. He must return home, if for a short while, very, very soon. And it should happen by his mother's birthday.

Minutes later, as they pulled up Mitch's gravel drive, Gabe slowed, then stopped. "Let's surprise him. I've done this before."

She turned off the headlights, rolled down her window and stuck her head out as they crept forward at a snail's pace. The Hyundai stopped again, just shy of the house.

"Come on, Nick. Let's see what this boy's up to. He'd better not be in his cups again."

Gabe put the car in park and they stepped gingerly toward the house and around its left side. Feeling the suspense build, Nicolás bit his lip and chuckled as he opened the door with the discretion of a burglar. He stepped aside, and in tiptoed Gabe. He placed his hiking backpack and survival knife on the table and followed as she lit their way to Mitch's bedroom with her smartphone's screen.

A violent thud sounded behind the door. A scraping across the floor followed, and a grunt, but one from high in the throat, something involuntary and pained. Gabe shot Nicolás a glance of great concern.

"Mitch?" Nicolás said.

"Mitchell?" she said into the door.

There was no reply, merely the bump of something against a wall. Gabe seized the knob and twisted.

"It's locked. Nick, we need to break down the door. Something happened. Something is wrong."

"I think so. Get ready," he stammered and backed up far from the door, then sprinted forward and thrust his foot as hard as possible at an angle against the old knob, which came loose. Gabe kicked the door once, and then once again. The door burst open and she leaped inside, followed by Nicolás.

Though the bedroom light was extinguished, the walk-in closet light was on. When they rounded the corner, Gabe cried out, and Nicolás swore. Donned head to toe in his formal Army uniform, Mitch dangled from a bedsheet noose attached to the pipe running just beneath the closet ceiling. His bloodshot eyes bulged, his grimacing face flushed deep crimson as spittle trailed from his mouth. A potent smell reached Nicolás's nostrils: the smoky but sweet scent of bourbon.

Nicolás imagined Esteban wincing in his gray pinstripe suit as the bullets entered his torso.

"Nicolás, get a knife! Get a knife, damn it! Run!" Gabe screamed as she grabbed Mitch about the legs and lifted. As she held his legs she attempted, without success, to jam her fingers between his neck and the noose.

As Nicolás shot from the bedroom toward the kitchen cutlery, he recalled his survival knife on the kitchen table. He snatched the knife and sprinted back into the bedroom. Gabe was swearing at the top of her lungs, still lifting the legs of the now purple-faced Mitch. Nicolás unsheathed the blade and slammed it against the bedsheet rope and sawed with all of the speed he could muster. He was grateful for the brand-new sharpness of the edge, for in less than four seconds, the bedsheet came apart.

"Let him down, let him down!" Nicolás screamed. Mitch's dress shoes thudded against the floor as he crumpled into a crooked, limp form, his eyed closed.

"Pull it off! Pull the sheet off!" Gabe yelled as she and Nicolás grabbed the sheet around Mitch's neck and yanked it loose.

Mitch breathed in deep heaves and kicked in a wild, frantic convulsion, propelling a strange, choking-like sound through his throat, as if he'd been drowning but at last shot to the surface.

He drooled upon the hardwood closet floor as his breathing slowed. Gabe rested her head against his chest as she held him about the shoulders, weeping aloud like a distraught child.

Nicolás stood, staring down at the prostrate form. Shock gave way to relief. He looked away, for he also felt a tinge of embarrassment. He had witnessed something so personal, a grave problem that he knew was surely a deep humiliation to his friend. And he knew that Gabe felt humiliation at weeping so. Never had he seen an adult cry in this way. He imagined that this is what a mother would sound like upon discovering her child dead. That town rumor came to his mind, that the two were secretly a couple.

"You were just going to leave all of us," Gabe said. "Are you just going to try until you succeed? Does Kat have anything to do with this? You know she's not worth it."

Nicolás snatched up the sheath from the ground and snapped the knife back in. He walked out into the living room, after flipping one of the light switches. Though he felt extreme relief that they had averted the suicide, standing in the bedroom with Gabe's weeping and Mitch's raw vulnerability had grown far too awkward. He collapsed onto the sofa, tossing the knife beside him. Running his palms down his cheeks, he sighed and stared into the fireplace. What should he and Gabe do, now that Mitch had taken this bold step?

A conversation sounded from around the corner, first in muted tones, the baritone occasionally surfacing in a sort of tired monotone, and then Gabe's voice, plaintive and pleading, then growing slightly deeper and more frustrated. An indiscernible argument ensued. Steps creaked across the floorboards of the bedroom.

The steps grew louder, then stopped just inside the living room. Nicolás turned around, his arm draped atop the back of the sofa.

"Mitch?" Nicolás said, then stood. "Hello, my friend. I am so happy to see you."

An unmistakable expression of humiliation played about Mitch's face. His eyes rose to meet those of Nicolás, for a sliver of a second, then sank again to the floor. Then he nodded and gave a coy smile—it seemed like one of embarrassed gratitude.

At his side, with one hand touching his shoulder, stood Gabe.

"Mitchell and I are going for a little ride. Up to Kalispell. I'm checking him into the hospital again."

"I'll accompany you," Nicolás said.

"No, no," Gabe said, "but thanks. Mitchell is embarrassed. And he and I need to have a talk."

More conversation? What more did she want to talk about? What he needed was medication.

As the crunching sound of the Hyundai faded in his ears, Nicolás sat staring at the fireplace, unable to rise. The suicide attempt shocked him, but in many ways, there was little surprise. He searched his memory for clues as to what would take Mitch from depression to a suicide attempt.

After a minute, he produced the first clue. It came amid that first conversation with José, when Mitch had delivered the odd joke.

"Northern passage, all right. That's what I'm waitin' for," Mitch *said, and clapped his hands once. "To be put out of my misery. And then my passage northward. Up to the hereafter."*

The second sign was that comment Nicolás had almost forgotten, on his first full day in Bigfork. As he sat in the café with Mitch, Freedom, and Stasia, after he had returned with his new ID card. Mitch had invited him to attend his combat training.

"How long does this—this class—last?" Nicolás said.

"Depends. Maybe three weeks. Maybe four. But whatever it is, you need the Mitch Intensive Training 101, like yesterday."

Nicolás laughed. "I can surmise what some of this involves. You do have my interest."

"Very well," Mitch said. "It ain't for the faint of heart. But weeks, months, years from now, you will thank me. If I'm still here, that is."

"Now Mitch," Freedom said. "Why would you say a thing like that?"

"Well," Mitch said, *searching the ceiling with his eyes. "What did Chaucer write? 'So long the life, the struggle so hard' or something to that effect. Except that he wrote it in Middle English."*

"I did not know you were so literary," Nicolás said.

Well there it was. It had been buried in the events of the next few moments, beginning with Jake appearing and insulting Mitch.

Perhaps we are all more vulnerable than we let on. Even the strongest among us.

Was not Mitch an example of what happens when that which tortures you finally overtakes you? The loss of his friend Adrian, his career and ambitions, his sobriety, and then his dignity within Bigfork. Then his love interest.

It was enough to push a fearless soldier to the ultimate surrender. Hell, Mitch had considered it before, as Gabe said.

Nicolás kept his eyes riveted to the extinguished embers in the hearth, as he began to ponder his own fate.

Would the darkness overwhelm him, in turn?

44

The next day at work proved grueling because of Nicolás's lack of sleep and, for some reason, they were deluged with lunch customers. But when the last diner departed, and he bused the tables, all grew calm again.

"All right men," José said, pointing at Nicolás and Oscar. "Good job at lunch. Glad to see you back at work, Aurelio. Now, just before we reopen for dinner, Oscar here will make a second attempt at glory. He's providing us with a mystery Salvadoran dish. I'm looking forward to it."

"And I, as well," Nicolás said with a smile.

"I actually have a few surprises in store," Oscar said as he began to pull the ingredients from the refrigerator and placed them on the counter.

José said, "Parker Wade—Burning Elk—he told me when he took Oscar to the grocery store in Missoula this weekend that Oscar went all out. So the suspense builds."

Lupe departed on an errand, and José tended to the bookkeeping in the rear office. Nicolás took out the garbage and cleaned the dishes for Oscar, then swept and mopped the dining room. Aromatic scents wafting and whirling about his nostrils grew more and more intoxicating. He discerned tomato sauce, garlic, sautéed onions, pork, cheese, and fresh broiled fish. Mere minutes after Lupe returned, Oscar's palm slapped down on top of the bell. Nicolás and José returned to the kitchen.

"This may be your first time, friends, for much of this," Oscar said. "But think of this as the cousin of Mexican food."

Nicolás set the table for four, and he, José, and Lupe took their seats. Oscar entered the dining room and placed a glass of water at the corner of each table mat. Then he returned and placed a full, steaming soup bowl atop each of José's plates, and added soup spoons to the settings.

"*Venga!*" Lupe cheered.

Nicolás stared down into his bowl of maroon soup. It did indeed smell celestial. He stirred it with his spoon and noted the whitefish, clams, octopus, squid, shrimp, and crabmeat.

"*Mariscada*," Oscar said. "Seafood chowder. *Buen provecho.*"

Nicolás slid his spoon under the steaming surface and brought it into his mouth.

"*Dios mio*, Oscar," Nicolás said. Other compliments arose from the table. He had been bested, but he did not care.

"Do you like it? Do you like it?" Oscar said, his face brightening like a growing fire.

"Of course we do," Lupe said with conviction.

"*Mijo*," said José, as he took another spoonful, chewed, and swallowed. He then mouthed the words with a slow, deliberate tone. "This is a work of art. This is magnificent, son."

"Thanks, everyone," Oscar said. Though his chest swelled with pride, his head bowed, his eyes watering.

"I want to know what is in this broth," Nicolás said. "First we should just—enjoy it. Devour it like wild beasts."

Oscar looked at Nicolás and released a giddy laugh. They ate with gusto for several minutes.

"Wait," Oscar said. "I did bring another surprise, from Missoula. Who wants the best Salvadoran beer?"

Everyone assented. Oscar disappeared into the kitchen, then reappeared with four frosty glasses and four open bottles on a tray, and served them to each diner.

"*Suprema*," Nicolás read the label. He took a sip, his eyes closed. "Supreme indeed."

When they finished the chowder, Oscar picked up the bowls. Then he collected the plates and disappeared once more into the kitchen.

He then distributed the plates, each one bearing two items.

"These are *pupusas* and *plátanos fritos*," Oscar said. "You might know the *plátanos* are plaintains, fried with caramelized sugar. The *pupusa* is like a thicker version of the Mexican tortilla. This one is filled with *chicharrón*. Pork ground into a paste, of course. And I also mixed cheese and refried beans into there."

They tasted each, and then lavished Oscar with fervent praise.

"But which dish is entering into the contest?" Lupe said.

"Well, the *mariscada*, I guess," Oscar said. "But the contest was not important to me. My goal was to make you fall in love with the food of my home country. So I bought the beer and made the two side dishes. And I wanted to repay José for all of those free breakfasts."

"Superb, Oscar," Nicolás said, sipping his beer. He thought of Mitch, and all of the danger, numbing, and pain that alcohol had brought his way. He wondered what his friend was doing at that moment, in the Kalispell rehab.

Nicolás stared at the bottle's label. "Not just superb, not just *suprema*. Oscar, you are now named—*Supremo*."

The name pained him a bit. After all, Nicolás always counted cooking among his top passions. Yet he felt Oscar merited the moniker, and he could not resist its humor.

"I guess so," said José. "When that seafood *caldo* warrants a solid nine point eight!"

Oscar cheered and clapped his hands once in delight.

They sat feasting on the *pupusas* and *plátanos*. After they finished, Oscar brought out desserts, placing at each setting a coffee mug filled with a custard-like substance topped with corn kernels and cinnamon.

"*Atol de elote*," Oscar said, as if he was himself mystified. "Corn pudding. Sugar, water, corn, corn starch, a bit of salt. The top is dusted with cinnamon."

Nicolás tasted the concoction, and was stunned into silence. He was happy for Oscar. He wanted to see him progress. But if Nicolás survived his strike on Segundo Cortez, what would become of him in Bigfork? Would he become this café's chef? Or the chef in José's restaurant in West Glacier? The others chatted and joked, and soon they cleaned the table and kitchen. Oscar stored the remaining *mariscada* in the refrigerator.

Customers started to trickle in, no more nor no less than a typical Monday evening. But Nicolás had been away from work for just enough days that he felt rusty. He was happy when the shift ended, and he found Gabe parked in the rear lot.

"I want to see Mitch," he said as the Hyundai rolled north. "We should go see him tonight. For many reasons."

"I was just going to mention that," she said. "Not the first time he's stayed up there. But he probably feels even more alone."

"And defeated, I would guess," he said.

"That, too," she said.

They drove in silence for several minutes. "You eat?" she finally said.

"I ate a little," he said. "You?"

"Not feeling it now, bud. Doesn't matter. Visitation period ends in an hour."

The silence returned. A half-hour later, they turned in the

ebbing twilight into a parking lot before a large rectangular edifice, very much a government building. Its bricks were fading into a dusty burnt sienna, its gloom only slightly alleviated by the white windowsills and panes.

As they walked down the halls, following the odd pairing of the pudgy nurse with the nearly skeletal doctor, Nicolás studied the walls and open offices. He observed the windows of patient rooms, some of them illumined within, a gowned patient visible here and there. A sound ensued within a room he had just passed: a drawn-out, despondent groan. Then from somewhere off to the left, a fierce argument. Then he realized it was not two or more people, but one man, arguing with himself in the same snarling, hoarse baritone.

Nicolás felt his head drooping, and he shook it as he stared down at his hiking boots squeaking across the shiny but worn linoleum floor. Fear and despair built within him, surely but a fraction of what others trapped inside here felt. His close friend was now among them. What would become of Mitch? Was this his final destination? Surely in America a history of alcohol abuse and even an attempted suicide would not merit a life sentence in a mental ward.

"Don't worry, Nick," Gabe said. "I know what you're thinking. But Mitch doesn't have to stay in this wing."

They turned down a hall, and then another. The doctor stopped before a gray door, punctuated with a small window, and turned to them.

"This is the addiction and recovery section," the doctor said. His large black eyes were striking with dark circles just beneath. "Much milder and more preferable environment, believe me, than what we just passed. I would advise you be relaxed, upbeat around him. No reminding him of anything negative or depressing. No teasing him about even the slightest thing."

The doctor gave three light raps on the door, then opened it, motioning them inside.

"Mitch? You have two visitors."

The room was a calm hunter green. Past a dresser topped with a flatscreen television, a gowned figure sat on the bed facing the window, slumping like a punished schoolboy. He did not move.

Nicolás shuddered. Was this actually Mitch? He recognized the broad shoulders, the dark hair slicked-back on top and buzzed on the sides. But something about this figure clashed with his memories of the man.

"Sweetie, it's us," Gabe said.

"Mitch, my friend," Nicolás said. Tears began to obscure his vision into the room. "I'm…so glad…to see you again."

The figure stared out at the streetlight-illumined parking lot a moment longer, then looked downward. He turned on the bed, slowly at first, and then faced them across the room. His shoulders bent in a slight hunch, his head drooped a trace to the side and downward as he glanced their way. Then some unseen weight drew the eyes downward to the floor between them. The face flushed a crimson shade. All about him loomed an air of the deepest humiliation, even more marked than Nicolás had seen in the living room the night before.

A slow and barely audible sound—Mitch cleared his throat. But no words came.

"I'll get a couple chairs," the nurse said, and disappeared.

"Mitch, you said you would be open to certain visitors," said the doctor. "Is that still the case?"

The voice finally came, weary but steady. "Thank you, Dr. Mays. Why don't you leave me with them for a bit?"

The nurse returned with the two chairs and placed them beside the bed. "We'll come back in about fifteen, twenty minutes? Good?" the doctor said.

"That will be great," Nicolás said, as he and Gabe took their seats.

The door shut. Half a minute passed.

"Hon," Gabe finally said. "I know you're embarrassed. We had to come. But I can see it plain as day—"

"Do you want to speak with Gabe in private? And then you can speak with me?" Nicolás said, looking Mitch hard in the face. Mitch pulled his gaze from their feet and looked at him, then blinked.

"Yes," Mitch mumbled.

"Gabe," Nicolás said as he stood and stepped toward the door. "Come and get me in a few minutes, in the hall."

"I'll do it," she said, then turned to Mitch and spoke in muted tones.

Outside the closed door, Nicolás began to pace. What would make Mitch stronger? He did not know.

How grateful he was for all his friend had done. Perhaps if he had made this gratitude known, Mitch would not have placed a noose around his own neck. He knew Mitch was troubled, but he had seemed so very strong, even powerful.

This had to be the time to do it. To broach the subject of his return to Veracruz. But first, to thank one of the two who had given him such power. And it was almost as if—Mitch had lost his power, and it had flowed into him...

The door opened. Gabe walked down the hall toward him.

"Hey, Nick," she said. "We had a good heart-to-heart. Tell you about it later."

"Great," Nicolás said as he passed her. "See you in a bit."

Mitch sat, his back this time to the corner. His shoulders still sagged, and his expression was almost meek. But what was undeniable was an aura of peace. As Nicolás sat, he spotted the slightest trace of a smile on his friend's face.

"Cervantes," Mitch said. "I knew you'd come."

"Of course."

"I'm sorry you had to see what you saw. And do what you did."

"Just don't worry about that, Mitch. Just heal yourself. To where you can be on Flathead again. Think of all those northern pike and whitefish, trout, salmon you will catch. And leading tours again. Doing the things you love."

Mitch fell silent again.

"That I love? My life has turned worthless. That's what Gabe doesn't understand. I don't get much enjoyment from it anymore. Others destroyed my career. Then I fell off the wagon here, many times. I've embarrassed myself. Horribly. Oh God, so many times before you met me. And now, what you and Gabe saw the other night. And prevented. I just don't matter anymore."

"No, Mitch. Of course you matter. And you will matter in the future."

"How in the hell have I mattered?"

"First of all, you matter very much to Gabe. You're her best friend, and vice versa."

Mitch did not reply.

"You've made a world of difference in my life. Right when I needed it most, you rented me a room. But what I really could not have received on my own was the training. You helped me get stronger than I have ever been. But somehow you lost your self-value, and your pride. And almost, your life."

"Yes," Mitch mumbled.

"Perhaps we didn't convey your worth to us, or to this community. Your depression increased," Nicolás said. "And all that drinking inflamed it. And then you felt the rejection by Kat."

Mitch did not reply for many seconds. Then he cleared his throat. "I will be free again. I'll get out of this rat hole."

"Will you attempt it again?" Nicolás said. "You will, won't you?"

"I won't," Mitch said. "Gabe made me promise her."

"But will it hold?" Nicolás said.

"Cervantes. So what's your plan? What are you thinking?"

"That is one very important matter I wanted to discuss. Though I'm here mainly to check on you. I—I must return to Veracruz."

Mitch's eyes widened. He straightened in his seat, his shoulders drawn back.

"Not for good, though," Nicolás said. "I want to be with Cassie. And my new friends, José, you, Gabe. And Lupe, Oscar. But you know what I must do first. I must do what I can, against Segundo Cortez. I have to at least get Ivan. I can't live a life in America without doing that first."

"Nicolás. You know your odds. You've got to look at the odds."

"I have. I may not return."

"You won't be able to. This is the last time I'll see you, Nick. I'm reminding you now."

"But I just might survive it, Mitch. And we will fish and camp and go to rodeos, and all of the bloodshed we have seen will be a memory. Maybe one day we'll be old men here. I have to do it. For my family. And to be able to live with myself. But I have to move now because my home city really needs it. It's breaking under them, under Segundo Cortez. No one has had the courage to attack them. Especially to attack Ivan. I do still love my people."

"I kind of like this, Nick. We're conspiring. But for the greater good." Mitch's face brightened with a knowing smile. Then his features relaxed into a poker face.

"Nick. You're gonna ask to tap into my collection, aren't you?"

Nicolás did not know how to reply. And what if Mitch refused? He could not complete the mission without one of Mitch's guns. He would have to steal one, and fast. Yet he knew he could never—would never—do so. And he would be just another Mexican thief in the minds of certain Bigfork whites, like Jake and Sheriff Press.

"Nick," Mitch said, leaning forward and dropping his voice to a whisper. Would this change everything? Was this the moment of truth? "Nobody understands your motives and your struggle more than I do. I want you to take that WASR pistol. It's called a pistol but it's really the shorter rifle with that pistol grip instead of the stock. You can fit that gun in your hiking backpack. But you need to wipe that WASR clean with alcohol and a rag, remove all of my prints. The second thing you can't forget: Take one of my tools, and file down its serial number. Otherwise if their police get it, it *will* be traced back to me. Load many magazines, after each round and each mag is wiped down in that same way. Take one of those .45s, too. Do the same to it. File it down, wipe it. Take your cash. I'll tell Gabe eventually, after you leave."

"Thank you," Nicolás said. "Thank—"

"You're catching semis down there again, aren't you?"

"I'll have to. I will start at the truck stop in Missoula."

"Good. I know there's one on the east side of town. You will have to wait until I get out, to drive you. Or Cassie can take you. But she won't if she thinks you are leaving to kill."

"I know. She will take me. But me leaving, it will be very hard on her."

"No doubt," Mitch said, looking him hard in the eyes. "Especially if you don't return. And you know that you can't expect to return. But whatever you do—never, ever let them catch you alive."

"Never," Nicolás said.

"Talk about suicide. Nick, you just might turn out to be the suicide here."

Nicolás clenched his teeth at the words.

Three knocks sounded at the door. It opened, slowly at first. The doctor and nurse stood inside the doorframe. Behind them stood Gabe, staring at Mitch and Nicolás with a solemn expression.

45

The SUV wound up the drive.

"So what was he like yesterday?" Cassie said.

"At first he was quite embarrassed by his actions," Nicolás said. "And being confined there in that hospital. Then he regained a trace of his old humor."

"How much longer do you think he'll be up in Kalispell?"

"I'm not sure," Nicolás said. "Weeks, most probably. He's on this new medication—an antidepressant. He's adjusting to life without alcohol. Like I'm now adjusting to life without cigarettes. Anyway, Gabe's visiting him now. She thinks he'll be home in a week or two. But the date's unknown."

"Wait, you *have* given up the cigs," Cassie said. "Babe, I can't smell smoke on you right now."

"Quitting is a trial, believe me," he said as he thought of all of his new discoveries. The headaches, the heightened senses of smell and taste. The mucousy throat and nose as if he was contracting a cold. The irritability, the impatience, the anxiety. All of it would end in a couple of days, Gabe swore.

"What made you stop?"

"You," he said. "You hate it."

Well, that was half of the truth. He envisioned *la migra* agents tracking him across the desert from his discarded cigarette butts.

"Wow, I'm impressed," she said, clicking her garage remote control, then parked inside. They headed through the garage into the house. Suddenly it was very cool—as if they had ducked into a cavern. They headed for the kitchen.

"So," she said, as she put her physician's bag on the dining table, "work was rough?"

"Not so much," he said. "But in a way, it was…"

"Nick? What do you mean?" She turned around to face him.

"Love," Nicolás said. "I may not be going back to work there."

"Babe, I don't follow."

"Ah, damn it. How do I say this? Cass, let's walk into the den and sit."

"Oh…okaaay," she said, a concerned look engulfing her face. "Would you stop this? Tell me what it is," she said, pounding her clenched fists onto her hips.

They sat in the cushioned seats that faced the fireplace.

"You're quitting? I thought—I thought José was considering you for opening up a new place. Or taking over the one now."

"He has been," Nicolás said. "It's just—I just—I may have that job, but I have to visit my family first. My cousins and aunts and uncles. I cleared it with José today."

"In Veracruz, of course," she said, half asking, half declaring.

"Yes."

"Why? You described how dangerous it is for you there. Your family murdered. That cartel. Why?"

"I just—I must. My family needs me, needs a visit. And you know I can't fly. My city won't even know I am there. I snuck out. I can sneak back in. This time dressed up as a homeless vagrant, head to toe. Now with this long hair, and this full beard that's getting longer."

"Sure you can. Your head will end up on a pole this time. Nick!" She shot to her feet and jammed a fist onto the glass lamp table. "Nick, you—you're so naïve! You know you should wait."

"My family needs me right now," he said, holding out his palms to her. "You know I haven't communicated with them by email or phone for a reason. Segundo Cortez must be tracking their calls, emails. They probably already hacked into my email. I have to visit them. Then you know I will return. You know I want to be with you."

"You won't be able to be with me because you'll be dead."

"Cassandra."

"I was a fool to trust you. A fool to love you."

"Cassie, it was not a mistake. I assure you."

"I guess I will find out."

Nicolás turned and walked three steps away. He felt an uncontrollable desire to pace. Something tugged at his arm, and he spun around.

"Damn it, Nick. Damn you," she said through tears as she jammed the bottoms of her fists against his chest. "I lost Sean, I lost Jake, and now I'm losing you."

He wrapped his arms around her, but she began to wail. She allowed her legs to give way, to become limp in his arms. He held her tighter, whispering her name in her ear.

"Please don't hate me. Don't be mad at me," he whispered. "Please do not regret."

Her wails became sobbing. He picked her up in his arms, stepped across the rug, and laid her onto a sofa. He got down upon his knees and began to caress her head with his left palm, gently smoothing her hair backward from her forehead.

After several minutes, she ceased weeping. Her eyes remained shut.

"What more do you want from me, Nick? Now that you've—destroyed my heart?"

"I want you to keep loving me—and to expect my return. One day, you and I and Mitch and Gabe will drive with Freedom and Stasia to Baja. We will surf and fish, camp—"

"Stop dreaming," she said, shaking her head.

He paused. "All right. There's just one more thing I need."

"What is it, Nick?" she said in a deadpan, her eyes still closed. "What more do you want to take from me?"

"I...I just need you to bring me back to Mitch's now. I must pick up my backpack."

"You're even packed?" Her eyes opened wide and she turned to him. "You've—you've been scheming."

"No, I have not," he said in a soft tone.

"You want to leave tonight? What—from where?"

"Yes, tonight is best. There's a certain truck stop. On the east side of Missoula."

46

Pantano rose from his desk and walked toward his study window. He would do it, at last. The following day, he would announce his retirement. First the memo, then the speech to the force. Articles and television news stories would follow. But within weeks he would be forgotten. No more threatening calls from the citizenry. And then—freedom.

He would repair his frayed marriage. Raquel would regain that passion for him—those kisses would no longer seem reluctant and forced from her end. He would spend more time with his entire family, and vacation for once. Segundo Cortez would leave him alone, for no longer would he be a threat. In fact, he would be harmless.

He would miss the money, no doubt. Both the salary and all of the bribes. But it was not worth his marriage, nor the rest of his sanity.

He scoured the lawn. So much to landscape. He had all of the plants in mind for months, just never the time. Unless he released his grip now.

Could letting go be this easy? Just mentioning it to Gustavo and his top men, and then emailing the memo would set it into motion?

Something inside him swore that in fact, it would not be this easy. That in letting go now, he could never respect himself. The citizens in the street might never again remind him, but he would have failed them. He would have aided and abetted their persecution and abuse, then surrendered, then deserted them. For him, there would be days, even years of tranquility and diversion. But there would also be shame, only interrupted by death.

His phone buzzed in his pocket. Its screen told him that his moments of contemplation were over. How would the conversation go, after that insane night at the hacienda, days before?

"Ivan," Pantano muttered into the phone, in a voice devoid of emotion.

"*Señor* Pantano," Ivan said, sounding upbeat. Strange.

Several seconds passed.

"I am calling for two reasons," Ivan said. "First, I apologize for my actions the other night, at my home. You came in good faith. You were disrespectful with your words, but I should not have reacted in that manner. Also, I should not have had my men lay a hand on you. I should not have ordered them to kill you. I should have just released you and the cop, and called it a night."

"I appreciate that," Pantano said. "Ivan, no one will tell you this. But I fear for your sanity. It's that, and the cocaine."

Silence. Pantano could hear Ivan clear his throat.

"Yes, you're right. Now for the other matter. This Sunday coming up, I'm holding another one of my brunches at the Café Cristal. My family and my top men all there. You're invited, a gesture of my goodwill, and my regret."

"You don't have to invite me, Ivan."

"No, I insist. I would like you there. I am sure Mother would, as well."

Strange.

"Though she surely won't attend," Ivan said. "You know she's become so reclusive."

"We will see," Pantano said. "I might be attending…not sure yet."

"We must coexist," Ivan said. "We must respect each other."

"I agree," Pantano said. "I will let you know."

"And one more thing. Don't even think of retiring," warned Ivan. "I have ears all over the department and this city. I caught wind of this. I'm telling you, I want you in that position. It's of benefit to my entire enterprise. After you go, there's no telling who will replace you."

"How did you—"

"Have a good afternoon, *Señor* Pantano," Ivan said. The call ended.

Pantano sat at his desk. Had he mentioned to one of his men other than Gustavo that he was mulling retirement? No matter. He placed his phone on the pile of papers. He must get his finances in order, ahead of his announcement. It was months overdue. He turned on his laptop and pored over his digital files.

An hour later, the phone buzzed again. Grijalva.

"What is it?" Pantano said.

"*Jefe*," Grijalva said. "Pilar and Bermudez. They were parked at a red light. Both were shot dead. No eyewitnesses. No *narcomanta* left behind."

Pantano pounded the pile of papers hard with his fist. And then twice more.

That bastard Ivan Méndez. No respect. No mercy. Just lies.

47

Nicolás wondered where she was at the moment. Several days had passed since that long parting kiss, but the memory never left his mind. Cassie...

He must force his thoughts onto other matters. He knew *la migra* crisscrossed this area with frequency. These days it was the most popular crossing area.

"Coronado National Forest." He recalled the sign from earlier that day, and smirked. If only the Spanish explorer could see what had become of this land. A battlefield not of swords, musketballs, and cannonfire, but of desperation, flight and pursuit, and ATVs.

Damn, it's one hot morning, he thought, as he sat under the tree. He knew it would only get hotter as he neared Veracruz. What did he expect? It was June, after all.

At least the cigarette cravings had ceased, sometime yesterday.

Nicolás turned to the spiky-haired crosser—in the torn, stained Las Vegas T-shirt—he had encountered a few minutes before. A boy of no more than eighteen, he crouched beside Nicolás in the shade, too on edge to rest. The border was so close.

"So what have you been doing in America?" Nicolás said.

"Rogelio, yes?"

"That's me. I built residential and commercial in Nevada," said Rogelio. "Three years away from my family in Nuevo León. Sent a ton of money to them, though. It was worth it, saved their house, and paid medical bills. But I can't stand to be away any longer. That's why I'm walking in one minute."

"Rogelio," Nicolás said. "It's almost the hottest part of the day. Wait a few hours, at least."

"Can't," Rogelio said, taking a swig from his water jug. "Pato, right?"

"Yes," Nicolás said.

"You said you've only been away a few months. It's been three entire years for me. It's become hell. I can't imagine how those people do it—those crossers away from their families for seven, eight years."

"You won't wait at least for the heat to break?" Nicolás said.

"Good luck on your trip, friend," Rogelio said, and extended his hand. "Nice meeting you."

They shook hands. Rogelio rose to his feet, drew in an audible breath, and launched himself—through the clusters of scrub and trees and rocks under the punishing glare of the sun— toward the border. Nicolás closed his eyes and prayed that no *la migra* lay in wait, and that the young man would not suffer heatstroke.

Minutes passed. There were no park rangers or *la migra* barking commands. No SUVs or jeeps or ATVs.

His thoughts migrated toward his own family, lost not from distance but to death itself. And he thought of the land he still loved, the land he would always love, the land that probably would swallow his own expired body in a matter of days. He knew what Rogelio meant. He could wait no longer.

But while Nicolás waited for the cool of twilight, his body

ached for rest. As his sleep had been so poor the last few days, he leaned back against the tree and closed his eyes.

Many hours later, he stirred awake, as the sunlight began to ebb. He drank deep from his own jug and jogged out into the open. Adrenaline pumped as hard through his veins as that moment, months ago, when he ignited that first Molotov cocktail. He increased his pace, sprinting as fast as he could wearing a tall hiking backpack, stuffed with the WASR, the .45 pistol, the few loaded magazines, cash, food, and water. If the rangers or *la migra* caught him, surely he would spend years inside an American prison.

Nicolás concentrated on pushing each leg before the other, moving with all the speed in his power, as if that was his only goal. His heart seemed on the verge of exploding as he spotted the looming, rusty metal beams of the border wall.

His breath sputtered through his burning throat, but he still forced himself forward, imagining a round tearing through his back. He powered on, ten, twenty, thirty meters.

And then something caught his eye. A horizontal mass upon the desert floor.

He stepped toward it, recognized its shape, and broke into a run toward it. As he neared, Nicolás knew it was Rogelio, lying on his back with an arm thrown halfway over his face. Had he passed out from heatstroke? Surely he had not been shot. He would have heard the reports of any gun.

He stopped a few meters from Rogelio. His eyes caught something moving from behind the body. A rattlesnake emerged into the light, fat and lengthy and with scales and a triangular head, a furious ruler of the desert that had stamped out an intruder.

Nicolás drew in a sharp breath. On Rogelio's neck, amidst the purple-black blotch of a bruise, the twin fang marks were obvious. There was another on his hand that rested at his side.

"Ah, damn it," Nicolás said. "Damn it all. Rogelio? Rogelio!"

There was no hope for the boy. He was already gone. At least two bites, one on the neck, probably many hours before. Nicolás mumbled a prayer, and then ensuring the snake was still several meters away, he turned and trudged toward the wall.

As he drew closer and it loomed taller, fear overtook him. What if the rangers or *la migra* appeared at the last moment, and thwarted everything?

Against his better judgment, Nicolás broke into a jog, though scouring the ground for rattlers. As he came upon the wall, he turned west, running alongside it, searching for one of the openings Rogelio had spoken of, either a spot dug under the wall or an aperture cut into it by the cartels with an acetylene torch or a hacksaw.

In the distance he heard some sort of engine. Good God, not now. Should he turn and follow the wall eastward? No, press on, at least for a minute or two.

The engine grew louder.

For the love of God, let there be an opening. Allow me to do your will. Permit me this last passage south. What would you prefer? That the evil triumph?

And like an answer from above, or perhaps even the punch line of some cosmic joke, his hungry eyes found an opening. From its surrounding metal, he could tell it had been torched. For once, a merciful deed by a cartel man's hand, even if unintended.

Nicolás pushed his pack through the aperture, ducked, and squeezed through.

My God, I thank you. I'm halfway there.

He once again lurched forward into a jog. Yet something snagged his boot. He pitched forward into the dust, scraping the palms of his hands, the bottoms of his forearms, and his kneecaps.

Ah, well. Still a much easier crossing than the Devil's Highway.

Pulling himself onto his elbows, he scrambled to a crouching position behind a prickly bush. As he paused, he remembered Rogelio. The desert had claimed the boy, just at the moment of his deliverance. His family would never know what became of him...

Tears crept into his vision, but he blinked them away. No time for grief—or rest. He knew he must continue toward the town lights, at once, for the park rangers and Border Patrol were no longer the ones he must evade. Now there were the Mexican police and troops—two groups much, much more fearsome. If he were caught with mere food and water and cash, they would be unpredictable, at best. But he must not forget: Those arms he carried were a one-way ticket to years in a Mexican prison or an early death.

At all costs, he must find a truck stop ahead in Nogales. Yet he had no idea where one was.

48

In a way the engine, reverberating through the semi's cargo hold floor, calmed his nerves. The entire way south through Mexico, he had caught only meager sleep, and none of it very good, much like his sleep between Montana and Arizona. But the hum of the metal floor beneath him allayed some of his worry. Yes, the semi was preferable to a train, for so many reasons.

His thoughts darted about, like bullets in a gunfight—surely like the gunfight that was to come. Those thoughts always returned to her. His love, the one love of his life, drawing farther away from his grasp by the second.

He knew he would never see her again. He just knew it. But he had to return to Veracruz. He had no other choice.

Yet he did have a choice. And that was the hardest part. But he did have another love—his home city. And he had to strike hard and fast in her defense.

Hours later, sleep did come. He felt himself falling into it.

The first dream was pleasant. It was, in fact, a memory. He worked the reel hard as the fish rose dripping out of Flathead Lake, swinging like a pendulum toward him.

The creature gasped and jerked and flailed as it descended

through the air and landed on the white plastic floor of the boat. Mitch swung twice with the wooden club. The movements ceased.

Nicolás pulled the hook from its lip, stood and held it before him, watching the drops slide off its sleek body.

"Pato Cervantes," Mitch said, his hands on his hips, shaking his head yet smiling with pride.

"Your first try, bud," Gabe said, nodding. "You scored a lake trout. Over twenty pounds. Maybe twenty-two, twenty-three."

"Does this mean I have good luck?" Nicolás said.

"Come on," Mitch said. "Let's take your picture."

"Here, lift your head up, Pato. Look my way," Gabe said, and her smartphone clicked.

And then Nicolás was there. The second dream.

It was a firefight. The cartel, joined by the police, had flanked him on both sides, as he lay on his stomach in the foliage, gripping his rifle. Bullets pierced him at once and he woke, screaming.

And then came the panic attack. His eyes darted around in the darkness, but could find no light entering the semi. The sharp scent of the crated onions was all around him. Sweat broke out upon his skin.

In his gut, Nicolás knew that his days were numbered. Segundo Cortez and Pantano's police would either shoot him or they would catch him alive. That must be how the story would end. Whatever happened, he could not allow the latter.

I suppose this is my own dark night of the soul. This is far, far more difficult than I expected.

His thoughts turned back, once again, to Cassie. He recalled one moment when hands covered his eyes, and he spun around on his heels and saw her before him, laughing. With his fist, he pounded the cargo hold floor, and began to weep.

He remembered that night riding home with Gabe, and she

had agreed with him that his character had much improved. Time and experience had helped him grow. But it was all for naught, if he was bound for an early grave.

How close he had grown to Gabe, to Mitch—his new siblings. He recalled Mitch's words in the mental hospital. *This is the last time I will see you, Nick.*

He blinked his eyes open, and waited for his vision to adjust. It was to no avail, for the cargo hold was utterly devoid of light. Through day and night, the entire trip, not a lone ray of light ever found its way in. His bathroom breaks every few hours served as a reminder that light and landscapes still existed in the world.

As he stared upward through the absolute darkness, he recalled that time when he lay with Cassie in the sheer darkness of her bedroom. No moonlight outside the windows, no nightlight in the hall, all lights extinguished within the room. When she told the story of her son's death, and Nicolás held her to his chest almost as hard as he could. And she had for the first time told him she loved him.

Then the thought presented itself. He could still turn back. And retrace his steps, reunite with Cassie and his friends, and just let it all go. Let Veracruz fend for herself. And somehow release his indignation over his murdered family, and leave it in the past. Then one day, many years in the future, he and Cassie, Mitch and Gabe could join Freedom and Stasia on one of their Baja trips. Fishing, camping, and Freedom could teach him to surf.

It was within his power to reverse course. But the stronger pull was that duty to help the city and its people. Suffocating under diabolical cartel members and rotten police officials. What about all of those prisoners who died in custody, their deaths never investigated? And the fact that, as Esteban swore many times, less than ten percent of Veracruz murder cases were ever solved, and few even investigated?

The people were grasping for any aid they could find. Even though so many of them had already gone to the dark side, years ago, becoming nearly as infected as so many of their police. His thoughts drifted to some of his peers in the faculty, and of those teachers in the *colegios*, who accepted bribes from wealthy parents. Then there was all of the embezzlement in local businesses, exposed weekly by the press. He thought of Carla de Echegaray, and her clandestine alignment with Segundo Cortez. Had anyone in the press revealed this? Did anyone care?

But still, in his city, so many remained who were very good. Like his mother had been. And Padre Manolo and Esteban. And Juan. And all of the good police and educators and parents. Not to mention the students. He must strike soon, and strike hard for them all.

His thoughts turned to that birthday party from his childhood. Esteban sat by his side. Several of his neighborhood friends and their parents, and Lucinda's friends, had gathered around the table. In its center was the giant *fútbol* cake baked by Lucinda.

My, that was a great day. Lucinda, Padre Manolo, and Esteban—they had all been so good to him, all of his life.

He began to feel something else. Rage. An animalistic fury, building to such a towering height, second by second, that it shoved all fear of pain and death, and longing for Cassie, far down below. He recalled another moment.

He had told Mitch: "I have a feeling that if I win this in the right way, Segundo Cortez will never be able to come after me."

"You might be right in that," Mitch said. "But there is something else. You must steel yourself to it. You must change part of yourself. A part deep inside of you that will come to almost love the clash of a righteous conflict. A fight worth fighting. And when you win, you must even come to love the brutality of it. Crushing the enemy, crushing evil with force. Think about that for a minute."

God willing, he would crush evil quite soon. Even if only a sliver of it.

But then there was another birthday his memory seized upon. Tomorrow was Lucinda's. If only this trucker drove faster. Would he arrive in time? Was it possible?

49

All evening and night he walked through the streets, the working-class neighborhood around him growing more impoverished. At last the cemetery came in sight, just thirty minutes before midnight. Yes, this was it. The Ovalde Cemetery and Mausoleum. The plots would be to the rear left.

There were few streetlights in this part of town, and none anywhere in sight. But he knew the cemetery by heart. Every All Souls' Day, or Day of the Dead, on the second of November, he had accompanied Lucinda and Esteban on a morning visit to these grounds. Lucinda placed food on her family's graves and whispered prayers in certain rituals, but she always ended up staying for hours, wandering from grave to grave, praying for strangers she never knew. In earlier years, he and his brother got permission to wander the grounds by themselves, and they would chase each other around the gravestones, through the canyons of mausoleums, and would hide behind crypts. Their energy spent, Esteban would follow him on a meandering route through the grounds. He would point out to his younger brother the names of the dead, especially those who had fought and fallen during the Revolution. Each visit, Esteban would ask him to find one gravestone commemorating a soldier who fought the invasion by the Americans, and then one who fought the invasion by the French, but he could never locate one.

Nearing the cemetery gate, he could at last make out its name on the cast iron arch. When he reached the cast-iron bars of the fence, he rested his forearms upon it, pretended to scour the cemetery within as he counted to ten. Turning his head in a casual manner behind him, he swept his gaze in a semicircular arc around the street. No one appeared, and no movement stirred. He removed his backpack and tossed it over the fence onto the grass. Then he climbed the fence, but a meter and a half in height, and swung himself over.

Once his feet contacted the earth, he recalled that sensation of his feet slamming onto the Arizona dust after he scaled the border wall in Sonoyta, months before. But unlike that moment, he pulled the pack onto his back and walked at first, for a couple minutes, until he was out of eyeshot. Then he started jogging through the field of gravestones, his pack swaying on his back. For he knew by heart the route to Lucinda's family plot, purchased near the best tree in the neighborhood. He reached the cinder path and turned left, picking up speed as he finally turned right and headed in his original direction. A minute later, he froze.

It stood perhaps twenty meters ahead of him. The massive tree, majestic even in the dim light of the crescent moon. The ceiba—the sacred tree of the ancient Mayans. In his youth, Lucinda would often tell Nicolás about the species, of its smooth light gray bark of its branches, and the thorny, light-gray bark of its trunk. And there it stood again, the branches broader than a man's shoulders, the base so thick four men could not form a chain and link their arms around it. He lurched forward into a run, and then made a slight leftward turn.

He slowed into a jog and collapsed onto the grass before the stone, and lay there for half a minute on his stomach, regaining his breath, gathering his courage. Drawing himself up onto his forearms, he raised his eyes.

Lucinda Orteaga Vélez
6 Junio 1961—30 Marzo 2015
"Y la luz en las tinieblas resplandece; y las tinieblas no la pudieron tomar"

Nicolás shot his arms forward and he released a whimper, his eyes blurring with tears. He loved that quote. Yes, John 1:5. "And the light shone in the darkness; and the darkness could not extinguish it."

He had made it just in time, with scant minutes left before her birthday ended.

Then he saw her face. Not before him, but within. Those warm smiling eyes again. She was near. She was there.

"Happy fifty-fourth, *Mamá*," he whispered, as a gust of wind blew leaves across the grass and touched his face. Was this her gesture?

By instinct, he jerked his stare to the left—to his mother's right side. He forced himself to breathe through his mouth in deep gasps. The gravestone was slightly smaller than his mother's.

Esteban Nolano Cuellar
27 Enero 1985—30 Marzo 2015
"Soldado de la Verdad"

Esteban Nolano—soldier for the truth, indeed. And commemorated with a beautiful stone, like Lucinda. This was surely a generous remembrance by Padre's parish.

Nicolás wriggled forward on his forearms and knees until he lay midway between the plots. He extended his arms forward until he touched each gravestone. The tears and breaths came faster as he recalled different moments with his mother and brother, and with Padre Manolo. Too bad he had no idea where he was buried. Perhaps in the cemetery of an abbey, perhaps for the Franciscans. Poor Padre—he felt he was neglecting the man. He probably would never see the gravestone, but he held out hope they would meet again—in the world to come.

For some reason, he remembered that day in the early nineties. Padre and Lucinda had brought him and Esteban to see the great *Museo Nacional de Antropología* in the nation's capital. They had posed for a photo in front of the entrance. Padre had made that funny squirrel sound he and Esteban loved, and when all four of them laughed, the museum guide snapped their photo.

He began to weep again. Yet somewhere in his misery, he was able to find sleep. For he woke in the wee hours, sprawled in that same position, each hand against a gravestone. It was not yet dawn on Sunday morning, but it was not far off. He must get moving—he could not let anyone see him sleeping in the cemetery. Surely it was the best place to sleep, until he located Ivan...

He had walked two blocks when he heard a car approaching from behind. His heart picked up pace, and he counted to three and turned. An old truck with a magnet sign on the door. A plumber. The truck zoomed on, and Nicolás continued toward downtown.

Nearly an hour later, as he traversed a lower-middle-class neighborhood, a car appeared in the distance. As it neared, and as his eyes strained, focused, he felt his heart resume its gallop. The police car approached at an even speed, then accelerated. Ten meters away it slowed, and then pulled up alongside him.

Nicolás forced himself to not act surprised, but to give a turn of the head, a peaceful smile, and a polite wave of his left hand.

The tinted window came down.

"Who are you, and where are you going?" the officer said in a stern voice. His eyes squinted at him through the dawn's light.

Nicolás inhaled.

Be calm, Nicolás, be calm. Finally put that imagination to use.

"Enrique Valdez, *Señor*. I lost my house and everything I own. Up in Xalapa. Bank foreclosed on me. I've been on the street for over a year. Been in Veracruz about a month."

The policeman stared him down with a skeptical expression, and then walked all over him with his eyes.

If the cop exits the car, you must draw and shoot. You cannot sprint with the pack. Hell, if the cop exits the car, it's game over. No prison or torture. You might as well draw the pistol and use it on yourself.

But he could not do it, draw the pistol on a random officer. How could he know if this was one of those who had been corrupted? If the man opened his door, he would drop the pack and run, his .45 still in his jacket. If they cornered him, he'd just have to take his own bullet.

Hold on, Nicolás, just keep holding on. One moment longer. Padre, Mamá, Esteban, don't let this end now...

The officer's lips pursed, then opened. Nicolás could feel his heart about to rupture.

"You know what you need?" the policeman said. "I'll tell you what you need. The Jesuit shelter downtown, on Calle de Rivera. Do you know the street? Two meals and a cot. Showers."

50

Pantano sat at the head of his kitchen table, watching his wife prepare the Sunday-morning coffee. He loved sitting and talking with Raquel. But today he could not bring himself to talk much. Raquel knew something ate at him, but she left him alone in his thoughts to work everything out. One of the many things he loved about her.

It was that damned Sunday brunch Ivan had invited him to at the Café Cristal. The insolent young man may have considered the invitation an honor he bestowed, but truly it was more of a burden. More and more, he could not bear the sight of the spoiled upstart who had come to rule through a climate of fear, even within his own family. The clan that would surely accompany him to yet another of those courtyard brunches. Pantano cringed at the thought of even another sight of them.

Perhaps he could play sick, and stay home. And watch old foreign films with Raquel again. And turn their house into a cocoon, shutting out the life he had come to detest.

But no, he should go to keep the peace. Or, rather, to keep up the charade.

Keep your enemies closer, and just attend the brunch. It's just a few blocks from the station, anyway.

Raquel set the full mug down on the table before him and kissed his forehead. "How about a Fellini movie this time?" she said. Her eyes were soft and mild as they had been that night he met her, forty years before. Those eyes still loved that part of him that remained good.

"Perhaps in a minute, I may join you, *amor*."

She nodded with a smile and disappeared into the den. He took up the mug.

It had become more challenging to even look Ivan Méndez in the eye, as of the last few months. His could feel his stomach turn. The way the young bastard talked to him, even before ordering his death those nights before. A mere thirty-two years old, and the words that slithered from his mouth had grown worse and worse.

Thirty-two. The same age as Ivan's classmate back in the *colegio*: Nicolás Nolano. He had at first helped search for the young man, after the arson incident and Arturo Méndez' heart attack. Yes, if the damned professor had not torched the warehouse and escaped, Arturo would still live, and his bloodthirsty son would be just a spoiled playboy. Veracruz would be more manageable. His job as police chief would be far easier, still with a trace of dignity in his last days before retirement. In many ways, the thought of Nolano filled him with anger.

Yet in a way, he respected Nolano far more than he was angry with him. The man merely tried to avenge the murder of his family, in whatever way he could.

And his family was a good one.

Padre Manolo had celebrated funeral Masses for Pantano's fallen officers. With notable devotion, and with impassioned homilies. Years ago, when his favorite lieutenant had been killed in the line of duty, he heard the *curandera* Lucinda said a novena for him, and performed one of her rituals for his spirit.

Esteban had proven a great annoyance, making his job so very much harder. What the hell was the man thinking, filing an actual suit against Segundo Cortez, against Arturo Méndez, earlier that March? An act of sheer insanity. Perhaps that family lived in a parallel universe. They always were eccentric. All four of them. Especially the *curandera*.

And the other Nolano, the literature professor, escaping after the arson. And then in the semis. How in the hell had he done it? Where in the hell was he now? Surely not foolish enough to return. And if he did, he would for sure end up shot or jailed. There could never be an escape again, by truck or train.

He must give Ivan an answer. Damn it, what should he say? His heart beat faster. How he hated this. No help from the federal police, no one. It was all his problem, his headache. Always was.

Pantano lost his grip on the mug, and it fell from his fingers onto the table, splashing coffee all over Raquel's linen cloth. He cursed aloud.

I've got the nerves of some of those I've interrogated. Or even one of those Segundo Cortez interrogated. Damn it all. I might as well be Ivan's prisoner.

51

Birds chirped, and locusts and mosquitoes buzzed in the brush above and around Nicolás, almost as if he had found himself amid some primeval symphony. A faint breeze blew in from the gulf, wafting over him the magnificent salt smell he so loved. From where he lay on his stomach, embedded just meters beside the sidewalk within the lush foliage, surely no one could see him. Yet his heart pounded faster and faster, in a breakneck tempo that frightened him. He had shivered in a fierce sweat for the last hour that Sunday morning as he waited there, his belly against the damp earth. Would it rain before his targets came into view? How could he have forgotten it was the wet season—May through October? A shower came on most afternoons, and sometimes lasted hours. Hurry, you bastards.

Would he have the mettle to do it? Would his heart give out, despite his mere thirty-two years?

Would he depart the world like Robert Jordan in Hemingway's classic? From that last class he had ever taught? Jordan, detonating the bridge, wiping out the enemy yet sacrificing his life in the process. While his lover lived on.

No, Jordan was a hero. And dying on the bridge was his destiny. But he must live—he must see Cassie's face again.

Then he thought of those words of Oppenheimer, the American scientist. When he saw the terrible product of his genius, the first thermonuclear detonation.

"Behold, I have become the destroyer of worlds," the man quoted from the *Bhagavad Gita* as he eyed the mushrooming inferno.

Surely today, he would destroy the entire world of Ivan Méndez.

Concentrate on breathing, Nicolás told himself. *Breath in, hard. Hold it. Now, release. Repeat.*

He heard steps, a rapid footfall. A jogger passed. Using his elbows, he pulled himself closer to the sidewalk. He adjusted the pack on his back, then tapped the large thigh pocket of his cargo pants that now held the .45, almost as if for consolation, then touched the magazine pouch he had fastened minutes before to his belt. Reaching back with his gloved hands, he pulled the WASR alongside him and then pushed it through the leaves before him.

They were there, across the street, seated together on the restaurant's patio. Ivan Méndez and his henchmen and some of his family. And Carla, of all people. He could not believe it. But then again, he could. Carla de Echegaray—he would make this whore of Babylon pay dearly for her treachery, her heartlessness.

It will have to be today.

It was a boon that he knew their custom, from Padre. A year before his family had resisted Segundo Cortez in any way, Arturo's wife, after a family baptism, had mentioned the Méndez Sunday brunches at the Café Cristal.

Nicolás had felt in his gut that Ivan would continue his father's weekly custom. He just wished the police captain was there. But in killing Pantano, would not a national manhunt follow, involving the federal police, the military? And who knew when he could ever encounter the police captain? But with Méndez, he still had a fighting chance at escape. He could always come for Pantano later.

He did not want to do it in front of the family. Still, the gods had left him no other choice.

His index finger found its way onto the trigger guard. Despite the glove, perspiration had dampened the grip in his right hand. Nicolás steadied the bottom of the grip with his left hand and attempted his best to forget the three bodyguards standing at the patio's border. He glanced along the iron sights, and aimed just behind Ivan Méndez' right temple. He held his breath, gritting his teeth. Once he took enough incoming fire, he knew he must drop the WASR if need be, take the pistol, and follow the escape plan back through the thick trees of the lot. And pray to whatever was watching up there that he evaded the police and cartel alike.

His hand shook such that he nearly dropped the rifle. Then he aimed it again at that same spot on Méndez' temple. He drew in a deep breath, and held it, praying for absolute stillness.

A memory surfaced in his mind, almost as if it were delivered to him from another realm, just for that moment. It was from that Saturday morning months ago at the Easter Week Festival, at the seaside café. The cumbia band struck into sound across the plaza. "Viva!" his mother cried, as she raised her hands in celebration, her face beaming. And then he felt a hand on his shoulder, and he turned and looked and saw his only brother smiling down upon him.

Nicolás gritted his teeth and squeezed the trigger. Ivan's head jolted and vanished behind a mist of crimson. A second later, Nicolás resumed firing, this time into the figures at the table. Bullets began to whizz around him, slapping the leaves and thudding into tree trunks. He raked the outside of the café, dropping all three guards. Again he aimed into the courtyard, spraying the henchmen with fire. Over and over he squeezed the trigger until he exhausted the magazine, then retracted it and slid in another from the pouch on his belt.

He shot forward out of the brush toward the courtyard and knelt just behind the wall, centimeters from the opening. He dove inside, onto his knee, and jerked the WASR before him. Women and children were huddled in the corner, up against the stucco wall. A man stood before them, his rifle pointed outward. Nicolás dashed the half-meter back around the corner.

Not that guard, not with those behind him. Now is the time, Nicolás. Turn and run.

He jerked around and sprinted back across the lane into the woods. He swung behind a thick tree and aimed back toward the opening in the stucco wall. A trio of men shot through the short corridor and he held fire, then released it, cutting down another man, and then the next two.

It's time again, Nicolás. To run for it, with all of your might. Time to let go.

He allowed the WASR to slip from his hand into the leaves.

Instincts deep within propelled his feet through the ground cover, branches and across the lot as he gripped the backpack straps across his shoulders. As he meandered through the trees, he heard no one in pursuit, only the cracking of twigs and the frantic rhythm of his own breath. At last he burst out onto the sidewalk on the other side. A police siren sounded nearby—he knew not where— though no patrol car appeared in the cluster of cars.

He pulled the pistol from the pocket of his cargo pants, and squeezed it in his palm. But he knew he was incapable of it— pointing it at a driver and commandeering a vehicle. And for the first moment, his plan was failing.

A police car appeared and sped closer. Then ground to a halt. Two uniformed men erupted from it.

"Drop the weapon! Drop your goddamned weapon!" one shouted.

What if they were from the faction of the Veracruz force that was good, unaligned with Segundo Cortez? He sprinted as fast as he could into an alley, mere meters away. But he could not drop the pistol.

He was halfway down the alley when a vehicle blocked the opposite end. Another siren, its blue and red lights flashing and whirling like tornados. Spinning around, he saw two officers approaching with a steady pace, sidearms drawn.

"Drop the weapon, *pendejo!*" one shouted.

By instinct, Nicolás jerked the pistol until its muzzle rested against his right temple. Mitch's warning replayed in his mind. He could not let them take him alive. They could—or Segundo Cortez would—torture him, murder him. Or confine him to jail. Hell on earth.

Strange—he heard gunfire in the distance, near the vacant lot beyond. Who was firing?

Two policemen neared him, guns drawn, from the opposite end.

"Lay the weapon down! Or I shoot!" one yelled.

"Drop it!" shouted another.

He held his breath. It was such a difficult leap. Mitch would do it, could do it.

In his mind, Cassie appeared, her broad, bright smile and sparkling eyes. She was his whole new world. If somehow he could survive, and return to her, he would find paradise.

It was far more difficult than the decision to return. Or the one in the semi, to not turn back. But he tossed away the pistol, and raised his open hands aloft.

"Now get down! Get the hell down, *cabrón!*" he heard as he sank onto a knee, then both knees, then his stomach. The steps hitting the pavement neared him as he whispered a prayer.

52

He woke. The floor beneath his back was so hard. Yes—the floor of the prison cell. He knew not whether it was day or night. Or what day it was.

Finally, he had found sleep. But now the nightmare returned. Those sounds again. Someone is being beaten. A man, pleading for mercy.

Nicolás muttered a prayer for the man, whoever he was. Soon his own time would come. He just hoped it would be swift. Ah, only thirty-two years. Now that death drew near, he realized how he so badly feared, hated it. Damn it all. He wanted a long, peaceful life, with Cassie by his side. And Gabe and Mitch not far away. He wanted to teach again. To inspire. To tell stories. But he would have settled for cooking for José. If only that were a possibility.

When they came to get him, he did not know who would be waiting. Pantano, or some *sicario*. But one thing was certain. It sure would not be Ivan Méndez. Or much of his high command. Or the six men he had dropped outside of the café. He must have wiped out about twelve men, total.

But what was that sound—that eruption of gunfire as he

stood in the alley? Would he ever know? Even if he asked, would anyone disclose it?

Heavy steps neared. How many men? It must be four, five by the sound of it. The cell door slid open.

He lifted his gaze, and rose to his feet, forcing himself to breathe in and out at a faster pace.

"You're coming with us," one snarled. The other slapped handcuffs onto one of his wrists, then the other. Then he was pushed out of the cell. The prisoners in the other were shouting. Some laughed, some spat insults, profanities. He recalled Dante's Inferno. Truly his was akin to one of its upper circles. He knew that something far worse lay in wait.

He gritted his teeth as his legs grew unsteady. As he walked he began to kick, pushing himself along.

"Nervous, son?" said one of the guards.

"Hmm," he forced himself to answer. "Frankly, not really. Not after what I pulled off yesterday."

"Shut the hell up, *mariposa!*" someone shouted, and he felt the punch in the head, just behind the ear, not very hard, but not too softly either. "We didn't ask for your reply, *Maria.*"

They trudged on in silence, as he grew lightheaded. One of the men opened wide the gray-metal door. Nicolás and the others stepped inside. They walked down another hall, this one less dim.

One of the guards opened a door, and Nicolás felt a hand on each shoulder blade, pushing him forward under the threshold.

Inside the room was a wall of opaque glass. Before this stood one of the largest men he had ever seen in Veracruz, tall and brawny in his green T-shirt. Beside him, in the center of the room, was a lone table. At its head sat a man of about sixty, dressed in a starched police officer's uniform, and with large, drooping eyes and short white hair that stood up on end. He recognized the man immediately from years of local news, both television and print. His other target.

"Nicolás Nolano!" Pantano said. "Welcome back to hell."

Nicolás noticed the smooth concrete floor was spotted with fresh blood.

"Take a seat right there, son," Pantano said, pointing at the chair at the opposite end of the table. Nicolás reached forward, both hands cuffed together, and pulled out the chair. He glanced at the large guard's face, as hard and immobile as stone, a tiny smirk upturning one end of his mouth.

Nicolás sat in the seat, and raised his eyes to Pantano.

"You surprised me, son, three times," he said, pulling a cigar from his shirt pocket and lighting it as he twirled it in his mouth. "First, that arson attack. Then you managed to escape. Then somehow you returned, with that rifle and pistol and the munitions. You know, you wiped out Ivan and his top men before we arrived. You got Raúl Segovia. Well, I guess you wouldn't know him."

"I guess I've been underestimated," Nicolás said.

"Perhaps," Pantano said and laughed. "You know, you've made things very hard on me. You put Arturo Méndez in his grave. Literally gave him such a shock it broke his heart. "

The twinkling, smiling expression in Pantano's eyes vanished. "You gave us Ivan Méndez, *cabrón*! A monster much worse than his father. You deserve to die, right now." Pantano spat the last words, his eyes flashing with fury.

Should he bite his tongue, hope to buy himself some time, and submit? No. Never.

"No," Nicolás said. "Kill me if you want. But you paved the way. You enabled Segundo Cortez. Arturo and his son. For years."

Pantano stared at him for several seconds, then laid his cigar in the large ashtray. He nodded at the guard. Nicolás felt the most powerful blow of his life directed across the left side of his face. His world spun like a top as his vision took in the room in a blurry swirl: Pantano, the guard, the toppling chair, and the black plexiglass windows.

Nicolás blinked his eyes open. He now lay on his right side, his left jaw smarting like it had been stabbed. His ear rang—it was more like a whistle.

"And keep in mind, boy, all he did was slap you with his palm," Pantano said in a slow and even tone. "Want to see what a punch is like from this man? Get back into the seat."

Nicolás pulled himself upright and eyed the man, who beamed down at him with a perverse, diabolical smile.

Could any man look more like the devil? He could only imagine how powerful his punch would be.

Nicolás lowered himself into his seat.

"I admit what you did yesterday was very bold," Pantano said. He puffed his cigar again. "I can't bring myself to believe you did it. Nicolás, the wide-eyed bookworm. I remember you from your graduation ceremony. My daughter was a few grades below you. We were there. About fourteen years ago. The woman and the man who raised you—they were good people."

"Do you recall my mother, and who she prayed a novena for? And performed the rituals for? So many years ago?"

"My memory is not so faulty, kid," Pantano shot back.

"She prayed for every one of your fallen officers. So how many men escaped yesterday, in the Café Cristal?"

"Well," Pantano laughed. "None, actually."

"I know there were some still inside when I fled."

"Many arrived after, as well."

"Was that the shooting I heard when I was arrested in the alley?"

"Well, yes," Pantano said with a nod. "That is when we lost two officers. Then we lost two more in the next half-hour. Eight of our men were wounded. Now you tell me where you acquired those weapons."

"I am sorry we lost officers yesterday, sir. They were my police, too. As for the guns, I borrowed them from a house in America."

"Don't lie to me. Or else. Why were the numbers filed down?"

"I'm not lying. And I didn't want the guns to ever be traced to their owner."

"Ah," Pantano. "*No importa,* anyway."

"So I guess," Nicolás said, "Segundo Cortez must have a new leader. Probably sitting his ass on his new throne in that old baroque hacienda."

"Well, not quite," Pantano said and looked at him with the utmost confidence.

"But your men fought with Segundo Cortez yesterday."

"It's a little more involved than that. We wiped out many of their people. At the café and at the hacienda both. The remainder we were able to arrest. They are in this very prison, in a different wing."

"So they will walk?" Nicolás said.

"Many would eventually, if I merely imprisoned them. I'll tell you the truth because you will die anyway. Night by night, I will have several disappeared, here and there, until there are no more. I've already had many of them disposed of today. Not one of their bodies will ever be found. And even if that were to happen, *no importa.*"

Pantano uttered the last two words with a casual wave of his hand.

"You say this because I'll be dead myself, anyway?" Nicolás said.

Pantano laughed, a confident but corrupt, twisted laugh. What more surprises were in store? What would they do to him, in the end?

"Nolano, I worked a favor for the *federales.* I've hoped for this for a long time. I tried to contain the cancer. It already infected my force. I did what I had to do, to maintain control. At least *some* control."

"So I opened the door for you to make your move," Nicolás said. "With my crazy act, yesterday?"

Pantano looked with smiling eyes up at the large man, then back at Nicolás. He gave a nod, barely perceptible and hummed in assent.

"You enabled my attack. When my men responded to the scene at the Café Cristal, two of my officers were shot. Maybe minutes after you were arrested. More and more backup appeared, both theirs and mine. And if you don't believe me —*Profesor*, there were seventy-eight of Segundo Cortez confirmed killed, and we arrested ninety-seven yesterday. The sole woman was Carla de Echegaray. She's one of the dead. We all knew her well. Or rather, except for you. You didn't know her that well."

"I suppose not. But that is most surely how Arturo knew where to find my brother and parents together, by themselves. She was the spy."

"And just when did you figure this out, genius?" Pantano said.

Nicolás paused. "I realized this in recent months. She was totally in bed with the cartel. In more ways than one."

A moment of silence ensued.

"Nicolás. You should know that, if I had known they were coming for your family, I would have done everything in my power to prevent it."

"I don't know if I believe that," Nicolás said in a measured, honest tone. A boot shot into his peripheral view to his left and a hard blow contacted his shoulder, sending him several meters onto the floor, once more onto his right side. Both shoulders shrieked in pain, inside his skin.

"Get up, son. Get in your seat," he heard Pantano say. "Gustavo, next time he gets it in the face. With the fist."

Once he had returned to his seat, he forced himself to raise his eyes to the police chief. Pantano met him with a grin.

And then Nicolás heard the words he had never expected.

"Nolano, you never knew the identity of your real parents. Would you like to?"

"Victor and Isabel Nolan. They—"

"Your father was one of those Irish-Mexicans from Central Mexico? Delightful tale spun by Padre Manolo and the *curandera*. To shield you from the painful truth."

"You don't know—"

"Oh, you'd be surprised what I know about this city, *chico*," Pantano said. "Little escapes me. The monster who fathered you was—Arturo Méndez. Well, he wasn't a monster at that time. He was still a cop. A good cop, actually. And we had even been best friends."

"There is no way..." Nicolás said, raising his voice an octave in an emphatic declaration. "I'm not buying what you're selling. You're just trying to make me suffer."

"So you're calling me a liar," Pantano said. Nicolás remained silent.

"He had this ongoing affair with this young graduate student at the university. I let him know it was wrong. She got pregnant, with you. Same year that Arturo's wife got pregnant with Ivan. The mistress dropped out, took a job in a library. Two years go by, and she and Arturo had Esteban. A few years later, she and Arturo were done. She returned to live near her family. On the west coast, near Mazatlán. No one ever saw her again. She left you and your brother Esteban with the orphanage.

"Know how a cop helped finance her apartment, and things, *chico*?" Pantano stepped closer. "First he started seizing cocaine and other drugs in arrests. To sell it himself. Then his moral code

—it just collapsed completely. Guy was on the take. Bribes made him look the other way as product was shipped out of the port. And trafficked north. No one knew, but I did. When I was promoted, I could not bring myself to advance his career. He had been corrupted so very much. He began to run operations on the side. He made his first kills. Around that time, he founded the cancer we know today. Segundo Cortez. You were about fifteen. You were classmates with Ivan in the *colegio*."

Nicolás could not bring his eyes up from the table. Shock, then horror spread through every fiber within him. He hung on to a lone, frayed thread of hope that this cop had conjured up this tale.

"Don't believe me?" he heard Pantano say. "Well, ever consider the similarities between Arturo and you, Esteban, and Ivan? The straight eyebrows, the ears on the small side? The narrow faces? The broad shoulders? That mannerism, how you people turned your head to the side when speaking to someone? It's real. I'm not a storyteller. Now you know this. Even Arturo's wife, Ivan's mother, does not know this. She never will, and she lives today. Your half-brothers you murdered yesterday—and even Jaime was involved with the dirty work, by the way—they never knew. No one did. Just me. And the two bighearted people who raised you."

No. It could not be. But it was. He saw it now—the truth had been there all along.

He remembered that day, seventeen years before. Ivan had invited him to his house. They played video games, and explored Arturo's bookshelves. He grew so entranced with one volume that Arturo surprised him by gifting him with it. Yes, the anthology of poems by Octavio Paz, the Nobel Prize winner. And Ivan could not disguise his jealousy. It never really was the same after that. In fact, Ivan became a different person to him altogether...

Nicolás slapped his hands onto his cheeks and let them slide down his face. Part of him would rather accept death than to continue. And yet—he remembered her. And the pain receded. Yes, there was still Cassie.

Nicolás said, "So what are you going to do with me?"

He caught the apathy and exhaustion in his own voice.

"I could do anything," Pantano said. "What do you deserve?"

"Well, especially after what I did yesterday—what I deserve is life. Hopefully a long one. And freedom. I want to live my life in America. With some new friends, far north of the border. You know, Chief Pantano, what I did I didn't do for revenge. That was only a small part of it."

"Then why in the hell did you do it?"

Just tell him the truth.

"Because Veracruz was hurting," he said, holding back tears. "I saw it on the Internet, on the news. Even though my new life was set, I had to act."

"I could see it every day, up close, Nolano. I just didn't know how to stop it. I did not know how to regain control. Neither the mayor nor I did. Almost half of my force was on the take. And yes, I have wavered. But now the mayor is completely bought. Cuevas is completely rotten. There is no hope for him, for his soul. And I can say out loud all of what I have said here today because I trust this man here. Gustavo's my favorite nephew. Ha. He should have played American football, for the Americans."

"There's only one thing I need to know," Nicolás said.

"I am sorry?" Pantano said.

"Surely you knew they were about to kill my brother. My only brother in the world. He was our district attorney. He was a law-enforcement official, like you and your nephew. He was trying to do right."

"Were you aware your brother looked the other way for a few years while Arturo moved his product? That he even dabbled in snorting the powder, from time to time? Oh! And then his better angel took over, and he went after the cartel. Through a lawsuit. Nicolás, your brother—you must admit. He was a fool. He was an idiot."

Outrage rose within Nicolás like a tidal wave—he could not quell or mask it.

"All lies! Rot in hell!" he yelled.

Some massive force connected with his left cheek. He felt himself flying sideways—as his world faded to darkness.

53

F acedown he awoke, the concrete floor cold on his skin. He heard the cell door slide open, footfalls. His jaw and head ached worse than it had that first morning in Montana. It was the second time he had been knocked unconscious. But it was worth it. Damn that rotten chief for belittling his murdered brother...

Hands gripped him underneath his armpits and jerked him upright, to his feet. His wrists once again felt cold handcuffs.

A cloth hood descended around his head and over his face. Hands gripped him by the nape of the neck, and the others grabbed him again by the arms, just beneath the armpits.

"Now you walk this way," a gruff voice said. "You're going on a little trip."

His heart began to thunder within his chest. What Mitch, then Cassie, then his nightmare in the last semi had foretold—it was morphing into reality. He would join the ranks of the disappeared. In some unmarked grave. Or at the floor of the gulf.

Jesucristo, if you exist, please have mercy on me. *La Virgen Maria*, please intervene. Esteban, Lucinda, Padre Manolo, if your spirits survived, please rescue me.

The cursing, taunts, and protests of his fellow prisoners filled his ears. In some of their cries he discerned warnings, that he was about to disappear, that this was his last night. Between the handcuffs and the hood, and being surrounded by the guards, he could not be more helpless.

If only he could take out a guard or two before that final moment.

So that was one hallway. Then came another. And now this one, the third. And another. Wait, hot summer air? I can smell the gulf. At least I'll have that to comfort me, in my last minutes.

A hand slapped onto the crown of his head, pushing him downward.

"Get in the car, now," the voice said, the same one he had heard moments before in the cell. He felt his way into the back seat.

"Remove the hood, or act up in any way, *cabrón*," another voice said, "and you will suffer even more."

As the engine growled to life, Nicolás could feel the car roll forward, then accelerate.

The car turned left, turned right, slowed, accelerated, and stopped from time to time. His heart did not slow its pace.

But the car did, and then broke to a halt. The momentum forced him to lean forward, then backward into the seat.

"The moment of truth," he heard Pantano say.

Now even the act of breathing was a task. In his chest and throat, he could feel his heart sprinting like a terrified rabbit. He just prayed that it would be swift. And without pain.

The front doors opened, almost in unison. Then the trunk opened. The door to his left opened a moment later. A massive hand grabbed his left arm and jerked him sideways.

"To your feet, *pendejo*!" It was the voice of Gustavo. Nicolás placed one foot, then another, onto the ground and stood. His legs were about to buckle.

"Walk him over here," Pantano said. "Look, over there."

The hand led him sideways, and then forward.

"Now, he stands right there," Pantano said in an authoritative tone.

The hand removed itself from his arm. He stood, straining with every fiber of his will to not buckle to the ground, and to continue the mere act of inhaling and exhaling. He could almost feel the bullets entering his chest and his brow. At least they were police, for unlike Segundo Cortez, they would only use bullets. No blade, no gasoline and match, no chainsaw. But the bullets would come, any second now.

"Remove it," a voice barked. Was that not Pantano?

The hood moved upwards over his face. He blinked his eyes open.

Before him stood Gustavo, hulking down over him, with Pantano mere steps behind. Nicolás cast feverish glances around him. It was a truck-stop parking lot. In the near distance were several parked semis and the bathroom and shower area.

Could this be real? They were releasing him? Or were they just taunting him?

He turned to face Gustavo and saw that he held his hiking backpack at his side.

"Relax, son," Pantano said. "I'm letting you go. You're lucky I am, after you spoke to me the way you did. You're lucky you aren't sinking to the bottom of the gulf right now. You hear?"

"You're setting me—"

"I told you I was. Can't you see where you are?" Pantano said. "Hey, boy, in the future, learn to respect your elders. Especially in front of their nephews."

"Thank…thank—"

"For what you did the other day, we all owe you. Veracruz owes you. God bless you. And God bless your mother with her novenas for my men. God bless the priest with his Masses for them. And bless your brother. I know I said what I said, but he was a very brave man, as well. Now, take back your pack. Everything is still inside. Minus the two guns and your magazines. Those now belong to the city, of course. I did throw in a chunk of cash for your trip north. Seized from some of my kills yesterday. Blood money, but it's still money. And one more thing. You never were wanted by the police, or charged. Local or state, or federal. Arturo and Ivan never officially reported your act of arson. It was an embarrassment to them, of course."

"So—so—I am not wanted? I can just, walk through a border checkpoint? With my Mexican ID and passport?"

"Affirmative. You were only wanted by Segundo Cortez. Yes, the cartel that's no longer a cartel. And yes, you could have walked through a border checkpoint months ago."

Nicolás could not believe it. To think he had given up on living, once the hood slid down over his face. Now he could even teach again. And emerge from the shadows.

"Very well, Nolano. Good luck to you," Pantano said, and nodded at his nephew. They walked back to the patrol car.

"Thank—thank you again," Nicolás said, nearly speechless.

The engine growled to life, and the car swung around and sped back down toward the highway. Nicolás stood in a sort of awkward silence. He did not move for many seconds.

A pair of lights beamed down the feeder road toward the truck stop. As they neared, it became clear. It was a semi.

Nicolás held both hands aloft and waved them in broad motions through the air.

54

As Mitch's truck sped north, Nicolás peered through the windshield at the familiar field beside the gravel road. In the distance stood her house, her SUV parked in the drive.

Mitch pressed harder onto the accelerator and the vehicle hurtled faster, sending gravel banging against the side of the truck.

About fifty meters from the house, Nicolás reached over and grabbed Mitch's shoulder.

"Enough," Nicolás said. "Just let me out here. Now."

The truck ground to a halt.

"Go on," Gabe said from the backseat. "Surprise her. Make her day. And her life."

"Yeah, boy," Mitch said with gusto. "Make her happy again, Cervantes."

The door burst open. As Nicolás's feet hit the grass, he began a steady jog up the lawn toward the house. He imagined he appeared to his soldier friends like an infantryman traversing a field toward an enemy installation. Except here, there was no enemy, no frontal assault. Was he not rushing to defeat separation? Over a month of separation from the heart that he loved.

He became aware of a female voice, shrieking. His feet froze as his ears strained.

It was not Gabe's voice—it was Cassie's. Yet ahead, the front porch sprawled, empty. But he heard it again—he heard his name.

It was behind him.

He spun around, his eyes focusing. A movement there, near the lawn's border with the pines. A hand waving, another grasping a shovel. He sprang into a dead sprint, across the grass, straight toward her.

She gasped, screamed at the top of her lungs, and repeated his name, over and over again as he neared.

"Nick! Nick! Nicolás! Oh my God!"

As she swept her hands back from her forehead and through her light auburn hair, he saw she had tossed off his black newsboy cap and her pale face was wet with tears.

She let the shovel fall into the grass and stood paralyzed, less than ten meters from where she could hold him forever.

He felt like a giddy boy, running as fast as his legs would allow. Perhaps she was recognizing that innocence, which, she had once said, drew her to him those months before.

"Wait, Nick, stop! Stop there!" she said.

He took two more steps and froze. "What? Why?"

She shook her head and made a motion with her index finger to approach.

"Come here, baby. Don't squeeze me, or knock me over. Something's growing in here." She patted her abdomen.

"Come again?"

"You got us pregnant, silly boy."

He stepped toward her and draped his arms around her shoulders. She shot up on the balls of her feet and gave him a deep kiss on the lips. He relished it, remembering her taste, then pulled his head back.

"I'm going to be a father! And everything's fixed. I'm getting my work visa, and will be a teacher again. And I'm not leaving you alone. Ever again."

They kissed again for an entire minute, and then she pulled him closer into a tight embrace. She opened her eyes and looked over his shoulder. They grew very wide. Nicolás turned.

Gabe and Mitch stood but a few meters away, their faces beaming with smiles, Gabe's elbow resting on Mitch's shoulder as he clapped.

Nicolás spun back around to face Cassie.

"What were you doing with the shovel?" Nicolás said. "Digging my grave?"

"Planting that tree there," she said. "A cedar, like the ones you loved in Glacier."

"Let me assist," he said, bending over and lifting the shovel from the grass. He deepened the hole with four thrusts, heaving the clods of dirt into the pile in the grass, and then took the small tree that they both lowered into the cavity.

"A new beginning. Here's to something we can look forward to," Nicolás said, smiling and raising his eyes to meet hers. Never had he seen such an expression, and he made himself pause and relish it—her lively eyes flashed at him with the greatest fervor and expectation.

ACKNOWLEDGMENTS

My sincere thanks go out to those who helped me bring this novel from dream to reality: my brother Ryan, my mother Sandra, the Novel In Progress writers' group, Astarte Sol, James Gutierrez, Maria Martinez, Carpio Bernal (Water Crow) of the Taos Pueblo, Chad and Janka Dixon, Pete Paulus, Ellen Sklarz, Danny Mamaril, Steve Krippner, Nick Krippner, and Ernesto Mendoza.

Many thanks to the artist Rafido, half a world away in France, for a great cover design.

Special thanks go out to Tiffany Yates Martin and FoxPrint Editorial. What a great experience it was, working with such an insightful and helpful developmental editor. Tiffany gave great advice and surely improved *The Second Cortez*—all while grasping my vision for the story, and encouraging me to follow my instincts and to stay true to my voice.

And last but certainly not least, thank you Lara Reznik and Enchanted Indie Press, and the eagle-eyed aviator (and decorated ex-fighter pilot) Tosh McIntosh, my production designer and manager, for your excellent layout and formatting work.

–C.W.

ABOUT THE AUTHOR

Born and raised in New Orleans and its suburbs, Chad has written for the New Orleans Times-Picayune, the Sewanee Purple, The Riverside Reader, The Baton Rouge Advocate, and most recently, Austin.com. After living in many cities and regions, he counts himself lucky enough to reside in the laid-back yet vibrant, creative city of Austin, Texas.

The Second Cortez is his second novel.